HarperChoice

MALICE INTENDED
By Ron Handberg

HarperPaperbacks
A Division of HarperCollinsPublishers

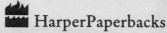

HarperPaperbacks

A Division of HarperCollinsPublishers
10 East 53rd Street, New York, N.Y. 10022-5299

This is a work of fiction. The characters, incidents, and
dialogues are products of the author's imagination and are not to
be construed as real. Any resemblance to actual events or
persons, living or dead, is entirely coincidental.

ISBN 0-06-101246-7

HarperCollins®, 📕®, HarperChoice® and HarperPaperbacks™
are trademarks of HarperCollinsPublishers, Inc.

Cover photo: Michael Goldman/FPG

First HarperPaperbacks printing: October 1997

Printed in the United States of America

Visit HarperPaperbacks on the World Wide Web at
http://www.harpercollins.com

❖ 10 9 8 7 6 5 4 3 2 1

To my wonderful grandchildren,
Nate, Sam, Tony, Zach, Kate, Allie, and Maddy

ACKNOWLEDGMENTS

My thanks to my wife, Carol, and my family for their continuing love, support, and encouragement; to my friends Nancy Mate, Carol Ellingson, Jack Caravela, Alan Cox, Dave Michela, Reid and Cindy Johnson, Debbie Olson, and Steve Stilwell for sharing their time, expertise, and suggestions. And, finally, to my editor, Jessica Lichtenstein, for her insight, skill, and patience.

MALICE INTENDED

1

Maggie first suspected trouble when she saw her own face staring back at her from the studio monitor. The face should have been Steve Cromwell's, the reporter she had just introduced.

One second, two seconds, three . . .

Smile confidently, Maggie told herself. Give 'em time.

Four seconds, five . . .

The screen suddenly went black, and the floor director began to hop around on one foot and point wildly. Trouble, for sure. Then came the clincher.

"Mayday, Maggie! Mayday!"

The words careened through her earpiece, stinging her eardrums and making her head flinch. The familiar but now frantic voice of Brett Jacobi, the ten o'clock news producer, came from the control room. "We've lost the live shot!" he barked. "We're coming back to you. Stand by."

Maggie glanced quickly at Alex Collier, her veteran coanchor, sitting calmly by her side. He managed a grin and a shrug, as if to say, "The ball's in your hands. Get ready to punt."

"Camera two, frame your shot," the show director ordered. "Square up on Maggie. Do it now!"

Maggie could see the studio cameraman struggling to focus on her. The seconds ticked by; the screen remained black. She could picture the chaos in the control room: Technicians scrambling to find the problem and solve it. Through the earpiece, she could hear a muttered, "Christ Almighty, the shit's going to fly."

Maggie sat back. Nothing to do but wait. It was not the first time this had happened, nor would it be the last. The technical gremlins loved to visit television newscasts at the worst times. The most she could do was stay calm.

Her earpiece crackled again. "Get set, everybody, we're coming back."

The red light flashed on above camera two, and once again her image appeared in the monitor. Then came the hand cue from the floor director. "We apologize," she said to the camera, showing no discomfort, "for the problems we're obviously having with Steve Cromwell's live report from Chaska on the search for the missing girl. We'll try to get back to Steve as soon as possible, but in the meantime, let me fill you in on what we know so far."

Thank God she had spoken to Cromwell shortly

before the newscast and knew the essence of his report. It was a lesson she had learned years before, after the first time she'd been left high and dry on camera with nothing to say and nowhere to go.

Ad-libbing easily, she said, "The three-year-old girl, Melissa Mackay, disappeared early this morning from her home, apparently wandering off unnoticed while her parents were eating breakfast. That was some fourteen hours ago, and nothing has been seen of her since."

She paused for a moment, then went on, unruffled. "Scores of volunteers have been searching all day . . . supported by helicopters, planes, and people on horseback. Tracking dogs have been brought in, and the governor has been asked to call out the National Guard to assist."

Brett's whispered voice came through the earpiece, calmer now. "Keep it going, Maggie. Keep it going."

He didn't need to tell her. "There are fears that the girl may have walked to the nearby Minnesota River, which is swollen from the recent rains. That's where the search is now concentrated, although darkness is making the task much more difficult.

"As we say, we'll return to reporter Steve Cromwell as soon as possible, but for now, we'll go to a commercial break and try to get our technical act together. Thanks for your patience."

The screen dipped to black and the first commercial popped up.

"Nice work, Maggie," Collier, her coanchor, said. "Couldn't have done it better myself."

"Thanks." She laughed. "But your modesty always amazes me."

Brett was in her ear again. "He's right, Maggie. Hell of a job. Saved our ass."

"All in a night's work," she said flippantly, although she was secretly quite pleased with herself. More proof, if anybody needed it, that she was more than just another pretty face reading the news. At least that's what she liked to tell herself.

Maggie found the envelope lying on her desk when she hurried back from the studio after the newscast: an ordinary envelope, eight and a half by eleven, partially hidden in the clutter of her desktop. It probably would have escaped her notice but for the green ink used to scrawl her name in large printed letters across its face:

MAgGie lAWrEnCE

And beneath the name, in the same ink and underlined:

PeRSonAl

Curious, she picked up the envelope and examined it, turning it over twice. No stamps, no postmarks, no return address or other markings. Strange, she thought, although God knows she got enough unsolicited mail from viewers who wanted an autograph, a picture, or some other favor from their favorite anchorwoman.

But this hadn't come in the mail.

Had it been there before the newscast? She didn't think so, although it could easily have been lost in the pile of old scripts, newspapers, and assorted journalistic debris that accumulated on her desk every day.

Still . . .

"Hey, Maggie! Move it." The call came from across the newsroom. Brett Jacobi, who was her best friend in the newsroom, stood by the door leading to the lobby. "The beer's getting warm. I've got your coat."

She gave him a quick wave. "In a minute," she mumbled as she quickly opened her desk drawer and retrieved the ebony-handled, gold-bladed letter opener she had received as a going-away gift from one of her buddies at the L.A. station she had left two years before.

One swipe of the blade split open the envelope at the seam. She pulled out two pieces of cardboard, sealed at each end by a small strip of tape. As she tore away one strip, a black-and-white picture spilled out, a glossy eight by ten, the image slightly out of focus and grainy, as though taken from a television screen.

Unable to see clearly in the dimly lit newsroom, she flicked on her desk lamp and slid the picture beneath it, leaning in for a better look.

The pain in her chest was piercing. She gasped for breath and clutched the edge of the desk. Her knees began to buckle, and she could feel the vomit rise in her throat. Collapsing into her chair, she breathed deeply, sucking in air like a marathoner, choking back the bile. Eyes closed, forehead pressed against the top of the desk, her mind tumbled.

How? Who? Why?

"Maggie, what the hell's the matter?" Jacobi was halfway across the newsroom, moving fast.

When she opened her eyes, she found Brett kneeling beside her, his expression reflecting both surprise and concern. Quickly turning away, she pushed the picture and the envelope out of sight beneath a pile of scripts. He took no notice; his eyes were fastened on her. "Christ, are you okay?" he demanded gently. His fingers were beneath her chin, turning her face toward him. "What the hell happened? You looked like you were going to take a dive."

She shook her head, unable to speak. By now, others in the newsroom began to gather around them.

"Shall we get an ambulance?" one of them asked.

"Get her to the Green Room," another suggested. "Let her lie down."

Maggie shook her head again, more vigorously now. "No way," she finally gasped. "I'll be okay. Just a fainting spell or something. Need to get my breath back, that's all."

Unconvinced, the circle continued to hover, clearly fearing another collapse. Brett was now standing behind her, gently rubbing her shoulders.

"Seriously," she said, surveying the group. "I'll be all right. This happens now and then. PMS or something. Really. Beat it, all of you."

One by one, the onlookers reluctantly moved away, glancing back as Brett pulled up a chair from an adjoining desk. "That's bullshit, you know," he said.

"What?"

"That this kind of thing happens to you. I would have seen it before. Or you would have said something."

His words were lost on her. She could think of nothing, could see nothing but the image on the photo. She closed her eyes, hoping to be rid of it, but the image stared back at her as though engraved on her retinas. There could be no mistake.

Her eyes snapped open. "My God, what about Danny?"

"What about him?" Jacobi demanded, his face only inches from hers. "What's gotten into you?"

"Nothing," she whispered, startled to find Brett still there. The passing seconds could have been hours. "But I've got to get home."

"He's with Anna, isn't he?"

She nodded, then turned away. The walls of her small cubicle seemed to close in, wrapping their fabric arms around her, squeezing, not allowing her to breathe.

"Then what is it?" There was a sharper edge to his voice now, impatience mixed with concern. "You look like a goddamned ghost."

She waited for her lungs to fill, then turned to face him. "Brett, forget about this, okay? I just had a spell of some kind, that's all. If you give me a minute, I'll be all right."

His eyes wouldn't leave hers. The gaze was so intense she could almost feel him inside her mind, fumbling around, trying to grasp her thoughts. She finally had to turn away again. He took the cue and stood up. "Better forget the drink," he said, not able to hide his frustration. Was there anger, too?

"I think so," she replied. "I'm not up to it."

She could feel him looming behind her, a full six-foot-five, slender as a stick, with arms and wrists hardly larger than hers. If he had just been three inches taller and forty pounds heavier, Brett had told her often, he could have played Division I ball. And who knows? Maybe the NBA. As it was, he'd been All-State at one of the suburban high schools and a star at a local private college, where bodily bulk had proved less important than finesse on the basketball court. That had been years ago, but he still talked and dreamed about what could have been—if only he hadn't stopped growing at seventeen.

Two years older than Maggie, Brett had been the first person in the newsroom to befriend her. From her first day, he had taken her under his wing, introducing her to others, making sure she knew where things were and what was expected of her. Part of his concern came with the job. As the producer of the station's major newscast, he had a responsibility to the new anchor. They would be a team, and the more comfortable he could make her feel, the better she would do. And any success of hers, he knew, would be his as well.

More than anything, though, there had been an immediate sense of kinship felt by both of them, although neither had ever tried to explain it to themselves or the other. However, from that first meeting, their friendship had flourished and deepened.

He dropped her coat on the desk and walked

away. Halfway across the newsroom, he stopped. "If you need me, just give a shout. Anytime. Okay?"

She gave another small wave, then turned and watched as he walked out the door, pushing one arm through the sleeve of his old college letter jacket, badly tattered but still worn like a woolen badge. For a split second, she was tempted to cry out, to call him back, to make him sit beside her and somehow share the horror.

But she knew that was impossible. Not now. Maybe never.

Minutes passed, she wasn't sure how many, before she finally stood up and glanced around the newsroom. Except for the overnight dispatcher, hunched over inside a glass booth monitoring the police and fire radios, and a janitor emptying wastebaskets, the place was deserted. The news day was over, the long night about to begin.

She couldn't remember feeling more alone.

Legs still wobbly, she walked slowly to the alcove where a pot of coffee waited, dark and simmering. She poured a cup, tasted its bitterness, and dumped the rest into a sink.

The dispatcher seemed to be dozing when she slid open the door to his glass cage and found herself surrounded by the constant chatter of the radios. "You awake, Lionel?" she asked, bending over him to be heard.

Lionel Heaton was a young university journalism student whose job was to make sure the station missed none of the assorted murders, fires, or accidents during the overnight hours. Startled by her voice, he sat up in his chair and turned to face her. "Wasn't sleeping, Maggie," he said, "just concentrating on the radios. Can hear 'em better with my eyes closed."

She managed a small smile. "Were your eyes open earlier, Lionel, when we were doing the newscast?"

"Sure, I was watching the show," he replied. "What's up?"

"You didn't happen to see anyone strange wandering around the newsroom, did you? Like over by my desk."

He shook his head slowly. "Not that I remember. But I wasn't really looking either. Like I said, I was watching the show on the monitor."

The dispatch room was located behind the assignment desk, elevated so that it had a clear view of most of the newsroom. But as she glanced through the window, Maggie could see that her cubicle was partially hidden by one of the square pillars supporting the ceiling.

Lionel was watching her. "Someone been messin' with your stuff, Maggie?"

"Something ended up on my desk and I don't know where it came from. Or who left it there. I thought you might have seen something."

"Sorry," he said, then quickly turned his attention back to the radios. The state patrol was reporting a three-car pileup on Interstate 94 in St. Paul.

She slid out of the glass booth as quietly as she had entered. One more stop.

The station security guard sat just inside the back door of the building, housed in a small office where he could survey the foot traffic coming and going. Employees gained access with a security card; anyone else had to get the guard's okay to enter.

Maggie posed the same questions to him as she had to the dispatcher. Any strangers in the building? Anything or anyone out of the ordinary?

Nothing unusual, he told her, although a small group had toured the building earlier. He had taken little notice, since someone from the promotion department had been in charge of the tour. He had simply let the people in and told them where to gather. No, he didn't know the name of the promotion person, but he thought she was new. He'd seen her only a few times before.

"No chance of anyone else getting in?" she asked.

"Not unless they've got a card."

"How about when you're off on rounds?"

"Then they'd have to wait until I get back."

Sounds good, Maggie thought, except that she knew someone could slip in the door as someone else was going out. She had seen it happen herself from time to time. "Okay," she said, realizing there was no more information she would get from the guard. "Thanks for your help."

"No problem, Ms. Lawrence."

What now? she wondered as she wandered down the hall and back toward her desk. Get the hell out of here, she decided. Get home, give Danny a goodnight hug, and think.

She knew that thinking would bring no easy answers tonight.

The night air was cool but not cold. Indian summer in Minnesota. The nicest time of year here, the natives were quick to tell her. And she agreed. Like winter in California, it was warm, but not too warm by day, crisp and comfortable by night. Her summer wear was not yet packed away, but with each day it was seeing less and less use.

Wouldn't be long, Maggie knew, maybe days, maybe weeks, before the temperatures would drop sharply and the winds would pick up out of the north, whistling across the state. Then the snow would come, flurries at first, or an icy rain that turned the streets and sidewalks into skating rinks. Then blankets of snow that would remain until spring. Sometimes a foot or more at a time. There was no telling exactly when it would begin—as early as Halloween, as late as Christmas—or when it would end, but come it would, of that there was no doubt. Two years in Minnesota had taught Maggie that much.

Still, when she had taken time to think about it, she wasn't sure she had made a bad trade: the sun of California for the snow of Minnesota. With the California sun, she'd learned all too well, came earthquakes and floods, mudslides, riots, and raging Santa Anna fires. And a society that seemed to be crumbling at the edges, plagued by too many people, too many problems, and too little tax money to deal with any of it.

In the end, she decided that while it was colder here, it was also cleaner and more civilized. More decent. A better place to raise her son. Until tonight.

She buttoned her light coat and began walking

to the parking ramp a block away. On her way out, the security guard had offered to escort her, but she had politely declined, in no mood for small talk, even for a block.

In one hand, she carried a tiny canister of mace, a nightly precaution she had adopted in California and maintained here, even though she had never had to use it. In the other hand, she held a small briefcase that contained an even smaller purse, a makeup kit, and assorted papers and other personal effects.

And the envelope with the green ink.

She had not opened it again. She couldn't. Not even in the empty newsroom. She couldn't escape the feeling of eyes in the walls. No one else must see it.

But someone else had. Someone had left it. Someone who must hate her.

2

When Maggie slipped into the apartment, she found Anna asleep on the sofa, her quiet snores mixing with the muted sounds of the television set across the room. No surprise, since it was the same virtually every night: Anna was unable to stay awake beyond the end of the news, and sometimes, Maggie suspected, not even for that long.

But who could blame her? Getting Danny settled down and into bed would exhaust almost anyone, let alone a woman well into her sixties, hampered by arthritis and suffering from a persistent bronchitis that Maggie guessed was really early-stage emphysema.

Anna lay on her back, hands folded on her

chest, fingers intertwined, as though she'd fallen asleep praying. Her gray hair was splayed across the pillow, her half glasses halfway down her nose, an argyle sweater covering her knees. Her fur-lined slippers were placed neatly by the side of the sofa.

After quietly hanging her coat in the front closet, Maggie tiptoed by the sleeping nanny, walked through the dining room and past the kitchen, and then proceeded down the long hallway to Danny's bedroom. The door was slightly ajar, as it always was at night, allowing the light from the hall to spill into the room. Danny insisted on it, wouldn't go to sleep without it, even when Maggie herself was home to put him to bed.

"Keeps the creeps out," he had told her more than once.

"What creeps?" she had asked. "There are no creeps around here."

He would never answer directly, but neither would he relent in his demand for the light. If he ever awoke in total darkness, he would cry out with a shrillness that brought Maggie out of the deepest sleep and left her sitting straight up in bed.

She knew, and others had assured her, that he would almost certainly grow out of whatever fears haunted his five-going-on-six-year-old mind, but his unwillingness to talk about those fears, the mysterious creeps he seemed to dread, still troubled her. Give it another six months, she had decided, and then seek some professional advice.

Pushing the bedroom door open, Maggie crept to the bed and knelt beside it. He lay facing her, pillow pushed aside with his head resting on one arm, breathing slowly, peacefully. None of his creeps bothering him tonight, she thought, wishing she could say the same.

"God, Danny," she whispered, "what have I done? What's going to happen to us?" The boy stirred slightly in his sleep, but his eyes remained closed. She kissed his cheek. "Could you ever forgive me? Can things ever be the same?"

She touched his hair lightly. More blond now than its natural brown, thanks to the summer sun. His skin still seemed as smooth as the day she had first held him to her cheek, but like his hair, his skin showed the effects of the summer just past. The tan had faded, but not by much.

The only flaw, if you could call it that, was an almost imperceptible scar at the base of his chin, the result of a cut suffered when he fell from a swing shortly before they'd moved from California. That and his somewhat protruding ears, which she was still sure his head would someday catch up with.

She never tired of watching him, especially as he slept. Never tired of the wonder that he was hers, that he had somehow emerged from her body so perfectly and had grown so quickly. He was, in every respect, her life, unchallenged by career or any other human being. Certainly by no man in her life since Danny's father, and now, even he was a fading memory.

Until now there had been no barriers to the new life she had tried to create for herself and Danny. Until the envelope arrived.

"Maggie, is that you?" The hushed voice came from just outside the door. "Are you in there?"

As Anna's backlighted figure appeared in the doorway, Maggie got to her feet and put a finger to her lips. Then she backed out of the room, taking a final look at her son before returning the door to its original position.

"I woke up and saw your briefcase by the front door," Anna said, still in a whisper. "I was expecting you later. Is everything okay?"

"Just fine, Anna," she replied, leading the way back down the hall. "I didn't want to wake you, and thought I'd spend a minute with Danny."

As Maggie flipped on the kitchen light, Anna—now clutching the argyle sweater around her shoulders—went to the refrigerator and opened the door. "There's some leftover chicken," she said. "You might want to heat it up. There's salad, too."

"I'm fine, Anna, but thanks. Have to keep my figure, you know."

"Posh," she offered with a small chuckle. "The Lord should have been as good to me."

Anna Sjogren lived just down the hall, in 202, a widow who survived comfortably on Social Security and the generous pension and savings left by her late husband. She had taken care of Danny, "for love, not money," since a few days after Maggie had moved in. "I don't know what I'd do without that boy," she'd once told Maggie. "He's a handful, believe me, but chasing after him keeps me young. The days I'm not with him seem awful long." Then she'd paused. "Doesn't seem like I ever had time to watch my own kids grow up."

Despite her arthritis and bronchitis, Anna remained a remarkably vibrant woman. Unstooped and with a spring still in her step, she had shown enough physical agility, patience, and mental stamina to keep up with Danny, which Maggie realized was no small task for someone half Anna's age.

Her mind was even quicker than her step: facile, retentive, and ever curious. She was Danny's teacher as well as his nanny, expanding his kindergarten education with stacks of her own children's books and tours of anyplace in the city she thought might challenge the boy's mind and imagination. There was hardly a museum, zoo, or library they had missed.

Danny had come to love her as he would a grandmother, although he sometimes bridled at the discipline and regimen she imposed on his young life. For Maggie's part, she was forever grateful she had found the woman, coming to love and trust her as much as she had always wished she could have loved and trusted her own mother.

"You feeling all right?" Anna asked, peering at her. "You look pale here in the light."

"Just a little tired, that's all," Maggie replied, hedging the truth.

"You push yourself too hard, between the job and the boy."

She shook her head. "Not much I can do about that, is there?"

"You could take more time off," Anna replied. "I don't think you've had a real vacation since you've been here."

Not exactly true, but almost. She had managed to squeeze in a week away earlier that summer, between the May and July rating periods, taking

Danny to a lodge in northern Minnesota where he could work on his swimming and learn how to fish. She was able to relax and enjoy the time with her son, but found little opportunity to be by herself or in the company of other adults.

Aside from that week, there had been only a few long weekends away, and those, too, with Danny in tow. She supposed she could have taken more time, but she was concerned with establishing her place at the station and in the market. The more time she spent on the air, the better, at least in the beginning.

"How was he tonight?" she asked as Anna prepared to leave.

"Same as ever. He can't seem to get enough of that video game. Wants me to play it with him, but my fingers just aren't nimble enough. He gets frustrated and so do I. Wish I could get him as enthused about a good book."

Maggie chuckled. "Don't expect miracles, Anna. They say those games help hand-eye coordination . . . and besides, he already reads better than anybody in his class."

Anna gave a small grunt as she walked to the door and then paused. "Same time tomorrow?" she asked.

"As far as I know," Maggie replied.

Their routine was set. On most mornings, Maggie was able to take Danny to kindergarten a few blocks away and be home with him for a couple of hours in the afternoon before leaving for the station. Anna took over then.

But, invariably, something would arise each week to break the routine and take Maggie away early: a promotional taping, a personal appearance or speech, an interview with one of the newspaper or magazine feature writers, a training session with the consultants, or a meeting at the station that she was required to attend. There always seemed to be something, duties that were as much or more a part of a news anchor's life as reading the news twice a night.

She sorely wished she could spend more time with her son, but knew that would be impossible anytime soon. Thank God for Anna.

"Well, goodnight, then," Anna said, closing the door behind her, leaving Maggie alone staring at the briefcase she knew she would soon have to open again.

She had just stepped out of the shower and into a light robe when she heard the telephone. It was on its third ring by the time she got to it, rushing to pick it up before it could bring Danny awake and out into the hallway.

"Yes," she said.

"Are you okay?" Brett's voice, with barroom hubbub in the background.

She glanced at the kitchen clock. "It's midnight, Brett, for God's sake." She had trouble hiding her irritation.

"Sorry," he said. "But are you okay?"

"I told you I would be."

"But are you?" he persisted.

She paused, collecting her thoughts, watching and listening for her son. Good, he's still sleeping. "Brett, listen to me. It's over. Something hit me, some bug or something. I don't know what. But it's gone now. I'm ready to go to bed. I'm—"

"I don't believe you," he said, cutting in.

"What?"

"I went back to the station. After you'd left. Lionel told me you'd been to see him. So did that security guard, whatever his name is."

"For God's sake, Brett," she protested.

"Maggie, I'm your friend, remember. Buddies. Long time, right? Now what the hell's going on?"

She said nothing, hoping the silence would discourage him. It didn't. "Is somebody bugging you?" he demanded.

"Brett, I can't talk about it. I won't talk about it. Even to you."

"Why?"

"Because it's too complicated, too bizarre. Trust me, will you?"

"Not this time, I won't. I know you too well."

She took three deep breaths. "Brett, I appreciate your concern, but I'm going to hang up now. It's late, I'm tired. Be a real friend and forget about all of this. I'll see you tomorrow."

"Hold on—"

Those were the last words she heard before she cradled the receiver.

Maggie wrapped the robe more tightly around herself and wandered aimlessly through the apartment, stopping to straighten a cushion on the couch, which Anna had used as a pillow, and to pick up the last of Danny's Legos that were still scattered on the carpet.

She turned off the TV and turned on the stereo, keeping the volume low. Whitney Houston, mellow and soothing.

The apartment was almost new, the complex

built just a year before she'd arrived in the Cities. With little time to look for a place, she had quickly settled on this south Minneapolis neighborhood because it lay in the midst of a beautiful chain of lakes and was not far from the station. Mostly, it was close to what she had been told was one of the best elementary schools in the city. That was the least she could do for Danny.

She knew she should be looking for a house, a real home for herself and her son. She certainly could afford it, but in these two years she simply had not had the time or the energy to search. Besides, moving might mean losing Anna, and she was not ready to face that prospect yet.

Give it time, she had told herself. Things will work out.

The apartment was spacious and beautifully decorated, the furniture and furnishings tasteful, and the appliances new. Security was tight, and her neighbors mostly friendly. Not much more she could ask for, she had decided.

Aside from the luxury apartment, Maggie tried to live frugally, unable to forget the lean, early years in California when she had struggled for every dollar. Since the television station paid for virtually all of her clothes and provided other perks and benefits, and since Danny required few expenditures, she was able to save much of each month's substantial paycheck—for Danny's college and for an uncertain future in an uncertain business.

Before moving, she had sold all of her furniture and other belongings that wouldn't fit into her '92 Caravan. Not that any of it was worth much anyway, but she viewed Minnesota as a place to truly begin her life anew—with the fewest reminders of the past.

The envelope had not changed. The green ink was still there, the scrawled letters as bold and frightening as before. Block letters, almost as a child would scribble them. A mixture of capital and small letters, each of a different size, with no apparent common characteristics. Almost like one of those kidnapping notes you see in the movies, clearly composed to disguise the identity of the writer.

Did that mean she might recognize the real writing? Not likely. And when had she seen green ink before?

Maggie sat at the kitchen table, biding her time, studying the envelope, delaying the inevitable. A cup of warm milk sat on the table to her left. She hated warm milk, but knew it might help settle her nerves.

Finally, she reopened the flap of the envelope and pulled the picture out, its backside facing up. She glanced down the hall to make sure Danny was not up, then closed her eyes and turned the picture over. Knowing now what she would see, she expected to be less shocked. But when she opened her eyes, she experienced the same piercing pain in her chest, the same feeling of fainting. Not from the picture itself, but from the horror it represented in her past and the pain she knew it could inflict in her future. For what it could do to Danny, to their lives.

The woman in the print was dark-haired and young—no more than a teenager. She sat atop a satin sheet, naked, spread-eagled, revealing all there was to reveal. A man, his back to the camera, also nude, sat beside her, his lips on her breast, his hand on her thigh, inches from her center.

The young woman's eyes were closed, a look of real or feigned ecstasy distorting her face. The distortion, the brunette hair, the age, and the milky quality of the photo made recognition difficult, but could not erase the reality.

The body and face were hers.

And she knew this picture was not alone. It was but one frame of many. Even now, she could visualize which came before and which would follow. All twelve minutes of it, imbedded in her mind, her share of a movie from hell.

As she studied the picture, Maggie was amazed that anyone else could have recognized her. Not now, twelve years later. She was so different. A girl then, a woman today. Her face had filled out, matured. The fake beauty mark on her right cheek was gone, and the dyed black hair had long since returned to its natural blond. To her, the girl in the picture could have been a stranger, another person, who bore only the slightest resemblance to herself. A young and distant cousin, at best. Yet someone else had seen through the years and the cosmetic alterations to discover her. Naked, there on the satin sheets.

For years, especially during those early years in Los Angeles television, she had desperately feared what had now come to pass. She had girded herself for exposure. Prepared for it. But it was not to be, and with each year had come a greater sense of relief and comfort. Not that she could or would ever forget it, but she allowed the film to slip further and further from her mind. She managed to convince herself that with the passage of time and with the hundreds of new adult films being produced each year, the greatest danger of exposure had passed. Perhaps the film no longer even existed.

The move from Los Angeles to the Twin Cities had given her an even greater sense of security. Twelve years and two thousand miles now separated her from the past.

How wrong she'd been.

Sleep would not come. The same hallway light that kept Danny's creeps at bay cast strange shadows on the walls and ceiling of her bedroom. Her eyes could not escape them and her mind would not rest. Tumbling, skittering from thought to thought, from place to place, like so many of the fallen leaves outside her window.

It seemed so long ago now. It was long ago, almost twelve years. She was sixteen, but claiming to be more. Lost in a lost city. A runaway, free of a brutal home, but captive in a world she was far too young to understand or control.

Broke. Scared. But proud of a face and body that had gained for her whatever affection and admiration there had been in her young life.

One film. Twelve minutes. Two hundred bucks. Enough for a month, living on the streets. Never again.

A nightmare of the past now part of the present.

She muffled her sobs with the pillow and tried to escape the shadows.

3

Sissy had talked her into it.

Sissy had no last name, at least none that Maggie ever knew. Sissy was just Sissy, one of six waifs who had somehow found each other on the streets of Los Angeles and who had for a time shared a corner of an abandoned warehouse in Hollywood.

How could she forget it? A two-story firetrap with leaky ceilings, splintered wood beams, crumbling walls, and greasy floors. The oil was everywhere, years of spilled oil and who knows what else, slickened by the dampness, the stench surrounding and penetrating everything within reach. Even the mice and rats, whose tracks they could see crisscrossing the oil slick, seemed to take on an oily hue. Every now and then they would find one of their small bodies mired in the muck.

Maggie would never forget the feel or the smell; it clung to her nostrils and seeped from her skin for months after she'd left the place. Even now, as she fought for sleep, the thought of it made her want to gag.

Besides Sissy, there were two other girls, Ginger and Rita, and two boys, Roger and Petey. All of them were, like Maggie, in their teens, on the run from their own particular demons, real or imagined. Strange that she could even remember their names after all these years, for she could recall little else about them. Except for Sissy. The others were now but vague shapes.

For a time, though, they had been her only family, sharing whatever food, money, or clothes they could hustle or steal. They were a frightened, suspicious, elusive, and cunning pack, dependent upon no one but themselves, forswearing the shelters, rejecting helping hands, fleeing from any effort to restrict or restrain them. Adults were the enemy, unless they could provide food or money with no strings attached.

Roaming the streets by day and night, they slept when they could. They loitered, panhandled, or shoplifted whenever they saw the chance. From time to time, one or more of them would disappear, sometimes for days, sometimes for weeks. Maybe they were in jail, drunk in an alley, or high on speed. No one ever asked or bothered to look. Eventually, they would come back.

Maggie was the last to join the group.

Sissy had found her—saved her, really—one night in an empty lot off Sunset Boulevard fighting off a drunken, black-jacketed punk who had mistaken Maggie's street-begging for hustling. In the darkness, he had dragged her from the street by her hair, stumbling over piles of debris, tearing at her clothes while trying to unzip himself.

She was on the ground, blouse in shreds, shorts around her knees, struggling, when Sissy emerged from behind a Dumpster. Maggie saw the knife before she saw the girl, the tip of the blade at the punk's throat just below the Adam's apple. He fell away in panic, crawling backward like a crab in reverse, never more than a foot from the knife. He begged for his life. She could still hear his guttural moans, more like a wolf's growl.

For Maggie, it was like awakening from a nightmare, an inky blur that was over in seconds. The flash of the knife, a spurt of blood, the screams of the man with a slashed cheek, running, falling, running again. His cries pierced the night, bouncing off the walls of the buildings on either side of them, and then finally fading away.

Sissy was beside her, kneeling, talking quietly, shushing the sobs. "Take it easy kid," she whispered. "It's over. The asshole's gone." While it was too dark to see her features clearly, Maggie could tell she was a girl of about her own age, dark-haired and wide-eyed with full lips and a dark space between two of her front teeth. Her face was dirty, and she smelled of sweat.

Maggie's choking sobs subsided, but her body continued to shake, the tremors uncontrollable. After struggling to pull her shorts up, she pressed

her knees against her chest, squeezing tightly, trying to control the convulsive twitching of her body.

"C'mon, get yourself together," Sissy finally
said, tugging at her. "That prick may be back with
friends. Better move it."

Maggie struggled to speak. "Who are you and
where did you come from?"

"I'm Sissy," she said. "How about you?"

"Maggie. Maggie Lawrence. Sissy what?"

"Just Sissy. Leave it there, okay?"

Maggie slowly got to her feet and yanked at her
tattered blouse, finding one button still intact,
enough to bring the frayed fabric together over
her breasts.

"Forget that," Sissy said, ducking into an alley.
"Come on."

Maggie followed at a half-run, past the Dumpster
and along a darkened, littered trail behind buildings and other empty lots, sidestepping piles of
rubble and trash cans. Maggie glimpsed the darting
of small bodies and hoped they were cats, not
rats.

After several blocks, they slowed to a walk, and
she caught up to the girl. "Can we stop for a
minute?" she gasped.

"In a while," Sissy replied. "We're almost there."

"Where?"

"Someplace safe. You'll see."

Ten minutes later, they walked into the warehouse, stepping carefully across the slippery floor
to a far corner—a walled-off space that apparently
had once housed an office of some kind. Cleaner
and drier than the rest of the building, its floor
was covered by old air mattresses, sleeping bags,

and piles of clothes, its walls filled with obscene graffiti. A Coleman stove sat in one corner, a rusted tin coffeepot atop it, surrounded by an array of battered pans, cooking utensils, and stacks of canned goods.

No one else was there.

"Not too fancy," Sissy said, surveying the room. "But we call it home."

"Who's we?" Maggie asked.

"Just some friends. You'll meet them."

There were five sleeping bags. Old tennis shoes were tucked into some of them, along with dirty shorts and T-shirts. Other pieces of clothing were piled along the wall or hanging from makeshift hooks.

By day, the room was lighted by two large windows high on the cement-block wall, windows steel-barred and so filthy and cobwebbed that sunlight had to fight its way through. At night, the only illumination came from a standing, three-way lamp—without its shade—in the center of the room, which Sissy later said Roger had salvaged from a dump and somehow fixed.

The lamp provided enough light for Maggie to get a better look at her companion. Shorter and heavier than herself, although well shy of fat, Sissy's body was solid and muscled, almost masculine, as though she had worked with weights. By contrast, her face was softer, more feminine, even without makeup and with the caking of dirt. Maggie decided that once cleaned up, with those full lips and sculptured body, she would be viewed—by men, at least—as quite attractive in a sexy, tart-like way. That impression would only be accentuated by what she wore: a thigh-high miniskirt and a Hard Rock Cafe T-shirt that barely contained her ample breasts and revealed more than a flash of midriff.

"You never gave me a chance to say thanks," Maggie said.

"No biggie. I kind of liked cutting that dude. Fucker had it coming. Might make him think the next time."

"I owe you," Maggie said. "And I won't forget it."

While she had been on the streets for six weeks, that night's attack was her first truly frightening encounter. Sure, she'd been hassled and propositioned a few times, even wooed by a couple of pimps, but until now she had always been able to tough-talk her way out of any serious problems or flee before the situations turned treacherous.

"Where have you been squatting?" Sissy asked.

"Anywhere. Everywhere. Usually in the parks or under the bridges."

"Where's your stuff?"

"In a duffel bag. I keep it in a Dumpster they never empty."

"Well, you're welcome to hang here. We've got room for one more."

Maggie looked around. Could she live in a place like this? The streets could be bad, but at least she had open space. Breathing room. This was like an overcrowded prison cell, only messier and smellier.

Sissy smiled, apparently reading her thoughts. "It looks for shit, but it's dry and safe. And no one's ever here, at least not all at once. Plus we watch out for each other."

Maggie debated. The attack could have been a sign, a warning flag she should not ignore. Maybe she had been lucky until now going it alone, relying on her wits and good fortune. Hell, she could have been killed tonight. It took her only a few minutes to decide. "Okay," she said. "Thanks. I'll give it a try. But no promises, all right? We'll see how it works out."

"Whatever," Sissy said. "We don't beg anybody to stay."

That was how it started.

It ended two months later when the warehouse burned to the ground. One of the boys, Petey, was alone at the time and was lucky to get out alive. The Coleman stove exploded as he tried to heat a can of soup, he told them later. Within minutes, the place was engulfed by towering flames—fed first by their clothes and sleeping bags, then by the oil and chemical residue that saturated the building. The walls and roof collapsed within an hour as firemen stood back and watched. Good riddance to an old and useless eyesore.

The few possessions Maggie and the others had owned disappeared in the flames. Not much of a loss, God knows, but the fire also managed to destroy the main bond that had held the group together. One by one after the fire, they took off in different directions, each leaving with little more than a perfunctory good-bye to the others.

Maggie and Sissy, however, decided to stick together.

That surprised no one. In the two months since the attack on Maggie, the two girls had become almost inseparable. Sisters of the street. They ate, slept, stole, and begged together; watched over one another; and shared secrets they had never before revealed to anyone.

Like Maggie, Sissy had fled an abusive home and two alcoholic parents. Unlike Maggie, she had been sexually as well as physically mauled and had somehow managed to shed the baggage of hate and anger that Maggie still carried. "They were pigs," she once said of her parents. "Plain and simple, pigs. They ruined my life as a kid. I'm not going to let them keep ruining it."

Pointing to a small but visible scar on her cheek, Sissy said, "See this? My dad did this to me. Slashed me with a razor, because I was standing too close to him when he was shaving. And I've still got burn scars on my ass end . . . from his cigarette. And those were the good times."

"Didn't you ever want to kill them?" Maggie had asked, recalling her own hysterical urges as a battered child.

"Hell, yes. Damn near every day. But I got over it. Fuck 'em. Forget 'em. They're animals. Pigs, like I said. Why should I wallow in their shit?"

Sissy was the bigger and stronger of the two girls, the more surefooted, resilient, and adventuresome. Maggie found herself becoming more dependent upon her, modeling herself after Sissy almost as a younger sister would. What Sissy did, Maggie did. Where Sissy went, Maggie went. What Sissy demanded, Maggie supplied. They lived on and off the streets—and on the edge. Sometimes it would be days between real meals. Nights would pass without shelter, often beneath trees or cardboard boxes in the rain. Their only clothes were on their backs until they could steal or beg more.

They were not proud. There was virtually nothing they would not do to survive, save one thing: They would not sell their bodies. But finally that, too, fell victim to the streets, to survival.

Maggie got out of bed and glanced at the digital clock on the nightstand. It was 2:20 A.M. and she still had not slept. Leaving her robe lying on the end of the bed, she slipped into the hallway, glanced quickly into Danny's room, and made her way to the kitchen. She opened the refrigerator, but saw nothing that looked appetizing. Unable to abide another glass of warm milk, she simply sat, staring into the darkened living room and listening to the seconds tick away on the clock above the sink.

Is there any time more still than the dead of night?

"We have to do it," Sissy said.

"Wrong. We don't *have* to do anything," Maggie replied. "And I won't do it."

They were sitting at a picnic bench, sheltered from the winter rain by the roof of the park pavilion. But the shelter, open on all sides, provided no protection from the chill that penetrated their bodies and kept them both shivering. It had been raining for three days, a hard, slashing rain that filled the parched reservoirs, but made life miserable. Especially for those who made their homes where they could find them.

"Look," Sissy persisted, "we haven't had shit to eat for two days. Our clothes are sopped, we're freezing our asses, and we've got no goddamned place to sleep."

"The rain can't go on forever," Maggie argued. "And it's bound to get warmer. This is California, for Christ's sake."

Sissy got up and walked to the edge of the shelter, cupping her hand to catch the water cascading from the roof. "It may go on for days," she said. "You know that."

Maggie could not remember being hungrier. The rain kept people off the streets or in a rush to get inside, making panhandling almost impossible. They had fished the last forgotten quarter out of every pay phone they could find and had been turned away from every fast-food joint where they'd tried to hustle a free meal. Even the garbage in the Dumpsters was soggy and inedible. "We could go to one of the shelters," she said.

Sissy turned on her heel. "No fucking way," she shouted. "I'm not taking any handout from those God lovers. Forget it."

Maggie sat quietly, cowed by the anger in Sissy's voice.

"It's two hundred bucks apiece," Sissy said, returning to the bench, "but it's both of us or nothing."

"Why me?" Maggie said. "He doesn't even know me."

"He's seen you with me. Says you give him a hard-on from half a block away. You want to know the truth, I think he's only taking me to get at you."

"My God, Sissy. Spare me."

"Come on! It's two hundred bucks. Think about it. Steak for dinner, for Christ's sake. We'll drink some wine, sleep in a real bed for a change. Get some new clothes. All for an hour's worth of work."

Maggie shook her head. "Listen to yourself. We're not going to be flipping burgers at some McDonald's. We're talking about a porno movie here. Getting screwed and who knows what else by guys we've never seen before. All on camera. It makes me sick to think about it."

Sissy edged closer. "Yeah, like you've never been screwed before."

Maggie turned away, saying nothing, unwilling to admit the truth.

Sissy kept up the pressure. "The guy is cool. And it's not some sleazy back-room operation. He's got a nice setup with fancy equipment and all that. He says it's more like an instruction movie, you know, showing the right techniques and shit."

"Sure," Maggie snickered. "And you believe that crap?"

"Why not? Besides, we can use fake names, and they'll make us up any way we want. Dye our hair, whatever."

"That's because they're afraid of getting busted. We're kids, you know. It's against the god-damned law."

Sissy got up and faced her. "I'm sick of talking about it. Hear me? If we keep sitting here, we could die of pneumonia. Or starve to death. We're going to do it. You owe me, remember? The fuckin' guy and the knife? Time for payback, Maggie."

Maggie stayed where she was as Sissy moved to

the edge of the pavilion, waiting. "It's now or never," she called back. "Come on or I'm baggin' you. I mean it."

Even now, twelve years later, Maggie could vividly recall her internal struggle. Although she knew she could somehow survive the hunger, rain, and cold, she wasn't sure she could again face being alone on the streets. Sissy had become the dominant influence in her young life, her protector and confidante. The thought of facing the next day, let alone the next week or month, without her by her side was beyond her imagination.

Maybe it was that. Maybe the cold and hunger had weakened not only her body but her resolve. Whatever it was, she found herself getting up and following Sissy through the rain.

As it turned out, the worst of Maggie's fears were realized anyway. They made the movie the next day. They were each paid their two hundred dollars, but then Sissy split without explanation, without a good-bye. Maggie never saw or heard from her again.

4

Danny was at the kitchen table munching on Frosted Flakes when Maggie struggled out of the bedroom, her eyes still filled with the sleep that had finally come. Exactly when, she wasn't sure, but she guessed it must have been close to 4:00 A.M. That meant less than three hours of sleep, a fact not lost on her head and body. Both ached, but she was determined not to allow her misery to show.

Not to worry. Danny hardly noticed her entrance; he was caught up in the cartoons that blared from the small TV on the kitchen counter.

"'Morning, kiddo," she said as she passed in front of him to reach the coffee, already perked thanks to an automatic timer on the pot. Filling her cup with one hand, she turned down the volume of the TV with the other.

"Mom!" Danny protested. "It was just getting good."

"You're not deaf, Danny. Nor am I."

It was not unusual for her son to be up before her, even when she got a normal night's sleep. He had quickly learned that the first to rise got to choose the breakfast cereal, meaning Frosted Flakes instead of Cream of Wheat, and controlled the television set, at least for a while, meaning cartoons instead of the *Today* show.

"Aren't you going to say 'good morning'?" she asked, leaning back against the counter, sipping the coffee.

"What?" His eyes were still on the TV set.

"Good morning, aren't you going to say 'good morning'?"

"Oh, Mom, c'mon. I'm trying to watch."

His hair was tangled, and his Power Ranger pajamas were drooping around his bottom.

"We've got to get dressed, kiddo. We're running late."

Without taking his eyes from the cartoons, he held up his half-empty cereal bowl. "I'm not done yet," he replied.

"Concentrate on eating and forget the TV. By the time I'm out of the bathroom, I want you in your clothes, ready to go. Hustle."

The bathroom mirror reflected the sleepless night and the demons that haunted her. Her skin was pasty and there were pouches beneath her eyes, the whites of which were streaked with red darts. Like I've been on an all-night bender, she thought ruefully.

She hoped a little makeup would help, at least enough to get Danny to school and herself back home. She rarely ran into anyone on these morning walks, but when she did, she knew they expected her to look as good in person as she did on their television screen. She would make a special effort to avoid any of those encounters today.

Shrugging off her robe, she started to slip into her underwear and sweats, but paused, again studying the mirror's reflection. Straightening up, holding her body erect, she examined herself, comparing the image to the body in the photo. The years showed, no doubt about it. The years and the birth of the child who now sat in the kitchen. A slight sag to her breasts, a small swelling to her stomach, thighs somewhat fuller than in those earlier years.

Still, it was a body that any woman her age would be pleased to possess, that any man would be pleased to know. She had worked hard in the little spare time she had to stay in shape, to keep the muscles toned and the weight off. The television business had demanded it, as did her own sense of confidence and self-worth.

Enough of that, she thought as she turned from the mirror and quickly slipped into her clothes. She took two more minutes to apply the makeup and was out the bathroom door. To her surprise, she found her son dressed and standing in the kitchen, his small backpack slung over one shoulder.

"Good for you," she said, checking him over. Shirt tucked in, belt on, shoelaces tied, jacket zipped.

"You said we were in a hurry," he said.

"We are, honey. We just have enough time to get you to school. Got everything?"

He nodded and moved toward the door. As Maggie followed, she was again struck by how he'd grown, how adult he'd become. A real little man, she thought, who, unlike many of his young classmates, had never shown the slightest hesitation about going to school, even on that first day when many others had cried and clung to their mothers. If anything, he seemed embarrassed that she insisted on walking him to school every day, often urging her to part a block away before the other kids could see them. Reluctantly, she had complied, but never turned for home before he was safely inside the school doors.

Today was no different. They separated down the street from the school, and when she leaned over to kiss him good-bye, he stiffened and quickly scooted away, shouting over his shoulder, "See you later, Mom. Meet you right here."

She waved and watched until the school doors closed behind him.

The newsroom seemed quieter than usual when Maggie walked in that afternoon. Not hushed by any means, but lacking the normal robust commotion she had become accustomed to both in Los Angeles and here. It's either a slow news day or my imagination, she decided.

But as she shed her coat and settled in at her cubicle, she sensed an even greater quiet and sidelong glances from around the newsroom. The

word had spread, she knew immediately. Here's
the anchorwoman who damned near fell on her
face last night, they must be thinking. What's her
problem anyway?

Ignoring the unwanted attention, Maggie busied herself tidying up her desk, which she had left
in disarray the night before. Old scripts went into
her file drawer, yesterday's newspapers into the
trash can along with the assorted and outdated
news releases. That left only her computer on the
desk, along with the framed pictures of Danny:
one as a toddler cuddled in the lap of an L.A.
Santa Claus, the other more recent, a profession-
ally posed shot of the two of them sitting side by
side by a fireplace in the photographer's studio.

That was her favorite, simply because it seemed
so *normal.* Mother and son, smiling, happy, content with themselves and each other. True, the
picture was missing a husband and father, but that
was hardly unusual these days. Half the people in
the newsroom were single or divorced, a few of
them—like herself—single parents.

Satisfied with the desktop, she walked past the
assignment desk to the coffee alcove and found a
freshly-brewed pot awaiting her. She had no more
than filled her cup when she was approached by
Teresa Jensen, George Barclay's assistant.

"The boss would like to see you," Teresa said.
"If you've got a minute."

"No problem," Maggie replied, carefully balancing the coffee cup as she followed Teresa
across the newsroom to Barclay's corner office.

George Barclay was the longtime news director of the station, the man who had discovered

Maggie laboring as a weekend anchor at one of the independent stations in Los Angeles and had persuaded her to come to the Twin Cities as the coanchor of the important six and ten o'clock newscasts.

She was hired to replace a woman named Barbara Miller, who had left the station after achieving almost overnight stardom in the market. Now anchoring at a network-owned station in New York, Miller was rumored to be the next host of the network's morning news program. Not bad for a Minnesota farm girl, no older than Maggie herself.

Miller was gone by the time Maggie arrived, but the newspaper critics wasted little time in noting, with more than a trace of sarcasm, the extraordinary similarities between the two women. Like Miller, Maggie was blond and blessed with a Scandinavian-like beauty that Minnesotans seemed to find so appealing. The critics forgot that Maggie, unlike Miller, was of English descent and had grown up on the streets of L.A., not in the farm furrows of Minnesota.

For a time, she chafed at the references to her as "Barbara's clone" or the "anchor look-alike," but then ignored them, convinced that if she did her job well and established her own on-air identity, those jibes would pass. Eventually, they did.

She was, in fact, able to build on Miller's success, increasing Channel 7's already dominant ratings. Hardly a week passed that she was not contacted by stations in other larger markets offering her a job. Many of those inquiries came at the behest of the other stations in the Twin Cities, eager to rid

themselves of a strong competitor. But Maggie
had a three-year contract that she was determined
to honor. In fact, for Danny's sake and for the sake
of stability, she hoped her tenure here would be
even longer, and she never hesitated to say as
much to the headhunters.

"Hello, Margaret. C'mon in."

Barclay sat behind his desk, hands folded neatly
in front of him.

"*Maggie*, George. It's Maggie, remember."

You could barely see the smile behind his
beard. Never relenting, he alone in the newsroom
continued to call her by her given name. Others
had tried, but were quick to retreat in the face of
her pique. Not George. He enjoyed tweaking her.

"Sit down, please," he said.

Only then did she see Brett Jacobi off to one
side, half-sitting on the window ledge, lanky legs
outstretched. She knew immediately what was
coming. "I don't want to talk about it," she said,
preempting the inevitable and making no effort
to disguise her irritation. "I made that clear to
Brett. He should have told you by now."

"What's that?" Barclay asked innocently.

"Don't play games, George. Please."

She watched for a reaction, but saw none.
Barclay was a hefty man, two hundred and fifty
pounds or more, she guessed. But from what
she'd been told, he'd once been even heavier, by
forty or fifty pounds. A heart attack waiting to happen. A few years of dieting and regular exercise at
the nearby YMCA had carved inches of the fat
away, but he remained a most imposing figure.

Imposing, too, was his reputation in the television

news business, a fact that had played a part in Maggie's decision to make the move to Minnesota. Known in the industry for his hard-nosed news sense and integrity, Barclay was one of a dwindling breed of news directors who cared more about substance than cosmetics, would cut no ethical corners to get a story, and demanded that his staff display the same kind of good sense and dedication that had marked his own career. He tolerated no fools and gave no special sway to the stars of the show—including Maggie.

"From what I hear," George finally said, "it doesn't sound like a game." His chair creaked as he leaned back, moving his folded hands from the desktop to his broad stomach, waiting.

Maggie shifted her glance from Barclay to Brett and back. "It's personal," she said. "Let's leave it at that."

"C'mon, Maggie—" Brett protested before Barclay waved him quiet.

"At least let me get things straight," Barclay said. "From what Jacobi tells me, you must have found something on your desk that you weren't expecting to find. That somebody must have put there. Whatever it was, it upset you, damned near caused you to keel over, the way Brett tells it. Says you looked like a friggin' ghost. Am I right so far?"

She shook her head. "This is ridiculous."

"Is it?" Barclay asked. "I don't have to remind you that you're a fairly important person around here. We have a lot riding on you. *I* have a lot riding on you. If something's bothering you . . . if you're in some kind of trouble, personal or not, I should know about it. You owe me that, don't you?"

Maggie took a moment before she responded. He was right, to a degree, but there was no way she could tell him what had happened. No way. "Only if it affects my performance," she said, finally. "And I hardly think it's come to that."

"So far," Barclay reminded her gently.

Brett uncoiled himself and stood leaning against the wall. "Maggie, admit it. You were more than upset. You were scared. That's why I came to George. If you're getting some kind of threats, if some kind of kook is out there, we need to know—"

"You're over-reacting, Brett. I told you that. I'm a big girl. If I feel like I'm in any danger, I'll let you know. This is a personal matter that I need to keep to myself for now."

The two men exchanged glances as she got out of her chair, coffee cup still in hand. "May I leave now?" she said.

Barclay nodded. "Keep in touch," he said as she walked out the door.

As Brett turned to follow Maggie, Barclay called him back. His face was grim. "So what do you think now?" he asked.

Brett settled into a chair and shook his head. "I don't know what to think. I only know what I saw and heard. I've never seen her shook up before, not like that. We've had shows explode in our faces, when everything that could go wrong went wrong, and she's never gotten flustered. Just look at last night, when we lost Cromwell's live shot. She was smooth as silk."

Barclay hoisted himself out of his chair and walked to the window, his back to Brett, hands deep in his pockets. "I suppose it could be just another of the crazies out there," he said. "God knows I've seen enough of them over the years. They get out of whack over the image on the television screen, fall in love, for Christ's sake, and then start doing stupid things like sending letters and gifts. Most of them are demented, but not dangerous."

"Don't forget the Iowa woman," Brett reminded him.

"I haven't," Barclay said, although he had tried to put it in the back of his mind. A young anchor-woman in a small Iowa market had been abducted months before, perhaps by an infatuated fan. She had not been seen since, and was feared dead.

"Maggie has seen her share of the harmless loonies," Brett said. "But this is different. Besides, she said it's personal, remember?"

"So what do you think we should do?"

"I wish I knew." Brett sighed. "Watch and wait, I guess. She obviously doesn't want any help now."

"You think someone's after her?"

"I can't imagine who, but somebody sure as hell has put a scare into her."

"Could it be an ex-boyfriend or something? She's not exactly open about her personal life."

"No way," Brett snapped. "I'd know about it."

Barclay turned from the window and studied him for a moment before speaking. "This is none of my business, but I'll ask anyway. I know the two of you are good friends, but does it, you know, well, go beyond that?"

Brett laughed. "You've got to be kidding."

"Do I?"

"You're right, it's none of your business. But I'll tell you anyway. No."

Barclay said nothing.

"Not that I don't wish it could," Brett continued. "We're about as close as two people can be without being . . . well, you know. She's never encouraged it, and I've never pressed it."

"But you'd like to?"

Brett got up and walked to the door. "I figure if she's ever interested, she'll let me know. Meantime, I don't want to screw up what we've got. And I don't want to see her get hurt."

"You're not alone," Barclay said, turning back to stare out the window.

Barclay's questions lingered in Brett's mind as he made his way across the newsroom and back to his desk. Although surprised that Barclay had raised the issue of his relationship with Maggie, he knew the same questions had been on the lips or minds of everyone in the newsroom at one time or another, although they were rarely raised in public . . . and almost never to his face.

Truth be known, if he would ever have the courage to admit it, he was hopelessly in love with the woman. Madly, totally, unwaveringly, and secretly in love. From practically her first day at the station. How could he help it? She was beautiful, sweet, talented and, as far as anyone could tell, invitingly unattached. Except to the boy, Danny, who seemed to consume almost all of her time and attention outside of work.

Brett had stood aside as others both in and out of the newsroom had made their play for her, watching with interest and abiding hope as she coolly but politely deflected the approaches. True, she went on an occasional date, but seldom more than once or twice with the same man. Early on, he had been one of those in line, but had quickly felt the same cool rejection. Unlike some of the others, however, he had learned as a very young man to never pursue a woman who showed no interest in being pursued. To do so, he knew, could spoil whatever slim chances might eventually exist.

So he had quickly retreated, dating other women from time to time, content with his deepening friendship with Maggie ... and with the hope that the friendship would someday ripen into the relationship he could now only dream of.

The promotion department occupied a part of the second floor of the station, tucked away next to sales and marketing and just down the hall from the offices of upper management. Maggie rarely ventured to this part of the building, known cynically in the news department as "management heaven," but she still had managed to become friends with the promotion director, a woman named Sophia Dromboski.

Sophy was at her desk, almost hidden away by stacks of videotapes, newspapers, and trade magazines. An unlit cigarette dangled from her lips, waiting for her twice-an-hour trip outside to light up. Smoking here, as in most buildings, was strictly prohibited, but that had not forced Sophy to break the habit.

"Screw 'em," she had told Maggie. "They can't

tell me how to live or die. Wish they'd mind their own fucking business."

Maggie knocked lightly on the door and walked in before Sophy looked up. "Got a minute?" she asked.

In her mid-forties, Sophy looked older: Her makeup was heavy and carelessly applied, the lipstick closer to orange than red and ranging well beyond the outline of her lips. Her hair, like her lips, was of some hue between red and orange. She admitted she had changed it so often over the years that she could no longer remember its original color.

Loud and profane, she was a character who reveled in her reputation for outrageous appearance and behavior. She was also one of the sweetest people Maggie had met at the station—and good at her job.

Sophy took the cigarette from her mouth and slipped it behind her ear. "You've got about three minutes," she said, glancing at her watch, "or you're going to have to stand out on the goddamned street with me while I have a smoke."

Maggie slid into a chair across the desk. "I won't take that long. I'm told somebody up here led a tour group in the station last night."

"Yeah, the new kid, Denise. Some church group, I think. You must have seen them wandering around."

Maggie shook her head. "I was back in editing for much of the night, doing a couple of voice tracks. Then to the studio. I didn't see anybody."

Sophy looked puzzled. "So what's the problem? Did you get ripped off?"

"Just the opposite. Somebody left something on my desk. I'd like to know who."

"Something?" The question hung in the air.

"That's not important," Maggie said. "Is this Denise around?"

"Not right now. She's off running an errand."

"What do you know about her?"

"Denise? Not much, actually. Seems like a sweet enough kid. We hired her right out of the university."

Maggie said nothing, looking past Sophy out the window.

"You think she might have something to do with this?" Sophy asked.

Maggie shrugged. "I don't know what to think. But will you have her call me? Or stop by?"

"Sure, but why don't you tell me more?"

"No thanks," Maggie replied with a slight smile. "Just have her call me, huh."

"No problem," Sophy said as she put the cigarette back between her lips.

An hour later, Denise showed up at Maggie's cubicle. "Miss Lawrence?" she said shyly. And when Maggie looked up, she added, "I'm Denise Parelli. Sophy said you wanted to talk to me."

"Sit down, Denise, and please forget the Miss Lawrence business. I'm Maggie to everyone around here."

Denise perched on the edge of the chair, appearing no less uncomfortable, almost ready to flee. It was her first meeting with a real anchorwoman. "Sophy said you asked about the tour group last night."

"That's right. Tell me about it."

"There's not much to tell," Denise admitted. "There were about twenty of them, people I mean, from Saint Raphael's church in northeast Minneapolis. A single's club, I think. I just showed them around, as I was told to do. Was there some problem?"

Maggie felt sorry for the young woman, so fragile and frightened, almost fawn-like, with wide eyes and a tremor in her voice. Any suspicions Maggie had about her quickly disappeared. "Relax, Denise. Please. Just tell me what time they got here . . . and when they left."

"They got here about eight. And left right after the news. Please, did I do something wrong, Miss Lawrence?"

Maggie let the name and the question ride. "Did you bring them in here, to the newsroom?"

"We walked through, that's all. I told them they had to be quiet, and not to touch anything. I didn't want them to bother anyone."

"Were you with them the whole time?"

Denise paused, thinking. "Except for a couple of minutes. I had to run to the bathroom."

Maggie considered what she'd heard, then asked, "Did you happen to notice anyone carrying an envelope, you know, a large manila one? With green writing on it."

Denise shook her head. "Gosh, not that I remember. Several of them were carrying things, briefcases and such. I didn't pay much attention."

"Do you have their names, Denise? The people in the group?"

"Only the leader, the one who arranged for the tour. And that's upstairs, in the office."

"Would you mind getting it for me? And his number, if you've got it. I'd like to give him a call."

"I'll be back in a minute," Denise said, clearly relieved to free. "You're sure I didn't do anything wrong?"

"I'm sure," Maggie said. "Just get me the name and number."

5

She had the name a few minutes later: Harry Carlisle.

She also had a phone number and a brief description of him: mid-forties, graying hair, about six feet tall with a sharp nose. "That's about all I can remember," Denise said. "Except that he had real bad breath. I thought I'd gag if I stood too close."

A middle-aged bachelor with bad breath, Maggie thought. Swell.

Now that she knew that much, so what? So he was the leader of a single's group. What did that mean? Probably nothing. Whoever left the envelope could have been anyone in the group. Or no one. She could hardly call Carlisle and ask for

the names of everyone in his group. How would
she explain that? And even if she got the names,
what would they mean? Was she supposed to
check out each one? Discover who among them
might like to sit around and watch old pornographic movies?

It was ridiculous and she knew it.

Even so, it would be nice to know a little bit
more about Harry Carlisle. He wasn't much, but
he was all she had. She dialed the number.

"Sinclair Engineering." A woman's voice, receptionist sweet.

"Mr. Carlisle, please," Maggie said.

"May I ask who's calling?"

Maggie paused. What the hell? "Maggie Lawrence
from Channel Seven."

She could hear the slight intake of breath at the
other end. Sweet voice knew the name. "One
moment, please," she said.

Maggie counted to fifteen before he answered.
Time enough to be told who he would be talking to.

"Carlisle here," he said, syrupy smooth. Syrupy
voice, smelly breath. Hard to picture.

"Mr. Carlisle, this is Maggie Lawrence from
Channel Seven. I hope I'm not disturbing you."

"Not at all, it's a pleasure to talk with you. I'm
sorry we didn't meet last night when we were at
the station."

"That's the reason for my call," she said.

"Really? How's that?"

Maggie knew she had to be careful, but she also
knew it was no time to be too cute. "Mr. Carlisle, I
have a little mystery on my hands. Somebody left
something on my desk last night. An envelope

with my name on it. The contents were quite disturbing."

"Really? I'm sorry to hear that." There seemed to be genuine surprise in his voice. "You think someone from our group might be responsible?"

"That's what I'm trying to determine. As far as I can tell, you were the only outsiders in the station last night."

"I don't know what to say." He was becoming flustered. "I can't believe that anyone in our group . . . we're from a church, you know. Saint Raphael's. I know most everyone quite well—"

"Please understand, Mr. Carlisle," she said, trying to use her most reasonable voice, "I'm not making any accusations. I just want to check out all of the possibilities."

"Can you tell me anything more . . . ?"

"The envelope was a large one, a manila mailing envelope. My name was written . . . scrawled, really . . . in green ink. Large block letters. Did you see anyone in your group carrying anything like that?"

No hesitation now. "No, no, I didn't. I almost certainly would have noticed. The women carried their purses, but most of the men, I think, left their briefcases and such in the tour room where we met. I know I didn't want to lug mine around the station."

"How many people in your group?" Maggie asked.

"Thirty-two in the club, but only nineteen took the tour. Some had to work, a few were on vacation. Pretty good turnout, I thought."

"Are there more men than women?"

"More women, I'd say. There usually are. I can give you an exact count, if you'd like."

"That won't be necessary."

She wanted to ask Carlisle what kind of company Sinclair Engineering was and what he did there, but she was interrupted by a signal from Brett Jacobi across the newsroom. She glanced at her watch. Four o'clock. Sweeps meeting.

"Mr. Carlisle, I have to go now, but—"

"Can you tell me what we're dealing with here? You said the envelope contained something, what, disturbing?"

"I'd like to tell you more, but I can't," Maggie said. "Perhaps we can talk further in the future."

"Be assured we'll be of any assistance possible. Our club is really quite reputable, the members quite nice . . ."

"I'm sure that's true," she replied, hoping to end the conversation. "I'll be back in touch if anything develops."

As she hung up, she felt some relief. He certainly sounded normal enough. But then, what could you tell over the phone? Or even face-to-face, for that matter? Perverts or stalkers don't necessarily stand out in a crowd.

Of one thing she was certain: Others in the St. Raphael's singles club would soon be aware of her call. And if the envelope had come from one of them, they would know she was wasting little time trying to trace it. For whatever that was worth.

By the time Maggie arrived at the sweeps meeting, most of the participants were already seated around a long table in a conference room just off the newsroom.

"Sorry to be late," she said as she slipped into one of the empty chairs.

"No problem," George Barclay replied, eyeing her carefully. "We're still waiting on a couple of others. Let's give them another minute or so."

As they sat waiting, Maggie's eyes were again drawn to the top of the conference table. It was hard to avoid, and the sight never ceased to amaze and amuse her.

Built on the cheap by the station's carpenters years before, the table's pine top now bore the carved initials of every person who had worked in the newsroom since the table's creation. Hardly a square inch of its surface remained unscarred.

As she was quick to learn, it not only served as a conference table, but as lunch table, poker table, and, some suspected, as an occasional platform for more exotic late-night adventures. No question, it was the favorite gathering place in the newsroom, the spiritual centerpiece of the place.

No one was absolutely certain whose initials had been the first to be inscribed, but newsroom lore pointed to Terrance McCarthy, a flake photographer whose TMC was spotted squarely in the center of the table. Unfortunately for Terrance, his carving skills far outweighed his photographic skills, and he was fired within a matter of weeks. But his initials had endured. And so had his name and legend. Even though few could remember the man himself, to everybody it was "Terry's table," and "Terry's room."

The table had come to be regarded as an eclectic work of art, with each new set of initials judged critically for its particular flare and flamboyance.

Maggie's ML, uninspired as she had to admit it was, was off to one end, squeezed between one of the producer's SW and a reporter's LT.

With the arrival of two more people at the table, Barclay said, "Okay, let's get started."

This was one of the few newsroom meetings that Barclay himself chaired, which spoke to its importance. At this and subsequent sessions, the subjects of the special sweeps series for the coming February rating period would be discussed and decided upon. While February was still months away, it was considered crucial to get an early start on researching and producing the stories. Indeed, the November sweeps series, which had yet to begin, had been assigned early in the summer.

As Maggie knew all too well, a station's ratings performance during the sweeps months was key to its news image and the flow of advertising dollars into the station coffers. Increasingly, the success of the sweeps was tied to the quality and appeal of the sweeps series.

Although Barclay never tired of berating the system, he was nonetheless a captive of it. "Why the fuck should we live and die by what we do in three sweeps months," he often ranted. "We ought to be judged by what we do all twelve months of the year."

You're right, George, the people in management heaven would sadly and patiently tell him, but that's not the way the world is today.

Besides Barclay, all of the key newsroom executives were at the table: the assistant news director, the executive producer, the assignment managers, and the producers of all the important late news programs. Maggie and coanchor Alex Collier were included as a matter of courtesy, but also because their ideas and opinions had come to be appreciated in the newsroom.

"We've got an hour," Barclay said, glancing at the clock above the door. "Where did we leave things?"

Stephanie Long, the executive producer whose squat stature belied her name, stood up and walked to an easel at one end of the room. She stretched to flip over a blank page, revealing another filled with a list of five story ideas. "This is as far as we got," she said as she ran her finger down the entries. "Number one. The safety of the seafood we buy in the stores. Thompson says he thinks we'll find traces of mercury and other toxic shit in some of it. But it's going to cost us a ton getting the lab work done."

She paused, waiting for reaction. Alex Collier didn't disappoint her. "Wayne Thompson thinks every goddamned thing in the world is toxic," Collier complained. "He's got a toxic fetish ... won't eat hardly anything that he doesn't grow in that garden of his."

"Cool it, Alex," Barclay cautioned with a grin. "You know that's what happens to environmental reporters."

Ignoring the exchange, Stephanie went on to quickly recite the other four items on the list: the effectiveness of a new security system at the Twin Cities International Airport; suspicions of nepotism in the state treasurer's office; the courts' apparent inability to protect spouses in domestic abuse cases; and, finally, little-known loopholes in the state's day-care licensing laws that could allow convicted felons to take care of kids. When she finished, the room fell quiet. All eyes turned to Barclay. "I've been thinking about these," he finally said. "They look good on paper, but we should again consider the risks."

"What do you mean?" Stephanie asked, a bit defensively.

"Look at the list," Barclay replied. "What if we spend months and a bucketful of money, but still find no shit in the seafood? What if there are no holes in the airport system? No felons in day care, no cousins or nephews working in the treasurer's office? There are no sure things on that list— except for maybe the domestic abuse piece, and that's hardly what I'd call an ass grabber."

Brett Jacobi spoke up from the other end of the table. "C'mon, George, since when do we do sure things? Every time we plan for one of these sweeps, we know we're taking a chance."

Barclay held up his hand. "Don't get me wrong. One or two may turn out, but I doubt that all five will. And we're going to need a solid five for February. We need to expand the list and be ready to dump the first one that doesn't show early promise."

Two or three more ideas were floated by the group, but only one seemed to generate any enthusiasm. They'd gotten a tip that a couple of farmers in southern Minnesota were adopting starving wild horses from Montana as an act of human kindness, then selling them for slaughter at five to six times the price they paid for them.

Horse meat, it seems, is a big seller in Europe, and so far, the government had failed to devise a way to check on the welfare of the horses they put out for adoption.

"How solid is that information," Barclay asked, "and will the story hold until February?"

John DeMaris, the assistant news director, shrugged. "Who knows? The network did a piece on the problem a couple of weeks ago, and we got the telephone tip about the two farmers a couple of days later. We're still trying to check it out."

"If we got a tip," Barclay groused, "so did everyone else."

"Don't be so sure," DeMaris said. "The tipster is a real fan, said he won't watch any other news. That he just *loves* Maggie."

Exaggerated groans came from around the table, which Maggie responded to with a slight bow and grin. "See," she said, "it's about time I get a little respect around here."

More groans and laughter.

Barclay waited for the room to quiet. "There is one other possibility floating out there," he said, "although I don't know if it will go anywhere. Much less be ready by February."

He suddenly had everyone's attention.

"Unbeknownst to most of you," he continued, "Jessica's been poking around rumors of a child pornography ring that may be operating in the suburbs."

Jessica Mitchell was a young reporter who had been with the station only a few years. Early on, Maggie had been told, she'd broken the story of a group of women vigilantes—led by a woman police lieutenant—thought to be responsible for the murders of several sexual predators who had escaped the law.

Barclay went on. "She got wind of the ring from some of her sources on the street, but she doesn't know much yet. She's just beginning the investigation, but there may be substance to the rumors. And it could involve a few names we'd all recognize."

A low whistle came from the other end of the table.

"This is strictly hush-hush," Barclay warned. "As far as we know, we're alone on this, and I don't want anybody blabbing about it over a beer. And don't bug Jessica. She's got enough to think about. I'll keep you posted on any progress."

Brett Jacobi leaned forward in his chair. "Who are we talking about here, George? What names might we recognize?"

"I can't say anything more right now, except for this: Word has gotten back to Jessica that some of the principals might be aware that we're sniffing around the story. That's why I've told you as much as I have. So . . . we'll just keep our guard up and our lips buttoned."

Maggie had sat quietly through Barclay's disclosure, attentive but uninvolved. Until his final words.

Only then did she think of the envelope.

She wondered if anyone else at the table heard the small gasp escape her lips.

6

Maggie was in makeup, as she always was fifteen minutes before the show, when Brett Jacobi knocked lightly on the door of the Green Room and walked in.

"I'll just be a minute," she told his reflection in the makeup mirror. "I know we're getting close."

"No sweat," he said, "but you may want to give Anna a call before you hit the studio."

"Anna?"

"I just picked up your phone. She'd like you to call as soon as possible."

Maggie swung around quickly in her chair. "Is it Danny? What's happened?"

Jacobi shook his head. "No, Danny's fine. She

said someone dropped off a package. Marked urgent. She thought you might want to know."

"Who dropped it off?" She tried but failed to keep her voice level.

"I asked her the same question, but she didn't know. Said she found it by your mailbox, just inside the outside door. She didn't see who left it there."

Maggie grabbed her news script and rushed past him, ignoring his trailing questions. She picked up a phone on a wall of the studio and hurriedly punched in her home number. It rang four times before her son answered. "Danny, I've just got a minute. Is Anna there?"

"She's in the bathroom, Mom. Want me to call her?"

"Please, Danny. Tell her to hurry."

As she waited, a floor director approached her. "Five minutes to air, Maggie. You should be on the set."

She waved him away, mouthing, "I'll be right there" at the same time.

A minute later, Anna was on the phone.

"Anna, listen. We have to hurry. Tell me about the package, quickly."

"I shouldn't be bothering you," Anna said slowly and apologetically, "but it seemed strange coming the way it did."

"Quickly, Anna."

"Well, it's one of those mailing envelopes, you know the kind."

The floor director was hovering next to her. "C'mon, Maggie. That anchor chair's going to look silly without you in it."

"It had your name on it," Anna continued, "but was marked personal. And urgent. No return address or anything."

"The writing, Anna. What color ink?"

"Funny you'd ask. I thought it was strange. It's green. It's been years since I've seen green ink."

Maggie closed her eyes and took a deep breath. "Anna, I have to go now. But please, don't open the package. Put it in the cupboard, high enough so Danny can't reach it. I'll explain later."

Anna agreed and Maggie hung up, just in time to have the floor director pull her by the arm and lead her to the set. They were counting down the final thirty seconds to air by the time she had her microphone and earpiece in place. It was at that moment that it suddenly hit her. *My God, they not only know who I am, but now where I live. They must have been following me, watching me. And they must know about Danny, too.* She choked back a cry as the Teleprompter came alive in front of her.

It came as no surprise to find Brett standing by the studio door as she and Alex signed off the newscast. "Nice show," he told both of them as they walked past and back toward the newsroom.

"I thought so, too," Alex replied. "Some real news in it for a change."

The two men stopped and continued to talk as Maggie walked on, hoping to outdistance the questions she knew would be coming. But Brett caught up with her as she reached her cubicle.

"Anything you want to tell me?" he asked.

She filed the script away and straightened the top of her desk. "About what?"

"About Anna's phone call . . . the package."

"There's nothing to tell."

"Nice try, but I saw the look on your face."

She slumped into her chair. "Brett, for Christ's sake, give me a break. You're getting to feel like my shadow."

He stared down at her, his expression revealing both hurt and anger. "You're right. I shouldn't be spending my time worrying about something that's none of my business. What the hell are friends for anyway?"

With that, he turned and strode away, leaving Maggie staring after him, trying to decide whether she should be angrier with him or herself. It was no contest.

On most evenings, Maggie was given two hours off between the early and late news, a time to relax and regroup so that, theoretically, she would appear as fresh and sharp at ten o'clock as she had at six. Many nights, when her other duties allowed it, she would make a quick trip home—to share a hurried supper with Danny and provide a short break for Anna.

But tonight, she knew Anna had taken Danny to her daughter's home for dinner. The daughter had a teenage son who had become Danny's idol and video game mentor. Maggie suspected they wouldn't be home until well after she had to be back to work. On one hand, it would be an ideal time to retrieve and inspect the package now hidden away in the kitchen cupboard. But she had no appetite for that. Not now. She was dead certain what would be inside the package and was in no hurry to endure another sharp dash of pain and humiliation.

Instead, she made her way to the station lunchroom, retrieved a raisin bagel and a carton of yogurt from the vending machine, and then walked two blocks to a small park surrounding one of the downtown high-rise apartment buildings. Finding a small stone bench next to a reflecting pool populated by oversized goldfish and other finned species she couldn't identify, she sat down and stretched her legs. Immediately, she could feel the tension begin to drain away, from her shoulders down to her toes.

The sun had not yet fully set, but had sunk so low that few of its rays could find their way between the skyscrapers of the center city. She sat in the shadows, munching on the bagel, breathing in the cool evening air between bites, occasionally dropping a few crumbs to the waiting goldfish. Ugly things, she thought, and far hungrier than she was. It wouldn't be long, she knew, before the fish would have to be moved so they wouldn't be encased in ice. She wondered idly where they would spend the winter; they sure as hell were too big for any fishbowl she'd ever seen.

Forget the damned fish, she told herself. Think about what you're facing. Analyze what's happened and what it might mean. Put aside the horror and decide what to do.

There were several possibilities.

Whoever sent the packages could be a crank, a porno pervert who had stumbled upon the old tape and somehow recognized her, deciding to launch a campaign of terror simply for the perverse fun of it. Or perhaps a right-wing zealot determined to make her pay for her past sins. If either was true, he might eventually tire of the game and leave her in peace.

She had little hope or confidence in that theory.

It could be someone bent on blackmail. She knew, as he must, the terrible damage the public exposure of such a tape could do to her career. Her reputation, both personal and professional, would be crushed, not only in the Twin Cities but anywhere else in the country she might try to relocate. Once public, copies of the pictures or the tape would follow her everywhere; she would find no safe haven from the snickers and the scorn. But if it was blackmail, why were there still no demands for money or other favors?

While she wondered whether any of the local newspapers would publish the pictures or even carry a story about the tape, she knew some of the national tabloids would love to get their hands on it. Forget the fact that she'd been sixteen at the time of the film, a penniless street kid who should have known better but didn't. It would make no difference. She shuddered at the thought of the possible headlines:

PORN QUEEN TURNS ANCHOR
or
ANCHOR TELLS NAKED TRUTH

Regardless of whether the story was ever published, the whispers would surely be there, first in every newsroom in the Cities, then in the bars, and before long in living rooms across the community. The living rooms of her viewers. How long would the station tolerate that?

And what about Danny? Perhaps too young to understand the scandal now, what about in the future? And how long could he escape the taunts of the other kids? The thought of it made her squirm.

But if the motive wasn't terror or blackmail, then what? Could it be someone inside the station, prompted by jealousy or spite or some other mysterious motive? She tried to think of enemies she may have made in the past two years. Not many, and none she thought might be capable of this. No real enemies, but not many real friends either. She had deliberately tried to stay apart from the cliquish camaraderie of the newsroom. She didn't fit in. She was a part of neither the single nor the married crowd. The fact is, she came to realize, she didn't really know that many people in the newsroom that well.

She suspected that some viewed her as aloof, even arrogant. She rarely attended station parties and never partook in the often inane ruckus of the newsroom, keeping largely to herself—open and friendly, but uninvolved. As far as anyone knew, she seldom dated and had never been seen with any man except Brett. And that in itself was viewed as curious: that the star anchorwoman would consort with a mere newsroom producer, no matter how experienced and respected he might be. Tongues wagged, but never openly. Maggie remained a mystery, and in a newsroom where knowledge is king and gossip the currency of choice, she caused untold frustration.

Behind her back, she had more than once been called the Virgin Mother Maggie.

Perhaps, she thought, there was someone she had unknowingly slighted in some way or who secretly coveted her job, someone who bore a grudge or ambition strong enough to want to terrorize her, to drive her away. She doubted it, but knew she would have to keep her eyes open.

And then there was Barclay's revelation at the sweeps meeting. Could the arrival of the packages have anything to do with Jessica Mitchell's child pornography investigation? It seemed unlikely, almost surely a coincidence. But Barclay did say that word of the investigation might have leaked. Could someone try to use Maggie's tarnished past as leverage to discourage the probe?

It's hopeless, she thought. There are just too many possibilities to consider, at least with what I know now. But it was frighteningly clear that this was only the beginning; two packages in two days pointed to more than some kind of perverted joke. But with what purpose? And what would come next?

As the last of the sunlight disappeared, she got up and made her way out of the park, walking slowly back to the station, thinking of only one immediate step she could take: defy Barclay's warning not to bother Jessica Mitchell about her investigation. The question was: How to do it? And when?

Aside from the perfunctory communication necessary between producer and anchor, Brett said nothing to Maggie before the late news. He kept to himself, stubbornly clinging to his computer, still smarting from the sting of her earlier rebuke. She approached him twice with needless questions about the script, hoping to thaw the icy silence, but his responses were curt and to the point.

Like the early news, this newscast went off without a hitch. Little news of importance had happened in the intervening hours, but with the repackaging and updating of the earlier stories, the newscast had at least taken on the appearance of freshness. On most nights, that was all you could ask.

Once they were off the air, Maggie went in search of Brett, checking first in the control room, where he had monitored the newscast, and then in the newsroom. He was in neither place, and no one could tell her where he'd gone.

"He took off like a rocket after the show," Lonnie Plunkett, the newscast director, said. "He was there one minute, gone the next."

After twenty more minutes of fruitless searching, she headed for the parking ramp.

Driving home, Maggie was barely able to keep her eyes open and on the road. Despite being almost alone in the late-night traffic, she had to struggle to stay alert and keep the car between the white lines. The fatigue and tension of the long day were taking their toll.

Her mind wandered. Back to the station, to Brett . . . who had fled without a word, now not only confused, but angry. And who could blame him? There was so much about her he didn't know.

While she had told him a fair amount about her more recent past—her years at UCLA and the time she had spent at the station in L.A.—he knew nothing of her childhood and her years as a runaway. Or the weeks after she made the movie, back on the mean streets, once again alone, resuming the solitary, scary life she had led before meeting Sissy.

But she could never forget them.

Picked up twice for shoplifting and once for pandering, she had spent several nights in a juvenile detention center, always refusing to speak or reveal her true identity for fear of being returned home. Frustrated by her silence, and bowing to the pressures of the overcrowded detention facilities, a juvenile judge had finally released her to a halfway house for troubled kids, which she promptly walked away from, never to return.

Back on the streets, she was faced with not only dodging the usual hazards, but the police and her probation officer, as well. For months she was on the run, scurrying like a frightened rabbit from warren to warren, keeping to herself, making few friends, trusting no one.

Until she met Elijah Robinson.

Elijah was a former pimp and recovering addict, a one-time drug dealer who was now a man of God, a black man with a heart of gold and a stash of cash from his dealing days that he was determined to put to a more God-like purpose. He ran a street ministry and soup kitchen in an old storefront just off Hollywood Boulevard that he called Redemption House, the kind of place Sissy would never have entered, no matter how desperate the circumstances or how empty her belly.

"Sure, they'll feed you," she used to tell Maggie, "but you'll pay a big price. Before you know it, they'll have you out on the streets, babbling from the Bible, hustling converts or singing in some fucking street-corner choir. Stay away from them."

Maggie had heeded the advice, even after Sissy had left her and even though she didn't fully believe it, steering clear of anyone or anyplace that seemed to want to trade food and comfort for access to her soul. For that reason, she never would have encountered Elijah had it not been for one of his kids, Celine, a six-year-old with chubby cheeks and cornrows who darted into the street after a ball as both a bus and Maggie happened to be passing by.

Without thinking, Maggie lunged after her, reaching the child only seconds before the bus did, pulling her to safety in the blare of the bus horn and the grinding of its brakes. The crushed ball beneath the huge wheels was sickening testimony to what could have befallen the girl.

Maggie didn't know who was the more shaken or hurt, herself or young Celine, but both ended up in a heap on the sidewalk, Maggie beneath the girl, both suffering from pavement cuts and bruises. Elijah, it turned out, had seen it all from the door of his mission and was the first to reach them—cradling the wailing child in his arms while trying to both thank Maggie and determine the extent of her injuries.

The worst of it was a badly-twisted ankle, which, when she tried to get up and walk away, would not bear her weight. She crumpled to the sidewalk again, crying out in pain, and before she could protest, she was helped into Redemption House by one of Elijah's disciples.

That was the beginning of the end of Maggie's life on the street. Unable to walk without help and with nowhere else to go, she grudgingly accepted the insistent pleas by Elijah to stay on at Redemption House, at least until she was back on her two feet. Enveloped by the family's warmth and gratitude, and enticed by a bed of her own and food without begging, she allowed the days to become weeks, and the weeks to become months—stretching to a full two years.

Redemption House became her home, a white girl welcomed into the bosom of the black family, soon becoming as much a child of Elijah and wife Cordelia as was any of their five children. Elijah became the father Maggie never had: Kindly and gentle, wise in the ways of the streets, a truly born-again Christian who had the wisdom and good sense to resist imposing his religious passions on her.

Nor did he seek to explore or expose her past or force her to return to her parents. He and his family simply accepted her for what she was: a runaway from an unhappy home who might well fall victim to the violence of the streets without their help. And who had, after all, saved their precious Celine from almost certain death beneath the wheels of the bus.

Elijah did persuade her to return to school, and within two years she had earned a high school diploma—with honors—and was offered the scholarship at UCLA.

While in high school, Maggie worked at the mission, earning her room and board by serving meals and scrubbing dishes in the kitchen. Years later, once she was out of college and earning a salary, she sent regular checks to the family—until she felt her debt had been fully repaid.

As she looked back on it now, those were the two happiest years of her then young life, secure and warm, filled with laughter and good cheer, where she finally learned to love and to be loved. Redemption House had redeemed her life and taught her that she had the intelligence and skills to face the world beyond the streets.

Although she maintained close contact with the family beyond her college years, the frequency of her visits slowed and finally ended when Elijah died of a stroke and his family scattered in all directions. Maggie still heard from Cordelia now and then, but had not seen her in years.

Elijah's death came two weeks after Danny was born . . . and six weeks before Maggie and the boy were suddenly abandoned by the man who had fathered him.

But that was another story . . . and more of her life that Brett knew nothing about.

Once back at the apartment, it was only after she had said good-bye to Anna and checked on her sleeping son that Maggie worked up the courage to pull the package from the upper shelf of the kitchen cupboard. As she suspected, Anna had been able to tell her little more about the envelope or its mysterious arrival, but to her relief, she did not appear overly curious or concerned about it.

Anna's only comment was, "You'd think people

would have the courtesy to include a return address."

As Maggie sat at the kitchen table inspecting the package, it came as no surprise to find it almost identical to the first. Same size, same markings. But this one seemed heavier. Bulkier.

With another furtive glance down the hallway, she tore it open. No wonder it felt heavier. Instead of a picture inside, she found a videotape. Unlabeled, but with a note attached, written in the same block-letter scrawl she had found on the outside of the two envelopes.

The note said simply:

ThERe aRe MORe WhEre tHis CaME FrOm.

7

It was almost ten the next morning when Maggie walked through the newsroom, aware of a few quizzical glances from colleagues not accustomed to seeing her in at that hour. She quickly brushed aside the questions while making her way to her cubicle.

She had hidden away the videotape the night before after looking at no more than a few seconds of the opening scene. It was enough to tell her that the tape was genuine. She could not bear to go further; she was in no mood to relive the horror of twelve years before. There would be time for that later.

As she sat down, she saw Jessica Mitchell working at her own desk across the room, near the door separating the newsroom from the videotape editing rooms beyond. Although Jessica's back was to her, Maggie could see she had a telephone tucked between her shoulder and ear while she typed furiously on her computer keyboard. Maybe not the best time to interrupt, she decided.

She wished now that she knew Jessica better, but was also quick to admit that it was a situation of her own making. Jessica was one of many people in the newsroom that Maggie had kept at a distance, not out of any dislike for the woman, but simply because she had chosen to keep newsroom friendships to a minimum.

Besides, they worked different hours and lived in different worlds, inside and outside of the newsroom. She was an anchor, Jessica a reporter, and while there was no caste system in George Barclay's newsroom, the two women had few opportunities to work together or socialize.

Jessica was single and involved with a young prosecutor she had met years before, while Maggie was single and a mother . . . and not involved with anyone. In short, they seemed to have little in common, and neither had ever made any real effort to connect.

To be sure, they had spoken on numerous occasions, and once or twice had had drinks together with others from the station. Even then, however, Maggie could not recall any lengthy conversations with the young reporter. But she was more than aware of Jessica's reputation. It was the stuff of newsroom legend. She knew that Jessica had narrowly escaped death in the pursuit of the vigilante story—the result of a harrowing confrontation with the leader of the group, who herself had died in an effort to prevent Jessica from getting the story and exposing the group.

Looking at Jessica, those kind of heroics were difficult for Maggie to picture. Barely over five feet tall and several years younger than Maggie, Jessica hardly struck one as a fearless figure. Shapely and petite, yes, but heroic, no. With short brown hair and eyes of an even darker brown, her face was open, friendly, and girl-next-door pretty, her cheeks and forehead speckled with freckles that were fading fast without the summer sun. Known around the newsroom for her smarts and boundless energy, Maggie could never remember seeing her sitting idly at her desk.

The vigilante escapade had not only won Jessica numerous awards and a special place in newsroom lore, but had served to set her apart from the rest of the staff. She now worked largely by herself on special investigative assignments, spared for the most part from the daily newsroom grind.

When Maggie looked across the room again, she saw that Jessica was no longer on the phone, but still hovering over the computer, her fingers dancing on the keyboard. She quickly walked to her desk and pulled up a chair. "Is this a horrible time to be interrupting you?" she asked.

Jessica looked up, a flash of surprise showing on her face. "No, not at all," she said hesitantly. "Just let me save this copy." She pressed a couple of buttons on the computer, then turned in her chair, smiling. "You can't trust these machines, you know. They seem to eat my copy faster than I can turn it out."

"I know what you mean," Maggie replied, although as anchor she wrote little and had never lost any of her words in the computer.

Jessica leaned back in her chair and stretched her arms, flexing her fingers to eliminate the keyboard kinks. "Now, what can I do for you?" she asked.

Maggie glanced around, aware of two other reporters within easy listening distance. "Can we go somewhere more private? Like the lunchroom? I'd be happy to buy you a Coke or a cup of coffee."

"Sounds mysterious, but I guess so," Jessica said as she logged off her computer and got up to join Maggie. Before they could take a step, however, she asked, "Are you feeling better? I heard you collapsed or something the other night."

"Word gets around, doesn't it?" Maggie replied. "But I'm fine. Must have been a bug of some kind."

Jessica gently pressed her for more details as they walked down the long hallway toward the lunchroom, but Maggie deftly sidestepped the questions, repeating that she felt better now and considered the attack a freak occurrence.

"Have you seen a doctor?" Jessica asked. "An episode like that can be sign of something more serious, you know."

Maggie shook her head, surprised at Jessica's concern and persistence. "No, but I'm due for a physical in a month or so. I'll check it then."

Several vending machines lined one wall of the lunchroom, while another wall was covered by large tinted windows overlooking the street, with the space in between filled by a dozen Formica-topped tables. A large-screen TV was mounted on the back wall, always tuned to Channel 7. When a Vikings or Twins game was on one of the competing stations, however, the channel mysteriously got changed.

At lunchtime, the room was often quite crowded, but now, at mid-morning, only one of the tables was occupied—by three technicians on coffee break. They gave only passing notice as the two women picked a table as far away from them and the television set as possible.

"Coffee, Coke, or something else?" Maggie asked.

"Coffee, thanks. With a little cream, if you can."

Maggie retrieved two coffees from the vending machine and returned to the table, pausing only long enough to allow Jessica to stir the cream in her coffee. "I know you're busy," she said, "and I don't want to waste your time. But I've got a couple of questions. Do you mind?"

"Depends on what they are, I guess. But go ahead."

Maggie could see her puzzled reaction, but forged ahead anyway. "I sat in on the sweeps meeting yesterday, and Barclay happened to mention that you're working on a story . . . something to do with child pornography."

"He did? Then he's a prick."

"Hold on," Maggie said quickly. "He warned all of us to keep it quiet, not to bug you about it—"

"That was nice of him," Jessica said, cutting her off. "But too many people may already know about it."

"Hey, I'm not here to get Barclay in trouble. And believe me, I'm not here to bug you. But when he mentioned it . . . well, I thought I might be able to help out."

"How's that?" The skepticism in her voice was unmistakable.

Maggie knew this question would come and that there would be no easy answer. She would have to lie, or at least skirt the truth. For now, anyway. "It's no secret," she said, "that L.A. is the pornography capital of the world. And I got to know something about it when I worked there. I thought it might be useful to you."

The skepticism was now evident in Jessica's expression. "I thought you just anchored out there. I didn't know you did any real reporting."

Maggie flinched at the words, although she knew there was more truth than fiction in them.

"Don't get me wrong," Jessica quickly added, "I think you're a hell of an anchor, one of the best I've seen. We're lucky to have you. But I never heard that you spent time on the street, doing the grunt work."

Maggie shrugged. "To be honest, I didn't do that much, not in my last couple of years. It was even worse there than it is here. Once you get put into an anchor chair, you don't have time for much else. Not with all the hoops they make you go through. I'm not complaining, mind you. It's what I think I do best. But every now and then, it would be nice to get your hands dirty on a real story."

Jessica did not appear convinced. "And you think my kid porn story might give you that chance?"

"I'm not sure. That's why I'm talking to you."

Jessica sipped her coffee and looked out the windows, saying nothing for what seemed like minutes. And then, "I'll have to think about this, Maggie. I like to work alone. And I hardly know you, or the kind of work you can do. And who knows what Barclay would say? He may want to keep you strapped to that anchor chair."

"I'll be happy to talk to him," Maggie said, "but I wanted to speak to you first."

They paused as the three technicians got up from their table and walked past them, mumbling something about time-code generators. Jessica waited until they were out of the door before turning back to Maggie. "Pardon the suspicion, but it still strikes me as strange, coming out of blue like this. You suddenly deciding you want to work on a story, and on this particular story. No hidden agenda here, is there?"

Maggie could feel the flush rising in her cheeks and fought to control it. "No, not really," she lied. "It's just a subject that interests me, that's all. Makes me sick, actually. And I'd enjoy working with you. Learning from you."

Jessica took a last swig of her coffee and got up. "I don't know, Maggie. Give me a day or so to think about it. Meantime, go ahead and talk to Barclay. He may put the kibosh on it, no matter what I decide."

"Fair enough," Maggie said. "Thanks for hearing me out."

"No problem. It's about time we got to know one another better anyway."

◆   ◆   ◆

Maggie allowed a day to pass before approaching Barclay. She found him alone in his darkened office after the early news, scowling at the television monitor across the room. She knocked lightly on his door. "Got a minute?" she asked. "Or is this a bad time?"

"As good as any, I guess," he growled, barely glancing at her.

She paused, taken aback. What the hell's wrong? Barclay's normal good humor had disappeared in a dark cloud. He was clearly out of sorts. "Maybe we should make it another time," she suggested.

"Nah, come on in. Flip the light on and pull the door shut behind you."

She did as directed and dropped into a chair close to his desk. His eyes had returned to the monitor, watching *Wheel of Fortune*.

"What's wrong, George?" she asked, hoping to break through the gloom. "Can't solve the puzzle?"

"Very funny," he said as he picked up the remote control and zapped the TV off. "What the hell's happening to us? Is that all we're covering these days, murders and drug busts? Jesus Christ."

So that's it. She shouldn't have been surprised by the question, coming as it did after a newscast that contained reports on at least four murders and three drug arrests, a not unusual number these days.

"You're just now noticing?" she asked.

He turned to face her, eyes narrowed with anger. "Of course not, but it's bugging the shit out of me. We're no different than anybody else. If it bleeds, it leads. I'm getting sick of it."

Maggie knew the murder rate in the Twin Cities had almost doubled in the two years she had been there, and now seemed to be increasing at an even faster pace. A day didn't pass without more bloodshed: blacks killing blacks, kids killing kids, husbands killing wives, and on and on. A never-ending river of blood flowing out there on the streets.

"I know what you mean," she said, "but we can hardly ignore it, can we?"

"I'm not sure it wouldn't be better for all of the meaning we give it. Let me ask you something. Do you remember the name of even one of the victims you just reported on?"

She shook her head, admitting she didn't.

"Do you think anybody else does?"

"Aside from their friends and families, probably not."

"What was it? Three of the four dead ones were kids, right? Do we know anything about them? Anything about how they lived, how they managed to get themselves killed? Were they good kids or bad kids? Good home, bad home? Do we even care? Shit, no."

Barclay picked up a paper clip from his desk and threw it at the monitor. "It's become a game, Margaret. A goddamned statistical game. We're keeping score. We report the numbers like the fucking sports scores or the prices on Wall Street. We don't care about the people, just the numbers. 'Chalk up another four murder victims today, bringing the year's total to'. . . It's bullshit, plain and simple."

He hardly paused for a breath. "It reminds me of Vietnam. You weren't around back then, but I remember how we used to report the latest body count damn near every night. So many American, so many VC killed and wounded. Up or down from the week before. We even had a little graphic all preprepared so we could slip in the new numbers with a minimum of trouble.

"But it's even worse now, with these murders. In Vietnam, like it or not, television brought the story smack into our homes. We saw some of those grunts getting killed, we could feel some of their fear, share some of the horror of the war. We may not have understood it or believed in it, we may have been misled by some of those fucking generals, but at least we felt a part of it.

"Now what do we see? A body under a sheet or being carted to the meat wagon, if our cameras get there quick enough. Maybe a splotch of blood on the sidewalk if they don't. Shoot a little tape and move on to the next one. We don't even pretend to understand what's happening out there on the streets . . . who all of these bodies belong to."

Maggie wondered how she had happened to wander into this harangue. She had never seen Barclay in a mood like this and wasn't sure how to react or what to say. After all, she didn't make the news decisions; she just read the numbers.

"There's hardly time to do personal profiles on every victim," she finally said. "So what do you suggest?"

"That's the problem. I don't know. That's why I'm so goddamned frustrated. I just know what we're doing now isn't right. Real people with real lives are dropping like flies out there, and we're reporting it as routinely as tomorrow's weather. Maybe we should just do weekly or monthly murder wrap-ups and forget about it."

He got up from behind his desk and sat on the edge of it, balancing his bulk carefully. He took several deep breaths and rubbed the back of his neck. "But enough of that. Forget about the tirade, okay? You picked the wrong time to drop by."

"No problem," she said, "but I hate to see you get worked up. It's bad for your blood pressure."

He smiled for the first time. "I appreciate your concern, but I have more than enough medical advice, thank you. Now what's up?"

"Sure you want to take the time?"

"Of course."

Maggie had decided to waste no words. "If she's willing, I'd like to work with Jessica on the child porn story."

His bushy eyebrows lifted. "Really? Why's that?"

"Because I think it's time I did a little reporting . . . and I'm interested in the subject. I think I could learn something." She quickly repeated what she had told Jessica about her experiences in L.A. and her eagerness to do something besides anchoring.

Barclay hoisted himself off the desk and returned to his chair, leaning back, clasping his hands behind his head. "I'm not sure you'd have the time. We need to keep you fresh."

"I'd make the time," she said, swallowing hard, knowing it might mean even less time with her son. "I really would like to help, if I could."

"You've talked to Jessica?"

"Briefly. She's thinking about it. But I knew I'd need your okay."

Barclay picked up a pen from the desk and toyed with it, twisting the cap on and off. "The last time one of our anchors got involved in a story, it turned out to be a hell of a piece. I'm sure you've heard about that."

Maggie had. Alex Collier, years before, had exposed a prominent local judge as a pedophile—just before he was to become chief justice of the state supreme court. Like Jessica's vigilante story, Collier's exposé had become the stuff of local legend.

"It took Collier off the anchor desk for weeks," Barclay said. "I'm not sure I can let that happen with you. There's too much at stake these days."

"I won't let that happen," she promised. "I'll fit it in around the anchor schedule."

"What about your other problem, whatever it is?"

"What about it?"

Barclay shrugged. "Nothing, I guess, except that you apparently have to deal with that, too. Plus a kid to take care of. You could be taking on more than you can handle."

"You may be right," she admitted. "But I'll never know unless I try."

Barclay studied her, obviously trying to decide.

"It would mean a lot to me, George."

He finally stood up and walked to the door. "Okay," he said, opening it and standing back. "If it's all right with Jessica, it's all right with me."

Maggie felt a surge of relief.

"But there's a but," Barclay said. "If I see it affecting your work on the air, the deal's off. I want you fresh, on top of your game. Okay?"

"Okay," she replied.

"And if this other thing, whatever it is, gets worse, I want to know about it. Okay?"

She swallowed hard. "Okay."

"Is that a promise?"

"Yes."

"All right. Now get the hell out of here."

8

They found the body the next morning.

It would have been but another of Barclay's anonymous killings, except that this victim happened to be young, female, and white. As a result, her murder became an instant, if short-lived, media sensation.

Hikers found the girl, naked and nameless, covered by brush off a pathway in a park west of Minneapolis. Because no clothes or other identification were discovered at the scene, it took two days to positively identify her: Penny Collins, age fifteen, a runaway from the small town of Eveleth on Minnesota's Iron Range.

On the day of the discovery, all of the television

stations provided extensive coverage of the crime—
reporting live from the wooded, taped-off murder
scene, breathlessly revealing what little the police
would say at the time: The body, bound hand and
foot, bore what appeared to be a single bullet wound
in the head. She appeared to have been there for
several days, although the time of death and official
cause would have to await the results of the autopsy.

No motive, no suspects, no clues that police would
admit to.

The investigation dominated the television
newscasts and the newspaper front pages for the
two days it took to confirm that the girl was a runaway and probable drug addict. A nobody. With
that, interest in her death faded quickly, and she
all but disappeared from the media's mind and
the public's view.

Had she been a suburban cheerleader from a
good home with friends, loving parents, and dot-
ing grandparents, the story surely would have lived
on for weeks. Or until the killer was found. As it
was, Penny Collins simply became yet another victim who had been lucky, or unlucky, enough to
attract more attention than most. A shooting star
whose celebrity ended as abruptly as her life.

Except to George Barclay.

He appeared at the morning news huddle as
somber as most could ever remember seeing him.
The outrage Maggie had witnessed in his office
nights before still smoldered. "We're not going to
forget this girl," he said, "not this time. I want to
find out everything about her. Her home, her
family. Her friends, if she had any. Why she was
out there on the streets, why she died."

Those around the table exchanged curious glances, but no one seemed ready to argue. Tangling with the boss in this mood might not be the wisest career move. But finally John DeMaris, the assistant news director, spoke up. "Why, George? The newspapers have already done some of that stuff."

"A half-assed job," Barclay snarled. "And now they've forgotten her, too. She's already history."

"That's because nobody gives a shit anymore, George," DeMaris argued. "She was just a street kid. There are hundreds of them out there. You know that. Doing drugs. Getting high. Panhandling or ripping people off."

"She was *fifteen*, John! A child, for Christ's sake. And she's dead, killed by some asshole the cops say they can't find. And you say nobody should give a shit?"

"I do." The words, barely audible, came from the doorway, where Jessica Mitchell stood quietly, unnoticed until then.

"Well, look who's here," Barclay said, as surprised as the others to find her there. "C'mon in, Jessica."

With some hesitation, she took a chair at the end of the conference table. Not normally included in these meetings, she appeared uncomfortable at finding herself there, with the others waiting and watching expectantly.

"So?" Barclay said, his expression urging her on.

Jessica shifted in her chair while casting a baleful eye on Barclay. "As George here was kind enough to inform some of you," she said, "I'm doing some preliminary work on a child porn story. I think this dead girl may fit into it somehow."

Barclay leaned forward. "What makes you think that?"

"Some work I've done," she replied vaguely.

"Your friend, right?" Barclay said. "The prosecutor?"

Jessica's face reddened. Everyone at the table knew she was living with a county prosecutor she had met and fallen in love with during her vigilante investigation. "Not this time, George. As far as I know, the cops haven't made the connection yet. Maybe never will. They've got too many murders on their hands right now."

"Then how?" Barclay pressed.

"Friends on the street. Leave it at that. It may not lead anywhere, but if anybody's going to be tracking this girl, I'd like it to be me. At least until I find out if she plays into my story."

"Speaking of your story," DeMaris said from the other end of the table, "where does it stand? Are you going to be ready for February?"

Jessica smiled and shrugged. "I have no idea, John. You know how it goes. Rumors, whispers, vague innuendoes. I'm trying to sort through it, pin some of it down. But it doesn't come easy, not with this kind of a story. It may never be ready."

"Anything we can do to help?" DeMaris asked.

"Funny you should ask," Jessica said. "Maggie Lawrence has offered to give me a hand, when she has the time."

"Maggie?" Several voices spoke in unison.

"What can I say? She wants to do it, and George says it's okay with him. That's all the help I think I'll need for now."

Barclay got up and moved toward the door. "All

right, then, here's how it stands: Jessica and Maggie will follow up on the girl for now, see where it leads. But we're not going to forget her."

"And keep quiet about all of this, okay?" Jessica chimed in. "I've got enough problems without leaks in the newsroom. Word of what we're doing may already be out there."

Maggie was among the last to learn of Jessica's and Barclay's decision. It was not until she arrived in the newsroom that afternoon and was almost immediately greeted by Brett. "Congratulations," he said as she sat down at her desk.

"For what?"

"You don't know?"

Maggie shook her head.

"They're going to let you play reporter. Jessica let it out at the morning news huddle."

"No kidding," she said, feeling a rush of excitement, but also disappointment that no one had bothered to tell her first.

"It came as quite a surprise to everyone," Brett said as he settled on the edge of an adjoining desk. "Including me. Why in the hell didn't you say something?"

"C'mon, Brett, you've hardly spoken to me in days. And besides, it was just a spur of the moment idea, and I really didn't think they'd go for it." She could see he was chagrined. "Perk up, Brett. I really did think it was a long shot. If someone had taken the trouble to tell me first, I would have let you know right away."

"So what's the deal?" he asked. "Why are you

getting into this? You're running yourself ragged as it is."

"I know, but it's something I want to do. You get stagnant sitting behind that anchor desk. I'll have to find the time."

If he was convinced, he didn't show it. He sat studying her, again giving her the feeling that he was trying to poke around inside her mind. She had discovered long ago that there was little she could hide from him, and until now, she had never really tried.

"Besides, it's a chance to work with Jessica," she said, tired of the awkward silence. "And I learned something about the pornography business in L.A. It seemed like a good fit."

"Really? Well, if there's anything I can do, let me know. If we're still talking, that is."

"For God's sake, Brett! Please. Lighten up."

He had walked about ten feet when he stopped and turned. "Anything new on the other thing? Any new packages?"

She shook her head without looking up.

A few minutes later, she spotted Jessica walking into the newsroom and moved to intercept her as she reached her desk. "I just heard the news," Maggie said. "It sounds like we've got a deal."

Jessica stopped and smiled. "If you're still interested and think you'll have the time. No second thoughts?"

Maggie shook her head. "None. I'll just have to make the time."

Jessica sat down at her desk and invited Maggie to do the same. "I'm not sure how much it will take, at least right now. Things are still pretty sketchy."

"When will you fill me in?" Maggie asked.

"Whenever you'd like. But I'd rather not do it here. Too many ears in this place."

Maggie thought for a moment. "Could we have breakfast tomorrow or the next day? After I get my son off to school?"

"Sounds fine. Tell me when and where."

They agreed to meet the next morning at a small coffee house a few blocks from Maggie's apartment. She had stopped there several times and knew it would likely be uncrowded at that time of day.

"There is one thing you could start on," Jessica said as Maggie got up to leave.

"What's that?"

"Call the local newspaper up in Eveleth and get them to send us everything they've done on Penny Collins."

Maggie was surprised. "The murdered girl?"

"Exactly. I'll explain tomorrow, but meantime, I'd like to learn as much as we can about her from the hometown folks. Find out who did the story up there. Sweet-talk them. They may know more about her than they've put in print."

"I'll give it a try," Maggie said as she headed back to her own desk. The time had arrived to do a little reporting.

Two hours later, when she'd completed her last phone call to Eveleth, Maggie looked up to find George Barclay standing by her desk, smiling down at her. "You've talked to Jessica?" he asked.

She leaned back in her chair. "Just after I got in."

"You're happy, I hope?"

"Sure, but it would have been nice to know about it before the rest of the staff."

Barclay shrugged. "It surprised me, too, when Jessica spoke up this morning. I wish she'd waited until the three of us could have talked. But it's too late to worry about that now."

"So what exactly did she say?"

Barclay quickly recited what had happened at the news huddle, including Jessica's theory that the dead Penny Collins might somehow be tied to the child porn story.

"So that's what's going on," Maggie said, more to herself than to Barclay. "I figured it must be something like that."

Before he could respond, the phone on her desk rang. She hesitated answering, but by then Barclay had turned and walked away, heeding a shouted summons from the assignment desk. She picked up the receiver on the third ring. "Maggie Lawrence."

The first sound she heard was loud static, jarring her eardrum and making her yank her head away. When she brought the phone back to her ear, the noise had lessened, but was still there, irritatingly insistent.

"Hello." She found herself almost shouting. "This is Maggie Lawrence."

The voice, when she finally heard it through the static, sounded distant. But more than that, almost electronic, a computerlike voice. "Did you get my gifts?" it said.

"*What?* Who is this?"

"Did you receive my gifts?" No computer, no way. A human voice, but electronically altered. It was impossible to tell if it was a man or woman, or to know how close or distant the caller might be. Across the street or across the country. Maggie was ready to hang up when the voice spoke again. "Were you surprised, *cunt*?"

Maggie sat stunned and speechless, feeling the shock and fear flow through her body. Her eyes made a quick sweep around her, but Barclay was across the newsroom and the nearby desks were deserted. Almost instinctively, she reached for the tiny recorder that could be plugged into her phone. Get this on tape, she thought. Quickly.

"What do you want?" she whispered as she struggled to untangle the cord and connect it to the receiver. "Why are you doing this?"

"Time will tell, won't it?" the voice said. "But you'll do what we ask, won't you?"

"Do what?" she demanded, trying to kill time.

"You'll know when it's time."

She finally got the tiny jack into the phone and turned on the recorder. Trying to keep her voice calm, she asked again, "What did you say? I can't hear with this static. What do you want?" She pressed the phone to her ear and checked to make sure the tape was rolling. But all she could now hear was the static. Then nothing. The phone was dead. The only voice on the tape would be hers.

He must have guessed what I was doing, she thought. Spooky.

Quickly dialing the station switchboard operator, she said, "This is Maggie Lawrence. Did you just put a call through to me? A couple of minutes ago?"

"No, Maggie. If you got a call, they must have dialed direct."

She hung up, only then feeling the sweaty film on the back of her neck and beneath her arms. Whoever it is, she thought, knows where my desk is, where my apartment is, and what my direct number is. No one outside of the newsroom or her small circle of friends was supposed to know any of those things. That kind of security for an anchor was routine and promised with the job.

What the hell's happening? Could someone in the newsroom be supplying the information? She quickly looked around her again, but found only the normal buzz of activity. No one seemed to be paying any attention to her.

For the first time since the first package arrived, Maggie felt genuine terror. True, before this there had been the dread and the humiliation, the uncertainty and the fear for her reputation and the future. The enemy, while out there, was anonymous, unseen, and unheard. But now there was an actual voice, disguised but human, a voice that had spit out the word "cunt," a voice attached to a body that was sitting out there somewhere, watching and waiting.

9

The Last Drop was one of the new-generation gourmet coffee houses that seemed to have sprung up everywhere, almost overnight. Located in Maggie's neighborhood, it was situated close enough to a small shopping center and one of the lakes to do a healthy business, especially on summer weekends when people enjoyed sitting at the outdoor tables sipping ice tea or cups of cappuccino.

Before long, the tables and umbrellas would have to be put away for the winter, but for now, they were still outside, hugging the street. Maggie arrived a few minutes early and, as she suspected, found only a few others there. With her pick of the tables, she chose one farthest from the shop's door and well away from any other customers.

The morning air was too chilly to be comfortable, but she guessed the rapidly rising sun and cups of steaming coffee would quickly warm her up. In the meantime, she wrapped her sweater more tightly around her shoulders and took a breath of the air that was as clean as it was cool.

Her car was parked just down the block, within view. She had decided the night before—after the frightening phone call—that she would drive Danny to school from now on, at least until she had a better sense of any potential danger. It might be silly, but she simply felt too vulnerable walking out in the open with her son.

Danny had protested the change vigorously, decrying the idea of being driven to the front door of the school in full view of his young classmates. Maggie persisted despite his noisy complaints, although she finally agreed he could alight at the nearest corner, where the school patrol stood guard.

After glancing at her watch, she spotted Jessica pulling into a parking space across the street, tucked inside a new Mustang convertible, fire-engine red with a white top and spoked wheel covers. The car's glistening finish caught the sun, the bright reflection momentarily blinding Maggie as Jessica hopped out and strode across the street.

"Nice wheels," Maggie said as Jessica joined her at the table.

"Want to help pay for it?" she laughed. "It cost me more than my folks' first house." She moved her chair into the shade and removed her sunglasses. "You been here long?"

"Just a few minutes. I knew I was early."

When the waitress appeared, they both ordered regular coffee, with cream for Jessica, and a bran muffin. They then sat quietly for a few minutes, their conversation limited to the weather and a few questions from Jessica about Maggie's apartment and her son.

"It must be tough," Jessica said, "raising a boy by yourself with the schedule you keep."

"Thank God for nannies," Maggie replied, and proceeded to describe Anna and the role she played in Danny's life. "I'd be lost without her, especially now, with this new project."

"If it ever gets to be too much, just let me know," Jessica said. "Believe me, I'll understand if you have to pull back."

Was that a subtle invitation? Maggie wondered. Was *she* now having second thoughts about the arrangement? Her demeanor, while friendly, was certainly guarded, her earlier suspicions and reservations still evident.

"I hope that won't happen," Maggie finally said, "but thanks anyway."

The waitress arrived with their coffee and muffins, then stood back, looking down at Maggie. "Aren't you on the news? Channel Seven?"

"Right you are," Maggie replied. "So is my friend here."

The waitress glanced at Jessica, but showed no sign of recognition. Then back to Maggie. "You're Maggie Lawrence, the anchor lady."

Maggie nodded. "Right again."

"Gosh, it's nice to have you here. What an honor."

"I stop by quite often, actually," Maggie said. "I don't live that far away."

"Well, I hope we'll see you again. Consider the coffee and muffins on the house."

Maggie protested, but the woman was insistent. "Just give me a wave when you want a refill."

When she walked away, Jessica said lightly, "I'll have to spend more time with you. I could pay off that Mustang in no time."

Maggie smiled. "Doesn't happen often, but I'm always embarrassed when it does. Makes me feel like I'm on the take."

As she began to munch on her muffin, Jessica asked, "Did you make those calls?"

Maggie nodded, still chewing.

"And?"

She swallowed and took a sip of coffee. "I'm not sure I learned that much, but I did talk to a reporter, a guy named Greg Newman, who covered the story for the local paper and knew the girl's family. Went to high school with her older brother, he said."

Jessica leaned forward on her elbows, listening attentively.

"You know most of it," Maggie continued. "The kid, Penny, ran away from home six or eight months ago, when she was only fourteen. Got herself lost in the city. This reporter says the family spent a fair amount of time down here looking for her, putting up posters, talking to the cops and other street kids, but got no help and never got a glimpse of her. She was just another runaway. After a few months, they gave up. Just sat back and waited for her to call. She never did."

Maggie went on to report that the girl apparently came from an abusive home and had run away before, the first time when she was only eleven or twelve. As she spoke, she could picture the child . . . the desperate unhappiness she must have struggled with, the urgent need to run, to get away, anywhere, but also the haunting fear she faced in doing so. Maggie had been there, and although she would never know precisely what Penny Collins had experienced, she could not imagine her life on the run being much different from her own. And while it was far too late, her heart went out to her.

Jessica broke into her thoughts. "Did this reporter say anything about drugs? Was the kid a user?"

"I asked, but he didn't know. Said it wouldn't surprise him, though, since a lot of the kids in town fool around with the stuff."

Jessica kept pressing. "Have they heard anything from any of her friends since the murder? Did any of them show up for the funeral?"

"The brother told this reporter, off the record, that the family got a couple of letters or notes. But nobody came to the services. It's a long way away, and they probably had no way to get there."

"Are there names?"

"Not that I know of," Maggie said. "The parents may have them, I suppose. I tried to call them, but there was no answer at the house."

Jessica sat back in her chair, ignoring the half-eaten muffin on her plate, her eyes fixed on something in the distance. Lost in thought.

"Barclay tells me," Maggie said, interrupting,

"that you think this Penny could have been mixed up in the porn business. True?"

Jessica's eyes came back to her. "That's what I'm hearing on the street. That she was part of a small ring of girls recruited to make some of the kid-vid porn shows. Fairly sophisticated stuff, I'm told. No low-budget home movies."

"You're told by whom?"

"That's the problem," Jessica replied. "It's all third- or fourth-hand. But the same thing is coming from enough different directions to give it some credibility."

"Who are the third and fourth hands? Other street kids?"

"A few, but mostly from the people working on the streets, the ones who are trying to get the kids into the shelters or back home. I've gotten to know a few of them the past couple of years.

"The rumors have been around for a long time," she continued. "Even back when Alex Collier was doing his exposé on the pedophile judge, I'm told. There was talk then of a kid porn ring, but nobody could ever get a handle on it. Not even Collier."

They paused as the waitress returned to refill their cups. The air had turned warmer, and the sun was now fully in Maggie's eyes. She shifted slightly in her chair to escape the glare and then asked, "So you think the girl's murder might be connected to this porn stuff?"

"Who the hell knows?" Jessica said impatiently. "In the world she lived in, anybody could have done it. I know the cops have all but given up the search. Nobody will talk to them. But it seems as good a possibility as any. Especially if she was trying to get out of it, or was ready to tell somebody about it."

Before Maggie could respond, Jessica added, "But, you know, I still don't get how kids can fall into that kind of a trap. If I was in their shoes, I don't care how desperate I was, I just can't see myself doing that. It's beyond me."

Maggie held her tongue, but was again struck by the huge gap that divided their lives. How could she expect Jessica to understand? Growing up as she did in a small Minnesota farm town, the daughter of prosperous and overly protective parents, never knowing hunger or abuse or endless nights without a roof over her head, a day without clean clothes and a warm coat.

"I wouldn't be so quick to judge them," she finally said. "You don't know how desperate these kids can get."

"And you do?" Jessica snorted.

Maggie hesitated. "Maybe," she said, almost in a whisper. "I got to know some of them in L.A. It's a tough life."

She immediately regretted the words as Jessica looked at her suspiciously. "You're sure there's something you're not telling me?"

Maggie turned away from the stare and reached for her sweater. "Nothing of importance," she lied. "I just don't think we can blame the kids."

"I'm not blaming them," Jessica said hotly. "I just don't think I could ever do it. Could you?"

By now, Maggie was out of her chair, ignoring the question. "I'd better get going," she said. "I have to run some errands."

Jessica watched as Maggie entered the coffee house to thank the waitress and then waited on the sidewalk as she emerged. As they crossed the street to Jessica's red Mustang, Maggie asked, "So what comes next?"

"Good question," Jessica replied. "You should try to find out more about the girl. See if there's any way to locate some of her friends. Maybe the fact that you're a TV celebrity will help."

"I doubt that many of her friends watch the news much," Maggie offered.

"Maybe so, but it can't hurt. We need to know who she was hanging around with, and where, and what she did with her days and nights. I've got a few leads, but they need to be pinned down."

Maggie wondered when she'd have time to do all of that, but knew she'd have to find it. She was committed. "How about you?" she asked.

"I'm going to keep working on the other half . . . the guys who might be running the ring. It's a pain in the ass, a lot of computer work, checking backgrounds, criminal records, and all of the rest."

"It's not going to be easy, is it?" Maggie said.

Jessica unlocked the door to the Mustang and got in. "It never is, but that's what makes it fun. You'll see."

The white convertible top was unfolding as Maggie walked to her own car down the block, wondering again what in the world she had gotten herself into.

10

Maybe it was the light morning traffic, or perhaps it was her increased vigilance, but Maggie had traveled no more than a few blocks before becoming aware of the car a block behind her. A white car, sleek and low-slung with a darkened windshield. Because of the distance and her own ignorance of car models, she could tell little else.

Had she followed a main thoroughfare, the car almost certainly would have escaped her notice. But after leaving Jessica, Maggie had decided to stop and pick up her cleaning at a shop not far from her apartment. The shortest route took her through a tangle of residential streets, including several stop signs and turns. After the second of

these turns, she caught sight of the car in her
rearview mirror. While that first glimpse gave her little pause, when the car remained after another
right and left turn, she suspected something might
be wrong.

Had she seen the car before? Had it been
parked near the coffee shop? She had no idea.

Quickly snapping the door locks, she slowed
her Caravan for a block, then sped up, watching to
see if the other car would maintain its distance. It
did. By now, she had no real idea of where she was
or what she should do. The neighborhood had
changed, the street names were no longer familiar, and she had lost whatever sense of direction
she had started with.

Should she pull over and let him pass? Try to
get a better look at the car, maybe the license
plate? What if he stops, too? Then what? No, keep
driving, she told herself. Don't panic. Find a commercial street with stores and gas stations and people, maybe a cop. Find a phone. Call Brett.

Perhaps it was a mistake. Maybe someone was
just being a jerk, having fun with her. Unlikely.
Whoever was driving seemed to make little effort
to escape detection. What did that mean? That he
simply wanted to frighten her? To reinforce the
telephone threats? If that was his purpose, he sure
as hell was succeeding.

She tried to concentrate on the car, to remember the lines of its body, the shape of its grill. It was
difficult, for most cars looked the same to her. She
regretted now that she had never paid more attention. The only distinguishing feature she could
see were two black bumper guards rising in front

of the grill, almost as you'd see on a police car. How long had he been following her? Did he see her drop Danny off? Having coffee with Jessica? The questions came quickly, one after the other, racing through her mind, all without answers.

Her eyes were off the mirror for only a moment when she felt the first jolt, sharp enough to throw her against the seat belt. She automatically hit the brake, then felt another hit, harder this time, accompanied by the sound of grinding metal behind her. Her car careened toward the curb, narrowly missing a parked truck. She fought to control the wheel, riding the brake hard.

Stop the car! she screamed at herself. Pull over!

The other car was no more than ten yards behind her, the driver invisible behind the tinted window. She could hear the roar of its engine, racing, as though revving for the next attack. The back of the Caravan fishtailed, and Maggie feared its top-heavy weight might flip it over. She tried to ease up on the brake and steady the wheel, like driving on ice, bracing herself at the same time for another hit, but none came.

From the corner of her eye, she saw a woman in a yard, a rake in her hand, mouth open, staring. Then she was out of sight, behind her. The Caravan steadied as it slowed, hugging the curb. The back window of the lift door was shattered, and she could hear metal dragging behind. Must be the bumper, she thought.

Where was the white car? She looked frantically in the mirror, but saw only the spider-web of broken glass. Looking over her shoulder, she saw it had dropped back, but was now coming up fast in the other lane, gathering speed as she stopped. It flashed past her. The only thing she saw was the large red lettering splashed on the trunk, like a JUST MARRIED scrawl.

Only this lettering spelled PORNO WHORE.

Shaking badly, her breath ragged and her stomach heaving, Maggie could only stare after the fleeing car, the scrawled words slow to work their way through her terror. "My God," she whispered when they finally registered. "Those dirty bastards." Then she leaned her head against the steering wheel and allowed the tears of fear and frustration to flow.

She wasn't sure how long she'd sat there, quietly sobbing, when she heard a sharp rap on the passenger window. Startled, she looked up and saw the woman from the yard down the street, still holding the rake, staring in at her. "Are you okay?" the woman shouted through the closed window. "Shall I call an ambulance?"

With a press of a button on the armrest, Maggie lowered the window. "I'm fine, I think," she said. "Just shook up a little."

The woman pushed her head through the opening. "I saw it all. It was crazy. He did it on purpose, you could tell."

"I know," Maggie said. "He'd been following me for blocks."

The woman walked around to her side of the car as Maggie opened the door and slowly got out. Her chest hurt from the snap of the seat belt and her head ached, but there didn't seem to be any other bodily damage.

"Are you sure you're all right?" the woman asked, watching her carefully.

She walked a few steps, testing her legs. Then she bent over, but felt no pain in her neck or back. "Yes, I'm okay. If I can just stop shaking."

"I'm Mrs. Anderson," the woman said. "Elaine Anderson. I live in that gray house with the brick trim."

Maggie shook her hand. "Nice to meet you, Elaine. Sorry it had to be this way."

"The police ought to be coming," Mrs. Anderson said. "I yelled at a neighbor to call 911."

"I appreciate that," Maggie said as she walked to the back of the Caravan to examine the damage, "but I don't think they'll be necessary."

The woman was by her side. "Sweety, it was a hit-and-run. You have to report it."

As Maggie suspected, half the rear bumper was ripped off, one end resting on the pavement. The back door was crushed, and the window splintered in a million pieces. "Bastards," she whispered.

"What was that?" Mrs. Anderson asked.

"Nothing," Maggie replied. "Just talking to myself."

Several other neighbors had emerged from their homes and stood quietly in a circle as a white Minneapolis squad car pulled up behind the Caravan. A lone officer, stomach bulging above his belt, stepped out and quickly surveyed the damage as he approached them. Before he could say anything, one of the neighbors shouted, "Aren't you Maggie from the news?"

Mrs. Anderson, the closest to Maggie, looked

again, recognition dawning. "You are, aren't you? Maggie Lawrence. I should have seen it right away."

Maggie had no time to respond before the officer asked, "What happened here? The call said a hit-and-run."

Maggie quickly spilled out the details, interrupted from time to time by the Anderson woman, who supplied her own version of the events she had witnessed. Neither of them, though, could describe the make, model, or year of the other car, only that it was white and low to the ground with big black bumpers.

"No license number?" the officer asked.

"It went by too quick," Maggie replied.

"There was something written on the trunk," Mrs. Anderson offered. "In big red letters. But I left my glasses in the house. I couldn't read it."

The cop looked at Maggie. She shook her head. "It all happened too fast," she lied. "I was just trying to get the car under control."

The officer examined her driver's license and made notes on a clipboard he had brought from the squad car. "You know anybody who might want to do this to you?" he asked. "From what you say, if he'd been following you, he must have known who you were. Got any enemies out there?"

She looked away, then back to the officer. "Nobody who would do something like this," she lied again. "It must have been some kook."

The policeman appeared skeptical, but handed her his card and started back toward his squad car. "We'll put out a description of the car, see what we come up with. But don't count on much. He's probably long gone."

"What about my car?" she asked.

"I'll request a tow," he said. "And maybe one of these ladies can call you a cab."

She walked back to him and took him aside. "Is there any way of keeping this quiet?" she asked. "I'd hate to see it end up in the newspapers."

"I understand," he replied, "but there's not much I can do about that. I've got to write up and file a report . . . and as you know, everybody has access to it. But don't be surprised if you get a call from one of the detectives. They try to keep an eye out for high-profile people like yourself. Especially with something like this. You're lucky to be standing there."

With that and a sympathetic nod, he drove off, leaving her there in the street, staring at the battered back end of her car.

"C'mon," said Mrs. Anderson, "I'll get us a cup of coffee while we wait for the tow truck. We've got to calm you down."

Good luck, Maggie thought, following her down the street to the gray house with the brick trim.

Things moved quickly. The tow truck was there before she could finish her second cup of Mrs. Anderson's coffee. And a cab got her to the nearest car-rental agency within a matter of minutes. The whole process was completed in plenty of time for her to get home and clean up before picking Danny up at the school guard crossing.

She saw nothing further of the white car or any indication of another vehicle that seemed interested in her whereabouts. She was able to breathe a little easier.

Danny was full of questions when he saw the

new car. Maggie patiently explained that she had had a small accident, that the Caravan was in for repairs, and that this Taurus wagon would have to do for the next couple of weeks.

"What kind of accident?" he asked. "Did you get hurt?"

She didn't want to lie to her son, but knew she had to stop short of the whole truth. "No, I didn't get hurt. But some man drove into the back of our car and then drove away without stopping," she said. "That's against the law, but he did it anyway."

"Was he a bad man?" her son asked.

"He must have been. The police are looking for him."

"Wow," Danny breathed. She could see that he wished he had been there.

"We've talked about this before, Danny, and you know that there are some bad people out there, like the man today. We have to be very careful."

"Is that why we're not walking to school anymore?"

"That's right, and after this—what happened today—we have to be even more careful. I don't ever want you outside by yourself, not without me or Anna."

"Never?"

"Never. You have to promise me that. If you want to play with your friends, you'll have to be inside or wait until Anna or I can be outside with you."

"I'm outside at school," he said smartly.

"I know, but one of your teachers is there. Stay with the other kids and never go near the fence or talk to anyone you don't know. That's a promise, okay?"

She could not escape the scowl on his face, but he gave her no further argument. Now she would have to figure out a way to give Anna the same warning without putting the fear of God into her.

Maggie held her breath as she walked into the newsroom that afternoon. While she harbored no hope that news of the accident would forever escape the notice of someone in the media—there were too many good reporters and too many loose lips in the police department for that to happen— she did hope that word would not leak too quickly, that she would have time to prepare for the inevitable barrage of questions that would come from Barclay, Brett, and others at the station.

Because of the star status the press gave television anchorpeople, she also guessed the newspapers and perhaps even the other television stations would be eager to do some kind of a story. If she wasn't careful, she could become a passing part of the news she was paid to report. How would she handle that?

She wished now that she had simply driven off, clanking bumper, shattered window, and all. But then she, too, would have been guilty of leaving the scene of an accident. Face it, she told herself, you're in a tough spot. Prepare for the worst.

To her relief, no one paid her special heed as she made her way to her desk. The newsroom seemed the same, although even the normal bustle would appear close to chaotic to anyone not accustomed to life under the news bigtop. Settling in at her desk, she found her message light blinking. Greg Newman, the Eveleth reporter, asking her to call. She quickly punched the number and heard him answer after the first ring. "Thanks for returning the call," he said when she identified herself.

"No problem," she said. "What's up?"

"Remember asking whether Penny's family had heard from any of her street friends?"

"Yes."

"Well, I spoke to her brother, my high school friend, after you called."

"Okay. Go ahead."

"He confirmed that they did hear from two of them. Short letters, notes really. He gave me copies."

"Really?"

"Because we're friends. I have them in front of me."

"Do they have names? Are they signed?"

"Yes they do."

"Addresses?"

"No. Just the names."

"Could you possibly fax them to me?" Maggie asked, crossing her fingers.

"I could, but I'd like to discuss a deal first."

"A deal? What kind of deal?" She crossed her legs.

"A cooperative deal," he said. "Sort of a quid pro quo."

"What do you mean?"

"Well, I figure you wouldn't be talking to me if you didn't have something going on down there.

You're a big-time news operation. Penny's murder was a big story up here, and if you're on to something new, I'd like to know about it. Before the AP or the Duluth paper does."

Maggie felt relief. "I don't see a problem with that, although I'll have to talk to our news director first. But you know that we're kind of casting about on this. We don't know if there's a new angle or not."

"I understand," he said. "But if it does turn into something, we'd like to have first crack at it after your broadcast."

"I'll get back to you, Greg. But could you fax me those letters now?"

"After I hear from you. Let's wait until then."

"Have it your way. I'll be back to you."

It was not until late afternoon—after she had completed her schedule of live news updates and recorded promotions—that Maggie managed to get Barclay and Jessica together. They met in Barclay's office, and Maggie quickly relayed the essence of her conversation with the Eveleth reporter.

"How important are the kids' names?" Barclay asked.

She shrugged and looked at Jessica. "Who knows? It's a start, at least. But we still may not be able to find them."

"If they knew Penny well enough to write a letter to her folks," Jessica said, "they may know stuff we need to know."

Barclay appeared doubtful. "Surely the cops would have talked to them by now."

"Don't count it," Jessica replied. "These kids are

elusive. And the cops have more murders on their hands than they can count right now."

Barclay turned to Maggie. "Okay, let's do it. I can't see a problem."

Before they could rise to leave, Teresa Jensen, Barclay's assistant, was at the door. "George, you've got a phone call. From some reporter at the *Star-Tribune*. He says it's urgent." With a glance toward Maggie, she added, "He says it concerns Maggie here."

Barclay gave Maggie a quizzical look as he picked up the phone. "Know what this is about?" he asked, covering the mouthpiece with his hand.

Maggie shrunk back in her chair. "I'm afraid so," she whispered.

11

Maggie squirmed under the intensity of Barclay's gaze as he took his hand away from the receiver and spoke into it. "Barclay here. Who's this?" He paused for a moment, then, "How goes it, Barry?"

Maggie gave an inquiring look to Jessica, who whispered, "It may be Barry Duncan, the *Trib*'s cop reporter."

Barclay's eyes never left Maggie as he listened to whatever the reporter was saying. Then his face seemed to darken. "No, I haven't talked to Maggie today," he said, staring straight at her. "I haven't heard a thing about it. Couldn't have been too serious, or I would have heard something."

Jessica leaned across to her. "What's he talking about?"

Maggie held her finger to her lips.

"You're going to go with the story?" Barclay said into the phone. "No, I can't comment until I talk to Maggie. You're sure you've got this right?"

Jessica leaned into her again. *"What is going on, Maggie?"*

Turning her head aside, Maggie whispered, "I had some trouble this morning, after I left you."

"What kind of trouble?"

"Somebody followed me from the coffee shop and banged my car around a little."

"Holy shit," Jessica muttered. "Are you okay?"

She nodded, her eyes back on Barclay. "No, Maggie won't be saying anything, either. Not until we've talked. I'm not even sure she's around. She has the night off."

Maggie's eyes widened.

"No, no," Barclay continued. "It was scheduled before all of this happened." Another pause. "I'm sure she's okay. I would have heard if she wasn't." Still another pause. "All right. Thanks for the call. We'll keep in touch."

He gently put the phone back on its cradle and then stood by the window, his back to the two women. "I don't like to lie to reporters," he said. "Even newspaper reporters. It goes against my grain."

"I'm sorry," Maggie said. "I was going to tell you when there was time."

"Should I leave," Jessica asked, making no move to do so.

"No need," Barclay said, turning to them. "You might as well hear this, too."

Maggie quickly told the story of the hit-and-run in as much detail as she could, but resisted saying anything about the painted words across the trunk of the white car.

"That jibes with what Duncan got from the police report," Barclay said. "You're sure you're okay?"

"I'm fine, but my car isn't. It's in the shop. Did the cops find the other car?"

"Not yet, I guess."

Jessica had sat quietly until now. "Did this come out of the blue? Somebody just ups and decides to bounce you around a little? I don't get it."

Maggie and Barclay exchanged glances. "Not quite out of the blue," Barclay said. "Maggie's had some other problems."

"Like what?" Jessica pressed. "What in the hell is going on here? If we're going to work together, I should know what I'm getting into."

Maggie waited, but Barclay's eyes urged her on. "I've gotten a couple of packages . . . anonymous. One was left in the newsroom, on my desk, the other was dropped outside my apartment."

"Packages of what?" Jessica asked.

"I can't really say, not now. But they were scary, threatening."

Jessica was simmering. "I knew it!" she hissed. "I knew something else was going on. Why didn't you tell me before? And does this have anything to do with my porn story?"

Maggie shrugged but didn't answer. Instead, she turned to Barclay. "There's something else, George."

"What now?" His patience, too, was clearly ebbing. She described the phone call of the day before without revealing its precise contents. "It sounded like the voice was altered somehow. I couldn't tell if it was a man or a woman."

"My God," Barclay said as he sank into his chair.

"Sounds like this woman needs some kind of protection," Jessica offered.

Barclay put his hand to his chin and slowly shook his head. He didn't speak for several minutes. Finally, he said, "First things first. Let's keep you off the air tonight. Between the police report and what you've told me, I'll write a short story for both shows. We'll play it down, but I don't want to get beat by the paper on a story involving one of our own anchors. And I'll talk to the cops, see what else we should be doing. Maybe we can hire a bodyguard for a while."

Maggie tried to protest, but he waved her quiet. "This isn't up to you, Maggie. Forgetting my personal feelings, you're worth a few million dollars a year to this company. I don't want to take any chances. Until we decide what to do, I'm going to ask Jacobi to stick as close to you as possible."

It was all happening too fast for her. Her world seemed to be spinning out of control. The police? A bodyguard? It was too much to absorb in that one moment. "I've got to think about all of this," she said, pleading.

"I don't want you to think about it," Barclay said with a scowl. "I want you to tell us what's really going on here, Maggie. What's behind it. We've waited too long already."

"I wish I could," she whispered. "It's too painful. Too embarrassing."

Barclay got out of his chair and knelt unsteadily

in front of her, grasping her hands in his. He teetered as he spoke. "We're not going to abandon you, Maggie. We want to help you get through this, whatever it is. We're your friends, you know. You've got to trust somebody."

Despite herself, she felt her eyes well. She closed them to hold back the tears. She had never cried in front of Barclay or anyone else in the newsroom and was not about to cave in now. She took a deep breath and got up, facing both George and Jessica. "Okay," she said, "I'll do it. But you've got to give me a couple of days."

"A couple of days, but that's it," Barclay said. "And keep your eyes open. I don't want you taking any chances."

Anna sat primly on the couch, knees together, hands folded in her lap, waiting patiently for Maggie to begin. Danny was in his bedroom, enticed there when Maggie moved the TV and his Sony Play Station from the living room to his bedside.

Since Anna had been given a sketchy account of the accident earlier, when Danny returned from school, she showed no surprise that Maggie came home from the station early. "I would think you'd want to be home after going through something like that," she said. "I don't think you should have gone to work at all."

She had fussed over Maggie, still suspecting she might be injured in some undetermined body part, and then insisted that Maggie rest while she prepared dinner. Dinner was over, and they had just finishing watching the six o'clock news, including Alex Collier's account of Maggie's mishap.

"We're sorry to report tonight that my coanchor, Maggie Lawrence, was the victim of a hit-and-run accident today. She was not injured, but police say her car was badly damaged after being rammed at least twice by another vehicle in a south Minneapolis neighborhood. Sources in the police department say it apparently was a deliberate effort to injure Maggie, and that they are now searching for the hit-and-run car and its driver. The car is described only as relatively new and white, with high bumper guards. Happily, we expect Maggie to be back with us tomorrow night."

Anna could only shake her head, still shocked that someone would actually want to hurt Maggie.

"It's not the first thing," Maggie told her now. "That package I got may have been sent by the same person. Someone who doesn't like me."

"How can that be?" Anna said, astonishment in her voice.

"It's too complicated to explain, Anna, but it could get worse. We need to talk about some changes that have to happen. To protect us from these people."

Anna started to cough, her bronchitis apparently worsened by her nervousness. Maggie waited until the coughing subsided. "Never let Danny out of your sight, Anna, not for a minute. I'm sure nothing will happen to him as long as one of us is around. But we can't leave him alone, ever."

Anna nodded.

"And please, don't open the door to anyone you don't know. No matter what they say. No solicitors, no deliveries. If anyone tries, call me or the caretaker right away."

"I understand," she said.

"If all of this is too frightening to you, Anna, please tell me now. We can certainly find someone else to watch Danny until this is over."

"No way, José," she said, gritting what Maggie had always suspected were false teeth. "It'll take more than this to scare me off."

"Okay, but I want you to think about it. And please don't tell anyone else, even your kids. We must keep this as quiet as we can. Everything should turn out okay."

Anna worked up a brave smile, but Maggie could tell it took real effort.

Brett showed up at the apartment door half an hour later. Maggie was not surprised to find him there, looking worried. "I just heard what happened," he said as she led him inside. "I got somebody else to produce the late show."

"It could have been worse," she said over her shoulder. "But I have to admit, it was pretty scary."

"No kidding."

They walked into the kitchen, where Anna was still putting away the dinner dishes.

"Hi, Anna," he said.

She turned with a smile. "Why, hello Brett. I was just about to leave."

"Not on my account, I hope."

"Oh, no. I'm all done here."

Anna had never made a secret of her admiration for Brett, nor had she hidden her hopes that he and Maggie might one day be more than just friends. "He's such a nice young man," she had often told Maggie. "I don't think you know what you're missing." When Maggie would protest, she would say, "You can't stay single forever. That boy needs a father, and you need a man."

Now, as she said her good-byes to Maggie and Danny, Brett pulled up a chair at the kitchen table.

"Can I get you anything?" Maggie asked. "Have you eaten? I can fix something real quick."

"No thanks, nothing to eat. But a beer, maybe."

She went to the refrigerator and returned with two beers, a Pig's Eye Lean for each of them. "So are you okay?" he asked. "No broken bones or anything?"

"Just a few bumps and bruises," she said, sitting down. "I'll be fine after a long, hot bath."

"Barclay's all worried about you. He thinks I should camp out here until this is all over."

"Stay here? At the apartment?"

"That's what he says. Thinks I can help keep you safe."

"George worries too much," Maggie said, but she had to admit it felt reassuring to have Brett there. Like his body, his face was long and angular, with teeth that were even and a glistening white. His hair was thick and brown, a brush without a part. High cheekbones seemed to almost meet at his brow, leaving his eyes, already a dark brown, hidden in a deep well that was hard to penetrate, giving him a brooding look, offset only when he smiled, which he managed easily and often. A pleasant face, she had decided long ago, not breathtakingly handsome by any stretch, but agreeable. Approachable.

Watching him quietly sipping his beer while trying to get his lanky body comfortable in the kitchen chair, she could not help but silently recall the only other man she had ever been as close to, albeit in an entirely different way. The man who had planted Danny's seed in her and with whom she had lived for two years in Los Angeles: Mick Salinas, who, like Sissy before him, had abruptly abandoned her just two months after Danny's birth—never to be seen or heard from again. There were no cards, no letters, no calls, no support for the child. He simply vanished, deserting his job and his other friends as quickly and mysteriously as he had deserted her.

"Where's your mind, anyway?" Brett asked, studying her from across the table.

The question startled her. "Back a few years, I guess."

She still wondered, although less often and in less agony with each passing year, where Mick could have gone, where he was now, and what she had done to drive him away. Was it the prospect of marrying her, of raising a son? Could that have been so frightening? Or was it something else? Some flaw in her that she could not see, but which others found and led them to flee.

It would have been easier, more understandable, more *acceptable* if there had been some hint, some clue before he left. But there had been none. He was there one day, attentive and loving to both her and the baby, then gone the next. For a time, she thought he must have been hurt or killed in some accident. Horrible as that would have been, at least it would have explained his disappearance, provided some comfort, some finality. But her frequent calls to the hospitals and eventually to the morgues had borne no fruit. For all she knew, he was still alive—somewhere. Mick Salinas, the father of her child, the only man she had ever loved.

"Are you going to tell me what happened today?" Brett asked, bringing her back.

"Of course," she said, and once again began the now familiar recitation, once again omitting any reference to the sign on the back of the trunk. Brett could only shake his head in wonder. "You could have been killed."

"I doubt that. We weren't going fast enough. But I could have gotten more banged up than I did. Thank God for the seat belt."

"And thank God Danny wasn't with you."

"Amen," she said.

Brett got up and walked to the refrigerator for another beer, offering Maggie one as well. She declined. "You have no idea who was inside the car?" he asked.

"The windows were black, Brett. There may have been more than one person inside, for all I know."

He stood with his back against the kitchen counter. "Barclay says you're going to tell us what this is all about. Is that right?"

"Yeah, but I need a little time."

"If what happened today doesn't convince you,

I don't know what will. It can't go on like this, Maggie."

"I know that," she said, "but it doesn't make it any easier."

Before leaving, Brett checked in on Danny, finding him sitting cross-legged on his bedroom floor, fully engrossed in his video game. "Hey, sport. How are you doing?"

Danny momentarily took his eyes from the screen. "Hi, Jake. Want to play some doubles with me?"

"Not now, tiger. I've got to get going. I'll take you on another time."

Danny grunted a reply and refocused his attention on the game.

In some ways, Brett had become Danny's surrogate father, or at least a favorite uncle, filling a void neither Maggie nor Anna was capable of filling. Whenever he could, Brett took time to teach the boy basketball at the neighborhood Y and often treated him to a Timberwolves game at the Target Center or a Twins or Vikings game at the Metrodome. To Danny, Jacobi was not Brett, but Jake, a nickname he alone had decided upon and which only he used.

For Brett, who had no nieces or nephews, the friendship with the boy had become an important part of his life. He had come to cherish the time they spent together.

From the doorway, Brett said, "Be good for your Mom, okay?"

"Sure," Danny mumbled, still lost in his own little electronic world.

Maggie was still in the kitchen when Brett made his way back from Danny's room.

"I think I've made a decision," she told him.

"What's that?"

"I'd like you, George, and Jessica to come over on Saturday morning. I'll try to explain everything then."

"You're serious?"

She took a deep breath. "I guess so. You've got to know sooner or later."

"Good," he said. "It can't be that bad."

"Don't count on that," she said.

12

The next morning, while Maggie was still at the apartment, George Barclay convened an impromptu meeting of the newsroom staff. While the crowd of reporters, photographers, and others milled about the room talking and laughing, Barclay stood impatiently on the edge of the assignment desk platform waiting for the hubbub to ebb. Finally, he shouted, "Let's cut the noise. This will take just a few minutes."

The room gradually quieted under his stern gaze. He waited until the only sound to be heard was the muted mumble of the police radios from the glassed-in dispatch room behind him. Then he began. "If you watched the news last night or read the paper this morning, you know that we had a serious scare yesterday. Somebody played bumper cars with Maggie Lawrence in an apparent attempt to hurt her or something even worse."

The fact that almost everyone in the room already knew about the incident did not deter the noisy reaction. A few questions immediately flew at him, but he held up his hands to deflect them. "She's okay. In fact, she'll be back on the set tonight. We still don't know who's responsible, but the cops are looking for the car and driver as I speak. You should know, however, that there have also been other threats against her."

This revelation *was* news to most of the staff and resulted in another clamorous interruption. "Quiet down!" Barclay yelled out. "Let me finish." Again, the commotion in the room slowly subsided. "At first," he continued, "we thought we might be dealing with just another one of those harmless nuts that live out there in TV-land, but the episode yesterday makes it clear that it's more than that. Someone is out to hurt her."

He leaned back against the assignment desk. "Believe me, we're doing our best to deal with the situation. We're going to try to protect Maggie, monitor her mail and phone calls, and increase security at the station. All of you can help in that regard by keeping your own eyes and ears open.

"But most important, leave her alone. This is troubling enough to her, obviously, without a lot of questions from all of you. The fact that she's willing to continue on-the-air is amazing in itself. So please act as normally as you can around her while we try to sort through this and get to the bottom of it. And spread the same word to the rest of the station staff." With a quick look across the newsroom, he concluded, "That's all for now."

Before he could leave the platform, however, the questions rained down on him. The first came from a young producer, Jane Higgins, who was standing right below him. "What are the threats about?" she demanded in a voice loud enough to be heard above the others.

Barclay again raised his hands, requesting quiet. "I can't tell you more, because I don't know more. I can only repeat that we're taking the threats seriously, especially after what happened yesterday. I'll try to keep you informed, but understand the sensitivity involved here. This is now also a police matter."

Another woman got up on a chair in the back of the newsroom. It was Cassie MacKenzie, the youngest reporter on the staff. "What about the rest of us?" she shouted. "Could this maniac, whoever he is, come after us, too?"

Shaking his head, Barclay said, "As far as we know, the threats are aimed only at Maggie. But it would pay for all of you to stay alert. There are a lot of crazy people out there. Report anything unusual to me."

With that, he waved off other questions and stepped down from the platform, making his way through the crowd and back to his office. Once there, he was not surprised to find Nicholas Hawke, his boss and the station's general manager, lurking and looking agitated.

Hawke closed the door sharply behind Barclay and sank into a chair across from him. "I was surprised to hear about this Maggie business on the news," he said, clearly upset. "You should have called me."

"Sorry," Barclay said, realizing he had fucked up again. "I've been hip-deep in shit since I first got the word late yesterday."

Hawke was not impressed. "You're the one who says we broadcast news, not excuses, George. I'm very disappointed."

Barclay shrugged and swallowed hard, holding his tongue. Saying anything further, he knew, would only fan the flames.

Hawke was a small man with a mind to match, puffed up and arrogant, whose relationship with his news director had been strained for several years—ever since anchor Alex Collier's exposé of the pedophile judge. As a friend of the judge, Hawke had tried everything within his considerable power to kill the story, finally failing because Barclay had conned him into leaving town at a crucial point. In the heat of his anger, Hawke had fired Barclay, only to later reconsider and apologize. Barclay agreed to stay on, but some of the bitterness and mistrust between the two lingered to this day.

"Keep the ratings up and your nose clean," Hawke once told him, "and we'll get along just fine. But don't forget again who runs this candy store."

A few years older than Barclay, Hawke was deeply tanned and turning gray at the temples. Always impeccably dressed, he was the only man Barclay knew who would wear no suit without a matching vest, complete with a draped gold watch fob that he constantly seemed to check. His shirts were heavily starched, his ties properly dimpled, and his Italian loafers brightly shined. Even his teeth sparkled. Given a pair of elevator shoes, he could have made the cover of *GQ.*

"I've been getting calls from members of our board of directors," Hawke told him now. "They want to know what's happening, what we're doing about this."

Barclay quickly recited what steps he had taken and which others he was considering. "We want to play this down. Keep a low profile."

"Play it down?" Hawke exclaimed. "Are you serious?"

"Of course I'm serious."

Hawke leaned forward, eyes glittering. "Don't you realize the potential for publicity here? The sympathy it could generate?"

"I'm not sure I understand where you're going with this," Barclay said, although he clearly did.

"Think about it, George. Glamorous anchorwoman, under siege. Threatened. Afraid to go outside. She and her small child held hostage by their fear."

Barclay's expression was disbelieving. "This isn't a goddamned made-for-television movie, Nicholas. For Christ's sake!"

"That's the point, George. It's not a movie. It's real. And it's here, happening to us. Think of all the interest it could generate going into the fall rating periods."

Barclay wanted to laugh, but fought to maintain a deferential tone. "With all due respect, Nicholas, I can't believe what I'm hearing. Maggie's safety is involved here. We can't turn this into some kind of publicity stunt."

"Nonsense," Hawke said. "I'm not talking about putting the woman in danger. I'd be an idiot. She's worth millions to us."

Barclay knew Hawke's estimate of her value was right. In her brief two years at the station, with the steady rise in ratings, she had become one of the most sought-after anchors in the country. He had heard indirectly that she was receiving inquiries from stations in other, larger markets virtually every week, some of them offering to pay off Channel 7 for the remaining year on her contract. Barclay also knew that the other stations in the Twin Cities would do almost anything to rid themselves of the competition, including sending tapes of Maggie to talent scouts and consultants across the country.

"Then what are you talking about?" he asked Hawke.

"Just milk the situation a little, that's all. Let a little information leak out. Keep it in the public's mind. With the network's shit prime-time schedule this fall, we're going to need all of the help we can get."

Barclay could only shake his head. He had to end this conversation, get Hawke off this track. "Let me think about it," he finally said. "I'll keep in touch."

"I hope so, George," Hawke said, rising from the chair. "I don't like being left in the dark." As he opened the door to leave, he turned and added, "Don't forget whose candy store it is."

Barclay hoped he didn't hear the "Fuck you, dirtbag" as he departed.

By the time Maggie arrived at the station at

mid-afternoon, she had been informed of the newsroom meeting and of Barclay's appeal to the staff to leave her alone. And for the most part, they did—except for a profusion of curious or sympathetic looks and several whispered expressions of concern and support.

Maggie accepted the good wishes with grace, at the same time wondering what the reaction would be if they knew the full truth. Before long, a few of them would. She shuddered again at the prospect.

Checking briefly with Barclay, she was told the police had made no progress in their search for the hit-and-run car or driver, but that additional steps had been taken to beef up security at the station. "There will be two guards at the entrances from now on," he told her, "and one more will be patrolling the garage. And we've canceled all tours of the building for the time being."

He did not mention his unnerving meeting with Nicholas Hawke.

"I appreciate all you're doing, George," Maggie said, "but I don't want it to get in the way of my job. I haven't given up on working with Jessica, and I'm going to need to be out and around."

"We'll see about that," Barclay replied. "Don't rush it. Let's let things cool down first."

When she returned to her desk, Maggie found a fax from Greg Newman, the Eveleth reporter. It contained copies of the sympathy notes from the two girls to the parents of Penny Collins, along with a scrawled message from Newman himself: "Glad we've got a deal. Good luck. Anything more I can do, let me know."

She had to squint to read the notes. The first

contained only one short paragraph and was
barely legible.

Dear Mr. & Mrs. Collins,

Was so sorry to here about Penny. Cuz she
was a nice girl and my friend. I hope they
catch the people who done this.

Sincerly,
Nadia Vaughn

The second note was longer and more thoughtful.
Also much more readable.

Dear Mr. and Mrs. Colllins,

Please accept my sympathies at the loss of
your daughter. It must be a terrible time for
your family and I feel badly for all of you.
   I only knew Penny for a short time, but I
thought she was a wonderful girl and a good
friend. I know she missed you and wished
things could have been different between
you. Now we can only hope she is at peace
with her Lord.

Your daughter's friend,
Amy Boyd

She read the notes again, then once more, studying
them carefully. Amy and Nadia, both friends of the
dead girl, apparently both street kids, yet obviously
quite different. Amy clearly was the more educated,

with better penmanship and a firmer grasp of the language. Not a misspelled word could be found.

What did that mean? That she was older? Went to a better school? Maggie had a feeling that Amy might be a city girl, Nadia from the country. But that was guessing. Newman had told her the night before, when she called to confirm their deal, that both letters had been postmarked in Minneapolis, but that neither carried a return address.

She carried the notes to Jessica's desk and laid them in front of her. Before she glanced at them, Jessica said, "Brett says you'd like us at your place tomorrow morning."

"Can you make it?" Maggie asked.

"I guess so. You're sure you want me there?"

"I'm sure," Maggie said without hesitation. "You should know what's going on . . . and besides, it will be nice to have another woman there."

Jessica gave her a curious look, then turned her attention to the notes on the desk. When she finished reading, Maggie outlined her own speculation about the two girls.

"You may be right," Jessica said. "But I'm not sure where that gets us."

"Neither am I, but if you'll give me the names of some of your streetworker contacts, I'll begin making calls. Someone may know where one or both of these kids may be."

"That's a start," Jessica said as she reached for her files. "You may also want to start calling everybody in the phone book with the same last name as the girls. Who knows? You could stumble onto their parents or one of their siblings."

"Okay," Maggie said hesitantly, aware of how enormous that task could be.

"We may also want to send you up to Eveleth to talk to Penny's parents and this reporter guy."

"I'm not sure Barclay will let me go anytime soon. He's being very protective."

"As he should be," Jessica said. "But maybe we can work something out."

An hour later, Brett was on the phone to her from across the newsroom. "Do you know a Harry Carlisle?" he asked. It took Maggie a moment, but then it came to her. The singles' tour leader, the bachelor with the bad breath. "Yeah," she replied. "Why?"

"Because he's on the other line. Want to take it?"

Brett, the phone monitor. "Sure," she said. "Switch him over."

The transfer took less than ten seconds. "Ms. Lawrence?" The same syrupy voice.

"Yes, Mr. Carlisle. What can I do for you?"

"I read about your accident. Thank God you weren't hurt."

"I appreciate that, Mr. Carlisle."

There was a significant pause, then, "Could this be connected with what . . . ah . . . you called me about earlier?"

"I don't know. Perhaps. Why do you ask?"

Another pause, even longer. "Mr. Carlisle, are you there?"

"Yes, of course. I'm sorry. I just don't know what to think."

"What do you mean?"

"Well, I talked to the group at our last meeting, after you called. Everyone was as shocked as I was, believe me."

"Yes?"

"But your accident made me think again."

"And?" She wanted to reach through the phone and pull his words out.

"Two of our new members were not at the meeting. None of us knew them very well, but both went on the station tour."

The information did not exactly bowl Maggie over, but it did catch her interest. "Perhaps they'll show up at your next meeting," she suggested.

"That's just it," he said, more urgently now. "Because of your call and the accident, I got curious. So I tried calling them. The numbers they gave us don't exist. Nor do the addresses they left. I tried to find them on a map."

She caught her breath. "You're quite a detective, Mr. Carlisle. Tell me about these two."

"A man and a woman. Both in their late twenties or early thirties, I would say. The woman called herself Eleanor Smith, the man Frank Edwards. But in light of the other misinformation, I suspect those aren't their real names."

"I suspect you're right," she said.

"I don't remember that much about the woman, frankly. Attractive, but a bit heavy for my taste. But . . . well . . . what should I say . . . well-constructed."

"You have any pictures?"

"I'm afraid not. They weren't with us long enough."

"And the man?"

"Six feet, or six-one. Muscular with a very small waist, I remember that. Brown, thinning hair. A mustache, very narrow. What do you call it? A pencil mustache? His face was pockmarked, as though he'd had a bad case of chicken pox or acne as a kid."

"Were these two together?" she asked.

"Not that I know of, although I remember now that they did kind of hang with each other during the tour."

"Give me a minute," Maggie said, taking the phone from her ear, thinking. Then, "If these two were new to your group, how would they know about the station tour?"

"That's easy. We try to spread the word in advance, you know, in an effort to attract new members. There was an item in the church bulletin, and we even put up a few posters. We do that before all of our special events."

She wanted to know more, but could think of no further questions at the moment. "Mr. Carlisle," she finally said. "Could you drop by the station early next week and bring whatever information you have on these two? I'd like to meet you and learn more if I could."

"I'd be happy to. Monday afternoon, say three o'clock?"

"Perfect," Maggie said. "I'll see you then."

Why was it, when she'd hung up the phone, that she had an uneasy feeling about Harry Carlisle's eagerness to help?

She'd have to think more about that. In the meantime, she had to prepare for her dreaded confession the next day.

13

For Maggie, it proved to be another almost sleepless night. Hour after restive hour she fought the fitful thoughts that held her brain and body captive and defiantly denied rest to either. Any semblance of normal comfort eluded her: The mattress which had so obligingly shaped itself to her body over two years suddenly turned to stone; the perfect pillows she treasured became too soft. The room was too cool or the bed covers too heavy. Her mind raced and her muscles refused to relax.

Twice during the night, she crept from the bedroom to the living room in the desperate hope that a few minutes of reading or staring at the muted àll-night shopping channel would numb

her mind and quiet the demons. Twice she
retreated to the darkness, feeling no relief, recalling nothing of what she had read or seen.

Now, as dawn approached, she still lay awake, on
her back, covers thrown aside, watching the light-
ening sky beyond the open window slowly push
aside the deep shadows of night. She was alert to
every sound: the first grating calls of the starlings
and the grackles astir in the trees and in the vines
scaling the walls outside; in the distance, the woe-
ful wail of an ambulance siren. On the street
below, the slamming of a car door and the squeaky
wheels of a trash can being rolled to the curb.

The world, like the birds, was awakening.

In a few hours, they would all be here, Barclay,
Brett, and Jessica, unsure of what they would hear,
but almost certainly expecting nothing like the
tale she would tell. *Could she do it?* She tried to
envision herself facing them, feeling their eyes,
seeing their shock and disbelief as she revealed
the most deeply held secret of her life. She had no
question that despite their feelings toward her
now, despite their advance assurances of support
and friendship, their view of her would be forever
altered. How could it be otherwise? And who
could blame them? Would her own reaction be
any different?

As she saw the first rays of the sun creep across
the windowsill, she again desperately searched for
other solutions, other options. But there were
none. The dawn cast no new light. More deception
would only bring more trouble. More danger. She
could not leave, and she could not go it alone. She
needed help, for Danny's sake, if not her own.

Slipping out of bed and into her linen robe, she quietly turned the latch on her door and tiptoed to the desk across the room. She unlocked a file drawer and pulled out the two hidden packages, turning them over in her hands, repelled once again by the scrawled letters in green. Would Barclay, upon hearing her story, demand to see their contents? To know what was at stake, to judge the potential damage to her and to the station? No way, she told herself. If he or the others ever saw the picture or the tape, it would be despite her, not because of her. Describing it would be humiliating enough, knowing they would see it—her, naked on the satin sheet—would be unbearable.

Why in God's name did she ever agree to do the film? Blaming Sissy wasn't enough. She knew that now. She could have walked away. There *were* other options then. Blaming her youth or her brutish parents or the tough life on the street was no answer either. Other girls in her same situation didn't end up on their backs, legs spread, under the lights.

There must be some chink, she decided, some genetic flaw in her character. Some tiny cell missing in her moral fiber. A flaw that would also draw her to a man like Mick, who would father her child and then abandon them both without so much as an apparent look back.

Enough of that! she chided herself. You are who you are, you did what you did. Regrets, yes, despair, no. Get this behind you. Get to the bottom of it and move on with your life, whatever that might mean and wherever that might take you.

Easier said than done, she knew.

By the time Danny was up and in the kitchen, Brett was there, too—having accepted Maggie's invitation to come early for breakfast. By then, she had already read the newspaper, cover to cover, consumed half a pot of coffee, and was breaking the eggs for scrambling. The bacon simmered in the frying pan.

"Damn, that smells good," Brett said, nose in the air, sniffing. He was still clad in the same baggy shorts, T-shirt, and Reeboks he wore every morning for his three-mile run. The white socks drooped around his ankles, making his pencil legs look even longer. Ichabod Crane without his horse.

"I don't want eggs," Danny complained. "I hate 'em. You know that, Mom."

"Tough luck, kiddo," she replied tiredly and too sharply. "That's what's going on the table. Make the best of it."

Brett turned at the tone of her voice. "Little edgy this morning?"

"I guess so. Sorry."

"How long have you been up?"

"Too long."

"Couldn't sleep?"

"Not much."

"Worried?"

"You could say that, yes."

Brett moved closer, out of Danny's earshot. "Relax, will you? We're your friends. We'll be here to help, if we can."

"I'm not sure you can," Maggie said as she stepped to the stove. "It's not that easy." She forked the bacon out of the pan, dumped the grease, and poured the scrambled eggs in. Handing him the fork, she said, "Stir these while I make the toast, okay?"

"No problem," he replied, bending to the task.

By now, Danny was in the living room, parked in front of the TV, the Saturday morning cartoons attracting his undivided attention. In less than an hour, he would be in Anna's hands, off on a trip to the Como Park Zoo.

When Brett spoke again, as Maggie buttered the toast, it was as though he'd been privy to her sleepless thoughts. "You should know, Maggie, that whatever this thing is, it won't make any difference to me. No matter how bad it is. It won't change anything."

She gave a short laugh. "Don't be so sure."

"I am sure. You are what you are today, regardless of the past." And then, chuckling, "Assuming you didn't kill somebody or bomb a building."

"A killer I'm not," she said. "Nor a bomber."

"Then we've got no problem."

"We'll see about that," she replied.

Barclay was the next to arrive. Maggie watched as he pulled into the parking lot, driving a decrepit Dodge Ram pickup that coughed blue smoke and appeared to be one gasp short of the junkyard. An advanced case of rust rot had eaten away most of the truck's fenders and lower body, and the whole thing leaned to the left, as though the springs on that side had finally surrendered to the weight of the driver.

"Oh, my God," she whispered as Barclay hoisted himself out of the truck. And then, shouting over her shoulder, "Brett, come see this! It's too good to believe."

Barclay was wearing a uniform of some sort, baseball or softball, she guessed. The pants were gray with black stripes and baggy, even on his body. The matching shirt was open at the neck, as tight as the pants were loose, straining the buttons and barely containing his girth. A baseball cap was perched precariously atop his head. Babe Ruth on his worst day.

Maggie stood aghast as Brett appeared by her side. "What the hell's going on?" he asked. Then he saw Barclay striding toward the door. "I'll be damned! Isn't he a picture."

"And look at his truck," she said, pointing. "I thought it might implode driving in. It may not make it out of the parking lot."

Brett shook his head and laughed, then quickly retreated to the bedroom to change out of his shorts and running shoes.

When Barclay appeared at the door, Maggie strained to maintain a straight face. "Did you bring your bat and ball?" she asked innocently.

"Very funny, Margaret," he said as he walked past her and into the apartment. "Nice place," he added, looking around. "I can see we pay you anchors too much."

She ignored the jab. "Seriously," she said, "what's with the uniform?"

He took off his cap and threw it on the couch. "I play softball on Saturdays. The Media Mites. We're in the playoffs."

She smiled. "The Media Mites?"

"The Old Timer's League," he said. "When you

want to talk on a Saturday morning, this is what you get, I'm afraid. We play in a couple of hours."

Maggie led him into the kitchen and offered him a cup of coffee. "And what position do you play?" she asked.

"Catcher. What else? Who better to block the plate?" He pulled out a kitchen chair and settled onto it, sipping the coffee. "Where's the baby-sitter?"

"You mean Anna?"

"No, Jacobi."

"He's back there getting changed," she laughed, pointing to the rear of the apartment. "He came right over after his morning run."

"And your boy?"

"Danny? He's with Anna, the real baby-sitter. They're off to the zoo."

She gave Barclay a quick tour of the apartment before they were joined by Brett and, a few minutes later, Jessica, who arrived clad in a pair of washed-out jeans, sandals, and an oversized Vikings sweatshirt. "Sorry I'm late," she told Maggie. "I got stuck in traffic coming around the lakes." Then she saw Barclay and squealed. "George, is that you? I didn't know this was a costume party. I would have brought my broom."

Once Barclay had again explained his uniform, less patiently this time, Maggie led them into the living room, poured coffee all around, and then grabbed a spot on the floor, facing them. Before she could begin, however, Barclay said, "I got a call from the cops this morning, at home. They found the car."

"Where?" The word jumped out of Maggie's mouth.

"Left in some alley in north Minneapolis. Illegally parked. A tow truck picked it up. Matches the description, complete with some front-end damage. Turns out it was stolen and the license plates switched. They're going to hold it for a couple of days before returning it to the real owner."

"Anything else?" she asked, recalling the scrawled words on the trunk.

"Not that they told me. We're welcome to go look at it, but I'm not sure what good it would do."

"Will they check it for prints?" Brett asked.

"Not for this kind of thing, they say. Besides, they claim that with a car this old there would be hundreds."

"So what happens now?" Jessica asked.

Barclay shrugged and glanced at Maggie. "Listen to what Maggie has to tell us, I guess, and take it from there."

All eyes turned to her. The moment she'd been dreading, the scene that had kept her awake most of the night. The living, breathing nightmare. She tried a brave smile, and when that failed, closed her eyes and rocked back, her hands clasped around her knees. The only sounds came from the grackles, still squawking outside her windows.

When her eyes reopened, Barclay was leaning forward in his chair. "It's not going to get any easier, Maggie."

"I know," she breathed. "I know." She pulled herself up straight. "I'm not proud of what I'm going to tell you. I can't tell you how ashamed I am. Telling you won't be easy and may take a while, so I hope you'll be patient."

Barclay and the others settled back in their

chairs as Maggie turned her eyes to the floor and spoke in a voice she hoped would be free of tremors and strong enough to be heard. She felt more nervous now than the first time she had faced a live camera in a television studio.

"You've all heard the unhappy childhood story a million times about other kids," she began. "Well, add me to the list. In spades. I won't bore you with all of the sorry details, but trust me that it was bad, real bad. Abusive home. Parents more often drunk than sober. A father who loved to beat on me, a mother who could only look the other way. No brothers or sisters, no pets, virtually no friends. Bad attitude, a terror at school, when I bothered to go at all."

She paused for breath. "As I think back now, it was like living in a kind of torture chamber. I can't remember a single happy moment, not one, not even at Christmas or at a birthday. Life was an endless string of drunken shouts and curses, of slaps and bruises. Of crying. My God, I cried. All the time, it seems like now. And prayed, night after night until I decided that God was as scared of my father as I was."

She felt her eyes welling again and took a quick swipe at a single tear which had found its way to her cheek. "When I was real young, the teachers used to ask why I never smiled, why I was such a sourpuss. If they'd only known. But back then, you never told, not the teachers, not even the few friends I had. I never dared to bring anyone home, and eventually I stopped getting invited to other kids' houses. I was a loner by the time I was ten."

As she took a sip of her coffee, she glanced up and found three sets of eyes fastened on her, unwavering. "To make this very long story as short as possible," she continued, "I finally got out. When I couldn't take it anymore, when I thought I was old enough to stand a chance on my own. I was fifteen when I took off. Stole a hundred bucks of my dad's drinking money and hopped a bus for L.A. It was like getting out of prison. Free at last."

Brett leaned forward and quietly asked, "Did your folks come after you?"

"Not that I ever knew. They were probably happy to be rid of me. I was in a lot of trouble by then. Fighting, skipping school, shoplifting, in and out of detention centers. Hell, it could have been days before they even knew I was gone.

"I only heard from them once. Years later, when I was on television in L.A. They came to the station to see me, but I told security to get rid of them, that I wanted no part of them. I have no idea whether they're dead or alive today, and try as I might, I just can't make myself give a shit."

"Sweet Jesus," Brett muttered. "So Danny will never know his grandparents?"

"That's the worst of it," she admitted. "It shouldn't happen to any kid. When he's old enough, I'll try to make him understand."

It was Barclay who spoke next, looking both confused and relieved. "Is that what you're telling us? That you've got a juvenile record? Is that the deep, dark secret? Christ, probably half the kids in this country have been in trouble with the law. I know I had a few scrapes myself."

"I wish it were that simple, George. But it's not."

"Then what is it?" he asked. "You had a rough childhood, I understand that. It's a horrible story and my heart goes out to you. I mean that, truly. But how does that fit into what's happening now?"

Maggie managed a small smile. "Coming to that, George. I told you it might take a while."

She quickly moved on, capsulizing in minutes the story of her months on the streets of Los Angeles, including her time living in the warehouse and of her continuing and deepening dependence on her friend, Sissy. "It's impossible to explain or understand now, even to myself, how Sissy became, in effect, the older sister or parents I never had. It shows just how weak I was, I guess. She guided me, she controlled me. She was so strong, so sure of herself, so . . . I don't know . . . cool and confident. And she had saved me from that jerk who tried to rape me. It was the only time anyone had ever tried to help me, and I felt a debt."

Barclay again interrupted. "So what does this Sissy have to do with things?"

"She's at the heart of it, George. But I can't ever hope to make you understand how desperate we were."

Maggie knew she was right. Words alone could not describe the hunger, the cold, the helplessness. No matter how eloquent, how gritty her depiction of their plight, they would not be able to put themselves in her place. To feel what she had felt then. Without that, they would never understand what happened next. But she forged ahead anyway, portraying in vivid detail that final afternoon in the cold and rain at the picnic pavilion. "We didn't know where we would eat or sleep. Or how long the rain would go on. We had no money, no home, no hope."

"So what did you do?" It was the first time Jessica had spoken.

Maggie took a deep breath and stood up, facing them. The moment had arrived. The room was absolutely silent. Even the birds had fallen quiet. Nothing, she knew, would be the same again.

"We made a pornographic movie," she said simply and with a touch of defiance.

14

The silence, if anything, became even more profound. The room stood still, as if the moment had been captured on videotape and the frame frozen in time. Barclay's mouth literally fell open. Brett's eyes grew wider than Maggie had ever seen them. Jessica fell back into her chair, her expression one of utter disbelief and distaste.

All Maggie could do was stand and watch. Suspended, out of the picture, an observer separated by space and time. Seconds that seemed like minutes passed before the frozen frame thawed. Barclay was the first to react, snapping his jaws shut and demanding, "You did *what?*"

Maggie slumped back to the floor. "I was sixteen, George. A kid, for God's sake."

Barclay was not assuaged. "Tell me again. You did what?"

Her eyes locked with his. "You heard it right the first time. I appeared in a pornographic film. A sex film, George. X-rated. Don't tell me you've never seen one."

Barclay buried his head in his hands and allowed a loud groan to escape. He could already picture the mocking tabloid headlines, could hear the public outcry and the jeers of competitors and colleagues, could see the livid face of his boss, Nicholas Hawke, spitting out his anger at him.

"My God," he whispered. "A fuck film. Jesus, Maggie."

Brett appeared to be in shock. His skin had paled, and he seemed to have trouble catching his breath. He tried to speak once, but choked on the words and fell silent.

Maggie didn't know what to say either. Their reaction was what she had expected. Shock. Disbelief. Disappointment. Anger. But that didn't make it any easier. Seeing Brett's stricken face caused the sharpest pain. His angel had lost her wings. Given the choice, maybe now he'd prefer that she *had* killed someone or bombed that building.

In the shroud of gloom, surprising Maggie, it was Jessica who saved the day. Forgetting for a moment their tense and uneasy relationship, she slipped out of her chair and flopped down on the floor next to Maggie, hugging her. Gone was any hint of the shock and disapproval of only minutes before. It was one woman coming to the rescue of another. "Is that all there is?" she asked slyly. "Shit,

I thought you had something *serious* to tell us."
Then she laughed. 'Til her eyes began to water.

The relief was immediate. All of the tension
that had built up inside Maggie for days exploded
into a series of giggles and then full-blown glee.
She laughed harder than she could ever remember; she couldn't stop, pushed on by Jessica's own
infectious mirth. They sat together on the floor,
hugging, laughing, crying, holding their stom-
achs, wiping away the tears, ignoring the two men
still sitting stoically on the sofa.

Barclay was visibly irritated. "I don't see anything fucking funny about this," he said harshly.
"Snap out of it, you two."

But there was no stopping them, and when they
continued to ignore him, doubled over with
laughter, he, too, found himself caught up in it.
Despite his every effort, the laughing tears began
to roll down his cheeks as well, lost forever in the
forest of his beard.

Brett was the last to capitulate. Even then, he
could only manage a sympathetic smile. But his
voice was back. "Are you guys crazy? Out of your
minds? How can you laugh at something like this?
This could ruin Maggie! Could kill the station."

That brought a brief pause, but then Jessica
countered with a giggle. "Don't be silly. Think
about it. We could have the first topless newscast
in town. Maggie could dance on the set."

More gales of laughter.

"All we have to do is talk Alex into it," Maggie
added, gasping for breath. "Does he have a hairy
chest?"

Even Brett thought that was funny.

Sanity returned a few minutes later.

They adjourned to the kitchen and sat around the square table. Beer replaced the coffee. Gravity replaced the levity. The whimsy was gone; reality was back. Nonetheless, Maggie felt a great sense of relief; the secret was out, for better or worse. The burden was no longer hers to carry alone.

Barclay began by asking questions about the film: What was it called? When was it done? Who did it? Was it widely distributed?

Maggie took the questions one by one, answering those she could calmly and concisely. The movie was called *Good-bye Innocence*, she told them, and was filmed in a small studio on the Strip some twelve years before. It was about ninety minutes in length and purported to tell the story of a group of small-town girls who discovered sex during their first week in a coed college dorm. She couldn't remember the real names of the producer or director, if she ever knew them, or of anyone else connected with the film. Only Sissy. And she had never learned her last name.

"So, what . . . ah . . . role did you play?" Barclay asked.

"One of the girls, Gigi by name. Cute, huh? As you might guess, the story really has no plot. It's simply a succession of girls getting, well . . . educated about sex is about the nicest way to put it. My part lasts about twelve minutes. No doubt the worst twelve minutes of my life."

She could see that Barclay was struggling with the unasked question. The heart of the matter. She decided to ease his discomfort. "I did everything, George. Or better put, I allowed everything to be done to me. You name it, I did it. Except I never touched the guy, not in any intimate way. I refused to do that, much to the director's dismay. They even threatened not to pay me."

Brett leaned across the table, gritting his teeth, focusing on Maggie, but seeing instead an entirely different image. One that he tried but failed to shake off, an image as vivid as the centerfold of *Penthouse*. He felt both repulsed and, despite himself, aroused. That other men, perhaps hundreds or thousands of others, had seen this woman as he had only dreamed of seeing her left him livid. "But how could you do any of it, Maggie?" he asked angrily. "What were you thinking? I just can't see it."

For the first time, she felt real rage. "I knew you wouldn't understand," she said, her voice almost a hiss. "I'm not making excuses, but you weren't there. You don't know what it was like. You never will . . . you never could.

"I did it for the money. I did it for what I thought then was survival. I did it because I thought Sissy would leave me if I didn't. I did it for a dozen reasons. None of them make any sense now, I know that. It seems stupid, irresponsible. Call it what you will. But I wasn't an anchorwoman, a TV star, then. I wasn't a mother. I was a naive, frightened kid on the streets of Los Angeles, literally without a dime to my name."

Brett started to respond, but she waved him quiet. "You know what's the saddest part?" she said, not bothering now to wipe away the tears seeping from her eyes. "I was a virgin at the time. Would you believe that? They didn't, Sissy didn't.

I don't think they'd ever seen one before. But it was true. For me, it was literally *Good-bye Innocence.* Nice, huh? What a way to have your first sexual experience."

"My God," Jessica whispered.

But Maggie wasn't finished. Her eyes flashed. "So don't get high and mighty on me, Brett. Or you, either, George. I did what I did, and I can't take it back now, much as I'd like to. I have to live with it, somehow try to put it behind me. For a long time, I thought I had, but alas, it turns out I haven't."

"Which brings us to the present," Barclay said in a calming voice. "The packages you received . . . the telephone call . . . the ramming of your car."

"Precisely," Maggie said, relaxing. "The first package contained a still photograph taken from the film, apparently off a TV set, the second was a tape copy of the film itself."

"No wonder you went nuts," Barclay muttered. "How would they have known it was you?"

"You've got me. I used a phony name and I looked quite different. I can hardly recognize myself. I was much younger, of course, my hair was a different color, and—"

"I hate to ask this," Barclay interrupted, "but can I see the tape? I'll need to—"

"Forget it, George! No one I know sees the tape, not if I can help it."

"Shit," he said, heaving himself out of the chair. "There's got to be something we can do. Find out who the distributor is . . . see how many copies are out there. Christ, I'll search every porn video store myself, if I have to. Buy every copy I can find."

"I doubt that you'd find any," she said. "It's been too long. The ones that exist are probably all in private hands."

Jessica spoke up for the first time. "So who do you think is behind it?"

Maggie puzzled over the question. "At first, I thought some pervert might be at work, some guy trying to get his jollies. Or maybe pure blackmail. But now, I don't know. Somebody is after something, I'm just not sure what."

"Which is why you came to me," Jessica said as Brett got up to retrieve another round of beers. "You thought the packages, the threats, might be tied to my child porn story." Maggie could hear the growing anger in her voice. "That's why you wanted to get involved. You *did* have your own agenda."

"I still think they may," she replied calmly. "When I got that telephone call, the voice said something to the effect that I would now have to do whatever they asked. To me, that either means money or some favor, and what favor could I do that would be worth all of this trouble? Except maybe to help kill your story when the time comes."

"How could you do that?" Jessica asked with disbelief.

"By telling Barclay here that it's a choice of either your story or my reputation and that of the station. Seems like fairly strong leverage to me."

Barclay sat up straight. "We'd never do it. Kill the story, I mean."

"But they don't know that," Maggie argued. "Whoever they are."

Both Jessica and Barclay shook their heads doubtfully.

"Think about it," Maggie persisted. "Who'd be more likely to discover me in a twelve-year-old film than somebody who's involved in child pornography? They've probably got a goddamned library full of old movies. And if they're after money or some other favor, like my body, why haven't they said so? They're waiting, that's why. To see what comes of all of this."

"But why try to hurt you?" Barclay asked. "Why ram your car?"

She could only shrug. "To tell me they're serious, I guess. We're not dealing with nice people here."

Jessica sipped her beer, and then, "She could be right, you know. Don't forget the Penny girl. If it's true that she was somehow involved in this porn business and they killed her, then sure as hell they're capable of knocking Maggie around a bit."

"Which brings us back to another point," Barclay said. "I'd like Brett here to move in with you for a while. Until we know you're out of danger."

Maggie began to protest, but Barclay cut her off. "You've got a spare bedroom, right?"

"Yes, but—"

"No buts, please. There's too much at stake here. Not only your safety, but that boy of yours, too. I want Brett to be near you every damn minute of the day."

Maggie looked plaintively at Brett, who said, "I think he's right, Maggie. We should have done it right after your car got rammed."

Maggie could see it was futile to argue, but said, "I think it's silly. I can take care of myself."

"Humor us, then," Barclay replied, glancing at his watch and then heaving himself out of the chair. "I'm sorry, but I've got to get to my game. Where do we go from here?"

There was silence at the table. No one had a quick or easy answer.

"Okay, then," he said, filling the void. "We'll go on as we have. We talk to no one about this. No one. Brett, you move in as quick as you can and keep a close eye on Maggie and the boy. Jessica, you and Maggie keep after the porn story, but take no chances. Hear that? First sign of trouble, you come running. Maggie, try to put this out of your mind, if you can. You're not alone anymore. I can't tell you what will happen if this gets public, but know that we're with you. Main thing is to keep you and that boy of yours safe."

He came around the table to give her a quick and clumsy hug, and then started for the door. Jessica and Brett took their cue from him and began to follow.

"One more thing," Maggie said before they could leave. "It may not mean anything, but whoever's doing this knows all about me. Where I live, the car I drive, where my desk is at work, my direct-dial number. It's weird."

Barclay paused by the door. "What are you suggesting? That somebody at the station . . . ?"

She shrugged. "I don't know. But none of those things are exactly public knowledge."

Barclay glanced at Brett and Jessica, then dismissed

the idea with a shake of his head. "Nah, that's not possible. I know everybody too well. Nobody down there would be part of something like this."

"Okay," Maggie said. "Just so you know."

She followed them out of the apartment. "Thanks for listening," she said. "I'm sorry to heap all of this on you. I appreciate your support. You made it easier than I thought it would be."

With another brief hug from each, they were gone, swallowed up in the fog of blue smoke from Barclay's old pickup.

Brett was back at the apartment a couple of hours later, a small satchel in one hand and a carry-on bag of suits and shirts in the other, slung over his shoulder.

Maggie led him down the hall to the spare bedroom. "Put your things anywhere," she said. "There's room in the closet and a few empty drawers."

"I'll do that later," he replied as he put the two bags on the bed and stepped back to look at her. "You're sure this is going to be okay?"

Maggie shrugged. "Barclay wants it this way. I still think it's silly, but I must admit it will be nice to have you here. I know Danny will love having you around."

They had agreed earlier that Brett would drive Danny to and from school and run whatever other errands were necessary, keeping Maggie inside and out of sight whenever possible. He would also continue to monitor incoming phone calls both at the apartment and in the newsroom, and he would check all mail before giving it over to her.

"I'm afraid you're going to feel like a prisoner here," she said.

"Not as much as you are, but maybe it won't last too long."

She smiled. "You know, I haven't lived with anybody for a long time. You're going to discover all of my bad features, my bad habits."

"What are you talking about? I already know most of them."

Maggie knew that Brett's living there would only cause more tongue-wagging in the newsroom, more speculation about the strange relationship between the star anchorwoman and the producer. That was okay. She didn't particularly care what others thought, but she had now begun to question her own feelings toward Brett. And she couldn't help but wonder if his feelings toward her had changed with this morning's confession about the movie.

She would have had to be blind—to say nothing of deaf and dumb—not to have known that he wanted more from her than mere friendship from almost the beginning. While he had never pushed for a more serious relationship, he had made it clear in a dozen different but subtle ways that he would relish one. At least, before today.

But not Maggie.

Still hurting from the heartbreak of Mick's unexplained flight in California, she had come to Minnesota fiercely determined to remain independent, to eschew any new romantic entanglements, and to concentrate on her job and raising her son. So far, it had worked, and she'd been grateful to Brett for not allowing his own ardor to spoil their friendship.

She fondly recalled his early and clumsy attempts to court her . . . and his deep disappointment when she fended him off, as she had so many others. But unlike the others, he'd accepted the rejection without rancor . . . and in the process remained her best buddy in the newsroom.

So what had changed? She couldn't quite define it, but something had. Perhaps it was this new situation, the potential danger she was facing. Or the fact that he was always there for her when no one else really was. Or perhaps it was simply the passage of time. In any event, she no longer saw him in the same brotherly light. There was a new awareness of his physical presence, a new stirring inside her that she at least had to acknowledge, if not respond to.

The rain began a few hours later. A cold rain that a few weeks later would almost certainly have turned to snow. A lot of snow, since the rain increased steadily as the afternoon progressed— from a light sprinkle to a heavy downpour, overflowing the gutters of the apartment building and forming huge puddles in the parking lot beyond. Like the day in the park with Sissy, when the heavens opened and stayed open.

Maggie stood by the window and watched as the streaks of lightning cut through the dark sky like slices of a fiery knife, then braced herself for the bursts of thunder, some strong enough to shake the panes of the window. Storms like this usually happened in the spring, not the fall, making her wonder if it wasn't some kind of ominous omen.

Anna and Danny were not yet home, no doubt off hiding from the rain somewhere. Danny had begged that they be allowed to take the bus home from the zoo, seeing that as more of an adventure than the zoo itself.

They're probably having a burger and a shake somewhere, she decided, waiting for the storm to pass. Still, she wished they'd call.

Her mood had darkened with the skies. The relief she'd felt that morning, after finally revealing her story, had slowly dissipated with the realization that nothing had actually changed. True, she was no longer alone with her secret, she now had allies, but the bad guys were still out there somewhere. So were the tapes. So was the threat.

Her creeping melancholy apparently was shared by Brett, who had hardly spoken to her again since he returned to the apartment. He had stayed close to his bedroom, emerging only occasionally to get something from the kitchen or visit the bathroom. She had made no effort to intercept him, knowing it would take time for him to sort through what he had heard that morning, to come to grips with the new vision of her. For him, she thought, it must have been akin to discovering that your sister is a whore or that your wife is sleeping with your best friend.

The pedestal he had so carefully erected for her in his own mind had just crumbled before his eyes.

Not that he wasn't forewarned. Lord knows she

had tried to prepare him, but how could he be expected to imagine the unimaginable? The idea that Maggie, his best friend, his idealized model of womanhood, living an apparently celibate life, could ever do what she had done must have struck him like one of those bolts of lightning out there.

It was not until later that night, after Anna and Danny were safely home and Danny snugly in bed, that Brett finally sought out Maggie. He found her in the living room, curled up in a corner of the couch, sipping a cup of hot chocolate and thumbing through a copy of *Redbook*. Just out of the shower, she had changed into her nightgown and woolen robe, fastened tightly around her neck for warmth.

The rain had finally stopped and the skies had cleared, turning the evening cooler and less humid, and leaving the apartment with a chill from the windows that had remained open most of the day. Frost was expected by morning.

Brett settled into a corner of the couch away from Maggie, his slippered feet stretched to reach the squat ottoman. He wore the same clothes from the morning: a pair of tan chinos, now well-wrinkled, and a sweatshirt bearing the emblem of a local golf club. He said nothing for several minutes, apparently content to stare into the distance and absorb the soft voice of Anita Baker emerging from the stereo. Maggie glanced at him once, then returned to her magazine, unwilling to begin the conversation.

Brett started to rise but then sat back down. "Can I look at it?" he asked suddenly.

"At what?" she said, momentarily thinking he meant the *Redbook*.

"The tape."

Startled, she cried out, "Of course not! Are you out of your mind?"

"I don't think I'll believe it until I see it," he said.

"Believe it, Brett. You don't need proof."

"Jesus, Maggie—"

She cut him off. "Remember this morning, Brett? You said no matter what it was, what I'd done, it wouldn't make any difference to you. 'You are what you are today,' I think you said."

He reddened at the reminder.

"I can't explain it any more than I already have," she said. "You'll either have to accept it or . . . I don't know, forget it and me, I guess. It's part of who I am . . . or at least of who I was. You've got your long legs, I've got my checkered past. Not much either one of us can do about it now, is there?"

She wondered again if she should destroy the tape. It would certainly prevent Brett or Barclay from ever seeing it, or Danny or Anna from stumbling upon it. But she knew it could someday be important as evidence, if it ever came to that. No, she decided, better to keep it locked up tight— but available if it was ever needed.

Standing now, Brett towered above her. "Is there anything else?" he asked. "Anything more you haven't told us? I'd like to know now."

Maggie sighed a deep sigh and laid her head back on the cushions of the couch, closing her eyes. Now that he knew about the film and her life on the street, there was no problem telling him about her years with Elijah and his family. But what about Mick, the runaway father of her child? The years of despair and self-doubt that followed his flight? Not now, she decided. It would be too much, too soon—not only for him but for her as well. She was simply too tired.

"Nothing like the movie, Brett," she finally said. "Mistakes, yes, bad judgments, yes, but nothing that would quite measure up to that."

"Good," he said. "I'll see you in the morning."

He was gone before she opened her eyes again.

15

As promised, Harry Carlisle arrived at the station promptly at three o'clock on Monday afternoon. Brett greeted him at the outer door and escorted him to the Green Room, where Maggie sat waiting.

"A pleasure to finally meet you," Carlisle said as he put down a thin brown briefcase and shook her hand. "I'm only sorry it has to be under these circumstances."

His hand, like his voice, was soft and moist and lingered for a moment too long in hers. Like gripping a slightly decomposed fish, Maggie thought as she fought the urge to wipe her hand on her skirt. But she recovered quickly. "Thanks for coming, Mr. Carlisle," she said, offering him a chair.

"Call me Harry, please," he said quickly. "Everyone else does."

"Okay, Harry. And feel free to call me Maggie." Then, with a quick glance at Brett still standing by the door, she added, "If you don't mind, my friend Brett here will stay with us. He's helping out with this little mystery of mine."

"Not at all," Carlisle replied easily. "I want to help, too, if I can."

Carlisle was as Denise, the shy tour guide, had once described him: in his forties, six feet or a shade more, with salt-and-pepper hair that was more salt than pepper. In contrast to his spongy handshake and silky voice, his features were sharp-edged, hawkish: a thin, beak-like nose; squarish chin; cheekbones high and pointed, stretching his skin; and lips that were narrow and tightly-drawn, as though he'd worn braces as a kid and was still afraid to show his teeth.

Not an entirely unattractive man, Maggie decided, his appearance helped by a well-tailored gray suit, a light blue button-down shirt, and a splashy paisley tie. Dapper and distinguished, she thought, even down to his tasseled loafers. Mindful, however, of Denise's earlier warning about his bad breath, she took a chair several feet from him. "I hope we're not taking you away from anything important at work," she said.

"No need to worry," he replied. "I own the place."

"Really? You own Sinclair Engineering?"

He smiled modestly. "It's a small company, about a dozen employees. We do consulting work for contractors who build bridges, mainly. Steel and concrete work."

Politely probing further, they learned he had worked his way up from an apprentice draftsman through the company ranks to a point, ten years later, that he was able to buy out the retiring owner, one Jeremy Sinclair. "We kept the old company name," he said, "but I'm the only shareholder."

Maggie's earlier impression of him on the telephone was borne out in person: He appeared to be open and friendly, if somewhat overeager, but definitely nonthreatening. If he's some kind of closet pervert, she thought, he's doing a great job of disguising it.

With more questioning, they also discovered he was one of the charter members of the singles' club at St. Raphael's, organized five or six years before. Never married, he told them, he got tired of the bar scene, and too old for it, anyway. He wanted to find a more substantial, lasting relationship, preferably with a nice Catholic woman.

"And have you?" Maggie asked, perhaps too boldly.

"Not really," he replied, unfazed by the question. "Dates, yes. A few short-term romances, but nothing permanent."

A little Scope might help, she thought wickedly.

"I continue to go because it's about the only social life I have, and because I keep hoping the right woman might come along."

He's certainly not bashful about his private life, Maggie thought. But it was time to move on. "So tell me more about these two people you mentioned on the phone, the ones who lied on their applications."

Carlisle reached into his briefcase and pulled

out two sheets of paper. "Here's what we have in writing," he said as he handed the papers to Maggie. Brett walked over and squatted next to her, scanning the documents as she did.

They were simple applications, listing name, age, address, telephone number, religion, employment, and other sundry facts. At the bottom of the page was an open space for the applicant to list his or her hobbies and other personal interests.

The woman, Eleanor Smith, had scribbled in three items: shopping, line dancing, and going to the movies. The man, Frank Edwards, was no more inventive; his list included watching sports on TV, fishing, and listening to rock-and-roll music.

"Not exactly intellectual giants," Maggie mused.

Harry smiled. "Those things are probably lies, too. Like the rest of it."

"You've checked all of this?" she asked, holding up the papers.

"As much as I could. Addresses, telephone numbers. Employment. Everything's phony."

Maggie sat back and reached for a small notebook. "Describe them again, if you would. I'd like to take notes this time."

Carlisle launched into another description of the pair, but added little to what he had already told Maggie on the telephone. When he finished, Maggie glanced at Brett. "Doesn't sound like anybody I know or have seen," she said. "How about you?"

Brett shook his head. "Afraid not," he admitted.

"There is one other thing," Carlisle said.

Maggie cocked her head. "What's that?"

"On the phone, you asked if we had pictures of these two."

"Yes."

"As I told you, we don't have any official pictures. You know, like head shots or portraits. They weren't with us long enough to provide them."

"So?"

"So after we talked, I got to thinking. I remembered that one of the other women on the tour, Pat McKenzie, took some pictures that night at the station. Snapshots. I remember the flashes. Irritated me at the time, but—"

Maggie interrupted him. "You think she may have gotten a shot of one or both—?"

Carlisle shrugged. "It's possible. She was taking lots of pictures, I know that."

"Can you get hold of them?" Brett asked quickly.

"That's the problem. Pat's in Mexico right now, on vacation. She'll be back later this week."

Maggie snapped her notebook shut, clearly disappointed.

"I'll call her as soon as she returns," Carlisle offered. "And get copies of the pictures to you as quickly as I can."

"We'd appreciate that," Brett said. "And could you do one other thing?"

"Of course. Anything."

"Talk to the other club members. See if anyone else knows anything more about these two. Maybe someone else got to know them better than you did."

"No problem. We meet again this week. We're having a dinner-dance."

"Good. And if anyone happens to see one or both of these people . . . you know, on the streets, in a store, or in a car . . . anywhere . . . let us know.

Maybe they could get a license number or something."

Carlisle picked up his briefcase and walked to the door. "I'll do what I can," he said. "But I wouldn't get your hopes up."

When Brett returned to the Green Room after escorting Carlisle out of the building, he found Maggie staring off into space. He sat down next to her and waited.

"You know," she finally said, "we could be chasing our tails."

"What do you mean?"

She turned to him. "These two mystery people could be lying about themselves for reasons that have nothing to do with me."

"Like?"

"Like what if they're just shy? Don't want anyone to know their real identities?"

"Unlikely," Brett scoffed.

Maggie paused, then, "What if they're married—"

"To each other?"

"No, no," she said impatiently. "Say they don't even know each other. They could each be married to someone else and are simply trying to have a little fun on the side."

She could see the doubt written across his face. "Seriously," she went on, "what better place for wayward married folks to meet single, eager playmates? Just claim you're single, give phony information about yourself so your wife or husband doesn't find out, and then go have a whee of a time."

"C'mon, Maggie—"

"It could happen," she persisted.

"That's a stretch," he argued. "You really think that both of these people would show up on the same night, then quit at the same time? Too much of a coincidence, if you ask me."

Maggie got up and turned to the makeup mirror, her back to Brett, fussing with her hair. In a casual voice, she asked, "Have you ever been to a singles' club? You must have."

Brett was taken aback. "Gimme a break, Maggie. I'm not *that* desperate."

She smiled into the mirror. "Maybe you should think about it. Harry said they're having a dinner-dance this week."

Suddenly aware of what she was thinking, he blurted, "Oh, no, you don't. Not me."

"Barclay would give you the night off," she said, turning to face him. "And who knows? You might meet someone."

"I've already met someone," he replied before he had time to think.

"You *have*?" she asked, not hiding her surprise. "Since when?" And then, after staring him down, "That's crapola, Brett. I would have known."

"You don't know everything, Maggie. But let's drop it. I'm not going to the goddamned dinner-dance."

She walked around him to the door. "Think about it. What if those two were to return? You'd see them firsthand, in person."

"They won't be back," Brett said. "Trust me."

"At least you'd meet some of the other members. Get to talk to them directly. Carlisle would help pull it off, I'm sure."

"Forget it, Maggie."

"I would go, if I could. But they'd recognize me. It would be all over the gossip columns."

"Sure."

"It might help, Brett. Give it some more thought."

George Barclay was in a grumpy mood and made no bones about it. Not only was it a Monday, which he'd always hated, but his lower back was giving him great pain, the result of being knocked flat on his ass at home plate on Saturday by a big bruiser, a goddamned newspaper guy at that. But at least he'd held onto the ball and managed to tag the fucker out. He took some satisfaction from that.

Adding insult to his injury, the game had been canceled by the rain while his Mites were ahead six to four—which meant he was suffering for nothing.

And if that misery weren't enough, there was Maggie. Her confession on Saturday pained him even more than his back. He had spent the rest of the weekend reliving her anguished words, wondering what to do. Worrying about it. About *her*. Debating the options. Trying to anticipate the problems. It was impossible. Too many things were unknown, unpredictable, beyond his control.

It was clearly a crisis in the making. Any fool, even an old fool like himself, could see that. The main thing he could do, he kept telling himself, was to try to keep her safe, out of harm's way. Beyond that, he could only watch and wait, be ready to react, helpless to do much more.

Already that afternoon he had taken calls from reporters for both the *Star-Tribune* and the *Pioneer Press*, asking for any new developments in the Maggie Lawrence case. Since they already knew the hit-and-run car had been found, Barclay could offer them little new information. "We're keeping a close eye on her," he had told them, "and trying to carry on as usual."

Even the cops had begun to show some interest. A detective called him that morning, asking for a meeting with Maggie. "The deputy chief's a fan of hers," the cop had told him, "and the papers are on his ass. He wants to know what's going on."

If you only knew, Barclay thought ruefully, but he went ahead and set up the meeting for the next afternoon.

And then there was Nicholas Hawke, waiting now outside his office door while Barclay pretended to be on the phone, killing time, thinking, letting Hawke cool his heels. He had debated telling him about Maggie's film, knowing he should. Hawke was his boss, after all, ultimately responsible for the station and its reputation. He should know. But Barclay could not bring himself to do it. Hawke would go crazy. Probably want to fire her immediately. And without question, he would want to see the film. Slimy bastard.

Barclay knew he was taking a big chance by remaining silent. Hawke's words, "I don't like being left in the dark," echoed in his mind. Keeping the secret could cost him his job, but the alternative was even worse.

"Fuck him," he muttered into the silent phone

and then hung it up, waving Hawke into his office.

"I don't appreciate being kept waiting," Hawke grumbled as he grabbed a chair and glanced at his pocket watch.

"Sorry," Barclay said with a shrug and a half-hidden smile. "I was on the phone."

Hawke settled back in the chair. "So what's new?"

"About Maggie? Not much."

"I hear they found the car."

Barclay nodded and told him what he could. "I don't think it's going to help much, though," he said. "Turns out it was stolen."

Hawke brought his two hands together, steeple-like, under his chin and stared across the desk at Barclay. "Have you thought about what I said the other day?" he asked.

Barclay avoided a direct answer. "As a matter of fact, I talked to two newspaper reporters today. They seem to want to keep the story alive."

"Good," Hawke said.

"And Maggie's going to talk to a detective tomorrow. The cops have taken a sudden interest."

"I thought they might," Hawke said. "I happened to bump into the chief at the club last week."

So that's it, Barclay thought as he shifted in his chair and grimaced from the pain. Forget what the cop told him. Hawke's been at work.

"What's the matter with you," Hawke asked, seeing Barclay's discomfort.

"Hurt my back."

"How?"

"Long story, but I'll be all right."

"I hope so," Hawke said as he got up and walked to the door, where he paused. "You're telling me everything, aren't you? No games this time?"

Barclay spread his arms in mock innocence. "Of course. What I know, you know."

Hawke stared at him hard for a moment, then left.

Maggie found Jessica in Computer Central, a fancy name for a small room set aside a year or so before for "computer-assisted reporting," the newest innovation—some would call it gimmick— in investigative journalism. Begun years before by some of the country's larger newspapers, the intensive use of computer technology in news reporting had now spread to those television stations which had the resources to buy the equipment and software and the brains to know how to use it.

Channel 7 was one of these, although Barclay was originally suspicious of its usefulness. "You find things out by talking to people and by digging through files, following the paper trails," he'd once groused. "Not by punching a bunch of buttons on a fucking computer."

But by now, even Barclay had to admit he was wrong. Although he still bristled at the name Computer Central, which he called "P.R. bullshit," and the heavy, high-tech promotion the station liked to give the concept, he had to acknowledge the computer could provide reporters with more information in minutes than they could get with weeks of pawing through dusty records. All at the touch of their fingertips.

Maggie pulled up a chair next to Jessica, who hardly seemed aware of her arrival. Staring at the computer screen, her fingers skipped across the keyboard, scrolling row upon row of information across the screen. Maggie watched in awe. She had seldom been in this room and had never used the equipment. Few of the reporters or anchors had. Because of the complexity of the process and the cost of using some of the on-line services, access was limited to people like Jessica, who had been thoroughly trained and knew what they were doing.

As she waited for Jessica's fingers to pause, she asked, "What are you up to?"

"Checking criminal records," she replied without taking her eyes from the screen.

"Whose?"

Jessica shot her a quick glance. "Names I've picked up," she said vaguely.

Maggie pulled her chair closer. "Where do you look?"

Jessica hit the PRINT button on the computer and sat back as the paper version of what was on the screen began to spill out of the nearby printer. "A couple of places," she said. "For one, the BCA keeps data on every criminal conviction in the state going back twenty or thirty years. Over 140,000 at the moment."

Maggie knew that the BCA, or Bureau of Criminal Apprehension, was a state investigative agency, akin to a state FBI, which helped local law

enforcement agencies in handling especially difficult or high-visibility cases.

"And then there are the state prison records,"
Jessica went on, "containing the names of almost
80,000 people who have spent time behind bars in
the state . . . again, going back many years."

"All of that's in the computer?" Maggie asked
with genuine surprise.

"In the database, yes, but that's not all. We can
also get county criminal records, state and federal
court records, and a lot more. It's truly amazing."

As Maggie listened, she couldn't escape a
dispiriting sense of her own inadequacy. Here was
a woman younger than herself who knew so much
more than she did . . . or probably ever would.
True, she spent the bulk of her time at the anchor
desk, but that was no excuse for her almost total
ignorance of this part of the business. She decided
then and there that once this was all over, she
would get herself educated.

Jessica got up and walked to the printer,
tearing off two feet of data the machine had
just spit out. "You tell me what you want," she
said, returning to her desk, "and I can likely get
it for you. Death records, social security numbers, credit report headers, telephone numbers
from any city in the country, drivers' licenses, the
list goes on and on. You name it and I can probably find it."

Maggie asked to see the printout. At first glance,
it looked like a bunch of gibberish running down
the left-hand side of the page. On closer examination, however, she could see that one name, Jeffrey
Axelright, repeatedly appeared—followed by data

she didn't pretend to understand. "What is this, anyway?" she asked.

"Jeffrey Axelright's criminal record," Jessica said. "Going back over ten years."

"Who's Jeffrey Axelright?"

"A convicted child molester. Pornographer. Been arrested a half dozen times on charges like that."

Maggie took back the printout and examined it. "Where did you get his name?"

"In his case, out of the *Star-Tribune*. We have every story they've ever done on disc, back to 1986. You feed the computer a key word or two, like "child pornography," and it will search the newspaper's files for every story ever done where those two words appear. Takes some time, but it's incredible what you can find."

"And they did stories on this Axelright guy?"

"Several. But I don't know what it means. I have lots of names, from dozens of sources, that I'm trying to check out. Axelright's just one. It's tedious and takes a lot of time, but there's always the chance you'll hit the jackpot."

"And have you?" Maggie asked. "Hit the jackpot, I mean?"

"Not yet," she replied, smiling. "But I'm still working at it."

Maggie shook her head in amazement and got up. "You have more patience than I do. I'd go crazy in half an hour."

"Once you get the hang of it, it's fun," Jessica said. "Like working on an impossible jigsaw puzzle. Trying to fit the pieces together without benefit of the overall picture."

It was not until Maggie was halfway across the newsroom that she thought again of something Jessica had told her. "You name it and I can probably find it." She stopped abruptly, debated for a moment, then returned to Computer Central. "Sorry to bother you again," she said from the door.

Jessica turned from the computer. "That's okay. What's up?"

Maggie hesitated, then said, "If I wanted to find out where someone is . . . someone I haven't seen or talked to for many years . . . who may not even be alive anymore . . . could you show me how to do that?"

Jessica looked at her curiously, but asked no questions. "Maybe," she said. "Is it a man or a woman?"

"A man."

"Unfortunately, we'd have a better chance dead than alive. We have access to national death records and Social Security claims, so I could probably tell you fairly quickly if the person is dead."

Maggie took a deep breath.

"If he's still alive," Jessica continued, "and is still using the name you know him by, well, there's still a fair chance of success. Using credit reports, telephone listings, whatever. It would take some time though, and could cost some money."

"The money's not a problem," Maggie said.

"Want to give me a name? I could do some preliminary stuff in my spare time."

"You don't have any spare time."

Jessica laughed. "Let me decide that."

Maggie leaned against the doorjamb, thinking. Did she really want to know? Did she care anymore? Would it make any difference?

Jessica was watching her expectantly.

"Mick Salinas," Maggie finally said, spelling the last name. "He's my age, twenty-eight, and his last known residence was in Los Angeles."

"Mick, not Mickey?" Jessica asked.

"Just Mick," Maggie replied. "As in prick."

16

Leaving Jessica at the computer, Maggie returned to her desk, ready to begin the quest for Amy Boyd and Nadia Vaughn, the two young friends of the murdered Penny Collins. But one glance at the local phone books told her instantly how enormous the task would be: There were at least seventy-five Boyds in the Minneapolis area alone, and about half that number of Vaughns, all of whom might have to be called. And that said nothing of St. Paul or the outstate area.

Talk about a needle in a haystack, Maggie thought. Thank God they're not named Anderson or Johnson.

Of the first dozen Boyd numbers she called, half were answered by answering machines and

the other half by people who either hung up
before she could ask her questions or said they
knew nothing about any girl named Amy.

Maggie kept track of the calls on her computer,
but soon realized that doing it alone could take
weeks. So she went to George Barclay, who quickly
agreed to provide the help of two station interns—
young college students who served as newsroom
gophers in return for a few bucks an hour and the
chance to rub shoulders with the professionals.

One was named Natasha, a heavyset young
woman who wore a shapeless dress and horseshoe
earrings that hung almost to her shoulders, the
other Justin, whose crewcut, ruddy cheeks, and
stand-tall bearing gave him the look of a young
Marine. Both appeared wide-eyed and eager, awed
by the chance to work side-by-side with the real
Maggie Lawrence. Little did they know what they
faced.

Maggie sat them down at her desk. "We're looking for two young girls," she said, reciting their
names and what little else she knew about them.
"As far as we know, both are runaways and both
may still be somewhere in the Twin Cities." Without
revealing more, Maggie went on to explain the
process. "We don't know where they're from, but
we need to talk to every person we can find with
either of those last names. Amy or Nadia could be
a daughter or a sister or a niece . . . some relative.
Keep track of every call and every response. If you
don't get an answer or you get a machine, try again
later."

Both interns sat straight in their chairs, listening intently.

"We'll start with Minneapolis. I'll divide the list in three. If we have no luck there, then we'll go to Saint Paul. Then . . . well, I don't know."

"What if they won't talk to us?" Natasha asked.

With a shrug, Maggie said, "Just keep track of them, I guess. Maybe I can try personally later on."

The other intern, Justin, apparently realized what could lay ahead and seemed to lose some of his earlier enthusiasm. "This could take a long time, couldn't it?" he said.

Maggie nodded. "And we may not learn anything, but we have to make the effort. It's important."

"Can you tell us more?" Natasha asked. "I mean, why you want to find them?"

"Not now," Maggie replied. "They're involved in a story Jessica and I are working on. For the moment, that's all you need to know."

The briefing over, Maggie found two available phones on one end of the assignment desk and provided each intern with a list of numbers they were to call. "Be polite but persistent," she told them. "And let me know right away if you get a lead."

By the time she walked away, both of them had phones to their ears, but neither looked especially pleased about it. This was not exactly their vision of the glamour of television news.

By nightfall, after several fruitless hours on the telephones, they called it quits for the day. "We'll try it again tomorrow," Maggie said as the two interns prepared to leave, clearly fatigued and frustrated. "Buck up," she told them. "We'll find them yet."

But she was not so sure. They had made about

half of the Boyd calls, but were able to reach only twenty-eight people—none of whom was able to provide any help. One of them did know of an Amy Boyd, but she turned out to be too young to fit the description of the missing girl. They had not even begun to call the Vaughn families.

She was beginning to wonder if it was worth the effort, and it was apparent the interns were wondering the same thing.

When Maggie and Brett arrived at the apartment after the late news, they found Anna waiting by the door. "It's Danny," she said, concern in her voice. "He won't go to sleep. Says he's waiting up for you. Poor kid can barely keep his eyes open."

Maggie pushed past her and rushed down the hall to Danny's room, followed closely by Brett and Anna. She found her son sitting up in bed, a large picture book open in his lap, the nightstand lamp providing the only light in the room. He appeared to be dozing, his head canted forward, chin almost touching his chest.

"Danny?" she said from the door. "Are you okay?"

His head snapped up, sleep in his eyes, momentarily confused. "Hi, Mom," he said, more awake now. "Hi, Jake."

Maggie walked to the bed and sat on the edge of it while Brett and Anna remained at the door. "What's the matter, kiddo?" she asked with a hug. "Anna says you won't go to sleep."

His words were muffled against her shoulder. "There was a man, Mom."

"What?" she said, pulling away. "Say that again."

"There was a man," he repeated. "In a car, outside of school. He kept looking at me. A creep."

"*What man*? When?"

"At recess. You told me to stay away from the fence, to watch out for strangers. Remember?"

"Yes, of course," she said.

Brett walked from the door and knelt beside the bed, leaving Anna standing where he stood.

"I haven't gone near the fence before. Honest, Mom." His eyes began to well. "But Johnny Tucker hit a ball right over there. In the corner, you know, by the slide."

She nodded. "It's okay, Danny. No need to cry."

"When I went to get it, I saw this man, sitting in a car. Staring at me. He had a mean face, Mom. Like he was mad at me." He sniffled.

"What did you do?" she asked, a tremor in her voice.

"I ran, just like you told me. But when I looked back, he was still there. Still looking at me."

"My God," she breathed.

"What did you do then, sport?" Brett asked.

"I told the teacher. Mrs. Goodwin. But when she started to walk over there, the man drove away. Fast. His tires screeched."

Maggie pulled him into her arms and held him tightly. "You did just fine, Danny," she whispered. "Just fine. You're a big guy."

Brett now sat with them on the bed. "What did the man look like, Danny? Can you remember?"

"Mean," the boy said, wiping his eyes. "A mean face. He had hair above his mouth."

"A mustache?" Brett said.

Danny nodded. "I guess so. And like warts on his face."

"Warts?"

"Marks," Danny said. He could be no more specific.

"Anything else?" Brett pressed. "What kind of car?"

"A black one," Danny replied. "It had white on the side."

"A white stripe?"

Danny nodded. "The car was long, like Batman's."

Anna walked into the room, standing next to the bed. "He wouldn't tell me any of this," she said. "Wanted to wait for you. He ate almost no supper. He's been fretting all night."

Maggie picked up her son, surprised again at how big he'd become. She could barely lift him. "That's okay, Anna. Let's go to the kitchen and get a dish of ice cream. Then we'll get this young man back to bed."

Danny managed to eat only a spoonful or two of the ice cream before his eyes began to flutter and he slumped in the kitchen chair. Brett carried him back to bed and Maggie stayed with him until he was breathing deeply and peacefully. The creeps were gone for the moment.

Danny slept later than usual the next morning and acted sluggish when he finally awoke. But otherwise, he showed no latent effects of his schoolyard encounter. Maggie debated keeping him home for the day, but finally decided that that might only increase his fears. Danny himself showed no hesitation about returning to school.

As a precaution, both she and Brett escorted him, seeing him safely inside the building before seeking out Mrs. Goodwin, the teacher who had supervised recess the day before. They found her in a room just two doors down from Danny's, surrounded by about thirty shouting and scampering first-graders. She quieted the class and then stepped out into the hallway, keeping the door ajar and a wary eye on the children. While cooperative, she could add little to what Danny had already told them. "It *was* a black car," she said, "and it did speed off when I started to approach it. But I had no chance to see the driver."

Brett pressed her for a better description of the car, but she was unable to provide it or to say how long it had been there. Or, for that matter, to confirm that Danny had been the target of the driver's surveillance. "I only know what Danny told me," she said. "We have dozens of kids out there that I have to keep an eye on. I didn't notice anything until Danny ran up to me, crying."

She said she had reported the incident to the principal and that they already had decided to ask one of the older students, a sixth-grader, to stick close to Danny during recess. "And we'll try to be more vigilant ourselves," she said, "but unless we keep him inside, that's about all we can do."

Maggie wasn't completely satisfied, but didn't know what else to suggest. She looked to Brett for other ideas, but he could only shake his head.

"I know this has upset you," Mrs. Goodwin said, "but you should know that it is not that unusual. To have strange men hanging around a school, I mean. It happens fairly often. That's why they put

up the fence several years ago. There are a lot of
weirdos out there, even in this neighborhood."

Maggie was tempted to explain her situation,
the special danger that Danny might be facing,
but decided it would probably not change anything the teacher or the school could do. "Just
watch him closely," she finally said. "That's all we
can ask."

"We'll do our best," Mrs. Goodwin replied. "I'm
sure things will be fine."

Walking back to the car, Maggie took a slight
detour and led Brett to the corner of the playground where the slide and swing set stood—the
spot where Johnny Tucker's ball had gone, where
Danny had seen the man. The chain-link fence
was about four feet high, bordering the sidewalk,
some ten feet away from the street where the long
black car had been parked. The street was empty
now.

They walked along the fence, Maggie dragging
her hand slowly along the metal bar on top. "Not
much protection, is it?" she said.

"C'mon, Maggie," Brett said, "you can hardly
put barbed wire on it."

"You think he'll be safe?" Her voice was tight,
strained.

Brett stopped and gently took her by the shoulders, turning her. "Yes, I think he'll be safe. No
one's going to hop over the fence and snatch a
kid. Not now, anyway. With what's happened. You
can't keep the boy in a closet, Maggie."

She pulled free of his grasp and resumed walking. "It's gone too far, hasn't it?" she said. "When
someone comes after my child. Maybe I should

just move on, Brett. Find another job, in another business. I can't put Danny at risk. Nothing is worth that."

"Don't be ridiculous. You can't run away from this." He paused, and then said, "Besides, we can't be sure that this guy, whoever he is, was zeroing in on Danny. Maybe Danny's imagination got the better of him."

"You believe that?" she asked.

"Not really. But it's a possibility."

Maggie stopped now and leaned against the fence, looking across the playground and toward the school. "I don't believe it, either. But you know, if I were a normal person, a real mother, I could send Danny away until I was sure he would be safe. To his father or his grandparents. But my life is so screwed up I can't even do that."

"Where is his dad?" Brett asked, broaching the subject for the first time.

"Who knows? I haven't seen him since Danny was a baby."

"Want to tell me about him?"

"Not now, Brett. Anyway, he's not worth talking about."

Brett wanted to push further, but the resolute expression on her face argued against it. And she left no opening. "Time to go," she said, turning quickly in the direction of the car. "I've got a date with a cop."

Driving to the apartment, Maggie suddenly let out a small whoop. "I just thought of something," she said. "Just now. This minute."

Brett glanced over at her. "What are you talking about?"

"Danny's description of the man in the car. The mustache and the warts."

"Yeah."

"Doesn't that ring a bell?" she demanded, grabbing his arm.

"Not exactly."

"Isn't that how Carlisle described the mystery man on the tour?" She released his arm and reached into her briefcase, pulling out the notepad she had used in the meeting with Carlisle. Paging through it, she said, "Here it is. About six feet, muscular, small waist, thinning brown hair and—get this—a small mustache and a pockmarked face."

A look of triumph spread across her face. "Pockmarks. Warts. Could be the same thing. And the mustache. Bingo!"

Brett appeared less sure. "It could be, I suppose."

"It *has* to be," she said, correcting him. "It can't be another coincidence."

"Maybe not," Brett conceded. "But I'd feel better if we had a picture."

"Maybe we will," she said. "Maybe we will."

The detective's name was Timothy McQueen, a trim, fresh-faced blonde with a dimple in his chin, no older—probably younger—than Maggie herself. Along with his firm handshake and quick smile, he was unfailingly polite—bowing slightly on being introduced and even pulling out a chair for Maggie as they met in Barclay's office. An Eagle Scout with a gun, she thought, a police poster boy.

Barclay insisted on sitting in on the interview,

claiming station policy required it. The detective did not object, and Maggie certainly felt more comfortable having him there.

"I've read the reports," McQueen said after the requisite small talk, "but must admit I'm still not clear on things."

"How's that?" Barclay asked.

"Who do you think we're dealing with here? A stalker? Some TV freak who's got it in for Miss Lawrence?"

"Make it Maggie, will you?" she said. "Miss Lawrence makes me nervous."

"If you're certain that's okay," he said deferentially, still the model of politeness.

"I'm sure."

"To answer your question," Barclay said. "We don't know."

McQueen moved his chair slightly so that he could face both of them. "Have there been other threats?" he asked. "Something other than this hit-and-run incident?"

Barclay and Maggie exchanged glances, an exchange not lost on the detective. "So there have been," he said. "Have you reported those?"

This guy doesn't waste any time, Maggie thought. Don't underestimate him.

"They weren't exactly threats," she said vaguely, not volunteering more.

"What were they then?"

She started to answer, but Barclay interrupted. "Maggie got some anonymous mail, strange stuff. Stranger than the normal junk that comes in."

McQueen leaned in toward Barclay. "What kind of stuff? You're losing me here."

"I can't really tell you," Barclay said. "It may involve an investigative report we're doing."

McQueen was startled. "I can't see it? The anonymous mail, I mean."

"I'm afraid not."

The detective stood up, shedding some of his decorum in the process. "Let me get this straight," he said, obviously annoyed. "First of all, someone tries to injure or kill this lady. Then she gets threatening mail. And you're refusing to tell me about it, or to show it to me?" Disbelief was in his voice. "How can I do my job?"

Barclay shifted uncomfortably in his chair. "Relax, Mr. McQueen. Please. You have to understand that we're dealing with a sensitive area here. We don't know what's going on. Or how serious it is. Someone may be trying to blackmail Maggie, or hoping to prevent us from pursuing a potentially explosive story. We just don't know."

McQueen sat back down, some of his composure returning. "Blackmail? For what?"

Barclay shook his head and shrugged. "Sorry," was all he would say.

"So what *can* you tell me?" McQueen asked.

After a whispered consultation with Barclay, Maggie described the envelopes she'd received without revealing their contents. "I'm the only one who's touched them," she said. "Maybe you can find some fingerprints."

"That would be a start," McQueen said, making a note in a small pad.

She also revealed the scare her son had received at school the day before, describing as best she could the car and the man inside, along with the protective measures the school was taking.

"I can have our squads in the area keep an eye out," he offered.

"I'd appreciate it, believe me," Maggie said.

Barclay also outlined the steps the station had taken to protect Maggie and her son, including the increased security, the mail and phone monitoring, and Brett's ubiquity. "You have to understand, Mr. McQueen," Barclay added, "that we're telling you all of this in confidence. We have to trust your discretion. We can't afford to see this in the newspapers. Even my boss is unaware of the other threats. We'd like your help, but we can't afford to have the word spread. It could put Maggie in even greater danger."

"Okay," he said, "but *you* have to understand that you're tying one hand behind my back. I can't force you to tell me everything, but I can tell you that you'd be better off if you did."

"Let us think about it," Barclay said.

That's where the conversation ended.

17

Maggie got two surprises the next day. The first came late in the afternoon when she spotted Natasha, the intern, dashing across the newsroom toward her desk. She had never seen a woman so big and so ungainly move so fast—a fifty yard dash from the assignment desk.

"I think I've got something!" she said as she pulled up, her chest heaving, her voice raspy. "I think I found her."

"Hold on, Natasha," Maggie said, moving back. "Slow down. Which one?"

"Amy. I talked to her cousin. Lives out in Shoreview."

"Way to go! Tell me what she said."

Still breathless, Natasha settled into a chair,

wiggling her bottom slightly to fit. "It wasn't a she, it was a he," she said, gulping air. "The cousin, I mean. He said Amy ran away about five months ago. Lived in Robbinsdale. A tenth-grader. Nobody's seen her since, although she calls home every now and then."

"Her parents have talked to her?"

"Apparently so. She won't tell them where she is, and they haven't been able to find her. But they think she may still be in the Twin Cities somewhere."

Natasha quickly gave her the name, address, and telephone number of Amy's parents, along with those of the cousin. "He's going to send me Amy's picture, too. He says they have several."

Maggie was elated, although she wasn't quite sure what it might mean. If Amy's family couldn't find her, how would she? But it was a beginning. "Terrific job, Natasha," she said with genuine admiration. And then, with a quick glance at the assignment desk, "How's Justin doing?"

He was still on the telephone, looking not at all happy. "We had a bet," Natasha said cheerfully. "On who would find one of them first. He owes me a buck."

Maggie laughed. "Well, get back to it," she said. "No resting on your laurels."

As Natasha got up to leave, she said, "I'm not sure it would help, but I know some of the kids who hang around the Uptown area. I used to myself. A lot of the runaways end up there, you know. Or at least pass through."

Maggie was aware of that, but she also knew it was one of the first places people looked for their missing kids. Amy could be anywhere. "That's nice to know, Natasha. Thanks. I'll let you know if I can use you."

The second surprise came an hour or so later, just as Maggie and Brett were leaving the newsroom for the studio to do the six o'clock news. "I've thought it over," Brett said. "I've decided to go to that damned dinner-dance of yours."

It was the last thing Maggie expected to hear. "Great!" she said. "But are you sure?"

"I'll hate it, I know that. It'll be boring as shit, but yes, I'm sure."

She grabbed his hand and squeezed it. "I'll call Carlisle tomorrow. He'll help set it up, I know."

They parted at the studio door. "I haven't worn a suit in months," he grumbled. "And I don't think I've danced since my high school prom."

"Then it's about time." She chuckled. "You'll make a dashing figure, I know. You'll wow all of those single women."

She wasn't sure, but she thought she saw the flash of his middle finger as she passed through the studio door.

Maggie wasted no time in following up on the Boyd lead. In the hours between the early and late news, she called the number Natasha had given her several times. The first two attempts went unanswered; the third and fourth triggered busy signals.

Finally, on the fifth call, the phone was answered by a man who turned out to be Amy's father, James Boyd. He proved aloof and suspicious when Maggie identified herself, and he quickly turned the phone over to his wife, Florence. She was more accommodating, but only after she was convinced it was *the* Maggie Lawrence on the line and that she wasn't calling with some dire news of her daughter.

"Have they found her?" she asked quickly. "Is that what you're calling about. Is she okay?"

Maggie assured her she had no news of Amy, good or bad, and that she was simply making a routine inquiry. The woman was relieved but curious. "I can't believe it's actually you," she said. "We watch your news all of the time." And then, "But how do you know about Amy?"

Maggie was deliberately vague about the purpose of her call and said that she would like to speak with Mrs. Boyd and her husband in person, if possible. After some hesitation, the woman agreed, but said her husband would not be there. "He can't stand to talk about Amy," she said. "It's too tough on him emotionally."

They set the meeting for ten o'clock the next morning.

Amy's family lived in a small rambler in a well-kept but aging neighborhood in the inner-ring Minneapolis suburb of Robbinsdale, just a few blocks from the sprawling North Memorial Medical Center—one of the largest hospitals in the Twin Cities.

Set well back in a tiny yard, the house was little different than any of its neighbors. All of the homes, Maggie guessed, had been built in the early fifties as part of the post–World War II building boom. Cookie-cutter structures, set apart from one another only by the color of their siding and shingles and the personal landscaping touches the owners managed to give to their lawns and shrubbery.

It was a neighborhood once proud if not fashionable, now struggling to maintain its appearance and dignity, but slipping slightly with each passing year.

Like others along the street, the Boyd home was in need of a fresh coat of paint, its white wood siding and black shutters blistered and peeling in spots. The sidewalk, where Maggie now stood, was cracked and uneven, the gaps filled by small tufts of weeds and bustling colonies of ants. But the grass and bushes in front and along the side of the house were well-trimmed, and the flower boxes beneath the windows and straddling the front stoop were alive with an array of geraniums and petunias. From the outside, she got the impression the Boyds were doing the best they could without the money to do more.

Brett had driven her to the house, but decided against going inside with her. "You two women will do better without me," he'd said. "I'll be back in an hour if you don't beep me first."

As Maggie picked her way past the cracks in the sidewalk, the front door opened and a woman she assumed to be Amy's mother stepped out onto the stoop, shading her eyes against the sun. "It is you, isn't it?" she said, smiling shyly and reaching to grasp Maggie's hand. "I didn't really believe it until just now."

Maggie returned the smile and handshake as

she was ushered into the house. "I appreciate your taking the time, Mrs. Boyd. Truly."

"I'm happy to do it if it might help find Amy," she said. "But please, call me Florence."

Maggie followed her into a small living room and through an adjoining dining room, both tastefully if frugally furnished. Everything appeared spotless, but, like the exterior of the house, the interior showed the effects of aging and a meager decorating budget. The carpeting was an old shag, a pathway across it worn and matted, and the cushions of the furniture sagged, the fabric showing the shine of years of wear.

"I've made some coffee," Florence said. "We can sit in the kitchen and talk."

"That's fine," Maggie said, following her, hoping to spot a picture of Amy as they went.

The girl must be a trailer in the family, she decided, since her mother appeared to be in her mid-to-late fifties. Short and plump, with a round face and graying hair tied tightly in a bun, she waddled more than walked as she led Maggie into a kitchen as clean and compact as the other rooms in the house.

While Florence poured the coffee, her hand shaking slightly, Maggie quickly explained her mission: to learn more about the death of Penny Collins and her life on the street before her murder.

"Isn't that sad," Florence said, interrupting her. "The Collins girl, I mean. When we first heard about them finding a body, we thought, My God, that could be our Amy."

She settled into a chair across the kitchen table

from Maggie, bending over to blow on her coffee, hiding the welling of her eyes. "I can't tell you how relieved we were when it wasn't," she whispered, "but I know what her family must be going through."

"We think your daughter knew Penny," Maggie said. "Perhaps quite well." She took a copy of Amy's note and showed it to Mrs. Boyd. "We got this from Penny's family and believe it was written by your daughter."

Florence dabbed her eyes with a tissue and raised a pair of half-glasses that hung from her neck. She studied the note carefully. "It does look like Amy's writing," she admitted. "She always had good penmanship and was a good speller."

"I understand that you talk to Amy now and then," Maggie said. "Has she ever mentioned Penny Collins? Did she ever talk about her murder?"

Florence shook her head. "Never," she said. "But it's been four or five weeks since she's called us."

Maggie sipped her coffee, then plunged ahead. "How about Nadia Vaughn? Have you ever heard that name? She may be another runaway who also wrote a sympathy note to the Collins family."

The woman appeared mystified. "I'm sorry. Amy's never talked about any of her friends. She simply calls to let us know that she's all right. She never tells us where she is or what she's doing. That's what makes it so maddening."

Emotion began to overtake her, but she went on to haltingly explain that after weeks of searching for their daughter, including posting pictures and walking and driving the streets endlessly, they had all but given up. "We couldn't afford to offer a reward," she said, choking back the sobs, "and the police weren't that much help. There are too many kids like Amy out there. I'm just grateful to know she's still alive, to hear from her now and then."

Before Maggie could respond, she went on, "But you know, I've never really stopped looking. No mother would. In the car, at the grocery store, at the movies . . . wherever I am, I'm always looking, always searching, always hoping that I might get a glimpse of her." The tears were now flowing freely, unnoticed and unimpeded. "Every time the doorbell rings, I think it may be Amy, coming home. But it never is."

Maggie sat back, not knowing what to say, chagrined that she had triggered this response. At the same time, she couldn't help but wonder if her own mother had ever felt a similar loss, had ever shed tears over her, had ever cared enough to search. Probably not, but she would likely never know for sure.

Finally, when Florence seemed recovered, Maggie asked if she could see a picture of her daughter.

"I'll have to get one out of the bedroom," she said, rising slowly from the chair. "I keep them in a drawer. My husband won't have one out in the open. He's quite bitter about Amy now. Says we gave her everything we could, and then she did this to us. Made our lives miserable. I've stopped arguing with him, although I have to admit it is hard to look at her picture every day and never know if we'll see her again."

As Maggie followed her to the bedroom, she learned that Amy was the couple's only child and, as she'd suspected, had been born late in their married life. A good kid, her mother told her, loving but headstrong, and a fine student until she got mixed up with the wrong crowd. When she and her husband tried to rein her in, she rebelled . . . and later, simply disappeared.

"How can a child do that to her parents?" she asked plaintively while rummaging through a dresser drawer. "Just abandon us like that."

Maggie swallowed hard, but made no response.

"Here's a good one," Florence said, holding up a framed eight-by-ten color photo. "The most recent one we have. It was taken after her confirmation."

Like her mother, the girl in the picture had round, heavy features, with short brown hair and striking blue eyes. Not pretty, but wholesome, flashing a smile that lit up the photo. "She's lost weight since then," Florence said, looking over Maggie's shoulder. "She was actually quite thin when she ran away. Said she didn't want to end up like me."

Maggie held on to the picture. "May I take this for a day or so?" she asked. "I'd like to make copies, then get it back to you."

Florence hesitated, then agreed. "It does no good sitting in the drawer, I guess."

"And let me give you my card," Maggie added. "It has both my office and my home numbers on it. I'd appreciate a call if . . . when you hear from Amy again. Perhaps she'd be willing to talk to me, in confidence, of course. You can tell her we're trying to find out what happened to Penny."

Mrs. Boyd took the card and tucked it into the pocket of her blouse. "Even if she calls, I doubt that she'll want to talk to you," she said. "She seems very suspicious of any adult."

"I understand, believe me," Maggie said, walking to the front door. "But I would appreciate it if you'd try. It could be very important."

Brett was waiting in the car at the end of the sidewalk. "Well?" he asked as Maggie slid into the passenger seat.

"Not much help," she said, quickly repeating what little information she had gained. "But I do have her picture," she added, "and I suppose there's a slim chance that she might call me."

As Brett drove, she sank back into her seat, frustration seeping through her body. What do I have? she thought. The names of two girls nobody can find, and even if they are found, may know nothing about how or why Penny died. That, plus the phony names and vague descriptions of two people at a singles' club who may or may not have anything to do with any of this, one of whom may or may not have been stalking her and her child.

Damn, she thought, I'm no further ahead now than I was at the beginning. I can only hope Jessica's doing better.

"What's next?" Brett asked, interrupting her pondering.

She shrugged. "God, Brett, I wish I knew. Keep looking for the girls, I guess. And hope for a break."

Brett glanced at her. "There's always the dinner-dance," he said with a scowl. "Maybe that woman's back from Mexico with her pictures."

Maggie took little hope in that. With her luck, the woman probably forgot to put film in the camera.

Two more days passed without a major development.

The two interns exhausted their attempts to find Nadia Vaughn in the Twin Cities, but now, at Maggie's suggestion, began searching the computerized telephone listings of the larger outstate cities like Duluth, Rochester, St. Cloud, and Mankato, calling any Vaughn they could find. Maggie had to give them credit; they did not surrender easily.

For her part, Maggie had been trying to contact the names Jessica had given her of street workers who dealt with runaways: social workers and volunteers from a variety of agencies and shelters who prowled the bus depots, shopping malls, streets, and neighborhoods in search of young people on the run—in hopes of getting them back home, or at least to somewhere safer than the streets. So far, they had been of no help in locating either Amy or Nadia. Nor did they have any firsthand knowledge of Penny Collins before her murder. "For every kid we run across," one of the workers told Maggie, "there are five or six we never see. They come and they go, like ghosts in the night. We're not in a high-return business here, but we do the best we can."

Jessica, it turned out, was having no better luck. She told Maggie she had made no significant breakthrough in her computer search, although she had narrowed the field of possibilities, culling out names of people who had died, were still in prison, or had moved out of state. "You'd be amazed at how many perverts and child pornographers we have out there," she said. "Dozens, scores of them. It's a wicked world, believe me."

Maggie could see the stacks of computer printouts on her desk. "At that first staff meeting," she said, "Barclay claimed this porn ring—if it exists at all—could include some names we'd all recognize. Is that true?"

Jessica cocked her head. "That's what I've been told."

"Like who?"

"I don't want to say, Maggie. Even to you. Not until I have some proof. I could smear innocent people."

Maggie was disappointed, but persisted. Pointing to the printouts, she asked, "Do you expect to find any of their names in the data?"

"No, I've already searched. None of the names I've heard about show any kind of felony record. At least not that I can find."

Maggie couldn't hide her confusion. "Then what *are* you looking for?"

"For anybody with a crim/sex record who might also have some connection with one of those well-known names. You know, campaign aides or contributors, volunteers, staff members. Whatever. Some tie to the big guys.

"I'm looking for a match," she went on. "Waiting for some name or names to pop out of the criminal records that also appear in the lists I have of party members or staff or financial contributors."

Maggie was beginning to see the light. She was also feeling a little stupid. "How long do you think it will take?" she asked.

"Could be forever," Jessica smiled. "Maybe sooner."

As Maggie was walking away, Jessica called after her. "By the way, if it's any relief, it doesn't look like your Mick the Prick is dead. At least he doesn't show up in any national death or social security records."

Maggie stopped and turned.

"But if he's alive," she continued, "I can't find him. Not yet, anyway. You think he may have changed his name?"

"I have no idea," Maggie said. "Anything is possible."

"Well, I'll keep looking," Jessica said. "But don't hold your breath."

Maggie wasn't.

18

When Maggie walked into the Green Room, she found Brett in front of the mirror, freshly shaved and hair brushed back, tightening his tie—a classic red-and-blue stripe that went nicely with his dark blue blazer and gray slacks. There was also a hint of Brut in the air.

Catching her reflection, he said, "Don't say a thing. Not a goddamned word."

She obeyed, but couldn't resist releasing a low wolf whistle.

"Cute," he said with a grimace.

She was hard-pressed to remember the last time she had seen him in a shirt and tie, maybe at a dinner the year before when they'd received an award from the Associated Press for the best local newscast. Even

then, though, the tie was off and in his pocket before
the dinner was over.

"I feel like I'm choking to death," he said, turning to her. "If God intended for us to wear these
things, he would have given us button-down skin."

Smiling, she moved closer to him and brushed
a few pieces of lint from the front of his blazer,
then circled him to do the same to the back. "You
look great," she said, meaning it. "You'll be the
hit of the party. You'll have to fight those women
off."

"Right," he replied gloomily. "Then why is it I'd
rather witness an execution?"

The singles' club dinner-dance was less than an
hour away, to be held in a small ballroom at the
nearby Hilton hotel. Since Brett had first agreed
to attend, he had changed his mind several times,
grumbling first about what it might do to his reputation if he was seen there, then bemoaning how
boring and belittling it was bound to be. "I'm no
good at small talk," he'd complained. "And I won't
know which fork to use, or whether my salad is on
the right or left. I'll probably make a damned fool
of myself."

Each time, Maggie had been able to reassure
him, gently reminding him of the importance of
the mission. "Besides," she had told him, "you're no
hick. You know which fork is which, and if you
do eat somebody else's salad, so what? You wouldn't
be the first."

As she expected, Harry Carlisle had been eager
to help, agreeing to introduce Brett as a friend,
but to refrain from revealing where he worked or
the true purpose of his visit—except to Pat

McKenzie, the woman with the pictures who was now back from her vacation in Mexico.

"I just want him to get a feel of your group," Maggie had told him on the phone. "To see and meet the others for himself, without getting their guards up. And to get copies of the pictures."

Carlisle said he would seat Brett between the McKenzie woman and another lady who had spent time on the station tour talking with the two mystery people, Eleanor and Frank. "With a little prodding," he said, "she might remember things about them that she hasn't told me."

Now, as Brett took a final glance at himself in the mirror and walked toward the door, Maggie said, "I'll wait up for you."

For the first time, he smiled, broadly and nefariously. "Who says I'll be coming home? I may find me a hot chick." Then he winked and waved.

But he did come home. And Maggie was there waiting, whiling away the time with George Barclay, who had escorted her to the apartment after the late news and had insisted on staying until Brett returned. They had split two games of cribbage and were in the middle of their third when the key in the door turned and Brett strode in. His tie was off, his shirt open at the collar, his blazer under his arm.

"Welcome back," Maggie said from the couch.

"Did you score, big guy?" Barclay asked with a smirk, putting aside his cards.

Brett scowled and threw his coat on a chair, then walked past them into the kitchen for a can of beer. They could hear the pop top snap open.

"It was miserable, if you really want to know," he

said, returning to the living room. "Everything I expected and more."

Maggie gave him a sympathetic smile and made room for him on the couch, saying, "C'mon, it can't have been that bad."

"Oh, yeah," he said, sitting and sipping the beer. "How would you like to spend half an hour listening to some lady talk about a three-legged cat named Stump? What he eats, where he shits, how he lost his goddamned leg? And that was just for starters."

Maggie burst out laughing. "That actually happened? You've got to be kidding?"

"Or try the woman who's lost two husbands in two years to cancer," he said. "She was citing statistics to me on just how rare a medical circumstance that is."

"Just how rare is it?" Barclay asked with a grin.

"Fuck you, George. You should have been there instead of me. They were about your age, for Christ's sake."

Maggie and Barclay sat back, waiting. Brett took a deep pull on the beer and kicked his shoes off before continuing. "When I walked into the room, I thought I must be in the wrong place. Everybody had to be in their forties, at least. It looked like a senior citizens' meeting." He shook his head, smiling at the memory. "They came to me like mice to cheese. I must be the first young face they've seen there in months."

"At least since Frank and Eleanor," Maggie offered.

"Oh, yes," he said, "Frank and Eleanor."

She leaned forward. "What did you find out?"

"Unfortunately, not a whole lot more than you already know. The woman Carlisle sat me next to at dinner, Harriet something or other, said the two were very quiet during the tour. Kind of stuck together, but made only perfunctory conversation with her or each other. She was put off, in fact, that they weren't friendlier. Said she wasn't disappointed when they didn't come back to the group."

"Did she notice either of them carrying anything, like an envelope?"

"I didn't think to ask her that," Brett replied, "but she made no mention of it. And nobody else I talked to seemed to know or remember much more. Most of the women, I'm sorry to say, were too busy coming on to me."

"You poor thing," Maggie said with mock sympathy.

"You should have seen them," he replied, shaking his head. "It was like being hustled by my mother's bridge club."

"What about the pictures?" Barclay asked.

Brett got up and retrieved his coat, reaching into the side pocket. "Here they are," he said, spreading a half dozen four-by-five color photos on the coffee table. "This McKenzie lady shot a full roll on the tour. I looked through all the prints and these are the only ones that show other people. The rest are of inanimate things in the building, like the studio and the control room."

Maggie reached across Brett to switch on another, brighter lamp, then bent over the pictures. Her head nearly collided with Barclay's. Three of the pictures were clearly posed, with various members of the group gathered in front of the studio cameras or standing alongside the empty news set, smiling as though they were actually on television.

"Forget those," Brett said. "Eleanor and Frank are not among them."

The next three shots were apparently not intended to include people, but in each case the camera must have moved or someone got in the way. Two of the pictures included parts of bodies or faces, partially blurred. The third, however, was clear, a full facial shot of a woman looking surprised. Startled.

Maggie held the picture under the light.

"Meet Eleanor," Brett said proudly. "Live and in color."

Maggie took a deep breath, then released it in a gush.

"What's the matter?" Barclay asked sharply.

"Her name's not Eleanor," she said. "Unless I'm badly mistaken, this is Sissy."

The two men stared at her, mouths agape.

"You're shitting us," Barclay finally said.

"*The* Sissy?" Brett demanded.

Maggie got up and knelt beside the lamp, holding the photo even closer to the light. "I'm almost positive," she said. "She certainly looks different, and I admit it's been a long time, but I don't think I could ever forget that face."

By turns, first Brett, then Barclay examined the photo as Maggie returned to the couch, sinking deep into the cushions. "Her hair's different and she doesn't have the gap between her front teeth like she did when I knew her," she said. "But the lips and eyes are the same. And do you see that small scar on her right cheek, just to the side of her mouth? She told me her dad did that to her, with a razor, when she was ten years old."

Still, the two men did not appear convinced. "You haven't seen her in twelve years," Brett said doubtfully.

She sighed and pulled herself off the couch. "Sit still," she said. "Don't move. Let me find something." Hurrying to her bedroom, she closed and locked the door behind her, quickly retrieving the *Good-bye Innocence* videotape from her file drawer and slipping it into the VCR beneath her TV. With the machine in fast-forward, she rolled through about twenty minutes of the tape until she found what she was looking for. Then she pushed the PAUSE button.

Returning to the living room, she asked Brett and Barclay to follow her and bring the picture. "I'm going to show you one frame . . . just one frame, mind you . . . from the movie, and you tell me if I'm wrong."

The three of them gathered around the television set, where a close-up of Sissy's face stared back at them. Brett and Barclay knelt in front of it, comparing the image on the tape to the picture in Barclay's hands. Their eyes moved back and forth.

Maggie stood back, her thoughts tumbling wildly, like rocks in a landslide, one landing on top of the other, then bouncing away. How could it be? How could Sissy have found her after all this time? And why?

She knew there could be only one answer to the why.

"It *is* her, isn't it?" Barclay finally said. "Look at the cheekbones and the nose. And you're right, that scar is in exactly the same place."

"Jesus Christ," Brett murmured.

Maggie turned off the TV and VCR and led them out of the bedroom and back to the living room. "So I guess we know now who dropped the envelope and picture on my desk," she said.

Brett flopped into a chair. "I don't get it," he said. "How could she be involved after all of this time? And how did she find you?"

"I've been thinking about that," Maggie said. "If she followed my career in L.A., she would know where I'd gone. My move here was in all of the papers, and even if she missed that, she could easily have called the station to find out where I'd moved. It was no secret."

Brett and Barclay were watching her intently.

"The rest is tougher. I have no idea what Sissy has been doing for all of these years. I told you, I haven't seen or talked to her since that day we made the movie. Maybe she stayed in the porn business and is connected to the people out here. Maybe she just ran short of money and figured I'd be an easy touch for a little blackmail."

"But nobody's made any money demands," Barclay reminded her.

"True," she said. "Which leads me to believe the other theory. Or maybe it's something else we've not thought about. Maybe she just wants to ruin me, out of jealousy of whatever, to spoil the life I've been able to build for myself."

"I don't buy that," Brett said as he got up and walked to the other end of the room. "It doesn't explain the other stuff. Your car getting rammed, the phone calls, the Danny scare. And what about the guy who was with her? Mr. Mustache."

She could only shrug.

It was Barclay's turn. "What I don't understand is this: Why would she risk coming to the station, risk being seen and maybe recognized by you? Why not let her friend drop off the envelope? That doesn't make sense to me."

"Nor to me," she admitted. "Perhaps she thought I wouldn't recognize her, or that she could duck away if they did see me. Or maybe she thought I wouldn't be there. Who knows how her mind is working?"

Barclay walked to the kitchen and helped himself to a beer. "So what do we do now?" he asked when he returned. "We know this Sissy was here, but we don't where she is now, or even if she's still around. To say nothing of her last name. And even if we did find her, what have we got? That she falsified an application to a goddamned singles' club? Big deal. There's no proof she had anything to do with that envelope, or anything that's happened since."

"I'd still like to find her," Maggie said. "Confront her, find out what's going on."

"Bad idea," Brett said. "It's better that she doesn't know that we know anything. Puts us one step ahead of them, it seems to me."

Thinking about it, she had to agree. But the idea that Sissy was here, somewhere in town, watching her, stalking her, still trying to control her life after a dozen years, was almost too much to bear. She had often wondered if the two of them would ever meet again, and if they did, where it would be and under what circumstances. Never did she dream that it could be like this.

"I've got to get going," Barclay said, putting aside the empty beer can and lifting his body slowly off the couch. "Unlike the two of you, I've got to be at work in the morning."

After a hurried good-bye at the door, he said, "Let's all of us sleep on this thing. Talk about it tomorrow. This is getting too bizarre to believe."

Barclay had been gone for an hour and Maggie was lying in bed, seeking sleep in the darkened room, when she heard the shower stop and Brett emerge from the bathroom down the hall. Debating, she waited a few minutes and then slipped from under the covers, tiptoeing past her sleeping son's room to the closed door of Brett's bedroom. She knocked lightly and asked, "Are you decent?"

"As decent as I get," he replied. "C'mon in."

She pushed the door open. He was stretched out on the bed, feet dangling over the edge, a copy of John Sandford's latest Minnesota thriller propped up on his chest. Hair still damp from the shower, he wore a pair of baggy old sweats that doubled as pajamas. The blue blazer was hung over the back of a chair.

"What's up?" he asked as she stood by the door, watching him without speaking. "Something wrong? You need something?"

She shook her head. "No, nothing."

He waited, trying but failing to avert his eyes

from the woman who stood before him, her body tightly wrapped in a modest but nonetheless revealing nightgown that hugged her hips and captured her breasts.

Finally, she said, "You're a good guy, you know that?"

"So my mother tells me," he replied lightly. "But thanks."

She walked slowly to the bed and sat on a far corner of it. "I'm serious. You didn't have to go to that dinner tonight. I know you hated it."

"I've had better nights, that's true," he said with a small smile, pulling himself up into a sitting position. He could see the dark circle of her nipples through the gown, the slight protrusion.

"And you don't have to be camped out here like this, day after day, night after night. You've got better things to do with your life."

He put the book aside. "It's not exactly a hardship, Maggie. And I wouldn't be here if I didn't want to be . . . and if I didn't think I needed to be." He paused then, looking at her curiously. "What's this all about, anyway?"

"I don't know," she said, sighing and looking away. "Lying there in bed, I just realized I don't say thank you very often. That I take you so much for granted—"

"What's new about that?" he asked with a short laugh.

"Nothing, I know," she admitted. "From the beginning, you've always been there for me."

Brett moved to the other corner of the bed, facing her but keeping his distance. "Look, Maggie. I'm here because I want to be here. I'm helping because I want to help. I don't need a lot of thanks; that's not what I'm looking for. I care about you and Danny. I want to see you get through this. That'll be thanks enough."

She sat quietly, reluctant to leave, but unsure of what to do or say next. Suddenly realizing how accustomed she'd become to having him there, how much she would miss him when he was gone. She could smell the shower freshness of him, could feel—for really the first time—the maleness of him. Not Brett, she told herself. C'mon, Maggie. But a slight shiver passed through her body.

He seemed to sense what was happening. "I think you ought to get out of here," he said. "Seeing you in a filmy nightgown in my bedroom is not exactly going to help me sleep better."

She quickly covered her chest with her arms. "It's not a nightgown," she said defensively. "It's a robe."

"Whatever," Brett said, grinning. "The effect is the same."

"I suppose you're right," she replied, getting up. "This is probably not very proper."

"Nice but not wise," he said. "At least not for me."

She started for the door, but then stopped. Returning to him, she leaned over and, for the first time, kissed him on the lips. She could feel his lips part slightly, could taste the minty toothpaste, could feel one of his hands slide across her hip, lightly. She pulled away, brushing his nose with her tongue.

"Thanks for being here," she whispered to him. Then she walked out, closing the door behind her.

19

Sissy was wearing nothing but the sheet that covered her, pulled up beneath her chin, draped across her body, revealing its peaks and valleys. She loved the feel of it, clean and soft, caressing her skin as she moved beneath it, making the tips of her breasts tingle.

She could lie like this for hours, she thought. Alone with her sheet, snug and sensuous.

But she knew it was not to be. Tony, the man across the room standing with a towel wrapped around his middle, would soon join her beneath the sheet—exploring her peaks and valleys, his hands as rough as the sheet was soft. Again, she would have to grunt and bear it, as she had so many times before.

"Hey, you need the bathroom?" he asked. "I'm taking a shower."

Without looking, she shook her head, her eyes fixed on the cracks in the ceiling, following them like so many lines on a map. They had been here a month, and this was already their fourth motel room. Keep moving, the man had told them. Never more than a week in any one place. Pick spots that are cheap and out of the way. Stay away from downtown or the Bloomington strip. Never use the same names, always pay in cash. Stay in your room or in the car, keep away from restaurants or other public places where you might be seen. Order room service or take-out.

Sissy had never met the man, not in person. She didn't know his name, just his voice—and that only by phone. A deep, throaty voice, official-sounding, authoritative, as if he were accustomed to giving orders. Because of that, and for lack of another name, he became the General to them.

The money they received was always in cash, always dropped off at a different spot, along with written instructions, if there were any. For the past week, since Tony had been spotted outside the kid's school, the only orders had been: "Sit tight."

The motels might be different, but the rooms were the same: sterile, stale, and nondescript, with fading wallpaper, carpets grimy from too many bare, dirty feet, and furniture that could have come from the Salvation Army. But Sissy was not fussy; she made only two demands: that the sheets be clean and the TV working.

She never missed Maggie Lawrence doing the news, carefully watching for any change in her on-air demeanor, any evidence of nervousness or fear. So far, she had seen none. Give the lady credit, she thought, she's not flustered easily.

Tony emerged from the bathroom without the towel, posing in front of the full-length mirror, pulling in his stomach, pushing out his chest, admiring his manhood, now hanging at half-staff. Sissy stifled a smirk. He is so proud of his thing, she thought, but she had seen better, lots better. She had never told him that. No way. He'd kill her.

He did have nice tight buns, she thought, and not a bad face, if you could forget the pockmarks. He kept the mustache well-trimmed and his hair short; he was obsessive about keeping clean. He showered at least twice a day, sometimes more. It could be worse.

As she pulled the sheet tighter around her neck, Tony walked to the bed and sat on the edge, absently picking at his toenails. "I'm getting tired of this shit," he said, looking up. "Bored out of my gourd. When is something going to happen?"

She frowned. "How do I know? It's your deal. We were told to wait."

She had known Tony Kolura off and on for years, since her early days in the porn business. He liked to call himself a producer, but the truth was he was little more than a hack, a hanger-on who had always been on the fringes of the business, an errand boy for the big-money guys who were at the center of the industry.

True, he had produced a couple of cheapie flicks a decade before, including one that Sissy had starred in, but as the business became more sophisticated, the capital requirements for studios and equipment more demanding, distribution more complicated, he had fallen by the wayside, doing whatever he could to make a buck.

She had lost track of him in the mid-eighties, when she left Los Angeles for San Francisco to ply her trade, selling her body in the Tenderloin and along the infamous Polk Street, years that included a few small roles in some of the adult films being produced by the Mitchell brothers and others in the Bay Area.

She even worked for a time at San Francisco porn houses, lap dancing for patrons, earning a dollar or more a minute for gyrating sensually in the laps of oversexed customers who sat in the darkened theater watching porn films.

Her dream had been to become another Marilyn Chambers, to star in a breakthrough film as big as Chambers's *Behind the Green Door*. But as Sissy was slow to discover, she had neither the chaste looks nor the unique skills necessary to move beyond the quickie, low-budget films that were being turned out by the dozens every month on the West Coast. And now even those roles had all but disappeared as younger, fresher women supplanted older veterans like herself.

"When's the next payment?" Tony asked as he pulled the sheet back and slipped into the bed beside her.

"Day after tomorrow," she said, sliding slightly away, hoping he'd get the message, but certain he wouldn't. "He said it would be waiting for us at the next stop."

That would be at a place called The Cabaret,

another small and inconspicuous motel located just a few miles south of this one. The cash would be there, she'd been told, in a sealed envelope, at the desk when they checked in. A couple of grand a week to be divided between them, plus expenses. Not a hell of a lot of money compared to what she had once earned on the streets and under the lights, but with the flush years now behind her, it wasn't bad for doing almost nothing. At least so far.

"And what are you worried about?" she asked with a feigned yawn. "You've got no place to spend it anyway."

"I will have," he grumbled, "once I get back to L.A. If I ever do."

She snickered and rolled over on her side, away from him, the sheet still tucked tightly beneath her chin. Closing her eyes, she pretended another sleepy yawn, knowing full well that it was a futile gesture. The bed creaked as he moved behind her and clamped one of his hands roughly over her breast. "Come here," he ordered.

"Jesus, not again tonight," she mumbled, twisting away. "Don't you ever get enough?"

He grunted and pulled her back, nuzzling her neck. The clipped hairs of his mustache were like a bristle brush against her skin, his breath a cave-like echo in her ear. She could feel his body tight against her back, pressing, probing, his flag no longer at half-staff.

Careful, she told herself. Resist, but don't refuse. Don't fight him, don't make him angry. Fake it again, as she had so many times before. Counterfeit climaxes, after all, were her business, bogus but believable orgasms. She couldn't count the times she had fooled the cameras—and her partners.

His hand moved from her breast to her stomach and below, spreading her thighs. "You're dry," he grumbled.

"Give me time," she hissed. "I'm not a goddamned faucet."

With rare exceptions, sex had long since ceased providing her pleasure. After all these years, her body and mind had grown numb and performed largely by rote, like the assembly-line worker who punches the same holes day after day. Sex to Sissy had become mechanical and methodical—and monotonous.

Especially now. With Tony. A month of making love to this man, sometimes two or three times a day depending on his moods and urges, had left her empty and exhausted. But she had little choice: She still needed him, and it was because of him—after all—that she was here, earning that grand a week. Surviving.

It was in the early nineties, after she had returned to Los Angeles from San Francisco, that Sissy ran into Tony again—at a drug rehab center, after both had been busted in separate crack sweeps by the LAPD. While she hardly remembered him, he had not forgotten her, and they spent the long days and nights of treatment getting reacquainted and reliving some of their early days in the business. Although she was relieved to find someone she knew at the center, she quickly discovered that Tony was as much of a loser then as he had been years before, an opinion only reinforced when he admitted he had spent the past three years in federal prison, convicted as part of a national ring producing and distributing child pornography.

The second encounter, two years later, came in the offices of Foxy Films, one of the scores of small-time studios churning out hardcore porn films for a growing audience across the country and world. In those years, adult films had moved out of the small, shabby theaters and corner bookstores with the blacked-out windows into respectable video stores in shopping centers and malls in virtually every major city in the country. The porn business had exploded, and the demand for videos had sky-rocketed, spawning a billion-dollar-a-year industry that gave birth to places like Foxy Films—and jobs for people like Tony Kolura.

Sissy was there to audition for a role in their latest offering, an epic called *Beavers Galore*, a two-day shoot that would bring her five hundred quick bucks. To her surprise, she found Tony conducting the audition. With coaxing, he agreed to give her the part, her first in more than two months. "This is a favor," he told her at the time. "The guy upstairs thinks you're too fucking old, but I talked him into it. Told him you and I went back a long ways . . . that you were a real pro."

She had heard it before, but still found it hard to believe. Too old, at twenty-six? Worn out, one producer had told her. "We want fresh faces, fresh bodies," he had said. "Better find another business, baby." But what? Despite kicking the crack habit, she was dead broke with no real prospects of a steady income. Her career in the film business clearly was ebbing, and she was loathe to return to the streets, hooking. It was too dangerous out there; too much disease, too many crazies as eager to beat or kill you as fuck you.

Another year passed before she saw Tony again. This time, he sought her out, finding her at a small club just off Sunset Boulevard. She was working for peanuts, stripping four times a night, hustling drinks between acts but refusing any after-hours action. "It's a fucking jungle out there," she told him. "I don't want to end up in a goddamned alley with a knife between my legs and some guy's initials carved in my chest."

After work and over coffee at a nearby all-night restaurant, Tony was quick to get to the point: He was out of work again, but had the prospect of a very lucrative deal. He needed her help.

"How's that?" she asked skeptically, knowing that at least one of his deals had landed him behind bars.

"You know Maggie Lawrence, right?"

Know her? Hated her was more like it. But how did he know?

"You told me in treatment," he said. "Remember? Said you hung with her on the streets years ago, that you made that movie together."

Sissy couldn't recall the conversation, but then again, the whole time at the rehab center was now a blur. Getting straight can do that to you. "So what if I do?" she said.

"I need the film," he said. "The one you did with her."

From her audition at Foxy Films, Tony knew that she kept copies of every film she had ever

appeared in. It was part of her deal with producers, to build a video portfolio to help land future
jobs. Tony had seen a sampling.

"For what?" she asked, staring at him over her
cup.

"Some friends of mine, business associates, are
interested in having it. They can't find it anywhere
else."

Business associates? Spare me, she thought. Probably
losers, just like him. She wanted to laugh in his face,
but controlled herself. "And you told them I had a
copy?"

Tony nodded. "I didn't think it was a secret," he
said.

Sissy had not looked at the film for years, but
knew she still had it, stashed away with the others.
Locked up. Doing her no good now. "Why would
these friends of yours want an old film like that?"
she asked.

Tony ordered more coffee, then said, "I can't
really tell you. But they're willing to pay top dollar
for it."

"Like what?"

"Five hundred . . . maybe a thousand, if we press
them."

She sat back, considering. While she had not
spoken to Maggie since the day they made the film,
she had managed to keep track of her—but always
from a distance. Through friends on the street, she
knew about Maggie's years at Redemption House
and that she had gone back to high school and
then on to college. Pulling herself out of the gutter,
making a success of her life.

While in San Francisco, Sissy saw or heard nothing

more of Maggie. Only after her return to Los Angeles did she find herself face-to-face with her on the television screen, watching as she read the news. Despite the shock of it, she was not really surprised. Maggie had always been smarter than the other kids on the street, and if anything, was more beautiful now than as a teenager. Maggie was utterly comfortable on camera.

Her earlier envy turned to outright jealousy. While they had started out as the same sorry sisters of the street, it was now clear that Maggie had managed to achieve everything that had so far eluded Sissy: Success. Money. Glamour. Respectability. While Sissy continued to spread her legs for a living, Maggie was apparently enjoying the almost perfect life of a budding television star.

"You got a problem with giving up the film?" Tony asked, cutting into her thoughts.

"You mean, do I give a damn about what happens to Maggie? Hell, no. She means nothing to me. Shit, I was going to send the film around myself a few years ago, when she working here in L.A. You know, to the newspapers or the other TV stations. That would have taken her down a peg or two. Burst that TV-star bubble of hers."

"Why didn't you?" Tony asked.

Sissy shrugged. "I don't know. I just thought better of it. Hell, she hadn't done anything to me. I was the one who walked out on her. I figured it wasn't her fault my life was all fucked up."

It took Maggie's baby to finally change her mind, to break her resolve.

For years, she told Tony, she had dreamed of having a baby of her own, for the chance to give a child the love and attention she had never had herself. "But then some asshole gave me a dose of syphilis, and the doc told me I could never have a kid. Not ever. So when I heard that Maggie had a little boy, I went ballistic. It was too much."

Tony was watching her curiously. "So what did you do?"

Sissy gave him a sinister smile. "I made an appointment with her boyfriend. Mick somebody. Told him I was an old friend of Maggie's, that I had important, confidential information about her that he'd want to know."

"He agreed to see you?"

"How could he resist? He was working at the CBS station then. Good looking guy, I'll say that for him. We met in his office. I showed him part of the film, Maggie's part. Wanted him to see what kind of woman was the mother of his kid. He went bonkers. I've never seen a guy get so angry. He was bouncing off the walls. Tried to grab the tape, but I told him there were others where that came from."

Tony grimaced. "Jesus, Sissy—"

"I loved it. Told him I wanted two grand for the film. Cash. Otherwise, Maggie's tits and twat would be all over town."

"What'd he say?"

"Not what I expected. Told me to go ahead, pass it around. He didn't give a shit if it was on the six o'clock news. Wouldn't give me a fuckin' dime. Damn near threw me out of the office, tape and all. Said if he ever saw me again, he'd have me arrested for blackmail. And I believed the bastard; he was that angry."

Tony was totally absorbed in her story. "Did you go after her then?"

"Nah. I knew she'd never go for it. And I didn't have the guts to face her anyway. I never did get any money out of it. But I heard later that the guy left her. Just like that. Her and the kid. Knowing that was almost better than the money."

As satisfying as the news might have been to Sissy, it clearly had no effect on Maggie's career. Sissy continued to watch her off and on until Maggie left the market, bound for a TV station in Minnesota, the newspapers said. For Sissy, it was a relief to have her gone. She was out of sight and out of mind.

Until now.

"So you'll sell me the film?" Tony said.

"I'll need to know more," she said.

"C'mon, I can't tell you more," he complained. "I just know they want the film."

"Who are *they*?"

"I told you, friends. People I've gotten to know."

He knows more than he's telling me, she thought. And if he's offering that kind of money now, there has to be plenty more out there. Play it cool, she told herself. Keep him guessing.

She finished her coffee and started to get up, but he quickly reached for her arm and pulled her back into the booth. "Where are you going?"

"Home," she said with a yawn. "It's been a long night."

"What about the film?" he demanded.

"I'll have to see if I still have it," she lied, "but if I do, it's going to cost your friends more than you're talking about. And I want to know what the deal is."

He slumped back, nervously clutching his coffee cup. "These people . . . the ones who want the film . . . don't like taking no for an answer," he said. "I told them I could arrange it."

Sissy was now out of the booth. "Too bad," she said. "You should have talked to me first."

As she walked to the door, he called after her. "Think about it, okay? I'll be back in touch."

Tony was back at the club the next night and the night after that. Each time, the bid price for the film rose by a few hundred dollars. And each time, Sissy said no, hoping and expecting still more. Finally, on the third night, he came with what he said was his final offer: Three thousand for the film. A thousand a week, plus expenses, for unspecified duties in the Twin Cities, where Maggie Lawrence now lived and worked.

"They want me to go to Minnesota?" she said, disbelieving, not even sure where the state was.

"Both of us. Together."

"What do they mean, unspecified duties?" she asked.

"We'll find out when we get there," he said. "That's all I know."

"For how long?"

He shrugged. "They didn't tell me. As long as it takes, I guess."

"To do what?"

He was getting angry. "You ask too many questions. I'm telling you, I don't know."

She hung back in the booth, debating. It sounded weird, maybe even dangerous. She didn't like the idea of partnering with a loser like Tony Kolura, but it was a lot of money. Twice what she was making now, getting naked four times a night in front of a bunch of leering old men. And who knows how long that might last? She could be out on her bare ass any day. Broke again.

Tony took an envelope out of his pocket and opened it, ruffling through a wad of bills inside. "There's a two-grand advance, if you agree," he said. "Three thousand more when you hand over the film."

She took the envelope and counted the bills. He was right, two thousand in hundreds. "What kind of trouble can this get us?" she asked. "No way am I going to end up in the slammer."

Sissy was no stranger to jail, having been picked up numerous times for pandering and soliciting, but she had never spent more than a night or two there and was determined not to risk more.

Tony retrieved the envelope and put it back in his pocket. "None, if we're careful. And do as we're told."

"What about Maggie?" she asked. "What happens to her in all of this?"

He shrugged. "She's not going to end up dead, if that's what you mean. I gather they just want to scare her a little."

"Blackmail her?"

"Something like that," he said. "But I told you, I don't know more."

Sissy thought for a moment, then said, "Give me the envelope."

"We've got a deal then?"

"I guess so," she said.

He handed her the envelope. "No changing your mind, you know. Not now."

She put the money in her purse. "I'll have the film for you tomorrow night. You get it when I get the extra three thousand."

"No problem," he said. "When can you leave?"

"In a week. No sooner. I have to give the club notice."

That was six weeks ago.

It was over as quickly as it began. Slam, bam, thank you, ma'am. Five minutes or less, she figured, from start to finish. Foreplay was not a part of Tony's sexual vocabulary, but that was all right with her. It would have only prolonged the ordeal. He was on his back now, snoring softly, convinced—she was sure—that he had given her as much pleasure as he had received.

Loser.

Sissy moved to the other side of the bed, as far away from him as the sheet would stretch. She felt raw between her legs and knew she should get up and shower, but could not work up the energy. Morning would be soon enough, she told herself.

If she had known that repeated sex with Tony would be part of the deal, she might have considered it more carefully, but by the time they got to Minnesota, it was too late to change her mind, and she had neither the strength nor the courage to fight him off. It was *his* deal, he had been quick to remind her, and she ought to be happy to show him a little gratitude.

Besides that, he could be a mean bastard. Downright dangerous. She had seen flashes of his

temper more than once and was not eager to irri-
tate him again. Keep him satisfied, she told herself, until this thing is over. Then take the money
and run.

But when would it end? She had no idea, but
she hoped it would be soon. As much as she liked
the money, she had no desire to spend the winter
in Minnesota. Or many more nights as Tony's
punch card.

20

The phone call came on the weekend—a beautiful Indian Summer Saturday, the cloudless sky a brilliant blue, the trees in the midst of their slow transition from summer's green to fall's marvelous mosaic of reds and yellows and golds.

Maggie was at home with Danny, both of them feeling cooped up and out of sorts, eager to be outside in the crisp air and warm sunshine. However, with Brett away tending to some personal errands, she was reluctant to venture too far from home.

So far, neither she nor Brett had mentioned the bedroom kiss again, as if each was slightly embarrassed about it or afraid to guess at what it might mean—or that talking about it might spoil the memory of it. Maggie was not sorry it had happened, although she certainly had not planned it. She could still taste the sweetness of the mint in her mouth. Let it ride, she told herself. See where it may lead.

"Can't we just go to the park?" Danny begged, knowing that some of his young friends from the apartment building or school would likely be there. "Do we have to wait for Jake?"

The park was just four blocks away, a collection of swings, slides, sandboxes, a jungle gym, and a wading pool now closed for the season. She knew the park would likely be crowded on a morning like this, and probably safe enough, but still she hesitated. "Let's wait another half hour or so," she said, "to see if Brett's back by then. If he's not, we'll go ahead."

Danny was momentarily pacified, but stayed close to the open window, looking out longingly, occasionally shouting down to one of his buddies below.

As it happened, the decision to wait was fortuitous. About twenty minutes later, the phone rang. She let it ring, waiting for the answering machine to click on, which it did after the fourth ring. "You've reached 555-0177," her recorded voice said. "Please leave a message."

There was a lengthy pause, then a small, tentative voice asked, "Is this Maggie Lawrence? My name is Amy . . . my mother—"

Maggie snapped up the phone, cutting off the machine. "This is Maggie," she said. "Is this Amy Boyd?"

There was another long pause. "Amy? Is that you? Please talk to me."

She could hear indecipherable sounds in the

background, like far-off laughter and talking, as though the caller were in the middle of a crowd somewhere. A crowd having fun. Then the voice came back. "I can't talk long, Ms. Lawrence. I'm with friends, and they're waiting for me."

"Amy, please, stay with me. I need to speak to you. It's about Penny."

"I know," the girl said. "My mother told me. She said you were nice, that I should talk with you."

Maggie pressed the phone close to her lips. "Amy, listen to me. I'm not trying to bust you. I won't try to get you home. But I need to talk to you. We're trying to find out what happened to Penny, to find the people who did that to her. We hope you can help."

"Nobody can help Penny," she whispered. "Not now."

"I know that," Maggie said. "But maybe we can help somebody else like her."

"Like me, you mean."

"Maybe."

After another long pause, Maggie asked, "Do you know Nadia Vaughn?"

"Yeah. She took off right after . . . you know."

"Took off where?"

"California, I think. That's what they say."

"Amy, will you meet with me? Name the time and place. I'll be alone. No one will know where you are, I swear."

She could again hear shouting in the background, more distinct now, closer. "Tomorrow," Amy finally said, sounding rushed. "At the Burger King on Central at three. You know where it is?"

"I'll find it," Maggie said.

◆   ◆   ◆

Brett argued against her going alone. They were sitting side-by-side, each squeezed into one of the park's swings, watching as Danny clambered up the side of the jungle gym across the way.

"I promised her I'd be alone," Maggie said. "I can't renege. She'd run for sure."

Brett pushed himself back with his long legs, then let the swing go. He sailed past her, feet straight out, gaining altitude, causing the swing set to squeal and groan. "Who knows what she's into," he said as the swing finally slowed. "Somebody besides her mother could have put her up to this."

"I don't think so," Maggie said. "She was too hesitant. Too scared."

Brett proposed a compromise: that he drive her downtown, get her into a cab, make sure she wasn't being followed, and then wait a block away, within view of the Burger King. After more discussion, she reluctantly agreed, but not without a promise that he would not interfere unless there was an obvious sign of trouble.

"If I see anything strange," he said, "I'm going to be there. Count on it. We're not taking any chances."

Maggie stepped out of the cab in front of the Burger King and—ever cautious—quickly glanced around her, relieved to see or sense nothing suspicious. Traffic on Central Avenue was light, and only a few cars were parked either on the street or in the restaurant's parking lot. Down the block, she could spot Brett's Explorer hugging the curb, the outline of his upper body visible through the tinted window, keeping watch.

She rarely came to this part of the city, but knew it to be one of the oldest sections of town, not far from the Mississippi River and St. Anthony Falls, where Minneapolis and its milling industry were born. A hundred years later, it was still home to many descendants of the first Eastern Europeans immigrants who had settled here: Poles, Russians, and Czechs, whose modest homes and mammoth orthodox churches maintained the ethnic character of the community.

She paid the cabby and stepped to the curb. Although yesterday's bright sunshine had disappeared beneath the clouds, she wore sunglasses and a scarf tied tightly around her head. Not really a disguise, but an effort to prevent anyone but Amy from easily recognizing her. There would be no time today for autographs or chats with admiring fans.

She shouldn't have worried; the restaurant was all but deserted. An old couple, still in their church clothes, sat in a corner booth sipping coffee, and across the way, a young guy in sweater and slacks was hunched over a book, totally absorbed. He ignored her entrance, and the old couple seemed to give her only passing notice.

Maggie checked her watch. A few minutes past three. She was on time, but where was Amy? She quickly stepped to the counter and ordered coffee, averting her face when the girl behind the counter showed a flicker of recognition. Hurriedly taking her coffee, she retreated to a table by the window—

as far as possible from the others in the restaurant, but where she could see, and be seen from, the street outside.

She waited. For thirty minutes and two cups of coffee. The old couple left and a few other people came and went, but still no Amy. Maggie wished now that she had brought a newspaper or a book, anything to help pass the time and appear less conspicuous sitting there alone. But it was too late to worry about that now.

Had she been stood up? Had Amy lost her nerve? It wouldn't have surprised her, knowing from her own experience how skittish runaways are. What would she do then? Go back to square one, she guessed.

Twice she caught a glimpse of Brett's Explorer passing by on the street, but she tried to ignore it. He must be getting worried, she thought. Or impatient. He wasn't alone. I'll give her fifteen more minutes, she decided as she returned to the counter, this time for a cup of hot chocolate. The coffee had made her even edgier.

Making her way back to her table, she passed by the young man with the book, apparently still as engrossed as he had been when she first walked into the place. Without looking up, he said, sotto voce, "Hang out a minute . . . she'll be here soon."

Maggie stopped short and turned. "What? Are you talking to me?"

The boy kept his eyes on the book. "Yeah. Amy's coming. She's running late."

"Who are you?" she asked, leaning down. "And how do you know Amy?"

He finally looked up, his eyes magnified by

thick glasses. "Hey, I'm a friend, okay? Just go back and sit down."

She was stunned. He'd been there the whole time, watching her, making sure it was safe. And she hadn't had a clue. But who would have? He appeared to be in his late teens or early twenties, the sweater, slacks, and glasses giving him the look of a bookish college student. Hardly someone who would be part the runaway street crowd.

She strode quickly to her table, but had no more than sat down when he picked up his book and went to the door. She watched as he stepped out onto the sidewalk and raised a hand, as though signaling someone. Then he walked away.

Minutes later, three young people emerged from a pizza parlor across the street. Two boys and a girl, from what Maggie could tell. All were dressed in ragtag outfits, the boys in jeans torn open at the knees and oversized sweatshirts that hung from their shoulders. One, with straggly, shoulder-length hair, wore laceless tennis shoes that flopped as he walked; the other, whose head was shaved clean, wore cowboy boots. Both had stubble beards and appeared—even at a distance—to be in desperate need of a shower.

The girl, whom Maggie assumed to be Amy, was wearing old army fatigues, gold sergeant's stripes still hanging from one of the sleeves. Her hair was cut short, topped by a baseball hat, its bill twisted to one side. She walked between the two boys, hand-in-hand with the one with long hair.

When they reached the door of the Burger King, the bald boy stayed outside, slumped against the wall, while the other came inside with the girl, warily taking a seat at the other end of the restaurant. The girl walked directly to Maggie, sliding into a chair across the table. "I'm Amy," she said simply.

"Thanks for coming," Maggie said, rising slightly from her chair. "I was beginning to wonder if you'd make it."

Amy glanced around her. "We have to be careful," she said.

There was a moment of awkward silence as they studied one another. Amy's mother was right: The girl *had* lost weight since the confirmation picture. She was now quite slender and surprisingly pretty, if you ignored the two gold rings piercing her nose. She had dark hair, unblinking blue eyes, and a long, narrow face that had thinned with her body and bordered on being gaunt. She wore no makeup, but, unlike her companions, seemed scrubbed clean.

"I thought you were coming alone," Amy suddenly said.

"I *am* alone," Maggie replied, surprised.

"Then who's in the Explorer? We've been watching it."

Maggie was taken aback. Hesitating, she finally said, "A friend. Someone who's worried about me. He won't bother us."

"I hope not," Amy replied, glancing over her shoulder. "I have friends, too."

Unlike her fearful demeanor on the phone, Amy now seemed absolutely composed. Wary, but unafraid. Maggie wondered what accounted for the change. Must be her two guardians, she thought.

"Can I get you something?" she asked. "Coffee or a Coke, maybe?"

"No, thanks. But a few bucks for dinner wouldn't hurt."

Maggie debated, but then opened her purse and pulled out a twenty-dollar bill. Barclay wouldn't approve, she knew, of her paying a source, but it was her money, not his, and he would never know anyway. "This is all I've got," she said, handing over the bill.

"That's great," Amy said as she stuffed the twenty into her fatigue pocket.

Maggie wasn't quite sure where to begin, and as she deliberated, the girl said, "I don't have much time."

"Then let's get to it," Maggie said. "We're trying to figure out what happened to Penny Collins. Not only who killed her, but why."

"Good luck," Amy said. "The cops sure as hell can't."

"Have the police talked to you?"

"Nah," Amy scoffed. "I've heard they're looking for me, but I wouldn't talk to them anyway. Most of them are assholes."

Maggie sat back in chair. "Then why are you talking to me?"

"Because you're not a cop, I guess. Penny was my friend, and I was scared shitless when she got killed. It shouldn't have happened to her . . . and I'd like to see the bastards who did it get theirs."

"Do you know who did it?" Maggie asked, leaning forward.

Amy shook her head. "You mean do I have proof? Hell no. But everyone who hung out with her has a pretty good idea of what happened."

Maggie said nothing, waiting.

"She got mixed up with some bad dudes," Amy continued. "Did some crazy stuff. She was a wild kid, always needed money to get crack."

"What kind of crazy stuff?" Maggie asked. And then, "Like making porn films?"

It was Amy's turn to be surprised. "You know about that?" she demanded.

"I had an idea," Maggie admitted.

Some of the confidence seemed to leave the girl. A tremor crept into her voice.

"So how much do you know?" she asked.

"Not as much as I need to. That's why I'm here."

"How do I know this is just between you and me? That I won't get involved?"

"You have my word."

"You gave your word that you'd be alone," she snorted.

Maggie shrugged. "That was different. He has to be out there. I'm not allowed to run around by myself."

"Why's that?"

She didn't want to get into it, but the girl was demanding an explanation. And she had to have her trust. Finally, she said, "There have been some threats."

"Against you? About this stuff?"

"I don't know. Maybe."

"Goddamn," Amy whispered with a slight shiver.

Maggie pressed on. "Were you involved in the films?"

"*Me?* No way. And I'm not a crackhead either. I don't do that shit."

"So what do you know?" Maggie demanded.

"I know that Penny and the other girl you asked about, Nadia, made a couple of films. Somewhere out in Edina, I think."

"Where is this Nadia from?" Maggie asked. "We've been trying to find her."

"Wisconsin, I think. Near Milwaukee, or maybe Madison. But I told you, she took off for California. Right after Penny got killed."

Wisconsin. No wonder they hadn't found her family, Maggie thought. "You know where in California?"

"No idea. She may have gone the other way, for all I know. She was scared."

"Because of what happened to Penny?"

"What do you think?"

Maggie took a breath. It was coming too fast. Slow it down. Get it right. "Let's step back for a minute," she said. "You said they made a couple of films. Somewhere in Edina, right?"

"That's what they told me."

Edina was a large suburb adjoining south Minneapolis, an old and wealthy bedroom community that was home to several shopping centers and commercial districts.

"Where in Edina?" Maggie asked.

"I don't know. Some warehouse or office building, I think. I was never there."

"Did you see the films?"

Amy shook her head. "No, but Penny told me there were five or six other kids involved, some of them younger than she was. Like twelve or thirteen, she said. That's what got her so pissed off. That they were just little kids, for Christ's sake. But she needed the money, so she did the second one."

"Then what?"

"I don't know. I didn't see her for a while. Then they found her body."

Maggie could see Amy was becoming impatient, edgy. When she started to get up, Maggie grabbed her hand. "Not yet, please." Although she settled back in her chair, Maggie knew she had little time left. "Do you think she died because of the films?"

"Maybe," Amy said, "but it could have been crack, too. I told you, she was into some messed up stuff."

"Did you ever hear any names? People connected with the films?"

Amy was now out of her chair and standing by the table as the boy with the long hair moved toward the door. "One time Nadia mentioned a Butch. That's the only name I ever heard."

"Butch? No last name?"

Amy shook her head. "I've got to go. I've probably said too much already."

To the contrary, Maggie sensed that she knew more than she was saying, but there was no stopping her now. She walked with her, stepping between her and the door. "How do I get hold of you?" she asked. "I may need to talk again."

Amy and the boy pushed past her. "You can't. Maybe I'll call you."

Then they were gone.

Maggie waited a few minutes and then stepped outside, waiting for Brett to pick her up. "They spotted me, didn't they?" he said as she slipped into the car.

"How did you know?" she asked, buckling up.

"One of them, the bald-headed one, gave me the finger as they walked by."

She laughed. "You're probably lucky they didn't pee on your car."

As Brett drove, she quickly reported on what she had learned. "If we can believe Amy, we know that Penny Collins was involved in porn films, two of them, and so was this Nadia, wherever she is. We also know that others kids, some younger, were, too."

"Younger?" Brett asked.

"Twelve or thirteen, according to Amy."

"My God," he breathed.

"We also know the films were supposedly shot in Edina, maybe in an office building or warehouse. But we don't know exactly where, and we don't know who was involved except for some guy named Butch. And how many Butches are there in the world?"

Brett was impressed. "I'd say you learned quite a bit."

"Maybe," Maggie mused. "But Amy says Penny was also heavy into drugs, and that could have been what got her killed."

"So what now?" Brett asked.

"I'm not sure," she said, suddenly feeling very tired. "Maybe it's time to put Jessica's computer into high gear. See if good old Butch pops up in any of her lists."

21

"You should have called me," Jessica said, obviously still miffed that she had missed Maggie's meeting with Amy. "I would have come in a minute."

They were sitting in Barclay's office, waiting for Barclay and Brett to break free from the afternoon news huddle.

"Take it easy, Jess," Maggie said. "She insisted that I come alone. She might not have shown up if they had seen two of us."

Maggie had called Jessica at home the night before, quickly briefing her on the meeting with Amy. Jessica had been angry then and had not cooled off much in the interim. "This is *my* investigation, you know," she said now. "My story. I don't like being cut out of it. Not with something like this."

Not *your* story, Maggie thought, quietly simmering. It's *our* story now. After all, it was through her efforts that they had found Amy and her mother, and it was she who had arranged the meeting. But she remained quiet, not wanting to further the argument or worsen an already shaky relationship. Instead, she waited patiently for Barclay and Brett to arrive.

"So what have we got?" Barclay asked once they had gathered around his desk.

Maggie carefully repeated the details of her meeting with Amy, omitting any reference to the food money she had given the girl or Jessica's pique.

"That's a hell of a start," Barclay said. "What's next?"

Jessica swallowed her anger and spoke up. "It's a long shot, but we're going to run the name Butch through the computer and see what turns up. But I'm not very hopeful. Butch sounds like a nickname to me, and the files aren't great on nicknames."

"I think we ought to jump on the Edina lead," Brett said. "If they're shooting the films out there, we should try to find out where."

"Edina's a big place," Barclay said doubtfully.

"True," Brett replied. "But Amy talked about an office or a warehouse. It could be equipped for this kind of thing. Maybe it's already a production house or studio of some sort. Hell, it could be in the Yellow Pages. It's worth a check anyway."

After more debate and discussion, a battle plan

was devised: Brett would pursue the location of the production house; Jessica would search the computer files for any lead to the mysterious Butch; and Maggie would resume her search for the missing Nadia, now that she had some clue to her hometown in Wisconsin.

For really the first time, Maggie felt a small sense of optimism, a hunch that somehow the pieces of the puzzle were slowly coming together.

Later that afternoon, Timothy McQueen, the detective, was back in Barclay's office. Maggie was there, too, summoned by Barclay.

"Sorry it's been so long," McQueen said, as polite as ever, "but I've been up to my neck with other cases."

"No problem," Barclay said. "What have you got?"

"Not much, I'm afraid. The envelopes Maggie gave me have no clear prints on them other than hers and the nanny's. Whoever left them must have wiped 'em clean and then used gloves."

Maggie slumped back in her chair, disappointed but not surprised.

"I also went over the car," McQueen said. "The one that rammed you." Maggie sat up. "Nothing there either," he added, "except for one thing."

"What's that?" Barclay asked.

"We found the remnants of some words on the back of the trunk. They had been wiped off, but not completely. Still some traces left."

"Words?" Barclay said, glancing at Maggie. She could feel her face redden; she had never told Barclay about the scrawled inscription.

"I went back to the original accident report," McQueen said. "One of the witnesses said she had seen some large red letters on the back of the car, but couldn't read them."

"So?" Barclay said, leaning forward over his desk.

McQueen stared steadily at Maggie. "They spelled 'Porno Whore,'" he said, lingering on each of the two words. "What do you make of that?"

She glanced at Barclay and then back to the detective. "I have no idea," she said with a shrug of her shoulders, feeling trapped.

McQueen kept his eyes locked on her. "You're sure? Nothing more? No connection to these threats you've been getting?"

Barclay was quick to intervene, deciding then that the detective deserved to know more. "We think we know one of the people who may be involved in all of this."

"Really?" McQueen replied. "Who and how?"

"A woman," Barclay said. "Someone Maggie knew years ago, in Los Angeles. Her name then was Sissy. We don't know if it still is or what her last name is, but we do have her picture. We think she may have dropped off the first envelope . . . maybe the second, too. But we have no proof."

"How did you get the picture?" McQueen asked.

Barclay briefly explained how the photo had come into their possession, but added, "The tour was weeks ago, and we don't even know if she's still in town. If she is, she may be with the guy who was stalking Maggie's boy outside of his school."

McQueen got out of his chair and leaned against the wall, looking perplexed. "Why would this woman . . . this Sissy . . . be threatening you? I still don't get it."

"And we still can't tell you," Barclay said. "I'm sorry."

McQueen shook his head wearily. "You're impossible, you know that? How am I supposed to help when you won't give me the full story?"

Maggie had one idea. "For starters, you could talk to the cops in L.A.," she suggested. "To see if they have any records on a woman named Sissy. You could fax them her picture. That could help."

McQueen sat back down and said, "Assuming they'd do it for me, which is no sure thing, and assuming there aren't dozens of women by that name in their records, what good would it do?"

"We might at least learn her last name. Find out what she's been up to . . . and who she's been mixed up with in the twelve years since I've seen her."

"You think she would have a record?"

"I'd bet on it," Maggie said.

"For what?" he persisted.

"Who knows? Pandering, prostitution, maybe worse."

"Sounds like she might be the porno whore," the detective said slyly.

"She could be," Maggie said, ignoring his slight smile.

She promised to get a copy of Sissy's picture to McQueen the next day, and he agreed to get back to them with any information as soon as he received it. "Maybe then you'll give me the whole story," he said.

"Maybe so," Barclay said. "But no guarantees."

As requested, Natasha and Justin, the two interns, were waiting by her desk when Maggie returned from Barclay's office. They didn't appear especially happy to be there. "I have a new lead on Nadia Vaughn," she told them. "She may be from either Madison or Milwaukee. We need to get back on the phones."

The interns exchanged glances. "I'm not sure I'll have the time," Justin said. "The schoolwork is piling up."

"This shouldn't take that long," Maggie replied. "Jessica has access to the phone books from both cities on her computer. She's getting all of the names and numbers now. There aren't that many."

As the two turned to leave, Maggie called Natasha back. "You once told me that you have friends who hang around some of the runaway squats, right?"

"A few, yeah."

"Do me another favor. When you have the chance, ask them if they've ever heard of a guy named Butch. No last name. He's not a runaway himself. He's older, but apparently knows some of those kids. Be discreet. Be cool, just ask casual-like."

"I'm not sure when I'll see them," Natasha said.

"Whenever you can. Just don't be too obvious. I wouldn't want word to get back to him that somebody is asking about him."

"I'll do what I can," Natasha said as she headed for the phones.

It took less than three hours.

When Maggie emerged from the studio after the early newscast, she found Justin waiting for her, his expression impossible to read. She saw both the flush of excitement and something else . . . what? . . . disappointment or pain?

"What have you got?" she asked as she pulled him to the side of the hallway.

He took a deep breath, then exhaled. "I found her," he said with a rush.

"Nadia?"

He nodded. "Her folks live in Madison. They were my tenth call."

"Good work," she said, surprised and pleased. "Did you talk to them? Do they know where she is?"

"That's just it," he said hesitantly.

"What do you mean?"

At that moment, Brett walked out of the control room and strode over to them. "What's happening?" he asked.

"Justin here found Nadia Vaughn's parents . . . in Madison."

"No kidding."

"There's a problem, though," Justin said.

Maggie had a fleeting sense of foreboding. "What kind of problem?"

He looked away, down the hall, then faced them again. His words were choked. "She's dead. Nadia Vaughn's dead."

"What?" She suddenly understood his look of pain.

"She committed suicide. Two weeks ago. The funeral was ten days ago."

Maggie felt her knees weaken as she grabbed Brett's arm for support.

"I couldn't believe it, either," the intern continued. "When they told me, I mean. They were so nice about it. Asked me how I knew Nadia, if I was a friend of hers. I probably shouldn't have, but I lied and said I was."

"My God," Maggie breathed, still holding tightly to Brett. "You're sure it's the right girl?"

"It must be," he said. "She was sixteen. Had been on the run, in Minneapolis, they thought, until she came home three weeks ago. They said she seemed depressed, but wouldn't tell them what was bothering her. Stayed in her room mostly, playing her old heavy metal tapes, until one night they noticed the music had stopped. They found her in the bathtub. She'd slit her wrists."

The image flashed into Maggie's mind and a shiver passed through her body.

"They told you all of this on the phone?" Brett asked, astonished.

"It was her mother. She wouldn't stop. It was like I was the first friend of Nadia's that she had talked to. And hell, I didn't even know the girl. It was weird. Like she was telling me about her graduation or something . . ."

The three of them walked slowly back to Maggie's desk, Justin filling them in with more details as they went. Nadia had been gone almost a year when she showed up at home, refusing to explain where she had been or what she had been doing. Her parents were so happy to have her back that they didn't press the issue. They just wanted to make her feel welcome, hoping she would eventually come out of her shell and talk to them. A week later she was dead.

Maggie sat at her desk, eyes closed. It was the last thing she had expected and still found it hard to believe. Two girls, both dead, one murdered, the other a suicide. Both involved in a kid-porn film. She had to know more. But how? She opened her eyes and reached for the phone, quickly punching in the number of Amy Boyd's parents. Florence Boyd answered on the second ring. "Oh, it's you," she said. "Did Amy call you?"

"Yes, she did," Maggie said. "I met with her yesterday."

"You did? How is she?"

"She seems fine, Mrs. Boyd. I appreciated your help in getting in touch with her."

Maggie briefly described her meeting with Amy, and then got to the point of her call. "It's important that I talk to Amy again, Mrs. Boyd. I have a very important message for her, but I don't know how to reach her. I know you don't, either, but if she calls you again will you tell her that?"

"Of course," the woman said. "Is she in some kind of danger?"

"No, no, I don't think so. But I do need to talk to her."

"If she calls, I'll give her your message," Mrs. Boyd said. And then, in a faltering voice, she asked, "When you saw her, did she say anything about us? About maybe coming home?"

"I'm afraid not," Maggie answered. "I'm sorry."

In words that were more of a sob, she said, "So am I."

Later that night, back at the apartment, Maggie sat curled up in a corner of the couch, slippered feet beneath her, robe wrapped tightly around her. Brett was on the floor, kneeling in front of the fireplace, watching as the first flames licked at the cedar kindling, reaching ever higher, crackling, sending sparks flying. Next came the split birch logs, hissing and spitting when the flames touched the bark.

An Arctic cold front, pushed along by strong northerly winds, had moved in during the day, tumbling the temperature to well below freezing and the wind chill to near zero for the first time that fall. Winter was clearly waiting around the corner, ready to pounce. And a touch of its chill had seeped into the apartment.

"That feels good," Maggie said as the heat from the fire found its way to her. "Smells good, too."

"You're lucky to have one of these," Brett said, tossing yet another log into the fire. "I wish I did."

They had been home for about an hour, having declined an invitation to join the rest of the night crew for a drink. Neither of them was in the mood. "I just can't get that girl out of my mind," Maggie said, hugging the robe even closer to her body. "I keep seeing her in that bloody bathtub. It's going to give me nightmares."

"I know what you mean," Brett said, moving from the floor to the couch. "It must have been horrible."

Maggie was so troubled that she had had

difficulty reading the news that night, stumbling enough, in fact, to prompt a call from Barclay wondering what the problem was. Once he had been told about Nadia's suicide, he seemed more understanding, but still disturbed. "This is what I was talking about in the office, remember?" he said to her. "I can't afford to have you distracted. You need to be at the top of your game."

She had mumbled an apology and assured him it wouldn't happen again, hoping she was right.

"Her suicide may have nothing to do with any of this," Brett said. "It could have been because of the drugs, anything."

"I know that," she said, "but that doesn't make it any less tragic. Sixteen years old, Brett. Who knows what she could have made of her life . . . if she'd just been given half a chance. The same with Penny. Two wasted lives."

Looking back now, there was hardly a kid she had met on the streets of L.A. who hadn't thought about suicide . . . or who hadn't known someone who had tried. Screw up a mind with enough drugs or despair or both, and that's what you get. Even Maggie herself had once considered it, before she had worked up the courage to run away. For a time, ending her life had looked like the easiest way to end the pain, to escape the horrors of her home. Although the temptation had passed, the experience made it easier for her to understand what Nadia had done. But no easier to accept.

She had never known Nadia, of course, but in a way, she felt as if she had—in the person of every other kid who had shared her life on the streets.

Booty and Babs. Hellfire and Jonas. Pinky and Hitler. The names came back to her now, even if the faces did not. And for every one of them, there were hundreds more. Thousands, if you counted all of the years that had passed since her own days on the street.

The crackling of the fire brought her back. She looked up and found Brett watching her. "You're way back when, aren't you?" he said.

"Sorry," she murmured, "I can't quite escape the memories. I never will, I guess."

"But you're here now."

She uncurled herself and moved across the couch to him. "Would you mind holding me?" she asked, snuggling against his shoulder. "I need to be held right now."

He put his arm around her, enfolding her, feeling the warmth of her body against his chest, the scent of her hair in his nostrils. Her eyes were hidden from him, but her deep, even breaths told him she was nearly asleep.

An hour passed. She did not stir. Nor did he. The fire was dying in the grate, the flames now only a flicker among the shimmering coals.

Brett could never remember feeling more content.

22

The flight from Minneapolis to Madison took less than an hour. Another twenty minutes by cab brought Maggie to a large two-story white colonial with blue shutters, set well back and almost hidden from the street by towering oaks and maples that clearly had been there long before the house. The overhanging branches made a tunnel of the curved driveway, which was still covered by a thick layer of unraked leaves that crackled and popped beneath the taxi's tires.

"Nice place," the driver said as he pulled up to the front door. "You live here?"

She dug into her purse for the fare. "No," she said. "Just visiting."

"Will you need a ride back to the airport?"

"Yes, but I don't know when," she replied, stepping onto the driveway. "I'll give you a call."

As the cab drove off, she stood for a moment looking around her. The cabby was right; it was an impressive home in a decidedly affluent neighborhood called University Heights, reflecting—she guessed—the status of Drs. Arthur and Dorothy Vaughn in the campus community. Both husband and wife, Maggie had learned, were Ph.D.'s, professors at the University of Wisconsin, Arthur in physics and Dorothy, or Dottie, as she liked to be called, in English. Nadia had been their only child.

Maggie had been as surprised by Barclay's approval of the trip as she was by the Vaughn's willingness to see her. But now that she was here, she wondered again if she should have come. She still didn't know what benefit or useful information might come of it, but in the days since learning of Nadia's death, she could not rid herself of the need to see and speak to the girl's parents. It became her mission.

After mounting the steps, but before she could reach for the doorbell, the door was opened by a slender woman with dark hair and a pale, almost pasty complexion that carried no hint of makeup. In her forties, Maggie thought, although she could be ten years older. "Miss Lawrence?" she said. "We've been waiting. Please come in."

Maggie shook her outstretched hand, as thin and fragile as one of the fallen leaves outside. "Thanks for seeing me," she said. "But please call me Maggie."

Mrs. Vaughn tried to smile, but couldn't quite manage it. She wore a black dress that appeared to be a size or two too large, hanging from her shoulders and belted tightly at the waist. She's still deep in mourning, Maggie thought, wondering at the same time how much weight she had lost since her daughter's death.

If anything, the interior of the house was even more impressive than the exterior. Once beyond the foyer, a large living room with a brick fireplace loomed to the right, a dining room half its size to the left, separated by a wide center stairway that curved gently to the second floor. The carpeting beneath her feet was soft and deep, a rich and spotless off-white that was either new or newly cleaned. She was almost afraid to walk on it.

"Let me take your coat," Mrs. Vaughn said. "My husband's waiting in the library."

As Maggie followed the woman around the staircase and through the kitchen to the rear of the house, she was struck by the utter silence and the unlived-in feel of the place. Aside from their own footsteps, there was no sound—not a radio or TV, not a squeaky floorboard or a noisy furnace. No magazines or newspapers lay about, no rug was rumpled, no picture askew. And while all of the furniture was lovely and perfectly in place, it appeared unused, like so many pieces on display in a furniture showroom.

Like the Vaughns, the house itself seemed to be in mourning.

As if sensing her thoughts, Mrs. Vaughn said, as they entered the library, "This is where we spend most of our time. It's more comfortable here." The wide windows of the library overlooked a backyard that went beyond the reach of the eye, populated by more of the soaring oaks and maples and bordered by Norway pines as high as the house itself. Maggie felt as if she were standing in the middle of a forest.

Mr. Vaughn rose from behind a large mahogany desk to greet her. He was as heavy as his wife was thin, with a white-fringed, balding head and ruddy, chubby cheeks, half-glasses clinging to his nose. Give him a beard and a red cap—and a smile—and he could play Santa Claus, she thought.

Two of the library walls were filled, floor to ceiling, with shelf upon shelf of books and papers, one wall apparently reserved for each of their academic collections. A third wall was used to display framed copies of their various diplomas and awards and an array of family pictures, none of which was close enough for Maggie to examine. A fire was blazing in the library hearth as Mr. Vaughn offered her a chair next to it. "Can we get you anything?" he asked. "Coffee or tea, perhaps. It won't take a minute."

"No thanks," she replied, settling into the chair. "I don't want to put you to any bother or take too much of your time. I'm just grateful you agreed to see me."

In her phone conversation with the Vaughns, she had again been vague in explaining the purpose of her call . . . or of her proposed visit. After expressing her sympathies at Nadia's death, she had told them only that she was researching a story that involved runaways and had come across their daughter's name.

Now, after some preliminary questions to Maggie about her job and the story she was pursuing, Mr.

Vaughn asked, "So how did you learn about our Nadia?"

She hurriedly explained the sympathy note that Nadia had sent to Penny Collins's parents, and how she had managed to locate another of Nadia's friends, Amy Boyd. "We're trying to find out how and why Penny Collins died," she said.

From their puzzled reaction, it was clear the Vaughns knew nothing of Penny or her murder. The story apparently had never reached the Madison newspapers, and their daughter must have told them nothing. "Are you sure Nadia knew this Penny person?" Vaughn asked.

"Quite sure," she replied, repeating some of what Amy Boyd had told her, but deleting any reference to the porn films. "We think she may have left the Twin Cities because she was afraid the same thing could happen to her."

Mrs. Vaughn leaned forward, disbelief in her voice. "You mean she was afraid she would be killed? Murdered?"

"Exactly," Maggie said. "From what we're told, she and Penny apparently became involved with some bad people. Perhaps with drugs ... and other things."

"What other things?" Vaughn asked sharply.

She had dreaded this moment, although she knew it would be impossible to avoid. If she was to get at the truth, she would have to tell the truth. But that made it no easier. "We think they both were involved in making ... ah ... adult movies," she finally said. "Films that involved children even younger than themselves."

Vaughn was on his feet, his ruddy cheeks now

aflame. "You're telling us our daughter was mixed up in child pornography?" he shouted down at her. "How dare you!"

As she recoiled from the outburst, Vaughn's wife quickly jumped to his side, calming him. "Arthur, please," she said. "Hear the lady out."

He sank back into his chair, trembling, breathing heavily. Maggie waited for a moment and then said, "I'm sorry, but I thought you'd want the truth. It's the only way we're ever going to get to the bottom of this . . . if we hope to find the people who preyed on Nadia and the others, who persuaded or forced them into something like this."

Mrs. Vaughn moved her chair closer to Maggie, her pale face a portrait of pain and sorrow. "You've got to understand what we've gone through the last couple of years," she said. "Nadia was all we had . . . and now she's gone. Forever. Do you have children?"

"A little boy," Maggie said. "Danny. He's almost six."

"Then you must know what we're feeling, what the parents of that girl, Penny, must have felt. The terrible loss, the horrible void in our lives. To lose any child is unimaginable, to lose one as we did is a nightmare that may never end."

She went on to talk freely about Nadia as a child, describing her as well-behaved but a slow learner, who came to hate school and began to skip classes before she was out of junior high. "She was physically very mature for her age," Mrs. Vaughn said, "and got involved with some of the older university students. That's when we discovered that she was using drugs."

Her husband broke in. "We tried everything . . .

tough love, counseling, a treatment program. We even sent her to live with her aunt in Green Bay, to get her away from the crowd she was hanging around with. Nothing worked. She finally ran away a year ago."

Maggie could only shake her head sadly. The story was all too familiar.

"But I can't picture her getting involved with pornographic films," Vaughn continued. "That just doesn't figure. She was never that kind of girl, I mean into sex and all. She never even had a real boyfriend."

Maggie's guess was that they wouldn't have allowed it. Judging from the flawless condition of the house, she suspected that Nadia had grown up in a very controlled, compulsive environment— one that she eventually had rebelled against, with now fatal consequences. "She probably did it to earn drug money," she said. "That's what her friend, Amy, thought." With that, she stood up and walked to the fireplace, turning her back to the flames, feeling the heat against the back of her legs. "When Nadia came home, did she ever talk about what she'd been doing in the Twin Cities, ever mention any names?"

The Vaughns shook their heads. "Nothing," the mother said. "Never. We tried to probe once or twice, but she wouldn't say anything. She'd just go to her room, shut the door, and turn on the stereo."

"Did she leave any kind of note, before she . . ."

The couple exchanged glances. "A brief one," Mrs. Vaughn said, her eyes welling. "It simply said that she was sorry and ashamed, and that she loved us. That was all."

"So you have no idea why she did this?"

"None," Mr. Vaughn said. "When she came back home, we thought there might be a chance that we could begin again somehow. But then she was gone . . . for good."

Maggie returned to her chair. "Would you mind terribly if I looked in her room? To see if she may have left anything that might help us?"

Mr. Vaughn heaved a deep sigh. "Except to pick out clothes for her funeral," he said, "we haven't been in the room. Neither of us is ready for that yet. The aunt I spoke of, the one from Green Bay, is coming down next week to help us sort things out . . . give away what we don't want to keep."

"I won't disturb anything," Maggie said. "Or, obviously, take anything without your permission."

After a whispered consultation, the couple agreed, and Mrs. Vaughn led her back to the front of the house, up the curved staircase to the second floor, and down the hall to the closed door of Nadia's room.

"We'll wait downstairs for you," she said, quickly retracing her steps before Maggie could open the door.

She wasn't sure what she expected to find, but it wasn't this. The room was practically bare, devoid of anything you'd guess a teenage girl might possess or treasure. There were no pictures or posters or dolls or stuffed animals, save one: A small, scruffy teddy bear that sat at the head of the bed, resting peacefully against the covered pillow. One of its glass eyes was missing, and Maggie couldn't escape the feeling that the other was watching her every move.

There were no knickknacks, no memorabilia, no apparent memories at all. Like the downstairs, the room looked as if it had never been lived in.

Closing the door behind her, she walked to the center of the room. In addition to the bed, there was a cherry dresser and a matching desk and bedside stand that housed a stereo receiver and tape player. The tapes, perhaps two dozen of them, were stacked on one of the lower shelves.

Opening the closet, she found on one side a grouping of blouses, slacks, and skirts, all carefully pressed, hanging neatly. On the other side, shelves filled with sweaters and sweats, more slacks and jeans, all nicely stacked and looking as though they'd never been touched.

The drawers of the dresser were just as tidily organized. Underwear in one drawer, socks and pantyhose in another, pajamas and nighties in a third. Maggie picked through them all, feeling more than a little odd doing so, but found nothing that could be of any help to her. Nor did the desk drawers reveal anything of interest.

Only as she was about to leave the room did Maggie think to look beneath the bed. The satchel was pushed to a far corner, requiring her to lay flat on her stomach to reach it: an old Northwest Airlines bag, dirty and battered with a broken zipper. She hoisted herself up and put the satchel on the desk, finally working the stuck zipper loose. Inside she found a T-shirt and a pair of dirty shorts, a bra and panties, a toothbrush, and a tube of toothpaste, squeezed dry. Beneath those items, several crumpled sheets of paper. Two of them were rough drafts of the simple note Nadia had written to Penny's parents weeks before. Poor thing, she thought, she had to practice to get it right. And still didn't. A third sheet listed several names and one address. None of the names meant anything to her, except one.

Butch. No last name, but at least an initial. Butch H.

Maggie waited until she reached the airport to make the telephone call. She caught Jessica at her desk, and after quickly describing her visit to the Vaughn home, revealed what she had found in the old flight bag. "One of the names on the paper was a Butch, last initial, '*H*,'" she said. "It might be the guy we're looking for."

"That could help, but I don't know," Jessica said. "Anything else?"

Maggie quickly ran down the other four names on the list and the one street address. "They mean nothing to me," she said. "But they're certainly worth a check."

"For sure," Jessica replied. "I should know something by the time you get back here. When does your flight leave?"

"In an hour."

"Good. Brett wants to talk to you. Hang on."

A moment later, she heard Brett's voice. "I probably shouldn't be telling you this now," he said, "but you got another one of those phone calls."

"What?"

"The electronic voice. He called again."

She shuddered, hearing the voice all over again. "When?"

"An hour or so ago. I've got it on tape."

"What did he say?" she demanded.

"Not much. Insisted on speaking to you. Got pissed off when I said you weren't available. He hung up when I pressed him for his name."

"You think it was a man?" she asked. "I couldn't tell."

"Sounded that way to me, but there was a lot of static."

Maggie slumped against the wall next to the phone, fighting off a sudden chill. "What else did he say?" she asked, trying to keep her voice calm. She could sense his hesitation on the other end. "Brett?"

"He said to give you a message."

She pressed the phone tighter to her ear. "What message?"

Another pause, then, "He said he's starting a fan club. Wonders if you'll autograph the picture he sent. Then he laughed."

My God, she thought, won't they ever stop?

"They're playing mind games, Maggie. Pure and simple."

"Maybe so, but it means they're still in town, they haven't given up."

"Did you think they had?" he asked.

"You can always hope."

"Forget about it for now," he urged. "I'll see you here at the airport."

"Check on Danny, will you? Make sure he's okay."

"I already have. He's fine. Just take it easy."

On the flight back to Minneapolis, Maggie closed her eyes, hoping to nap, but her mind was fully awake, grappling both with the implications of the latest phone call and the lingering thoughts of the Vaughns sitting alone in their funeral chapel of a home.

What was the purpose of the call? Simply to keep her on edge, she guessed. To let her know she had not been forgotten, that the threat remained, whatever its purpose. Playing mind games, as Brett said. Could they possibly know, Maggie wondered, that we're making progress, getting closer? But how? Could Amy Boyd have said something to someone? Did one of her boyfriends talk? Possible, but not likely. Maybe McQueen, the cop, or someone in the newsroom? Even more unlikely.

No, she decided, chances are that the timing of the call was accidental, an out-of-the-blue attempt to keep the pressure on, to keep her thinking, worrying.

In that, at least, they were succeeding.

As for the Vaughns, well, she had mixed feelings. She had left the house as quickly as possible after discovering the flight bag and the papers, despite the Vaughn's efforts to get her to stay a while longer. She blamed an early flight, but the truth was she was suffocating in the silence and the sorrow. She could understand the trauma of their loss, and sympathize with it, but was uncomfortable with their apparent decision to quietly wallow in it. Both said they had taken leaves of absence from their teaching jobs and had made no plans for the future. From what Maggie could tell, they were intent on sitting in their silent, well-ordered house, grieving.

She could only wish them well and hope that they would come to grips with their loss and get on with their lives. She had promised to stay in touch, to let them know the outcome of the investigation, but she made no guess as to when that might be.

Brett was at the gate when Maggie emerged from the jetway. Smiling, he grabbed her briefcase and began leading her down the long concourse. "Welcome home," he said. "Everything okay?"

"I guess so," she said, and then quickly described her meeting with the Vaughns. "It was kind of spooky, actually. I was happy to get away."

Brett told her that Jessica had briefed him on what Maggie had found in the flight bag.

"Has she tracked down any of those names?" she asked.

"Not by the time I left, but she was hard at it. The old computer was smokin'."

Maggie laughed. "And no more phone calls, I hope."

Brett shook his head. "No, just the one. I've got the tape in the car. You can listen to it on the way to the station."

"I'm not sure I want to hear it," she said grimly. "It'll just make me jumpier."

As they walked through the parking ramp to the car, Brett said, "We just added one of those caller ID gadgets to your phone. We should have done it before, but now, at least, we'll know where the next call comes from . . . if there is a next call."

Before she could reply, the cellular phone in Brett's pocket buzzed. "Yes," he said as he put the phone to his ear. He listened for a moment, then said, "I'll tell her."

Maggie looked at him expectantly.

"That was Jessica," he said. "She said to tell you she may have hit the jackpot."

23

Sissy was pissed. And slightly worried. Tony had left the motel more than two hours before to make the telephone call and was still not back. It should have taken him no more than an hour, unless he had run into trouble or was just fucking off. Either way, it left her agitated.

Sitting at the bar in the motel's dingy lounge, she sipped a ginger ale and listened to a Randy Travis tune on the jukebox. She was alone except for the bartender, who was at the other end of the bar chewing on a toothpick and flipping through a *USA Today*.

She knew she should be back in the room, staying out of sight, but the walls had closed in on her again and she had had to escape. She had long since watched all of the movies on the motel system, and by now had read every magazine and book in the place. The threadbare carpeting in the room was wearing even thinner from her constant pacing. If she dared, she would have loved to sneak away and shop, but since Tony had the car, the bar was as far away as she could get. The nearest store was blocks away, and it was too damn cold to walk.

The ashtray in front of her was overflowing as she reached for yet another cigarette. She had been off the damn things for a year, but had begun to smoke again to help pass the endless hours of waiting. Her chest felt like a furnace, and the hacking cough was back. Screw it, she thought, lighting up again.

So far, she had been left pretty much alone in the bar, although two young executive types on a several-martini lunch had made a boozy, half-hearted attempt to hustle her. Her curt "Fuck off" had sent them scurrying.

She glanced again at her watch. Where the hell is he?

If anything, Tony was even itchier than she was. He prowled the room like a caged cat, growing surlier by the day. Unless he was on surveillance duty or a special mission like today's, he left the room only to get the morning paper or arrange for their take-out meals, filling the rest of his days with sleep and watching the endless string of daytime soaps and talk shows.

To Sissy's delight, his sexual appetite had diminished to almost nothing. He apparently had grown as bored with her as he had with everything else. He wanted desperately to get back to the warmth and freedom of California, but knew he didn't dare to leave before the mission was completed.

When that would be was anyone's guess. They'd heard from the General again the day before. An envelope had been left at the front desk, the clerk didn't know when or by whom, containing both their money and a typewritten letter reciting the message to be delivered to Maggie by phone. It also promised more action in the near future. "We are nearing the end of this endeavor," the letter said. "You have done well thus far. Be patient and be alert."

What that meant neither of them could guess. Tony still claimed not to know who their employer was or what the final objective of the mission would be. Sissy didn't fully believe him, but repeated efforts failed to shake it out of him, and they both took heart that it could soon be over.

As she looked up, the bartender put down the paper and sauntered slowly to her end of the bar. Slightly-built and balding, he wore oversized horn-rimmed glasses that seemed to slip farther down his nose with each step he took. As he approached, Sissy was tempted to reach out and push them up. "Want another ginger ale?" he asked.

"I guess so," she replied with a glance at her empty glass.

He took the glass, threw in some ice, and filled it. "You staying here?" he asked, making conversation.

"Yeah, but only for a few days."

"On business?"

"Right."

He emptied the ashtray and swabbed the top of the bar with a rag smelling of Lysol. "Where you from?"

"New York," she lied, swiveling on the bar stool, turning her back to him as she looked toward the door, hoping he'd take the hint. The last thing she needed now was idle chatter with a goddamned bartender. But he was not easily discouraged.

"I've got a brother in Queens," he said. "Works in a bakery on LaSalle Street. You know the area?"

"Afraid not," she said. "I live in Manhattan. Never been to Queens."

"Too bad. He makes great bagels. Best in the borough, he says. Even got a mention in some magazine. Scones, too. He sends us a box every year for Christmas."

Before she could marvel at his good fortune, the swinging doors to the lounge opened and Tony walked in, pausing briefly to allow his eyes to adjust to the dim light. When he saw her at the bar, he quickly moved to her side. "What are you doing down here?" he demanded in a whisper.

The bartender moved away, dragging the smelly rag along the bar as he went.

"Waiting for you," she said. "Where the fuck have you been?"

"Making the phone call. What did you think?"

"For two hours?" she said, challenging him. "Give me a break."

He looked away. "It takes time to hook up the equipment, you know."

She knew he was lying, but decided not to press him. It would just piss him off. If she had to guess, he had probably stopped at the Indian-owned casino located just a few miles from the motel. He loved to gamble and for once had plenty of money in his pocket, with nowhere to spend it. He'd better hope the General didn't find out.

"So what about the call?" she asked.

"Some guy answered her phone, but wouldn't let me talk to her. Or maybe she wasn't there, I don't know. It could have been that guy that's living with her, the tall, skinny guy. Kept asking me who I was."

"Did you give him the message?"

"Sure, but it didn't get much of a rise out of him. I don't know what's going on."

"They're protecting her, that's for sure," she said. "I wonder if she's told them about the film?"

Tony shrugged. "She must have told them something. I've yet to see her or that kid of hers alone."

By now, they were well aware of Maggie's daily routine. In the beginning, they had taken turns watching her, always from a safe distance. Taking the kid to school, leaving for work, returning home. Early on, before Tony rammed her car, she had always been alone. Not now. Never.

Tony signaled the bartender and pointed to Sissy's drink. "Give me on of those, too, will you?"

"What's next, do you think?" she asked once the bartender had poured the drink and retreated to his end of the bar.

"Got me," he said. "More pressure, I'd guess. Keep the bitch on edge."

"For what, though? I just don't get this. They're paying us two grand a week to scare her a little, to keep her on edge? It doesn't make sense."

"They must have their reasons," Tony replied vaguely. "I just wish they'd get it over with. Forget the money. I want out of this fucking place."

She knew it was futile to probe further. Tony had never told her who made the original contact with him or who had paid for the film. He claimed they were just "go-betweens" who had nothing to do with the people pulling the strings.

"Let's get out of here," he said with a final gulp of his drink. "We should be back in the room."

Sissy glanced at the clock above the bar. No wonder he wanted to leave. It was time for *Oprah*.

About the time Sissy and Tony left the bar, Nicholas Hawke was storming into George Barclay's office, not bothering to knock, slamming the door behind him. Barclay was on the phone, but quickly cut off the conversation. Hawke's anger was evident: Flushed face, reddened neck, laser eyes. What now? Barclay wondered.

"What the fuck's going on, George?" he demanded, standing stiffly by the door.

"What are you talking about?" Barclay replied.

"I just got off the phone with the chief," Hawke said. "He tells me our friend Maggie is getting blackmailed."

McQueen, the bastard.

"We don't know that," Barclay said, more defensively than he would have liked.

"Oh, yeah. What about the anonymous mail, the phone calls, the spying on her kid? I didn't know about any of that."

Shit, Barclay thought, McQueen must have spilled everything. Thank God he didn't know about the film. "We don't know what those things mean," he finally said. "There have been no money demands, no nothing."

"You don't know or you won't say?" Hawke asked, finally sliding into a chair across from Barclay. "The chief says you're stonewalling that detective of his."

"That's bullshit! We've told him everything we can."

"What haven't you told him?"

Barclay was being squeezed. "Things we think are too sensitive at the moment."

"Why haven't you told me?"

"Because there's nothing definite, nothing you can do. Maggie's getting harassed, no doubt about that. But we don't know why."

That was true as far as it went, but Hawke was clearly looking for more. "We think it could involve one of our investigations," Barclay continued, trying to choose his words carefully. "It could be a big story, and we don't want to fuck it up."

"What kind of investigation?" Hawke demanded. "Not about another one of my friends, I hope," an obvious reference to Collier's earlier exposé of the pedophile judge.

"I hope not, but I'd rather not go into details. It's still too early."

Hawke would not let him off the hook. "The chief says it has something to do with Maggie's past. He claims they're checking on some woman's police records in L.A."

"That's true," Barclay said.

"So? What about her past?"

Barclay was again torn. Hawke had a right to know, no question about that. If their places were reversed, Barclay would be asking the same questions. Still . . . he didn't fully trust the man. He had too many buddies in high places and a proven inability to keep his mouth shut, especially after a few shooters at the Club. In the end, Barclay couldn't bring himself to reveal the full truth. Not yet. "She had some trouble as a kid," he admitted. "She was a runaway, lived on the streets for a while. Has a juvenile record. It's not the most flattering image for a high-profile anchor."

"No shit!" Hawke spit out. "Our Maggie? A juvenile record?"

"Afraid so, but it was a long time ago."

"What kind of record?" Hawke asked.

"I'm not really sure," Barclay said. "Loitering, shoplifting, that kind of thing, I guess."

Hawke sat back in his chair, considering. "It would be a pity if it got out," he said, "but what the hell? She was only a kid. I think we'd survive it. You really think that's what the blackmail is about?"

Barclay simply shrugged his shoulders, not willing to lie outright. "We think they may be trying to put pressure on her so that she'll put pressure on me . . . on us . . . not to pursue the investigation. That's our theory anyway."

"Sounds flimsy to me," Hawke said, eyeing him carefully. "Who else knows about this?"

Barclay named Brett and Jessica. "We're trying to keep the circle small. The fewer people who know, the better. That's why I've been hesitant to involve you. Until we know more."

Hawke rose slowly from his chair, apparently satisfied. But he couldn't leave without the last word. "From now on, I don't want to get my information from the goddamned police chief. I want it from you. Understand? Let me judge whether it's important or not, okay?"

"If that's the way you want it," Barclay said, reminding himself at the same time that he ought to be updating his résumé.

As soon as Hawke was out the door, Barclay picked up the phone and dialed McQueen's number. "This is Barclay and you're an asshole," he said when the detective answered.

There was a pause as the words sank in. "Who are you calling an asshole?" McQueen demanded. "And what are you talking about?"

"My boss just left," Barclay said. "He's been talking to your chief. He knows the whole fucking story. I thought you were going to be discreet."

"So that's it," McQueen said with a sigh. "I'm no one-man department, you know."

"What do you mean?"

"I have to go through channels. I needed an okay upstairs to go to the L.A. cops for a records search on that woman. The chief got wind of it and put the screws to me. What the hell was I going to do?"

"Who else knows what you're doing?" Barclay asked.

"My immediate supervisor, that's it. I've kept it as quiet as I can."

Barclay settled down. "Okay, okay," he said. "What have you found?"

"Nothing yet. They said they'd get back to me as soon as they could. I may hear something tomorrow."

At that moment, Brett Jacobi stuck his head in the door. "Maggie's back from Madison, and Jessica says she's got something on the computer."

Barclay returned to the phone. "I've got to go," he said, "but keep in touch, okay?"

Then he followed Brett across the newsroom.

24

Jessica was at the computer, Maggie by her side, when Brett and Barclay came through the door of Computer Central. Barclay wasted no time or words. "What have you got?" he asked, checking the computer screen.

"Maggie got a last initial for a Butch in Madison," Jessica said, glancing over her shoulder at him. "Found it in the dead kid's room."

"What initial?"

"An '*H*,'" Jessica said, returning her gaze to the screen.

"So?" Barclay said.

"So I went back to the list of names I'd accumulated from the Bureau of Criminal Apprehension's database. Concentrated on the *H*'s. There were only four that had extensive crim/sex records in recent years. Henderson, Hendrick, Holmgren, and Hustad. But just two of them—Hendrick and Holmgren—had any convictions dealing with child pornography. The other two had been sent up for rape and indecent exposure."

She hit a button on the keyboard and the name of John Hendrick appeared on the upper left of the screen, followed by a long list of information running below it.

"What's all that?" Barclay asked, as unfamiliar with the appearance of the data on the computer readout as Maggie had been. "It's gobbledygook to me."

"Hendrick's criminal history," Jessica said, with a touch of triumph in her voice. "Fresh from the BCA's database." She reached to the side of the desk and handed Barclay a long roll of paper. "I've already printed it out for you," she said.

Barclay studied it, with Maggie and Brett peering over his shoulder. "I thought we were looking for a Butch," he said.

"His nickname," Jessica said. "That's why the computer didn't spit it out before. It doesn't deal in nicknames."

Barclay held up the printout. "Translate this, will you?"

"In a minute," she said as she handed him another length of paper. "This is from the Corrections Department's database, listing anybody who has served time in one of the state prisons over many, many years. Our friend Mr. Hendrick is among them, too."

Barclay laid both printouts on the desk, puzzling over them. "What was he in for?"

"He served almost ten years on a variety of crim/sex charges, including two for possession and distribution of child pornography. The last one was twelve years ago, and he's been out of prison for nine. Clean since then."

Barclay pulled up a chair next to the computer. "You said you found his name in one of your earlier searches?"

"Sure, but it was one of dozens. It didn't mean anything then. Didn't match up with the names on any of the other lists I was trying to match . . ."

"I'm still not following you," Barclay said impatiently. "What other lists?"

Jessica gave him an exasperated look. "How easily you forget, George. Because the original rumors dealt with some unnamed public official, I've been searching every public source I could find for the names of politicians, campaign officials, legislative staffs, state and county office rosters, corporate bigwigs. That's what I've been doing for the last few weeks, putting a master list together and trying to find a match with the criminal data."

"Okay," Barclay said, "I think I'm with you now."

Jessica went on. "Nothing matched up under the name Hendrick, but then I checked the local Hennepin county records, which unlike the BCA and the Corrections Department does list the known aliases of convicted felons. Lo and behold, I discovered that one of Hendrick's aliases was John Hemrick, H-E-M-R-I-C-K. When I tried to match that name to my other list, bells started to ring."

"What bells?"

"Figurative bells, George. There's a John Hemrick who works for Martin Duggan."

"The attorney general?" Barclay said, amazed. "C'mon, not Marty."

"He's listed as a campaign aide. But I'm told he's kind of Duggan's personal errand boy. Political point man."

"You're sure it's the same guy? This Hendrick?"

Jessica smiled slightly. "Not positive, but when I called the AG's office and asked for Butch Hemrick, they told me he wasn't there, but at the campaign office."

"Christ Almighty," Barclay muttered as he slumped back in the chair.

Until now, Maggie and Brett had remained silent, as engrossed in Jessica's recitation as was Barclay. But Maggie finally spoke up. "Duggan has to know that the guy has a criminal record. They must do background checks there, of all places."

"You'd think so," Jessica said. "But he is using an alias."

"So what does it mean?" Brett asked.

Jessica got up and stretched. "It may be too early to tell," she said. "But it certainly seems strange. The first thing we have to do is to make absolutely sure that this is the same Butch that Amy and Nadia were talking about, the one involved in making the films. Then, it seems to me, we have to see if Duggan himself has any connection to it . . . or if Hendrick is a rogue working on his own, or for somebody else."

"Duggan can't be involved," Barclay said. "He's tough, but he's Mr. Clean, for Christ's sake."

Martin Duggan was in his third term as attorney general, a highly successful criminal attorney at one of the Twin Cities' leading law firms who had given up his law practice ten years before to campaign for attorney general. A staunch Republican in a largely Democratic state, he had said at the time, "I want to give something back to the public. The state has been wonderful to me and my family, and it's time I repay the debt."

Buoyed by his impeccable record and large infusions of his own cash, he was easily elected on his first try, then reelected by ever larger margins twice more. There had even been talk of a possible bid for governor in the next election, two years away.

Maggie asked Jessica, "Was he one of those that you'd heard whispers about?"

"No, not a peep," she said. "That's what's so surprising."

"There must be some mistake," Barclay said. "Shit, I've even been to a couple of press parties at Duggan's house. He's got a beautiful wife, a couple of grown kids. He's so clean he shines."

Jessica shrugged. "Maybe so, but he may have an ex-felon, a child pornographer, working for him. And he's the chief law enforcement officer of the state. Explain that."

Barclay made no response, but immediately thought of Alex Collier's investigation of several years before—when he exposed as a vicious pedophile the chief judge of Hennepin County on the eve of his elevation to the state supreme court. Could it be possible? That another high-ranking state official was involved in something similar?

"Let's get Collier in here," he said.

"Collier?" Brett said. "Why?"

"Just get him," Barclay ordered.

Brett left the office and a few minutes later returned with the anchorman in tow, looking mystified. "What's going on?" he asked, glancing at the others in the office.

"Grab a seat," Barclay said.

Collier did as he was asked. "Whatever it is, I didn't do it," he said with a smile.

Barclay leaned back in his chair, in no mood for jokes. "Think back," he said. "When you bagged Judge Steele, was there any talk then, rumors even, of any other government official involved in his little games?"

"Directly involved?" Collier asked. "No, but—"

"But what?" Barclay pressed.

"Don't you remember? We kept hearing rumors about a child porn ring, but we couldn't connect them to Steele and never had time to pin them down further. Then they died away. We never could get a handle on it."

"Did Martin Duggan's name ever come up?"

"The AG?" There was no hiding the surprise in his voice. "No, not a whisper." He surveyed the circle of faces around him. "Are you telling me Duggan is looking dirty?"

"We don't know yet," Barclay said hurriedly. "But one of his aides may be."

Collier let out a low whistle. "I do know Duggan was one of the judge's friends," he said, "but so were a whole lot of other people in high places."

"So how do we prove this Hemrick is the right Butch?" Maggie asked.

"If he's that close to Duggan," Brett said, "we must have tape of him somewhere in the library. At least we can find out what he looks like."

Brett volunteered to talk to Mike Overby, the station's veteran state capitol reporter, to help track the tape and find out more about Butch Hemrick. "Mike must know the guy," Brett said. "He spends every day at the capitol."

"Be careful what you tell him," Jessica urged. "Everybody's so tight over there they squeak."

"Don't worry, I know."

Barclay got up to leave. "Anything else?" he asked.

"Yeah," Jessica said. "The address Maggie found in Nadia's flight bag."

"What about it?"

"I haven't had a chance to trace the ownership through the city and county records," she said, "but I know that this part of France Avenue happens to be in Edina. Remember Edina?"

"Let me take that one," Maggie said. "I can drive out for a look after the early show."

"Not without me," Brett said. "If George here can get somebody else to produce the late show."

"I'll take care of it," Barclay said as he made his way to the door. "And you take care of yourselves."

The first snow of the season began to fall as they drove the station's van out of the basement garage and onto the street. The flurries of tiny flakes, more like sleet than snow, actually, were caught in the van's headlights—glistening, diamond-like—for an instant before disappearing into the darkness.

"Say hello to winter," Brett said, flicking on the heater and the wipers.

"I'd rather not," Maggie replied, sighing. She knew it would be coming sooner or later, but still, the prospect of five or six months of snow and sometimes bitter cold, of short, dark days, was distressing. It must be her California bones, she decided, or maybe her warm California blood, but she simply could not abide winter like the Minnesota natives. Many of them, Brett included, seemed to savor it, the harsher the better, as some kind of test of their human spirit, of their will to survive the worst that nature could deliver.

Even Danny had fallen in love with winter, and he was no native. He could hardly wait for the snow and all that came with it: the sliding and skating, and the skiing that Brett had begun to teach him the year before. If she was to continue to live here and enjoy it, Maggie knew that she would have to change. The weather certainly wouldn't.

"We may get two or three inches tonight," Brett said with a touch of anticipation.

"I heard," she said tiredly. "And it's not even Halloween yet."

"Don't worry, it'll melt. It's too early for the snow to stick."

They swung onto the freeway and headed for the exit at 46th street, which would take them through south Minneapolis and into suburban Edina. They weren't that far from Maggie's apartment, but there would be no time to stop.

"Speaking of Halloween," Brett said. "What do you plan to do?"

"Danny's already asking about a costume. Wants to go as Superman. I suppose I'll have to take him around, trick-or-treating."

"That could be a little dangerous," he said.

"On Halloween? Not likely. And remember, you once told me I can't keep him in a closet."

Ten minutes later, they were at the intersection of 50th and France, a bustling shopping hub of upscale shops and trendy restaurants. But few people were on the streets braving the weather. "It's a couple of blocks this way," Brett said, pointing south.

The snow came harder and the bright lights of the shopping area disappeared, making it difficult to see the buildings along the street. Brett slowed the van as both peered into the darkness. "It must be right about here," he said, pulling up to the curb. They sat quietly for a moment, listening to the hum of the heater and the swishing of the wipers. "You stay here," Brett said, opening the van door, "while I look around."

"No way," Maggie said. "I'm coming, too."

They locked the doors of the van and stepped along the sidewalk, pulling their collars up to shield their faces from the wind-driven snow. When they drew closer to the entrance of the building, they could see the address: 5206. "This is the place," Brett said.

A five-story brick building with a darkened entryway. Finding the double doors locked, Brett pressed his face against the glass, staring into a small, dimly-lit lobby. Two elevators were to the right, next to a small security desk that was now unmanned. "Just an ordinary office building," he said, turning to Maggie—who was huddled in a corner, escaping the snow.

"Let me look," she said, joining him at the door.

As they both stared into the lobby, a voice suddenly

sounded in the darkness behind them. "Can I help you folks?"

By reflex, Maggie grabbed Brett's arm as both turned. They faced a broad-shouldered man in a parka, his features all but hidden beneath the parka's hood. "Nasty night to be out," he said. "The building's all locked up. Everybody but the cleaning people have gone home."

"Who are you?" Brett asked, straining to get a better look at his face.

"Building security," the man said. "Making my rounds. Is that your van there?"

"Yeah," Brett said.

"You're from Channel Seven?"

The station decals on the side of the van were unmistakable. "Right," Brett said, kicking himself for not using one of their own cars. Stupid move, but too late to correct it now. "We're looking for a video production house. We were told they had offices here."

"What's the name?" the guard asked, making no effort to remove the hood or to step into what little light there was.

"We don't know," Brett admitted. "We were just given the address. We thought they might do some work for us."

Maggie stood behind Brett, saying nothing, averting her face, hoping she would not be recognized.

"There are a lot of offices here," the guard said. "I don't know what they all do."

"Is there a building register in the lobby?" Brett asked. "I hate to have come all this way for nothing."

"Sorry," he said, "I can't let anybody in now. You'll have to come back tomorrow."

Brett decided to take a flyer. "Butch isn't around then?"

There was a slight pause, a few seconds too long. Then, "I'm afraid I don't know any Butch. Sorry."

When it became clear nothing more would be accomplished, Maggie pulled on Brett's arm. "Let's go," she whispered. "I'm freezing and this is creepy."

As they walked toward the van, they heard the guard through the darkness. "Now you all have a nice night, hear?"

It took only a few seconds for the wipers to clear the windshield. The guard still stood by the front entrance, watching as the van pulled out into the street.

"What did you make of that?" Brett asked.

"Just what I said, it was creepy. I never could get a look at the guy's face."

The snow was melting almost as fast as it fell, turning the street to slush.

"Did you notice the pregnant pause when I asked about Butch?"

"Yeah," she said, "but that could mean anything."

Brett drove without speaking for several minutes, navigating the rutted roads, retracing their steps back to the freeway and then on toward the station. Finally, he said, "Well, one thing's certain. If there is a Butch, and if he has something going in that building, he'll sure as hell hear that somebody from Channel Seven was there poking around."

"I'm not sure that's good," Maggie said. "I mean, maybe it's too early."

Brett shrugged. "You may be right, but let's hope not."

25

It was well after midnight when the telephone rang, reverberating like a rifle shot through the quiet, darkened apartment. Maggie was brought out of a deep sleep, momentarily confused and disoriented, not knowing for a split second if she was awake or dreaming. She reached for the bedside lamp and the phone at the same time, snatching up the receiver before it could ring again.

"Yes," she said, still groping for the lamp switch.

"Maggie?"

"Yes. Who's this?"

She heard the door of Brett's bedroom open down the hall just as she found the switch, lighting the bedroom.

"Amy Boyd," the voice said. "Did I wake you up?"

"Amy? No, no," she lied, shaking the sleep off. "I was still up."

Brett knocked lightly on her bedroom door, then pushed it open. Bare-chested with drooping sweatpants, he appeared both groggy and puzzled. Maggie waved him in, then returned to the phone. "Amy? Are you still there?"

The girl's voice was hesitant, hushed. "Nadia's dead."

Maggie was caught by surprise, and it took her a moment to respond. "I know," she finally said. "I was trying to reach you. Did you talk to your mother?"

"No," Amy said. "I just heard about it. She committed suicide."

"I know. I saw her parents."

"You did?"

"In Madison. She lived in Madison."

"Why did she do it?" Amy asked.

"They don't know. No one does."

She could hear Amy's quiet sobs on the other end of the line. "Amy? Could we meet again? To talk this out?"

"I don't think so," she whimpered.

"Please," Maggie said. "We may have a lead on this Butch person, the name you mentioned at the restaurant. Remember?"

"Yes."

"Did you ever see him? This Butch? It's very important."

"Maybe," she said haltingly. "But not close up."

Maggie again felt—as she had at the Burger King—that Amy was holding out on her. "We hope to get a picture of him, Amy. It would really help if you could identify him."

"You told me I wouldn't have to get involved," she said.

"It wouldn't be much. Just looking at a picture."

When there was no response, Maggie said, "For Nadia's sake. And Penny's."

Another moment of silence. Then, "I'll call you tomorrow. At the station."

Maggie put the phone down and stared off into space, thinking.

"Is she okay?" Brett asked.

"Not really," she said, repeating the side of the conversation he did not hear. "Poor kid, she sounds really scared."

"Can't blame her, suddenly discovering another of her friends is dead."

Maggie sat staring into the darkness beyond the window. The snow had stopped, but the wind continued to blow, the gusts rattling the panes. "This will sound dumb, I know," she said finally, "but I wonder if she would come live here when this is all over?"

"Amy?" Brett exclaimed. "Here? Are you serious?"

She turned to face him. "She's a lot like I was at her age, Brett. Confused, frightened. With no place to go."

"She could go home," he offered.

"Not a chance," she said. "Not now anyway."

She sat cross-legged on the bed and patted a spot next to her. "Come here," she said. "Maybe I can make you understand."

He did as she asked, not knowing what to

expect. Maggie had not had time to put on a robe, leaving her body covered by only a sheer silk gown. If she was aware of it or felt uncomfortable, she didn't show it. The same could not be said for Brett. He had trouble keeping his eyes on her face and his breathing even.

"Who knows what would have become of me," she said, "if somebody hadn't cared enough to get me off the street when I still had a chance to make something of myself."

"Who are you talking about?" Brett asked.

"That's what I'm about to tell you," she said, launching into the story of Elijah Robinson and the years she had spent with his family at Redemption House. The tale took almost half an hour, and when she'd finished, she said, "It was a safe haven. It gave me time to get my head on straight. Without Elijah, I'd probably be dead . . . or another Sissy."

"I doubt that," Brett said. "You've got too many brains, too much gumption for that to happen."

"Don't be so sure. You didn't know me then, or what it was like. I was going nowhere fast—until Elijah got me pointed in the right direction. Maybe I could do the same for Amy."

"I hope you'll think long and hard about it," Brett said as he got up to leave. "But what the hell? It's your place and your life."

Watching him walk toward the door, seeing his bare back and the sweats hugging his thin hips, she came to a sudden and surprising realization. She didn't want him to leave. Not now. She wanted him there, beside her. Touching her. She could still taste the mint of his mouth.

He turned at the door and gave her a small

smile and wave. "Hope you can get back to sleep," he said. "I'll see you in the morning."

"Wait a minute," she said.

He paused, questioning. "What?"

Careful, she told herself. Are you sure? Taking this step would mean no quick or easy retreat. She couldn't do that to Brett, not after everything he had done for her. But it was more than gratitude she was feeling now. It was real desire, for the first time in a long time. "You don't have to leave, you know," she said, finally.

"Pardon me?" he replied, puzzled.

Her eyes were on him. "I said you don't have to leave. Not if you don't want to."

He cocked his head. "You know what you're saying?"

"Uh-huh," she said as she pulled back the covers on the other side of the bed.

He glanced at the open door behind him. "What about Danny?"

"You probably should close the door," she said, smiling.

Without his eyes leaving hers, he pushed the door shut behind him. "You're sure about this?" he said, not even certain that he was.

He got his answer when she reached to turn off the light.

By the time Brett felt his way back to the bed, she had slipped under the covers and out of her gown. She found his hand in the dark and held it to her cheek, letting him feel the warmth, then moved it beneath the covers and on to her breast, cupping it there as the nipple hardened.

"My God," he whispered, his throat dry.

She lay still, savoring the sensation as his fingers began to move beneath her hand, ever so slowly and gently, tracing the soft curves so lightly as to not be there at all. She felt the cover being pulled back, his warm breath on her other breast. Then his lips. And his tongue, flicking.

God, she thought, it's been so long. I'd forgotten it could be like this.

He kissed her eyes, her cheeks, the tip of her nose, her parted lips. Their tongues met and retreated. Then met again. Circling, exploring, inside and out. The bed covers were now all of the way to her waist and his hand was on her stomach, tracing the outline of her ribs against her smooth skin.

"You have a wonderful body," he breathed. "Like I've always imagined."

"And you have wonderful hands," she whispered back. "Please don't stop."

As if acting on their own, her legs spread slightly and her back arched as his hand moved down her body, pausing here, then there. Never in a hurry, caressing, massaging. She could hear her own breath quicken, then her convulsive gasp as his fingers found the moist center of her.

She reached out for him, only then realizing he was still clothed. "Let me touch you, too," she pleaded. "Please."

He pressed his mouth to her ear. "We can't, Maggie. It's too risky. I don't have anything. I never expected—"

She pulled herself upright. "I do. Take off those sweats, and don't you dare move."

He heard her leave the bed and move to the door. The crack of light from the hallway spilled in as she slipped out. Then the bathroom door opened and closed. He pulled off his sweats and lay back on the bed, eyes closed, body trembling, still not fully believing this was actually happening. Fighting to remain calm, he could not rid himself of the fear that he would disappoint her. Spoil the chance. While he had had one or two fairly serious affairs in the years before Maggie came to the station, he certainly did not consider himself a master at the art of lovemaking. Far from it. And he had never before made love to a woman he felt this strongly about, so the prospect of possible failure haunted him.

She was back inside the room, carrying a small lighted candle, placing it on the bedside stand. Kneeling beside him on the bed. Holding him, caressing him. "Oh, yes," she murmured, slowly increasing the pressure, the speed. It was exquisite, explosive. His hand found her as well, and in seconds the room was filled with their soft moans and small cries. His fears disappeared.

Maggie's, too. Any qualms had vanished with his first gentle touch. It felt right. *He* felt right. Her hands began to move as his had, across and up and down his body, skimming the smooth skin, the flat stomach, the lean but taunt muscles, always returning to the hardness of him. Delighting in his small shudder when she did. For her, there was no shame, no second thoughts. Who ever said friends can't be lovers, too?

Then she was on top of him, slowly settling down on him. Soft and warm, enfolding him, filling her. She rocked forward. Then back. Lifting, falling. Her hair was in his eyes, her lips on his, skin warm and touching. Hips moving, thrusting. Then faster, ever faster.

Later, much as he tried, he could not recall the precise moment of climax. The final seconds were a fiery blur, unlike anything he had ever experienced before or would ever hope to experience again.

She was lying, spent, on top of him, as both breathed deeply, filling their lungs.

"Am I crushing you?" she asked softly. "Should I move?"

"No, please," he said. "Stay where you are."

He wasn't sure how long they would lie like that, but for him, it could have been forever. And while his mind was filled with the wonder of her, try as he might, he couldn't chase the wayward thoughts away. Is this what she had done in the film? No, he told himself, she said she had never touched her partners in any intimate way. Could he believe that? After what she had done to him? And what about Danny's father? Who was he and how good had he been? Better than himself? He had to be. And why did she have the contraceptive so handy? Had there been others?

Forget it, he thought. She's a grown woman and a mother, not a cloistered nun.

When the candle finally flickered out and with Maggie asleep, he rolled her gently to her side and lifted himself quietly from the bed. He kissed her softly on the cheek and made his way silently back to his own bedroom.

♦   ♦   ♦

"How did you sleep?" Maggie asked innocently as he walked into the kitchen.

"Never better," he said.

"Me too," she replied, grinning. "It was wonderful."

Aside from that small exchange, neither of them spoke of the night before as Maggie prepared breakfast and Brett readied himself for his morning run. But their shared glances and passing touches said more than words. Danny, of course, noticed nothing, intent as he was on the TV cartoons.

When Brett returned from dropping Danny off at school and his three-mile jog, Maggie was waiting, a small towel wrapped around her. "I waited to shower until you got back," she said. "You interested?"

He didn't need a second invitation.

Mike Overby was waiting impatiently at Brett's desk when he and Maggie arrived in the newsroom that afternoon. The legislature was not in session, but the governor was due to hold a news conference shortly, and Overby was eager to be on his way. "What's on your mind," he asked gruffly as Brett pulled off his coat and hung it next to the desk. "I've got to get back to Saint Paul."

"Cool your jets," Brett said. "And grab a chair."

The oldest reporter in the newsroom, Overby was pushing fifty, with graying hair and an expanding waistline. He had covered government and politics for the station for the better part of two decades, a survivor who had outlasted four news directors and more reporters and producers than he could count. He sat atop the union seniority list, which meant he'd be the last on the staff to be fired or laid off, if it ever came to that.

In short, he was untouchable . . . and not about to take guff from anyone.

"We need some information, Mike," Brett said, "but this conversation can't go beyond this desk. Deal?"

"No problem," Overby replied, looking suspicious.

While not the best on-air performer, Overby possessed an encyclopedic knowledge of state politics, including scuttlebutt on more skeletons in more closets than he'd ever admit to. He guarded his turf jealously and resented any attempt to intrude.

"Tell me what you know about John Hemrick, on the AG's staff."

"Butch? Not much to tell. He's Duggan's behind-the-scenes guy, his political runner. I never see him much, except at the conventions, working the floor."

"Did we ever get him on tape?" Brett asked.

"I suppose so. I could check the files. But why the interest?"

"I can't tell you right now."

"Why not? It's my beat."

"But it's not your story. I'll fill you in as soon as I can."

Overby's face began to redden in anger, but he held his tongue.

"What do you know about Hemrick's past?" Brett asked. "How and where did Duggan find him?"

"Damned if I know, although I heard at some point that he came from out-of-state. I've never asked, because it never seemed important to know."

"You know where he headquarters?"

"Splits his time, I think. Between Duggan's office at the capitol and the campaign office, somewhere in Edina."

"Edina?" Brett couldn't hide his surprise.

"Yeah, they opened it several years ago. I've never been there."

Brett paused to jot down some notes. He would have to check the office. Then, "What about Duggan himself?"

"What about him?" Overby asked, even more suspiciously.

Brett shrugged. "I don't know. Is he as clean as everyone claims? Any rumors about him? Skeletons rattling around?"

"Where are you going with this?" Overby demanded.

"Relax, Mike. Just answer the question, okay?"

"Is this part of the secret mission I keep hearing about?"

"What do you mean, secret mission?"

"The thing that Jessica and Maggie are involved in? The big investigation. The rumors are all over the newsroom."

Brett was caught off guard, and it took him a moment to recover. "I don't listen to rumors," he finally said. "Now what about Duggan?"

"He's a damn nice guy," Overby said. "Best AG the state's ever had, if you ask me. Even the Democrats admit to that. He's rich, but I don't hold that against him. Clean as your mother's wash, as far as I know."

Brett pressed on. "Has anybody ever really investigated him? Poked around his past?"

"This is fucking ridiculous," Overby said, rising from the chair. "I'm sure every one of his opponents has picked his bones clean and found nothing. The guy's a jewel, I'm telling you. Besides that, he's a pretty good friend of mine."

As he started to walk away, Brett called after him. "Remember our deal. No talking about this, to anybody. And I'll need that tape of Hemrick."

"You'll get it," Overby shouted back. "When I damn well feel like it."

26

When Maggie looked up from her desk, Timothy McQueen was striding across the newsroom in a hurry, coming in her direction. She got up to meet him halfway. "You're looking for me?" she asked.

"Barclay's not in," the detective said. "Is there someplace we can talk?"

Maggie led him to the Green Room and shut the door behind them. "I got a report from the L.A. cops," he said, his words rushed.

"Good," she said. "But why don't we sit and talk."

He took a chair across from her. "You were right. This Sissy, it seems, is something of a celebrity on the West Coast, in both L.A. and San Francisco, it turns out. As soon as they saw the picture, the vice cops knew who she was."

"Really?"

"Her last name, by the way, is McGowan. But she has a stage name, too. Get this: Missy Marvelous."

Maggie couldn't hold back the laugh. "No kidding?" she said, giggling despite herself. She could see the name in lights.

"She's a stripper, at least she has been for the last few years. She's got a long record, but nothing violent. Everything from prostitution to lewd and lascivious conduct, along with one bust for cocaine possession."

Maggie was not surprised, although she had never known Sissy to do drugs. At least not when she'd been with her. "Do they know where she is now?"

McQueen checked his notes. "Her last arrest was a couple of years ago, for hooking. The last anybody saw of her, she was working at a joint on the Strip. But she dropped out of sight a couple of months ago and nobody seems to know where she went, even the other women who worked at the club."

"The time frame fits," Maggie said. "Anything on the guy she's with?"

"Not a word."

"Sissy McGowan," Maggie mused, turning the name over, seeing if it felt right. Could be, she decided.

"One other thing," he said. "I'm also circulating her name, picture, and description to all of our squads. Saint Paul, too, along with the suburban departments. To pick up and hold on suspicion of stalking."

"Really? You can do that?"

"Based on what you've told me, sure. That doesn't mean we'd actually charge her, but we can sure as hell bring her in for questioning."

While Maggie held little hope of that happening, she was intrigued by the thought of seeing Sissy again, of confronting her. But what would she say? What could she prove? Not much at this point, but still, it could take some of the pressure off of her and put it on Sissy. Who knows what that might bring?

McQueen leaned forward in his chair. "Now it's your turn. Barclay said you might be ready to tell me what's really going on here. I do need to know."

She guessed this would be coming, but hesitated to say anything without Barclay's okay. But he wasn't there, and it was clear that the detective had done his part and deserved to know what he was dealing with. Still, she hesitated.

"Well?" he asked, clearly impatient.

She got up and walked to the other end of the room, deliberating. Could she do it again? Repeat the whole sordid story? It was one thing to confess to her friends, quite another to someone who was all but a stranger to her. But maybe that will make it easier, she decided. Like she was telling him a story about someone else.

"Okay," she said. "but you've got to give me your word that it will go no farther without our specific approval. Not to your boss, not to anybody. Until we say okay. Is that a deal?"

He nodded, but said nothing.

In somewhat abbreviated form, and without

embarrassment, Maggie told him of her life on the streets of L.A. and of the film she had made with Sissy. Then of the packages and the phone threats she had received. "Obviously, if the film is ever made public, my career here is over. Maybe everywhere. It would follow me."

If McQueen was shocked, he didn't show it. "You still don't know what they want?"

"Not really, but as we told you before, it may be connected with an investigation we're doing. They may be trying to pressure us to kill it."

"What's the investigation?"

"That I can't tell you," she said. "You'll have to talk to Barclay."

The detective stood up and walked to the door. "Okay. Thanks for filling me in. I'll keep working on it, and I'll let you know if there are any developments. I hope you'll do the same."

"We'll try," Maggie said, following him out.

Once McQueen was out the building, Maggie went in search of Jessica and Brett, finding Jessica camped out in the computer room. "Have you seen Brett?"

"Yeah, he left about twenty minutes ago," she said.

"Left for where?"

"For Edina. It turns out that Duggan's campaign office is in the same building that you guys went to last night. Quite a coincidence, huh?"

"Goddamn," Maggie muttered. "Did he go alone?"

"As far as I know. Unless he took a cameraman."

What's to worry about, Maggie told herself. It's broad daylight and there are bound to be plenty of people around. Still, she couldn't completely dismiss her concern.

"The property tax records show the building is owned by Pioneer Properties, a private company," Jessica said. "Appraised at two million dollars."

Maggie sat on the edge of the desk. "Who owns Pioneer Properties?"

"That's what I'm trying to figure out now," Jessica said. "The corporate ownership records on file with the state aren't accessible by computer, so I've put in a couple of calls. I should know something soon."

Maggie then quickly reported what McQueen had told her, and also a synopsis of the late-night call from Amy.

"You think you'll hear from her again?" Jessica asked.

Maggie could only shrug. "Who can say? I sure hope so."

By the light of day, Brett had no trouble finding the Edina building again. He came alone, and to avoid the mistake of the night before, drove his Explorer. He found a parking place half a block away.

Hoping the same security guard was not on duty, he approached the building boldly and then passed through the glass doors as though he had legitimate business there. If anyone asked, he had decided to say he was searching for potential office space and would like to inspect any vacancies.

Fortunately, there was no guard at the security desk, leaving the lobby to himself. He quickly made his way to the building register, searching for any name that could connote a production studio or video service. He ran his finger down the list, quickly finding the Duggan Campaign Office, but seeing nothing else of interest. There were law offices, accounting firms, a temporary service, and other companies that appeared genuine enough. Four floors and nothing suspicious.

Disappointed, he was about leave when he thought of something he had noticed the night before. To check himself, he walked back outside and stood in the street, away from the face of the building, counting the rows of windows. He was right. There were five rows of windows, but only four floors of offices. What was on the fifth floor?

Returning to the lobby, he called for the elevator. It took a couple of minutes, but then the doors opened and he stepped inside. Looking quickly, he saw there was a button for each of the four floors. But for the fifth floor, there was just a keyhole. No sign or other indication of what was there. Just the slot for the key.

"Can I help you in some way, sir?"

Brett's head snapped up. Standing in the open elevator doorway was another security guard, not as tall or as broad as the one they had encountered the night before, as polite but no friendlier.

"Maybe you can," Brett said quickly, stepping out of the elevator. "I was trying to check on available office space here. But I can't find the building manager's office."

"Rentals aren't handled from here," the guard said. "The owners have an office downtown."

"Whereabouts?"

"The Baker Building. Pioneer Properties. They're in the phone book."

Brett started to move toward the entrance. "You don't happen to know if there are any vacancies, do you?"

"No, sir. That's not part of my job."

With one hand on the door, Brett took a chance. "I couldn't help but notice that there are no offices listed on the fifth floor. Are they using that space, do you know?"

The guard seemed to stiffen. "No, sir, I don't. You'll have to check downtown."

"I'll do that. Thanks for your help."

As he walked back to the Explorer, Brett again studied the building. He couldn't be sure, but it looked as if all of the windows on the fifth floor were draped.

When he got back to the station, two things happened in quick succession. First, he got a call from Mike Overby at the capitol, saying he had found tape footage of John Hemrick, taken on the floor of the state GOP convention the year before. The video librarian, he said, should be bringing it to Brett any minute. He again pressed for more details of the investigation, but Brett put him off.

"I'm going to Barclay on this," Overby threatened. "If it involves the capitol, I should know what's happening."

"That's fine with me," Brett said. "But I doubt if you'll get anywhere."

"We'll see about that," Overby said, slamming the phone down.

Ten minutes later, Brett intercepted a call for

Maggie from Amy Boyd. "Hold on a second," he said, "I'll find her."

Amy reluctantly agreed to meet Maggie again, the next morning at the same Burger King. She promised to be on time and to try and identify the picture of Butch. "I shouldn't be doing this," she said, the fear apparent in her voice. "If they ever find out—"

"Hold on, Amy," Maggie interrupted. "Who are *they*?"

"Never mind," she said quickly. "I'll see you tomorrow."

Maggie decided it was time for a meeting. Too many things were happening with everyone going in different directions. It was time to compare notes and decide on future strategy. Barclay agreed to meet at a nearby Italian restaurant after the early news. They found a round table near the rear of the place, well away from any other customers.

After ordering, Maggie began, starting with Amy's agreement to meet the next day and then summarizing her meeting with Timothy McQueen.

"You actually told him about the film?" Barclay said. "How wise was that?"

"He promised to keep it to himself," she replied. "And besides, he's done a hell of a lot for us. He deserved to know."

Brett broke in. "What if the cops do luck out and pick up Sissy? Would we confront her? What the hell would we say?"

"She'd at least know that we're on to her," Maggie said. "Give her a scare, maybe chase her out of town. We might also get a line on the guy she's with."

Barclay said, "Let's not get ahead of ourselves. We'll face that decision when we have to. I doubt that they'll find her anyway."

Brett quickly reported on his conversation with Mike Overby. "He's pissed that he's not in on this, but he did find video of our friend, Butch." He pulled out several copies of a photograph and passed them around. "I had these stills made from the videotape."

Barclay studied the picture. "I've seen this guy before. He was at one of Duggan's press parties. I never talked to him, but I know he was there. Who could forget that face."

One glance at the photo revealed what Barclay meant. A long, deep scar reached from the corner of the man's right eye, across his cheekbone, and down to his chin.

"Jesus, that's gross," Jessica said. "I wonder how it happened?"

"Who knows?" Brett said. "Maybe in prison."

Aside from the scar, there was nothing especially unusual about Hemrick's features: narrow face, close-set eyes, a somewhat protruding chin. "If Amy really saw this guy," Maggie said, "the scar should give him away."

After their food was delivered and the waitress gone, Brett described his visit to the Edina office building, including the mystery of the fifth floor. "It may be nothing," he said, "but it would be nice to know what happens up there."

"You think it's the film studio," Barclay said.

Brett shrugged. "Why else would Nadia have kept that address? I doubt that she was working for the Duggan campaign."

Jessica asked, "So how do we find out what's there?"

"I'd like to do some van surveillance for a few days," Brett said. "See who comes and goes."

They all looked at Barclay, who would have to make the decision. "Let me think on it," he said. "I don't know if we can spare the people."

Then it was Jessica's turn. "I'm afraid I don't have much to report," she admitted. "I'm still waiting on the ownership report on the Pioneer Properties, and still trying to track down the other four names on Nadia's list. I should have it all in a day or so."

They sat quietly until Barclay finished the last of his lasagna. He wiped his chin and patted his ample stomach, clearly satisfied with the fare. Maggie wouldn't have been surprised to hear a big burp.

"I'm worried about Overby," Brett said. "He's sitting over at the capitol stewing. I know damn well he'll be bitching about this, and I'm afraid he could say something to somebody who matters."

"I'll talk to him," Barclay said as he took a final swipe with his napkin. "He'll keep his mouth shut."

Brett wished he could be as certain.

27

This time, they forgot the charade and made no effort to hide Brett's presence. He dropped Maggie off in front of the Burger King and again parked his Explorer a block away, engine idling. He had wanted to go into the restaurant with her, to meet Amy himself, but Maggie had argued against it, still afraid that Amy could be easily spooked.

Once on the sidewalk, a quick glance told her that Amy must already be inside. Her skin-headed friend was again outside, standing guard by the door, shivering without a coat. He barely glanced at her as she walked past, but she heard him mutter, "Fuckin' hurry up, okay?"

Amy was sitting at the same table, from a

distance looking no different than she had before. She wore the same fatigue jacket, the same baseball cap, its bill straight now. Her other friend, the one with hair to his shoulders, was occupying the same seat at the other end of the restaurant.

It was as if no time had passed since their last visit.

Maggie walked to her table, but before sitting, she asked, "May I get you and your friends something?"

"No, we're okay," Amy said. "But I could use some more food money."

Maggie slipped into her chair. "Let's see how far we get first, okay?"

Amy shrugged. "Whatever."

On closer examination, she appeared even thinner now than before. What's more, dark circles had formed beneath her eyes and she was fighting a persistent cough. She looked as though she hadn't slept in days. "Are you okay?" Maggie asked.

"I'm fine," she replied, without much conviction. "I think I'm getting a cold."

More likely pneumonia, the way it appeared. Maggie guessed the worsening weather must be getting to her. Squatting in summer is one thing, in winter something else. "Do you have a roof over your head?" she asked.

"Some nights. But I move around."

"How about a coat? Something besides that?"

Amy glanced down at her thin fatigue jacket. "Not yet," she said, "but I'll get one."

Maggie got up and walked to the counter, ordering four hot chocolates. She carried one to each of

Amy's companions, who grunted their thanks, and brought two cups back to the table. "This should help you warm up," she said.

Amy nodded and sipped the cocoa, blowing on it to cool it. "Tell me about Nadia," she finally said.

Maggie quickly reported on her visit to Nadia's parents and on what she had learned about Nadia's death.

"She slit her wrists?" Amy asked, grimacing.

Maggie nodded sadly. "In the bathtub. She left a short note, saying she was ashamed and sorry."

Without warning, Amy began to weep, the tears sliding, unchecked, down her cheeks. Maggie tried to ignore them. "I also found a scrap of paper," she said. "That Nadia left. It had several names and addresses on it. Butch was one of those names." She pulled a picture from her purse, one of those Brett had made from the videotape, and put it on the table in front of Amy. "Is this the man you saw? The one you think was called Butch?"

She wiped the tears away with her sleeve and held the photo close. Then she looked away. Maggie thought she detected a slight shudder in the slender body. "Is it?" she asked again.

"I think so," Amy murmured.

"You *think* so?" Maggie pressed.

The girl sat speechless for several seconds. Then, fixing her gaze on Maggie, she said, more firmly, "I'm sure. That's him. It's the scar."

"Good," Maggie said. "How close did you get to him?"

Amy again said nothing, glancing over her shoulder, as if planning an escape. It was then the truth suddenly dawned on Maggie. She took a deep breath. "You were in the movies, too, weren't you, Amy? That's it, isn't it? That's why you're so afraid! Look at me. Please."

Amy turned to her. The tears were gone now, replaced by an expression that was a mixture of shame and defiance. "I only did one. Just one. He tried to get me to do the second one, but I told him to fuck off. But Penny and Nadia didn't. They said they needed the money for their goddamned smack."

Maggie sat back, waiting.

"They would have been all right," she continued. "But something happened."

Maggie straightened up. "What happened?"

Amy began to sob. Short, painful bursts. "In the second film. One of the other kids, a little girl, only twelve or thirteen, got hurt real bad."

Maggie reached across the table and touched her hand. "Take it, easy, Amy. You're okay." And then, "This girl, how did she get hurt?"

"She started to bleed, hemorrhaging, you know, down here, between her legs. She almost died."

Maggie closed her eyes in disbelief. "Penny told you this?"

"No, Nadia. After Penny was killed, and just before she took off. She was so ashamed. She said she would never forget that little girl, how scared and hurt she was."

"What happened to her," Maggie asked. "The girl, I mean."

"Nadia wasn't sure. I guess they had their own doctor treat her or something. And they must have paid off the girl's parents. I don't know about that."

"Do you know her name?"

Amy shook her head. "Nadia never told me, and I never saw her. I just heard what happened."

My God, Maggie thought, can this be true? In this city, in this day and age? Baby rapers? Butchers? It had to be. Why would Amy lie to her? Why would Nadia lie to Amy? No question, her tears and her fears were real. And her two friends were dead.

She waited until Amy's sobs subsided, then asked, "Were they afraid Penny would talk?"

"Nadia thought they might have caught her trying to steal a copy of the tape to take to the cops. That's what she told Nadia she was going to try to do."

"And Nadia thought she might be next," Maggie suggested.

Amy nodded. "I guess that's why she told everyone, even me, that she was going to California when she really wasn't. She just wanted to disappear."

As Maggie glanced up, she saw the boy from the back of the restaurant walking toward them. "You okay?" he asked Amy when he reached the table.

"Yeah," she said. "I'll just be a minute."

The boy retreated to another table a several feet away, but out of earshot.

"Who else knows about this?" Maggie asked. "What you've just told me?"

"Nobody, not even them," Amy said with a gesture toward her friends. "They just know I need looking after."

"We've got to get you to the police," Maggie said. "They have to know about this."

"Yeah, like they're going to believe some

fucking street kid with rings in her nose. Anyway, all I know is what Nadia told me, and she's dead. I have no other proof."

"But you were in one of the movies," Maggie argued.

"The cops don't have the movie. They'd just have my word. And if it ever gets out that I went to the cops, I'd end up just like Penny."

"They would protect you," Maggie countered. "And if they don't, we would."

"I can't," she whispered. "My folks would die if they ever found out."

Maggie got up and came around the table, pulling a chair close to the girl. "You can't just walk away from this. They could do it again. They may be doing it now, for all we know. You've got to help us stop them."

Amy buried her head in her hands.

"Your folks may never need to know. And if they do find out, I'll help you deal with them. You won't be alone, I promise."

The girl didn't move. Maggie debated, then said, "This may not mean much to you Amy, but I was once on the streets just like you are. In Los Angeles, many years ago. For months, living like you're living, squatting, scavenging, doing whatever I had to do to stay on the run. I even made a film, not unlike the one you made."

Amy's head shot up, eyes wide.

"It's true, only I was about the youngest kid in it. I'm still carrying the guilt, but I got past it somehow, got on with my life. But I might never have gotten off the streets if someone hadn't pulled me off. It's not too late for you."

Amy got up out of the chair. "I have to think about this. I don't know what to do."

"Call me, Amy. Please. Let me know where you are." Maggie quickly scribbled her address on the back of one of her business cards. "You can come stay with me if you'd like," she said, handing her the card. "I have the room, and you'd be safe there."

Amy paused to take the card and then started for the door, her friend behind her.

"Wait," Maggie said. She got up and took off her coat, a new and expensive car coat that she just bought weeks before. "Take this, please. It's warm and there's money in the pocket. Take care of yourself and get well."

She held out the coat, and after a moment's hesitation, the girl walked back to take it. "Thanks," she said. "I'll let you know."

Barclay's office was crowded, and the atmosphere was tense.

"We've got to call McQueen," Maggie argued, her voice a notch below a shout. "The cops have got to know about this."

"Not so fast," Barclay replied, "and cool down."

"Maggie's right," Jessica said, stepping forward. "This has gone beyond a news story."

"Sit down, all of you," Barclay ordered.

Maggie and Jessica dropped into chairs across from his desk, and Brett settled on the window ledge. "Let's think about this rationally," Barclay continued. "This Amy is right. All we have is her word and the word of two dead girls that this Butch is involved in the films and that some young kid got badly hurt in the process. We don't have the films, we don't have other eye witnesses, we don't know who the little girl is. What the hell are we going to tell McQueen . . . and even if we do tell him, what is he going to do?"

"He could provide some protection for Amy," Maggie responded, still angry. "She's alone out on the streets, facing who knows what."

"Would she be better off with protection?" Barclay asked. "Seriously? From what you say, nobody aside from you, and now us, knows what she knows. It seems to me that she's almost safer this way, at least until we know more."

Brett spoke for the first time. "He could be right, Maggie. We'll need more before the cops are going to do anything."

Maggie scowled. "So how are we going to do that? And when? I don't know how long Amy's going to stick around. She's scared stiff."

"I've got a couple of ideas," Brett said.

All eyes turned to him.

"Remember the other night, Maggie, when the security guard at that building told us nobody was there but the cleaning people?"

She nodded. "I guess so."

"Let's find out which cleaning company does the work there," Brett continued. "Then see if we can get somebody to go to work for them. Get inside the place, maybe up to the fifth floor. Those companies are always looking for new janitors."

"Why not the guard company, too?" Maggie offered.

"Not bad," Barclay admitted. "But who do we get inside?"

"Let me try to figure that out," Brett said.

Jessica got up and passed a sheet of paper to each of them. "I finally got the ownership information on the building," she said. "This is a roster of the board members of Pioneer Properties."

Each of them studied the list of names, but they recognized none of them. "I didn't either," Jessica said. "But my computer did. The third name on the list, Anthony Higgins, happens to be the finance director of Martin Duggan's campaign. That's why the campaign office is in that building, I'd guess."

"Fine, but where does that get us?" Barclay asked impatiently.

Jessica shrugged. "Just ties it that much closer to Duggan himself, I suppose. He could even be a hidden owner, for all I know. It wouldn't be that unusual in a privately held company like this."

Barclay got up and walked to the door, a clear signal the meeting was about over. "One more thing," he said. "I've okayed the use of the surveillance van for two days. Brett can arrange the staffing."

"Only two days?" Brett protested.

"I'm already up to my ass in overtime," Barclay said. "That'll have to do for now."

Across the river in St. Paul, capitol reporter Mike Overby wandered into the offices of Attorney General Martin Duggan. It was not unusual to find Overby there; he tried to visit each of the state offices at least once a day when the legislature was not in session, searching for story ideas or the latest tidbit of political gossip.

But now he was on a special mission.

He hated to get beat on any story—by the news-papers or, especially, by one of the other TV stations. Even worse, by his own station. Assholes. The only way to avoid it, he knew, was to make the regular rounds and check his trusted sources.

No one in Duggan's office paid him particular heed as he stopped by the desk of receptionist Carol Peters, who was busy on the phone. He waited patiently until she was finished, spending the minutes scanning the material on her desk upside down. It was amazing how many good sto-ries he had discovered that way over the years, but today he saw nothing of interest.

"Hey, Michael," the receptionist said. "What's up?"

"That's my line," he replied with a grin. "Anything new around here?"

"Not that I know of," she said, "but hell, I just answer the phones."

"Is Stringer around?" Brian Stringer was Duggan's press secretary, a former wire service reporter who was another of Overby's close friends.

"Should be in his office," she said as she answered yet another call. "Feel free."

Walking past her desk and out of the reception area, Overby made his way back through the maze of the attorney general's complex, finding Stringer in his small office, hunched over his computer. "Hey, flack, how's it going?" he said.

Stringer looked up. "Not now, Mike. I'm busy putting words of wisdom into Mr. Duggan's mouth."

"I'll bet they're real pearls," Overby said as he took a chair next to Stringer's desk.

"I'm serious. I have to finish this speech. I don't have time to bullshit."

"Neither do I," Overby said. "I'll just take a minute."

Stringer growled an expletive, but punched a couple of buttons on the computer to save what he was writing and turned to face Overby. "What do you need?"

Stringer still wore the crewcut the Marines had first given him thirty years before, and which he had never bothered to let grow out. It was brushed up straight and stiff, held that way by a dab of butch wax. His face, like his body, was thin, the skin sallow, as though it rarely saw the light of day. His fingers were stained yellow from too many years of smoking, another vestige of the Marines he had never discarded.

"We're old friends, right?" Overby said. "You can talk to me off-the-record."

"What are you getting at?" Stringer asked suspiciously.

Overby paused a moment, then asked, "Is something going on around here? Something hush-hush, something I should know about?"

Stringer was clearly puzzled. "What the hell are you talking about?"

"I don't really know, but I got a whiff of something, and it doesn't smell good."

"You're smelling your own farts." He laughed. "Nothing's going on here, except for the usual crap."

"Duggan's not in some kind of trouble?"

Stringer suddenly got serious. "Is this on the level? You've actually heard something? Like what?"

"I told you, I don't know. I thought you might."

Stringer shook his head. "Nothing, and I'm being straight with you."

"Okay," Overby said, getting up. "That's good enough for me. Get back to your words of wisdom."

"Let me know if you hear anything more," Stringer said.

Overby was out the office door, but then stuck his head back in. "I forgot," he said casually, "but do you have a bio on John Hemrick? The newsroom is asking for one."

"On Hemrick? Why?"

Overby shrugged his shoulders. "Got me. They must be planning for the conventions or something."

"I don't have one," Stringer said. "But I'll ask Butch. He should."

"Don't bother," Overby said quickly. "I'll call him myself."

Stringer waited a few minutes, then put a call in to Carol Peters, the receptionist. "Has Overby left yet?" he asked.

"He just walked out. Want me to try to catch him?"

"No, no," he said. "That's okay."

He knew Mike Overby well enough to know that something was brewing. He didn't ask those kinds of questions without a reason. And Stringer was paid to not only put words in Martin Duggan's mouth, but to spoon-feed him any information that was potentially important.

Stringer logged off his computer and went in search of the man himself, the attorney general.

28

Martin Duggan was not a man to fuck with. Brian Stringer knew that as well as anyone, having served as his press secretary for the past six years. Duggan didn't like problems, and was quick to jump on the unlucky messenger who happened to place one in his lap. Stringer knew that, too, and approached the AG's office with more than a little trepidation.

By any measure, Duggan was a towering figure. Large of stature with an IQ to match, his stentorian voice, rugged good looks, and cocksure attitude made him a dominating presence wherever he went, the kind of man who could turn heads and quiet a crowd whenever he entered a room, the kind of lawyer who could intimidate almost any jury he would ever face. To say nothing of opposing lawyers.

Although he had gained a few pounds since his days as a University of Minnesota linebacker in the Gopher glory years of the early sixties, his six-foot-three frame carried the extra weight well. He took great pride in his body, religiously working out at the health club three times a week, and could still outlift and outrun other men many years younger. At the office, he seldom wore a suit or sports jacket, the better to allow an appropriate display of his bulked-up muscles and trim waist beneath his shirt. It was not unheard of to catch him unaware, posing as a bodybuilder would in front of a mirror that dominated one wall of his office.

When Stringer found him, he was slipping into his topcoat, ready to leave for the day. Stringer knocked lightly on the doorjamb and nervously stepped just inside the office. "Can I grab you for a minute before you take off?" he asked.

Duggan glowered at him. "Can't it wait until tomorrow? I'm already late for my racquetball game."

"It could, I suppose," Stringer said, "but I think you'd want to hear this now."

Duggan threw the topcoat on the desk and glanced at his watch. "You've got five minutes, and it better be good."

Stringer walked to the desk and stood stiffly, almost at attention. Years of working for the man had made him no more comfortable facing him. Although Duggan never displayed it publicly, his inner circle was intimately aware of his ferocious temper. Everyone on the staff, including Stringer, had felt the sting of his rage at one time or another, and no one was eager to precipitate another tantrum. Because of this, Stringer had considered quitting a number of times, but always chickened out. After all, the money was good and other job prospects for an over-fifty former wire service hack were not great. So he simply tried to keep a low profile, out of sight, out of mind—and out of trouble.

"I just had a strange visit from Mike Overby of Channel Seven," he said.

"Strange how?" Duggan demanded, suddenly more interested.

Stringer quickly recapped the visit by Overby and the questions he had asked. "He didn't come right out and say it, but I got the feeling he thinks there may be some kind of scandal brewing around here."

"That's ridiculous!" Duggan snorted.

Stringer shrugged. "Of course, but I thought you should know about it. Overby doesn't usually waste his time chasing phony leads. He's too good a reporter."

Duggan wandered to a window overlooking the capitol grounds, rubbing his hands together as if to warm them. "Well, he's chasing his tail this time," he finally said. "He'll find no fucking scandal in this office. We run a tight ship here."

"I know that," Stringer said as he started toward the door, his five minutes almost up. "But I guess forewarned is forearmed."

Before he could leave, however, Duggan turned and asked, "What else did he say?"

Stringer paused, thinking. "He also asked if we

had a bio on John Hemrick. Said the newsroom wanted one, apparently to plan for the conventions."

Duggan turned back to the window, but not before Stringer caught the flash of surprise on his face. "The conventions are a year away," he said.

"That's true, but the stations do plan well in advance. Especially now that there's talk about you and the governor's race."

"Did you give it to him? Hemrick's bio?"

"I don't have one," Stringer said. "I've never even seen one. But I offered to call Hemrick for one."

"And?"

"Overby told me not to bother, that he'd call Hemrick himself."

The truth was that Stringer, like others in the AG's office, knew precious little about John Hemrick. They knew he worked for the Duggan campaign, but because the attorney general kept the office and campaign staffs separate, they had little idea of what he did in the four years between campaigns. Fund-raising was the best guess. Although seldom at the capitol, he clearly had the AG's ear, and was therefore viewed with respect—and some fear—by staff people like Stringer.

Duggan was now back at his desk. "Thanks for stopping by, Brian," he said. "I appreciate the information. Keep your ears open."

"No problem," Stringer said, pleased to be escaping with both of his balls intact.

Duggan waited until the office door closed behind Stringer before picking up the telephone. Using his private line, he quickly punched in a seven-digit number and waited.

"Butch? We need to meet."

"What's the problem?" said the voice on the other end of the line.

"I just had Stringer in my office."

"Yeah."

"He says Overby from Channel Seven was poking around, asking questions about some scandal in the office. Wanted your bio."

"It doesn't surprise me," Butch said.

"Why's that?"

"Because they were out at the Edina office the other night, supposedly looking for a production studio."

"How do you know that?" Duggan demanded.

"One of the security guards told me. They even mentioned my name."

"Jesus Christ!" Duggan exploded. "Why didn't you tell me?"

"Because I didn't want to worry you. I can handle it."

"You can handle shit!" Duggan fumed. "How did they find out?"

There was a pause. "I'm not sure yet," he finally said. "But I've got a good idea."

At that moment, there was a light rap on Duggan's door, and his secretary poked her head in. Duggan held the phone away.

"I'm leaving, Mr. Duggan," she said. "Is there anything else you need?"

"No, no," he said, waving her away. "Have a good night."

Then back to the phone. "I've got to go," he said, "I'm already late for the club. But I want your ass over here tomorrow. I want to know everything you're doing. You got that?"

"Sure, but I'm telling you, don't sweat it."

The advice came too late. Duggan could already feel the drops of perspiration rolling down the back of his neck and under his arms.

Sissy was sprawled on the bed, absorbed in the latest issue of *Cosmo,* when Tony walked in the door. "Man, it's freezing out there," he said with a mock shiver. "And it's not even the fucking winter yet."

She smiled. "You'd better get a heavier coat, buddy. We may be here 'til Christmas."

"No goddamned way," he said. "The Eskimos can have this place."

Sissy got up off the bed. "So how did it go?" she asked.

"It worked," he said. "I found a kid." Then he laughed. "But it cost me a buck."

They had gotten the new instructions the day before. The General was taking a different tact, one that Sissy found troubling. It was one thing, she thought, to go after Maggie, but something else to target the boy.

Tony shared none of her concerns, however. He was just happy to get out of the motel, to be doing something. As for the boy, well, tough shit. A job is a job.

29

Danny was dressed and ready, waiting for Brett to finish in the bathroom and drive him to school. He stood by the door, shifting from one foot to the other, obviously eager to leave. Maggie watched him from the kitchen. "What's the hurry, kiddo?" she said. "You're early."

When he didn't respond, she crossed over to him. "What's the matter, Danny?"

"Nothing," he said without looking at her.

She studied him. Now that she thought about it, she realized he had said next to nothing since he woke. He had even ignored the cartoons and had not complained about his eggs for breakfast. She knelt next to him and turned his chin toward her. "Look at me," she said. "Is something wrong?"

"No," he said, pulling away. "Where's Jake anyway?"

"He'll be here in a minute. Is there a problem at school?"

"No," he said again, shaking his head. But she could see his lips purse and his chin begin to tremble, a sure precursor to crying. Taking his hand, she pulled him away from the door and led him to the couch. She felt his forehead, but there was no hint of a fever. "C'mon, young man, 'fess up. What's going on here?"

He tried to pull away, but she held him firmly. "Maybe you should stay home."

"No way," he said.

"Then what is it?" she demanded, losing her patience.

The tears began. "A boy gave me something yesterday," he said, sniffling. "Something naughty."

"What?" She took him by the shoulders, looking into his eyes.

"A naughty picture. A naked lady."

She could feel her heartbeat quicken, the familiar pain in her chest. "Where is it?"

He reached into his backpack and pulled out an envelope. She knew without looking what it would contain, but she pulled the picture out anyway. It was the same one that had been left on her desk. "Who gave this to you, Danny?"

"A boy at school. He's in fifth grade, I think. I don't know his name. He said a man gave him a dollar to give it to me."

"Did he look at it, the boy who gave it to you?"

"I don't know. I don't think so."

She pushed the picture back into the envelope

and took her son into her arms, holding him tight. "It's okay, Danny. You did nothing wrong. I'm glad you told me."

Had he recognized her? Apparently not, or he surely would have said something. She took some comfort in that, but it did little to assuage her anger.

"Why would he do that, Mom?" His face was against her shoulder, his words muffled. "Why would he give me a naughty picture?"

"It wasn't the boy," she said. "It was the man who gave it to him. He's a bad man."

Brett walked into the living room, but stopped short. "What's going on?" he asked.

Looking over Danny's shoulder, she said, "Nothing. Everything's okay now. Right, son?" She held him at arms length, looking into his face. The tears had stopped. "Are you okay now? Ready to go to school?"

He nodded and picked up his backpack. The envelope remained at her side.

"I'll see you after school," she said with a final hug. "You just forget about this."

"Okay," he said and followed Brett out the door.

Once they were gone, Maggie tried to calm herself and consider her options. She certainly would have to tell Brett what had happened, but she decided against trying to identify the boy who had given Danny the envelope. After all, he was an innocent messenger, and searching for him would only lead to further questions and explanations. She had no doubt who had given the boy the picture, the same man who had been in the car watching Danny. Sissy's cohort.

Picking up the envelope, she again took the picture out, careful this time to hold it along the edges. Maybe McQueen could find some prints. She turned it over, and on the back there was a scrawl of words, written, not printed this time. They said: "Is this the legacy you want to leave your son? Think about it."

If they only knew that was all she could think about.

Several hours after Maggie had told him what had happened, Brett still found it difficult to control his rage. At the time, he'd been angrier than Maggie had ever seen him. "Those chickenshit bastards," he had stormed, "picking on a kid like that. Using him as their fucking messenger. I'd like to kill the assholes."

She had tried to calm him, but even now, as he drove the station's surveillance van toward Edina, he was still fuming, having trouble concentrating on the road. Not only was there the anger and concern over Danny, but the recurring image of the picture Maggie had finally shown him. Try as he might, his mind would not release it, the sight of her sitting there nude with some guy fondling her. He could only imagine what had come before and what had followed. It made his stomach turn.

"Are you okay?" The voice brought him back. Tamara Swain, the photographer assigned to the van, was sitting next to him, staring. "It's like you're in a cloud."

"I'm fine," he said quickly, glancing at her. "Just daydreaming, I guess."

He could understand why Danny had not recognized his mother in the picture; he barely did.
She looked so different, not only younger but,
with all the makeup, harder . . . and what? . . .
experienced. That's what troubled him the most,
the pleasure he saw in her face. Although he knew
it wasn't true, that she hated what she had done,
he could not erase her rapt expression. Especially
now that he had now seen it himself. If she was, as
she claimed, faking then, was she faking now?
With him?

"We're getting close, aren't we?" Tamara said,
again bringing him back.

"It's right over there," he replied as he slowed
to a stop and then backed into a parking place
across and down from the building.

The surveillance van was an old, nondescript
Chevy panel truck, rusted around the fenders and
badly in need of a paint job. Small, one-way windows were located on each panel, along with the
faded words, JORDAN PLUMBING. The truck had
actually belonged to the plumbing company years
ago, before Channel 7 had bought it specifically
for surveillance duty. The engine and other vital
parts had been replaced and were now kept finely
tuned.

Inside, the walls of the truck were padded and
lined with shelves of electronic and communica-
tions equipment. Tamara busied herself setting up
the camera on a tripod, positioned in front of the
one-way glass. The camera could be fitted with a
variety of lenses, including a nightscope capable
of capturing useable images in the darkness.

Brett wasn't sure what to be looking for, so he

simply told Tamara to shoot anyone who came in or left the building. Especially anyone who looked like they were a teenager or younger. He also showed her the picture of Butch. "And we'd like to find out who cleans and guards the place," he said. "So keep an eye out for any truck that looks like it may belong to a janitorial or security service."

The photographer had been told nothing more about the nature of the assignment, and was wise enough not to ask questions. This was strictly a need-to-know operation.

One thing bothered Brett. There was also a back entrance to the building, and he had no way of covering it and the front at the same time. He decided to divide the van's time between the two, knowing he would run a risk of missing something in the process. Maybe he could get Barclay to splurge for another pair of eyes.

"All set?" he asked the photographer.

"All set," she said. "Let 'em come."

"I just thought of something," Maggie said, walking in on Jessica at the computer.

Jessica didn't look up. "What's that?"

Maggie waited until she had her full attention. "Remember that Amy told me that the little girl in the film, the one who got hurt, was treated by their own doctor?"

"I guess so," Jessica said, leaning back in her chair.

"That list you gave us the other night, the one with names of the board members of Pioneer Properties."

"Yeah."

"One of them was a doctor, remember? A Henry Klinkle."

Jessica retrieved the list from the desk and studied the names. "You're right," she said. "We don't know what kind of doctor, though."

"It would be nice to find out. See where he practices and whether he has any kind of record with the medical licensing board."

"I'll give it a try," Jessica said, making a note to herself as Maggie started to leave. "Wait a second," she said. "There's something else."

Maggie stopped at the door, waiting.

"I've finished the run on the other four names Nadia had. Three of them have one kind of drug conviction or another. Either for possession or distribution. Two of them just got out of jail. They must have been Nadia's drug contacts."

"And the fourth one?" Maggie asked.

"Clean as a whistle. In fact, he's at the downtown Y, some kind of street worker, I'm told. Works with wayward kids."

"Like Nadia?"

"Maybe."

"What's his name?" Maggie asked.

"Jonathan Cassidy. I already tried to reach him, but he was out on his rounds."

"I'll try him again," Maggie said. "Maybe he'll stop by for a visit."

The hours passed slowly in the van. It didn't take long to run out of conversation with Tamara, and the van radio didn't provide much company either. Brett's eyes were tired from the constant watching, and his shoulders and back ached from too much hunching over inside the cramped quarters. What's more, he had little to show for all the discomfort.

They had moved the van twice, once to deflect possible suspicion about it sitting in one place too long and again to get a better view of the rear entrance and the fire escape that climbed along the back wall. Now they were back in front. A number of people had come and gone in their time there, but all of them appeared to be businesspeople going about their daily routines. There had been no sign of Butch or anyone else that Brett could recognize.

Darkness was fast approaching when another panel truck, newer but not unlike their own, pulled up in front of the building. The words CLEAN SWEEP, INC. were painted on the side, next to a cartoonish depiction of a long-handled broom being pushed by a little man in coveralls.

"Here we go," he whispered.

"I've got it," Tamara said, crouched behind the camera.

Two young men, one black, one white, and a white woman got out of the truck and went around the back of it, opening the rear doors. They took out what appeared to be three vacuum cleaners and two large satchels, which Brett guessed could carry cleaning supplies. They closed and locked the doors and disappeared through the front entrance of the building.

"That answers one question," Brett said as he jotted down the name on the truck.

Tamara stood up and stretched. "How much longer do you want to go?" she asked. "I haven't eaten since noon."

"A few more hours," Brett said. "I'd like to see what happens at night."

"Then I'm going for a burger," she said. "There's a Wendy's down the street." When he hesitated, she added, "The camera's all set up and focused. You just have to push the button."

"Okay," he said, wishing he could get a breath of fresh air himself.

Another hour passed. Then another. The burgers were gone, but the odor of fried onions lingered in the van. Brett had twice used the cellular phone to report to the station, checking with both Maggie and the fill-in producer of the ten o'clock news. There had been no new developments, he'd been told.

It was now fully dark, and with the night came colder temperatures. The van's heater was working, but they could still see their breath inside. Tamara was not only chilled, but anxious to be done. "Let's give it a while longer," Brett urged. She responded with chattering teeth.

He continued to watch the fifth floor, but half an hour later, after seeing no sign of lights or activity, he said, "Let's get out of here," satisfied they would learn nothing more that night.

"Wait a minute," Tamara said, her eye pushed against the camera eyepiece.

A car had pulled up directly across the street from their van, just behind the cleaning truck. Two men got out and stood on either side of the car. The nightscope gave Tamara a better view than Brett could get with the naked eye. "I think the guy on this side is the one in the picture you showed me," she said. "The Butch guy."

"Let me see," Brett said, edging her aside, replacing her behind the camera.

She was right. Even the darkness could not hide the facial scar from the scope. Tamara got back behind the camera, panning as the two men walked to the back of the car into somewhat better light and opened the trunk.

"What about the other guy?" Brett whispered. "Can you make him out?"

"Let me focus," she said. Then she let out a long, low whistle.

"What is it?" he demanded.

"I can't believe this."

"What?"

"It's Clyde, for Christ's sake. Clyde Calder."

"No way," he said. "Are you sure?"

"Look for yourself," she replied, moving aside.

He again positioned himself behind the eyepiece, straining to see. She was right.

Clyde Calder was a Channel 7 photographer, one of the most senior on the staff. "I'll be a son of a bitch," he mumbled.

"You'd better hope he doesn't look this way," Tamara said. "He sure as hell knows this van." She was behind the camera again, watching as Calder pulled a large case out of the trunk and set it on the sidewalk. Then he reached for something else and put it down next to the case.

"What's he got?" Brett whispered.

"I'm not sure, but from here it certainly looks like a tripod and a camera case, just like the one over there," she added, pointing to the case in the back of their van. "Clyde must have a freelance job."

"He must have," Brett agreed.

"I take it that's not good."

"You got that right," he replied, and then added, "You can't breathe a word of this, Tamara. Not a goddamned word, to anybody. Okay?"

"You got it," she said.

They watched as the two men entered the building, carrying the case and tripod. Then, a few minutes later, the lights on the fifth floor came on.

At the apartment later that night, Brett and Maggie sat huddled together on the couch, warmed by one another and by a fire blazing in the hearth. He had already briefed her on the evening's excursion, and they were now cuddling quietly, lost in thought as they watched the flames dance, casting strange, leaping shadows on the walls of the darkened living room.

"Isn't it time you told me about Danny's father," Brett said, breaking the silence.

When she made no reply, he thought for a moment that she might be asleep. "Maggie?"

"I heard you, Brett."

"Well?"

"It's a long story," she said. "I don't know if I have the strength to tell it."

"Try," he urged. "I think I deserve to know."

She pulled away from him slightly and looked into his eyes. "You're right, you do."

After getting up to put another piece of oak on the fire, she returned to the couch, but sat apart from him, kicking off her slippers, curling her legs beneath her. "His name was Mick Salinas," she said. "I say 'was,' because I'm not sure if he's still alive, and if he is, whether he's still using that name."

She decided against mentioning Jessica Mitchell's computer search for him.

"We met in college, at UCLA. We were both majoring in journalism and were in several classes together. He was what we college girls used to call a hunk, dark and almost Hollywood-handsome. Looked a lot like Tom Cruise, actually, and we all thought we'd see him in the movies someday. He had that kind of aura about him, that kind of . . . well, sex appeal or whatever it is.

"For a time, we were simply classmates, not even friends. We'd say hello in the halls or in class, but that was about all. Then, to my total surprise, he started to pursue me, and I do mean pursue. Everywhere I was, he was. In class, after class. In the library, on the mall. It was really the first time any man, to say nothing of this Adonis-like creature, had really paid that much attention to me, and, of course, I was overwhelmed, swept off my feet."

Brett broke in. "That's hard to believe, that no man had—"

"It's true, trust me. Maybe it was because of what I'd gone through on the street, I kept in a shell. I was shy, withdrawn, maybe even afraid of men. Certainly not comfortable around them. I figured most of them just wanted a quick screw anyway. But

Mick was different. Kind, considerate . . . and interested in more of me than just my body."

Maggie uncurled her legs and walked to the kitchen, bringing back each of them a can of beer. Brett said nothing as she settled back on the couch, slowly sipping from the can. "We started to date," she continued, "and before too long, we were living together, off-campus. I was absolutely, totally in love . . . and I thought he was, too. We studied together, we played together, we . . . did everything together. It was a very happy period in my life."

Brett hadn't touched his beer, hadn't taken his eyes off of her. "Are you sure you want to hear all of this?" she asked.

"I'm sure," he said, but she could see that he was having a hard time of it.

"I'll make it brief," she said, trying to remember where she had left off. "We graduated at the same time and both got jobs right away, Mick at Channel Two, the CBS station, as a producer, and me at one of the independents, as a trainee. Life was very good, about as good as it could get, I thought at the time. I was working, I was in love, and before very long, I was pregnant."

"But not married," Brett interjected.

"No, not married. We talked about it, but it didn't seem that important at the time. We were still young, and neither of us was ready to make that kind of a commitment."

He shook his head. "A baby's not a commitment?"

"Danny was hardly planned," she said. "It did make the situation more complicated, and, to be honest, I did hope the pregnancy would push us toward marriage. But Mick wasn't ready yet, and I wasn't ready to lose him by pushing too hard. So we went on as before...Danny was born, a healthy eight-pounder...and the future looked bright." She took a deep breath. "Until two months later, when Mick disappeared."

Brett sat up straight. "What?"

"Just like that. There one day, gone the next. No good-byes, no explanation. Poof! Disappeared into thin air. Left his job and everything else behind. I haven't heard from him or seen him since."

Brett stared in disbelief, but before he could speak, she went on to describe her desperate search for him, the months spent looking and wondering and worrying. "I guess I could understand him leaving me," she said, "but the baby? *His baby?* His son? How can any man do that?"

Brett had no answer, but quickly asked, "You have no idea why he left?"

"I've spent the better part of six years thinking about it, Brett. Wondering what I might have done. And I don't have the answer. The only thing I can tell you is that he was a very possessive man. He'd guard me like I was his own personal treasure, go crazy if he saw another man looking at me wrong. Or me looking at another man. Maybe I did something to send him off the deep end. I just don't know."

He took her back into his arms, holding her, stroking her hair. "Did he know about your life on the street, about...?"

"He knew about everything except the film. I couldn't tell him about that."

Brushing back her hair, he kissed her forehead. "Maybe he found out about it," he whispered. "That could have done it."

"I've thought about that, too. But how could he have found out? And wouldn't he have given me a chance to explain? It doesn't make sense."

They watched as the fire shrunk to glimmering embers. Brett tried to imagine how any man could leave this woman, to say nothing of the boy. He must have been out of his mind. "Danny must ask about his dad," he said.

"Not until a year or so ago, when he got old enough to understand that other kids had fathers and he didn't."

"What have you told him?"

"I've lied. I've told him his dad has died and gone to heaven. For all I know, it's the truth, but when he's older, I'll tell him the whole truth."

Brett wanted to ask one more question: Could she ever love another man as she had once loved Mick? But he decided against it. He was afraid of her answer.

30

It was morning. Amy Boyd and her two friends had just exhausted the last of Maggie's money on breakfast at McDonald's and were now sitting on a bus bench near Calhoun Square, considering how to spend the rest of their day and how to find money for their next meal. They had long since hocked everything they owned of any value, and none of them was in the mood to go back to panhandling. At this time of day, and with the onset of colder weather, there weren't that many people on the streets anyway.

"I could sell the coat," Amy said. "It's damn near new."

"And freeze your ass," the long-haired boy,

whose name was Rocky, replied. "And shit, you wouldn't get more than a few bucks for it."

As it was, they had begun taking turns wearing the coat Maggie had given Amy. Trading it back and forth, depending on who was the coldest or who complained the most.

"You could give the lady another call," the other boy, Popeye, said, referring to Maggie. "She must have more money than she knows what to do with."

Before Amy could respond, she felt a sharp tap on her shoulder. Startled, she turned to find the man named Butch hovering above her, staring down at her. None of them had seen his approach. "We need to talk, sweety," he said, moving quickly to the front of her, blocking any escape.

Rocky jumped up to intervene, but was roughly pushed aside. "Move on, asshole," Butch said. "This is none of your business."

The other boy, Popeye, stepped back, fists clenched, but cowed by the venom in Butch's voice. "You, too, baldy. Piss off before somebody gets hurt."

Looking at the man, neither of the boys was eager to take him on, nor was there time to even consider a joint attack. Squat and muscular, with biceps the size of their calves, he was clearly someone to reckon with, an impression reinforced by the scowl on his face, the anger in his eyes, and the vivid scar that flared across his cheek.

Amy tried to push her way past him, but was caught and slammed back on the bench by one of his bulging arms. "I told you we needed to talk," he said, sitting next to her, the arm still around her, holding tight.

Rocky and Popeye backed off, standing to one side, uncertain of what to do next. Rocky fingered a switchblade in his pants pocket, but hesitated to take it out. After all, it was broad daylight, and who knew what the man had in *his* pocket. As they hesitated, Butch glanced up. "I told you to beat it, hear? I need to speak privately with this young lady."

Amy knew she could scream and struggle and perhaps bring help, but he would only find her another day or night, when the risk of getting hurt was even greater. Better to hear him out now than later. "It's okay, you guys," she said. "Do what he says. I'll be all right."

The two boys retreated about twenty feet and plopped down on the curb, never taking their eyes off of her. Rocky now had the switchblade out of his pocket and in his hand, flicking it open and closed, but Butch appeared to take no notice, his full attention on Amy. "Nice to see you again," he said in a calmer voice, but without slackening his grip. "What's it been, three or four months?"

"Something like that, I guess," she replied, trying not to show her fear.

"What have you been up to?" he asked.

"Nothing much. Hanging out, trying to keep warm."

"Nice coat," he said, fingering the lapel. "Feels expensive. Where did you get it?"

"A friend gave it to me. Felt sorry for me, I guess."

Butch loosened his hold slightly, but still kept her in place. "You must have rich friends," he said.

Amy shrugged, but said nothing, chilled to the bone despite the coat.

"Who have you been talking to lately?" Butch asked.

"What do you mean?"

"Just what I said."

She shrugged again. "Just the normal people. Friends on the street, you know . . ."

Butch took her chin and pulled her face around, holding it no more than six inches from his. "You heard about Nadia, didn't you? Poor kid. Tough way to go."

"I heard," Amy mumbled, unable to take her eyes off the scar.

"Way too young to die," he whispered. "Penny, too."

He released his grip on her chin and she quickly turned away. "Did you talk to Nadia before she left?" he asked. "Being good friends and all."

"Never saw her, never talked to her," Amy lied. "First thing I heard, she was dead."

"You're sure of that? You haven't talked to anyone else about our little film project?"

"No one," she answered. "Why would I?"

"No television people? No reporters?"

Amy turned back to him, feigning shock. "You've got to be kidding?"

His eyes bored into hers. "Do I?"

"I may be on the streets," she said, "but I'm not stupid."

Butch freed her from his grip and she quickly moved away on the bench. "I hope you're not lying," he said, smiling now. "It would be too bad if I find out you are." Then he reached for his wallet and pulled out a fifty-dollar bill. "This is a down payment on our next little project. And a small reward for keeping that pretty little mouth of yours shut. Understood?"

Amy nodded as he pushed the bill into her coat pocket. "And tell those friends of yours," he added with a glance at the two boys, "that if they ever pull a switchblade on me, they'll end up eating it. You got that?"

Amy swallowed hard, but said nothing.

As he stood up and began to walk away, he paused, looking back at her. "Nice coat," he said. "Very nice."

From the looks of him, Jonathan Cassidy could have been living on the streets himself. He was unshaven and unkempt—and probably unwashed, Maggie guessed as she watched him enter the station lobby. His clothes were no more impressive, as dirty as they were old, one step removed from the ragpile. A tattered flannel shirt torn at the elbows and missing more than half of its buttons, baggy khaki pants held up by a rope, and a pair of beat-up sneakers that Nike would have been ashamed to call their own. And while he wore no coat, he did have a purple woolen scarf wrapped securely around his neck.

"Jonathan, I'm Maggie," she said, walking up to him. "Thanks for coming."

"No problem," he replied, shaking her hand. "Glad to help, if I can."

Maggie guessed that he was in his early twenties, although he could easily have been older. His hairline had receded early, leaving him with a high forehead and the remainder of his hair swept back and tied in a ponytail. He wore tiny wire-framed glasses, the lenses like miniature monocles barely covering his eyes.

Maybe it was the scruffy beard or the grungy clothes, but he strongly reminded Maggie of the grubby undercover cop in television's *Hill Street Blues*.

As if reading her thoughts, he said, "Sorry I didn't have time to clean up. I've been out roaming the streets."

In an earlier conversation with the director of the downtown YMCA, Maggie had been told that Cassidy was one of their most effective street workers, in part because he looked and lived the part of the kids he was trying to help. He had been a runaway himself years before and knew most of the habits and haunts of today's street kids. "He's probably the most trusted guy out there," the Y director had told her. "He's got a way with those kids that few others do. They'll talk to him, at least. And he's gotten way more than his share of them off the streets."

Maggie led Cassidy from the lobby and through the halls to the Green Room, where Jessica was waiting. Although neither remembered it until then, it turned out they had met years before, when Jessica was developing a story on juvenile prostitution.

"So what can I do for you?" he asked once the small talk was out of the way.

Without explaining why they wanted to know, Maggie asked if he recalled a girl named Nadia Vaughn.

"Of course," he said, "but I haven't seen her for awhile. Why do you ask?"

"Then you haven't heard?" Jessica said.

"Heard what?"

"That she's dead. A suicide."

His mouth fell open and he slumped over. "You're shitting me," he finally said.

"I wish I were," Jessica said. "Maggie visited her parents in Madison two weeks after she died."

Cassidy hesitated, then said, "I was going to say I can't believe it, but the truth is, I can. She was a very unstable young woman, worse than most of the kids out there. Although I never saw her taking any, I'd heard that she was into drugs—"

"She was," Maggie interjected.

"Doesn't surprise me. Did she take an overdose?"

"No," Maggie said. "She slit her wrists in the bathtub."

Cassidy grimaced, but said nothing more.

"I found a slip of paper she had hidden away," Maggie continued. "With several names on it. Yours was one of them."

"Really?" he said. "And the others?"

"Mostly drug dealers," Jessica said. "From what we can tell."

"And somebody named Butch," Maggie added. "Know of him?"

"I've heard the name, but have never seen or met him. The kids talk about him. A bad dude, from what they say."

"Bad how?" Maggie persisted.

"I can't really tell you, because they've never really told me. They just try to stay clear of him."

Maggie got up and wandered to the other end of the Green Room and back. "Why would Nadia

have kept your name on that list?" she asked.
"Were you that close to her?"

"No closer than I am to many of the kids, but
she did leave something with me. Maybe that's
why."

"Left what?" Jessica exclaimed.

"I have no idea. A bag, a Target shopping bag,
I think. Asked me to keep it until she got back. A
lot of the kids do that, since they're always on the
move and have no place to keep things. I make a
handy storage locker, and it doesn't cost them anything."

Both women were now on their feet. "You have
no idea what's in the bag?" Maggie asked.

"Of course not. It's taped shut. But I would
never look anyway. It's a matter of trust."

"But Nadia's dead," Maggie argued. "Surely you
could open it now."

Cassidy appeared puzzled. "Why all of this
interest in Nadia? I don't understand."

Maggie and Jessica exchanged a quick glance,
and after a brief consultation, Jessica explained
that they were investigating the death of Penny
Collins and that Nadia could be a link to her murder. "It could be very important to know what's in
that bag," she said. "Even crucial."

"Then perhaps the police should have it,"
Cassidy offered. "Or her parents. I wouldn't feel
right just handing it over to you."

Maggie knelt by the side of his chair, using her
most persuasive voice. "Look, Jonathan. Nadia's
parents gave me free access to the girl's room.
That's how I found the slip of paper with your
name on it, hidden away beneath her bed. I

promise you, we'll pass on any personal effects to her parents, but we need to look at the bag first."

"As for the police," Jessica quickly added, "they don't have the foggiest idea of what we may be on to here. We'll let them know, of course, if it turns out to be anything, but it's still too early to tell."

From the expression on his face, Cassidy was feeling trapped and undecided. He took off his glasses and rubbed his eyes. "I don't know," he said, looking from one to the other. "Maybe I should talk to my boss first. Let him decide."

"Do that," Jessica said, "and it's just like going to the cops. That's what he'll want to do. The safe thing. But it could be the worst thing, believe me." Then she knelt on the other side of his chair, across from Maggie, and tried a new tact. "I didn't screw you over on the juvenile prostitution story, did I? I kept the faith, didn't I? I honored the commitments I made to you. Right?"

Cassidy nodded. "I have no argument with you. You played it straight. But this is different. I'd be giving you something that doesn't belong to me."

Maggie heaved a deep sigh and got up. "We can't force you to do anything," she said. "We can only tell you that you might be holding the key to something very important. Please think about it."

"I will," he replied. "I'll call you tonight or tomorrow."

It was mid-afternoon when Butch Hemrick walked into the office of the attorney general and found Martin Duggan in his shirtsleeves, parked behind his desk. Duggan had cleared his calendar for the rest of the day, and now sat waiting. "Well," he said impatiently, before Butch could close the door behind him. "What have you got?"

Hemrick sauntered across the office and slumped into a chair opposite Duggan's desk, ignoring the AG's testiness. "I'm not sure, but one of those kids must be talking," he said, going on to describe his morning encounter with Amy Boyd. "She denied saying anything to anyone, of course, but she was pretty tight with both the Collins girl and Nadia Vaughn. She might have heard something about the second film."

Duggan swore and swiveled in his chair, his tightened neck muscles evidence of his anger. "But how could anyone tie it to this office?" he demanded. "None of those kids know you by anything but Butch, and they sure as hell don't know that you work for me."

Hemrick shrugged. "Nobody has proof of anything, Marty, or they would have done something by now. Worst case, they've got the word of some runaway kid. Period. It could be this Amy or one of the others. You're worrying too much about this. I'll keep digging and shut off the leak."

Duggan jumped out of his chair and almost crawled across the desk, nostrils flaring. "Don't tell me I'm worrying too much!" he snarled. "It's my career, my reputation, my fucking *life* we're talking about here. Don't try to sugarcoat it. I've got reporters snooping around, hinting at some fucking scandal. I want it stopped!"

Hemrick sat back, unruffled by Duggan's tirade. He had seen similar tantrums too often before. "I told you I'd get to the bottom of it," he said. "And I will. I've got as much to lose as you do. You want to stay in office, I want to stay out of prison. We're two peas in a pod, Marty."

Duggan knew that Hemrick had him by the short hairs. Again. Would it ever end?

Duggan had first heard of John Hemrick— then John Hendrick—in the middle of his first term as attorney general. That's when he found Hendrick's letter, marked PERSONAL & CONFIDENTIAL, stuffed into the edge of his locker at the health club. He had no idea who had left it there, but as he opened it, he was not especially surprised to find it written by an inmate at the Stillwater State Prison. Many prisoners wrote to him, pleading their innocence or asking for favorable consideration from the state pardon board, of which the attorney general was a member. But Hendrick's letter was different. "You don't know me," he had written, "but I think you knew my cell mate, Junior Adair. Remember him?"

Duggan didn't need a reminder. If Minneapolis had a drug kingpin in the early eighties, Adair was it. An extraordinarily powerful and ruthless figure in the underworld of the time, he was said to control more than 70 percent of the drug traffic into the Twin Cities, and was probably responsible for half of the drug killings.

"I should say my former cell mate," the letter went on, "since I'm sure you know that Junior died in a knife fight here in prison a week ago."

Duggan not only knew, but had silently rejoiced at the news, feeling a huge surge of relief. Indeed, given the opportunity, he would have gladly paid whoever was on the other end of the knife. Hendrick's letter had anticipated his reaction.

> I suspect you were not especially saddened by his death, but you should know that Junior and I were very close. We kept no secrets from each other. I trust you know what I mean.

Duggan knew what it meant, all right. It meant that a secret Adair had carried with him, a secret that could destroy Duggan, had not died with him. That it was now in the hands of the man who had written the letter.

> I suggest that you arrange to visit me here at Stillwater. Use whatever pretext is necessary. We have several issues to discuss. I will give you one week before I provide the news media with an exposé the likes of which they have seldom seen.

Duggan would never forget the feeling of desperation as he read the letter. It was like a ticking bomb.

> I have no doubt that you will check me out, but I would not allow that process to delay your visit. Nor should you make any effort to restrict or silence me. I have made arrangements to deal with such an eventuality.

Duggan did as Hendrick expected—ordering a quick but discreet investigation of the man, discovering him to be a two-time loser, a child pornographer in the middle of a five-year-sentence. And, indeed, a former cell mate of Junior Adair. But the investigation could not answer the crucial question: How much did he know?

Years before, while still in private criminal practice, Duggan had represented Junior Adair in one of his early and celebrated drug trials. A key witness for the prosecution, an undercover cop by the name of Henry Sealoff, had—on the eve of the trial—disappeared without a trace. Without Sealoff's testimony, the prosecution was left with largely circumstantial evidence, which gave Duggan a chance to win a quick acquittal for his client. It was another feather in Duggan's already well-feathered hat.

At the time, it was speculated that Sealoff, the missing witness, had either been killed by one of Adair's minions or—more likely—paid off with some of the drug lord's hidden riches. Despite the conjecture, however, no one would ever guess that the highly-respected Martin Duggan would have played a role in the cop's disappearance, let alone that he would have arranged for and delivered the payoff.

Only three people knew: Adair, Duggan, and Sealoff, who was now believed to be living sumptuously somewhere in Latin America or Europe. Adair was now dead, but he had been replaced on the list of three.

Looking back on it now, of course, Duggan could not believe that he had actually agreed to be the bagman. But he had little choice. Basically an honest man, fiercely devoted to his career and family, his only prior professional sins had consisted of cutting a few ethical corners in his ambitious ride to the top of his field. And what defense attorney had not done the same?

He capitulated, in part, because of his genuine and total fear of Adair, who was convinced that only Duggan could get access to the undercover cop, and who had made not-so-veiled threats against Duggan and his family if he failed to carry out the money mission. As his attorney, Duggan was acutely aware of the kind of violence Adair and his followers were capable of, and he simply could not work up the courage to defy the threats, to put himself and his family at that kind of terrible risk.

Besides, there was the money. Two hundred thousand dollars over and above his defense fees. Dirty money, to be sure, but in those days a nice windfall, even for a successful lawyer, but especially for one already with his eye on political office.

Much as he might regret it now, the deed was done. Sealoff was bought off, Adair was acquitted, Duggan's family was safe, and he was a wealthier man.

But that was not the end of it. Before Sealoff took off for places unknown, Adair forced him to sign a letter, acknowledging the role Duggan had played in the payoff. Adair kept the letter as a receipt of sorts for the money he had expended, never allowing Duggan to forget that it was in his possession.

Two years later, Adair was again on trial, but by

then, Duggan was attorney general and unable to assist in his defense, legally or illegally. Adair was convicted and sentenced to twelve years at Stillwater, a term Duggan—again under threat of exposure—was working to shorten at the time someone put a knife into Adair's belly.

Now, as he sat across the desk from Hemrick, Duggan could not forget their first meeting inside the walls of Stillwater prison. "Call me Butch," Hendrick had said as they faced one another for the first time. "I'm glad you could make it."

Duggan had brushed aside any small talk and quickly got to the point. "What do you want from me?"

Hendrick had held up a copy of Adair's letter. "Out of here," he'd said smugly. "As quickly as you can manage it."

That was the beginning. Because of his power and position on the parole board, Duggan was able to free Hendrick within a matter of months, convincing the board that Hendrick had responded well to sexual offender treatment and that he had taken a personal interest in his further rehabilitation.

But as Duggan had suspected from the beginning, that would not be the end of it. Not as long as Hendrick held the letter. Within the next year, Hendrick—now Hemrick—had demanded a position on Duggan's campaign staff. Then, the next year, the use of the fifth floor of the Edina building, which Duggan controlled through a complex corporate structure. He had made no effort to conceal the use of the facility from Duggan or to keep all of the profits for himself. In fact, as treasurer of the Duggan campaign, he was able to move money around under the guise of campaign expenses or contributions—laundering the dirty dollars while also escaping some of the constraints of the state's campaign finance law. All in all, from Hemrick's point of view, the arrangement had worked well over the years.

As much as Duggan detested what Hemrick was doing, he was helpless to interfere. He kept his distance from the fifth floor and had never seen— had never wanted to see—one frame of any film that Hemrick had made. The very thought of it made him gag. But he could do nothing more. Not only was there the letter, but now his unwilling but undeniable complicity in the porn business and campaign finance violations.

He had learned to live with the guilt, but not with the constant fear of exposure, knowing what it would do to his beloved family and, of course, to his career and any hope of becoming governor. In an effort to assuage his conscience, he became the architect of Minnesota's tough laws on pedophilia, including legislation that required the registration of every released sex offender and the notification of any community they chose to settle in. But it was never enough.

"So what do we do about Channel Seven?" Duggan asked now.

"I've already got Calder, the photographer, poking around the newsroom," Hemrick said, "but so far, he hasn't been able to pick up anything. Rumor has it that there's some kind of special investigation going on, but that's as far as he's been able to get. They're keeping a tight lid on it."

"You're sure this Calder's not the leak?" Duggan asked.

"Positive," Hemrick said. "He's into me so deep he couldn't shovel his way out. He likes the slot machines, but the slot machines don't like him. Don't worry about Calder."

Duggan pushed away from the desk and stood up. "I don't like the sound of it," he said. "You'd better pull back and hunker down for a while."

"And cancel the next shoot?" Hemrick exclaimed. "No way. Everything's set. The kids and crew are lined up and the distributors are waiting. I can't back away now."

"Then make it the last, hear me?" Duggan snapped. "No more until I say okay. You got that?"

"Back off, Marty. You don't give me orders. Besides, I told you, I'll take care of things."

"That's what you said the last time," Duggan snarled. "And that Collins girl ended up dead."

"Purely a coincidence," Hemrick said with a small smile.

31

When Maggie walked through the door of Barclay's office, she found Brett and Jessica inside, almost chin to chin, arguing loudly and angrily—with Barclay standing to one side, trying to restore order. "It's time I got out from behind the computer," Jessica was saying, "time I got to do some real work on this story. It is my story, you know . . . at least it was at one time."

Maggie stepped inside. "What's going on?" she asked, hoping to be heard above the fray.

The argument stopped momentarily as all three turned to her, surprised by the interruption. "Nothing that a little rational discussion won't solve," Barclay said, "if these two would sit down and shut up for a minute." As they did, Maggie shut the office door and grabbed a chair for herself.

Jessica turned to her. "Somebody has to get inside that Edina building," she said, more calmly now. "I want it to be me. Brett thinks it should be him."

"With all due respect to your fair gender," Brett said, "the cleaning company's a hell of a lot more likely to hire a man as a janitor than they are a woman."

"Listen to yourself," Jessica snapped, her voice rising again. "That's sexist bullshit, and you know it."

Barclay rose from behind his desk. "Okay, both of you. Quiet down. Let's think about this." He waited and sat back down, the chair groaning beneath him. "Brett's probably right that a man would stand a better chance of getting the job, but Jess also has a point—it is her story. What's more, Brett, two of the security guards working the building have already seen you. What if you do get in there and they recognize you?"

"Jessica could have the same problem," Brett argued. "They may have seen her on the air."

Jessica scoffed. "I haven't been on the air in months. Besides, a little makeup can turn me into a different person. It can't make you any shorter."

Maggie wanted to be careful not to take sides, but she felt compelled to get one gnawing thing off her chest. "Jess, this is the second or third time you've talked about this being your story."

"It is my story!" she blurted.

"Then what are we all doing here?" Maggie asked heatedly. "Don't we own a piece of it, too?"

Jessica's voice softened. "Of course, but I don't want to keep getting pushed aside while the two of you have all of the action. I want inside that building."

Maggie shook her head. "Who knows how many buildings this company cleans? Getting hired doesn't mean either one of you would ever get inside that particular place."

"But we've got to try," Brett said. "How else can we see what's on the fifth floor?"

Maggie smiled wryly. "We could ask our favorite photographer, Mr. Calder, to take us on a tour," she suggested. "Or maybe we could borrow his key."

"Fat chance!" Jessica said.

The problem of what to do about Clyde Calder had already been thoroughly discussed. And Barclay was still in a state of shock. Not until he saw the tape of Calder and Butch outside the Edina building was he convinced that Calder might actually be involved in the porn ring. Even now, however, he couldn't rid himself of doubts. "The guy has worked for this company for twenty-five years. He's one of our best. How could he get himself caught up in this?"

"He loves to gamble, George," Brett said. "You know it. So does everyone in the newsroom. He makes no secret of it. He must need the money."

Maggie did not know Calder well, although she had worked with him on several occasions. She knew only that he was divorced with a couple of grown children and shared a bachelor pad with another of the photographers. While he had always been pleasant to her, he kept to himself and never said much, letting his camera speak for him. He was capable of shooting wonderful video that had won numerous awards.

"Remember, weeks ago," Maggie said, "when I suspected that someone in the newsroom must be leaking things about me . . . my phone number, address, and the rest of it. Clyde may be our man."

Barclay could only shake his head. "Knowing that you might end up getting hurt? I just can't believe it."

"The fact remains," Brett said, "that he's doing some kind of work for this Butch character. I think we should confront him . . . threaten him if need be to get what we need."

"Not yet," Barclay insisted. "I need to know more. We can't be accusing him with what we have now. He'd go crazy and so would the union. I've told Harvey to put him on a short leash, and to keep him the hell away from this story at all costs."

Harvey Campbell was the photo chief, the person directly responsible for supervising all of the photographers. He was also one of Barclay's trusted lieutenants.

"So that leaves the cleaning company," Jessica said. "I say let me give it a try. What can we lose?"

"Maybe you," Brett shot back. "If they figure out who you are."

Barclay waved him quiet and took only another moment to decide. "Okay, Jessica, but I want you wired, and I want Brett outside in the truck. Any problems, he comes running. Deal?"

"Deal," she agreed, with a triumphant sideward glance at Brett.

◆   ◆   ◆

The offices of Clean Sweep, Inc. were housed in a
shabby building on East Lake Street, stuck
between an abandoned movie theater and a discount carpet store. The large window facing the
sidewalk was cracked down the middle, held
together by a long strip of duct tape. A small HELP
WANTED sign was placed in the left hand corner of
the window, next to the door, which held its own
little sign, PUSH HARD TO OPEN.

Jessica took heart from the HELP WANTED sign as
she paused outside the building, watching as Brett
parked the surveillance van across the street, well
within range of the tiny wireless microphone
attached to her bra. Fitted with a black wig, dangling earrings, workboots, and a pair of oversized
jeans, she had hardly recognized herself in the
mirror. She thought she looked every bit the part
of an out-of-work cleaning lady.

Leaning hard against the door, she was able to
push it open, finding herself in a small reception
area overseen by a large, florid-faced lady working
at a desk behind the counter. Two men were also
there, slouched on folding chairs pressed against
one of the walls. As she stepped to the counter,
the woman looked up from behind the desk.

"I saw the sign in the window," Jessica said. "I'd
like to apply."

With effort, the woman lifted her body from the
chair and moved wearily to the counter. Jessica could
smell her cheap perfume from three feet away.
"You got any janitorial experience?" she wheezed.

Jessica reached into her purse and pulled out a
piece of paper with the hand-written names of
three other cleaning services, retrieved from the

Des Moines, Iowa, Yellow Pages. "Not around here," she said. "I just moved up from Iowa. But you're welcome to check these out," she added, hoping—and trusting—she never would. "I'm sure they'll give me a good reference."

The woman studied the list, her eyes shifting between the paper and Jessica. "We only pay six bucks an hour," she said. "And no benefits. We employ people as independent contractors. You'll have to pay your own taxes."

"That's fine with me," Jessica said.

"And we don't provide uniforms," the woman added.

Jessica nodded. "That's okay, too."

"When could you start?"

"Anytime. The sooner the better."

"Can you work nights?"

"I guess so. Where would I be working?"

The woman pushed a one-page application form and a pen across the desk to her. "We handle several buildings on this side of town. It'll vary from night to night."

Jessica took the form and stepped to the other end of the counter, filling it out with a pre-arranged phony name and address, along with other particulars such as age and Social Security number. It took her only five minutes to complete the form and return it to the woman, who quickly glanced at it and put it aside. "How about tomorrow night?" she said. "Seven o'clock, here. One of our crew chiefs will take it from there."

"I'll be here," Jessica said.

◆   ◆   ◆

When she returned to the station, without the wig and other accouterments, Jessica found Maggie in the Green Room with Jonathan Cassidy, the Y street worker. On the table in front of them was a large bag from a Target discount store, its top still sealed with tape.

"Glad you got here," Maggie said to Jessica. "Did you get the job?"

"No problem," she replied. "I start tomorrow night."

Cassidy appeared confused. "You have a new job?" he asked, peering at Jessica through the tiny lenses of his glasses. "You're leaving the station?"

"No, no," she laughed. "This is a part-time night job. They don't pay me enough here, you know."

Apparently unsure if she was serious or joking, he decided not to press the matter. Instead, he said, "I've decided to give you the bag. With the promise that you'll pass the personal effects on to Nadia's parents."

"You have our promise," Maggie said. "I'll see to it personally."

"I didn't sleep much last night thinking about it," he continued. "I'm taking you at your word that it could be important, and that you'll go to the cops if it will help solve Penny's murder—"

Maggie cut in. "Did you know her? Penny Collins?"

"Not really. I saw her only once, a couple of weeks before she died. She was with Nadia at the time, now that I think about it, squatting in one of those abandoned grain elevators off Washington Avenue. I never knew her name, and didn't even realize she was the one murdered until I saw her picture in the paper."

Maggie took the bag off the table and, with a glance at Cassidy, tore the tape away. Opening it wide, she first pulled out a heavy sweatshirt with a Minnesota "M" stenciled on the front, then two old issues of *People* magazine, a grimy pair of tennis shoes, one without laces, and a box of costume jewelry.

Then, at the bottom of the bag, wrapped in a pair of jeans, was a videotape cassette. "I'll be damned," Maggie muttered with a knowing glance at Jessica.

Cassidy leaned forward for a better look. "Is that what you were looking for?"

"We didn't know what we were looking for," Jessica said, "but it could be."

There were no markings or labels on the cassette. However, the fact that it was buried in the bottom of the bag certainly indicated that Nadia was attempting to conceal it from a casual inspection of the bag's contents.

"Are you going to play it now?" Cassidy asked.

"I'm afraid not, Jonathan," Maggie said. "Sorry."

"I can't see it?"

"Not now, at least. It could be important to the investigation we told you about."

Cassidy was clearly disappointed, but didn't argue further. "You'll let me know what happens?"

"Absolutely," Maggie said. "But, please, don't say anything to anyone about this, okay? It could be dangerous."

"*Dangerous*? Are you serious?"

"Yes. It could be."

"All right," Cassidy said. "I just hope I did the right thing."

"Trust us," Jessica said. "You did."

With Cassidy gone, Maggie and Jessica began to search for a screening room private enough to view the videotape. "If this is what we think it is," Jessica said, "I'm not sure I want to see it."

"I know what you mean," Maggie replied. "But somebody's got to look at it."

"Maybe we should wait for Barclay and Brett."

"Forget that," Maggie said. "It would be worse with them here."

After several minutes, they were able to locate a vacant editing room with a lock on the door and no windows. Once inside, Maggie slipped the tape into the playback machine, but then both women hesitated, neither prepared to roll the tape. They looked at each other for courage until Maggie finally gave in, muttering, "What the hell," as she hit the START button.

The first scenes showed four girls, all teenagers or younger, in pajamas, giggling, shouting, engaged in a mock pillow fight on a large double bed. Then the film's title, *Pajama Party*, was superimposed over the pictures. It soon became apparent that they were looking at a professionally-produced product: The scenes were well-lighted, -shot and -edited; the graphics and video effects state-of-the-art; even the background music was well-orchestrated and recorded in stereo.

No doubt about it. This was no back-alley production.

What followed the opening scenes were forty minutes of pure pornographic filth. Three boys, as young or younger than the girls, invaded the pajama party, and before many minutes had passed, all of the children were naked, engaged in sexual acts that would make most adults blush. There was no plot to the video or any attempt at narration, but simply a succession of explicit sex scenes among children who should instead have been worrying about their first date or first kiss.

Maggie and Jessica could only sit stunned, morbidly spellbound, but sickened by what they saw. "I can't stand this," Jessica said, halfway through the video. "I want to throw up." They stopped the tape machine twice to give themselves a chance to recover and regain their composure, then several more times to study specific frames that clearly showed the faces of each of the children.

Within the first few minutes, they recognized—from pictures they had seen—both Penny Collins and Nadia Vaughn, who, although young themselves, still appeared older than the other two girls in the video. "My God, they can't be more than twelve or thirteen," Jessica said with disbelief.

"This must be the second film," Maggie said. "Because Amy's not in it. That means one of those other girls must be the one who got hurt."

As the tape ended, they sat back, lost for the words to describe their shock and anger. "Seeing this has to bring back bad memories for you," Jessica finally said.

Maggie could only nod.

"Was your film anything like this?"

"Not that different," she admitted. "Technically,

it was not nearly as sophisticated, but otherwise, yeah."

"It must have been a horrible experience."

"You got that right," Maggie said. "It will always be with me, I know that now."

"But you survived it."

"That's yet to be seen, I'd say."

"Well," Jessica said, "I just want you to know that I admire what you've done. How far you've come. It's taken a lot of guts. I would hope some of these kids can do the same."

"It may be too late for them," Maggie said as she reached for the machine to rewind the tape. "But we've got to make sure there's not more. We've got to get the bastards who did this. No matter what it takes."

"You don't have to convince me," Jessica replied. "Barclay and Brett are going to go crazy when they see it."

Maggie wondered how many copies of this tape or the one before it were now in circulation, and how many others like them were making the rounds in the pornographic underworld. Probably more than she or the public would ever imagine, since she knew efforts to investigate and prosecute the makers and distributors of child pornography were uneven, at best. It was a secret world that few had been able to penetrate, one that yielded enormous profits to those who managed to stay out of the clutches of the law.

And now, of course, the purveyors of child porn were taking their product to the Internet, where detection and prosecution were proving to be even more difficult. For all Maggie knew, single frames from this tape could already be out there in cyberspace.

Jessica broke into her thoughts. "How do you think Nadia got hold of the tape?"

Maggie got up and stood by the door. "Amy Boyd told me that Penny Collins may have died trying to steal the tape. She must have found it and given it to Nadia before she was killed. That's the only thing I can figure."

"But why would Nadia leave it in the bag?"

Maggie shrugged. "She must have planned to come back. Who knows what she was thinking at the time? She must have decided on suicide after she got home. We'll probably never know."

Their conversation was interrupted by a sharp knock on the door. Maggie quickly retrieved the tape from the machine and held it behind her back as Jessica unlocked the door. Brett was standing outside. "Someone said they saw the two of you come in here. What's going on?"

"Close the door," Maggie said as she held out the cassette and explained how it had come into their hands, describing it in some detail. "It was awful, Brett. You can't imagine." As he took the cassette from her, Maggie added, "Barclay should see it, too. And we should get still shots of each of the kids off of the videotape. Maybe we can figure out a way to identify the others."

"First thing we've got to do," Brett said, "is to get some copies made. We don't want this tape disappearing on us." Then, with a grimace, he said, "You're sure I have to see it?"

"You don't have to, but you should," Maggie replied. "It may make you ill, but it will also make you mad as hell. And we need to be mad as hell right now."

Brett took the tape and left, in search of Barclay.

32

Halloween fell on a Saturday. The weather was cool, but not cold. Most of the earlier snow had disappeared, although the streets and sidewalks remained icy and slippery in spots. Not the best night for the kids to be out trick-or-treating, but a far cry from a Halloween night of several years before–when Minnesota was buried beneath more than a foot of snow. Although Maggie had not been there at the time, people never tired of telling her stories of the Great Halloween Blizzard.

Danny was already in his Superman costume by mid-afternoon, long before the promised time of departure. "We have to wait until it gets dark," Maggie told him. "When the other kids are out. That's half the fun."

While accepting her edict, he could not pull himself from the window, patiently waiting for the sun to set and watching for the first sign of any other child on the streets in costume. A small plastic pumpkin with a carrying handle was already sitting on the kitchen table, ready to be filled with whatever goodies he could harvest door-to-door.

For his part, Brett still questioned the wisdom of venturing out with the boy after dark. "I don't know, Maggie," he said, "with everything that's been happening, I'm not sure this is the smartest idea."

She understood and shared his concern, but could not bring herself to deny Danny the fun of a Halloween night. "All of the kids in school have been talking about it for weeks," she told him. "And he remembers last year and all the stuff he got."

Because of the tight security at their own building, there would be no kids coming to their door. Which meant that both Brett and Maggie would be free to accompany Danny on his rounds— giving Maggie an even greater sense of confidence. "We'll just keep a close eye on him," she said. "I'm sure everything will be okay, if we can just stay awake long enough."

Brett was stretched out, half-asleep on the couch. "Amen to that," he mumbled.

The two of them had been out late the night before, attending an impromptu and raucous celebration at a nearby bar, shared by more than a score of other staff members, including George Barclay. The October rating period was over, and Channel 7 had scored another impressive victory, increasing its share of audience in each of its four daily newscasts, but most impressively at ten o'clock—which, from a sales and prestige point of view, was the most important newscast of the day.

They were now reaching more than forty percent of the news viewing audience, an almost unheard of figure in the highly competitive television news wars. It was only the latest in the string of rating successes since Maggie had arrived in the market, a fact not ignored by Barclay in his somewhat tipsy party speech.

"With all due respect and thanks to Alex Collier and the rest of you," he said, shouting over the noise in the room, "I think we should pay a special tribute to Maggie Lawrence. Since she's come to town, we've gone from a twenty-eight to a forty share in the late news, and damn near that much in the early slot."

Maggie was at the back of the bar, hardly able to hear Barclay's words when applause suddenly broke out around her and she found everyone looking and smiling in her direction. She leaned toward Brett. "What is he saying?"

"That you're a star," he replied with a grin. "I'd go for a raise right now."

But Barclay had not yet finished. "Especially in light of what's happened lately, I think we all owe Maggie a debt of gratitude. As you know, this has not been an easy time for her, with the threats and all, yet she's not missed a night on the air." Weaving slightly, he managed to raise his glass of beer in a swooping toast. "To Maggie," he said, "may she be with us for years to come!"

Maggie quickly found herself surrounded by

people she worked with but didn't know that well, feeling their pats on her back and their boozy breath in her face, hearing words of congratulation, sincere but often slurred. She looked for Brett to come to the rescue, but he was now across the room, deep in conversation with someone whose back was toward her.

Smiling graciously but self-consciously, she thanked the well-wishers and slowly backed away, retreating to a more isolated section of the bar, hoping to escape the unwanted attention. But George Barclay got to her first, wobbling, his beer held unsteadily in his hand. She had never seen him tight before.

"Not trying to run away, are you?" he said. "Enjoy the party."

Maggie continued to back pedal. "The speech wasn't necessary, George. I don't need to be singled out. It makes me uncomfortable."

"Savor it while you can, Margaret," he said, clearly feeling little pain. "Fame can be fleeting, you know."

"Especially in my case," she added wryly.

He paused, cocking his head. "You know I didn't mean it that way."

She smiled. "I know, George."

Maggie realized this was neither the time nor the place for a serious discussion, especially considering Barclay's condition, but since she had not talked to him since Brett took the *Pajama Party* tape, she couldn't resist asking him if he had seen it.

He could only shake his head. "I thought I was going to puke right there in the office," he said more soberly. "In all my years in this business, I've never seen anything like it. And I've not lived an especially sheltered life. It's hard to believe the thing was made here. Kind of puts 'Minnesota nice' to shame, doesn't it?"

She slid into a booth and pulled Barclay in next to her. "Who knows how many more they've made," she said plaintively, "or plan to make in the future. We've got to stop them, George. We need to put everything we've got into this."

"Who can argue with that?" he replied. "But we still have to run a daily news operation, Maggie. Keep those goddamned ratings up. October was important, but as you well know, the November ratings are the crucial ones. The ones that Hawke and everyone else up in management heaven will be watching."

He didn't have to remind her. She knew the newsroom staff was already badly stretched, humping to cover the breaking news of each day while also working on the November and February sweep series. There was little more support Barclay could afford to give them. "Then maybe we ought to call in the cops," she said. "Now that we're sure this kind of thing is happening, we can't let it go on."

Barclay eased his bulk out of the booth. "Maybe you're right," he said. "But I want to give it a few more days, at least. See what happens."

Sissy and Tony waited until late that Halloween afternoon before pulling out of the motel parking lot and heading toward south Minneapolis, Tony at the wheel of a black Buick LeSabre—the third car they'd rented since arriving in Minnesota.

"This seems stupid to me," Sissy said, huddled against the passenger door.

"You read what the note said," Tony replied. "We do what we're told to do."

Sissy scoffed. "Damned dangerous, too. Even if we do find them, we could end up running down some innocent little kid, for Christ's sake. And you know damn well that the cops are going to be out and around on a night like this."

Tony pulled onto the interstate, not bothering to respond. Sissy had been harping at him for days, demanding to know what the hell was happening and when it was going to end. He had no answers, but could not convince her of that. She was certain he was holding out on her, and he had long since given up trying to deny it.

"I would never have signed on for this deal if I'd thought we'd still be here at Halloween," she said. "I'm getting blisters on my butt from sitting around all day."

Tony scoffed. "It's better than shaking your ass and twirling your titties up on some stage, isn't it?" he said angrily. "And I don't see you turning down the money."

Both were accumulating more cash than they had seen in years, although Sissy remained convinced that Tony had blown some of his at the Indian casinos on his rare trips away from the motels. As nice as the money was, however, their frustration over the waiting and the secrecy of the mission was growing by the day, wearing them down.

"Remember the General's note a couple of weeks ago," Sissy said. "The one that claimed we were nearing the end of this business? What the hell's happened?"

Tony could only shrug, his eyes on the highway, watching for the right exit.

"If they think we're scaring her," she continued, "they must not be watching the news. She's cool as can be, like nothing's bothering her. It's amazing."

"Maybe that's why we're still here," Tony offered. "Maybe that's why we're doing what we're doing tonight."

"You'd better hope we don't kill somebody in the process," she said.

Maggie and Brett stood on the darkened street, watching as Danny walked up to the first house, a small one-story structure a block from the apartment building. Two carved pumpkins, candles burning inside, sat on the stoop, flanking the door, goblins on guard. Danny gave a quick glance back at them and then pushed the doorbell, which was immediately answered by an older lady, pincurls in her hair.

From the street, they could hear his "trick-or-treat," and the woman's animated response. "My goodness, it's Superman!" she squealed, opening the door wide enough to drop a couple of pieces of candy into Danny's plastic pumpkin. "You take care now, Superman. Don't you fly away."

As they walked along, moving from house to house, they met dozens of other children, some in costume, some not, laughing and chattering, swinging their bags of goodies. Danny was enjoying every minute of it, rushing back from every stop to tell them what he had gotten—grousing about the pennies and the apples, gushing about the Mars bars and Baby Ruths.

Maggie couldn't remember seeing him more excited. After all, he had been living a sheltered, controlled life for the past several weeks. While he seldom complained, she knew that he was feeling confined, unable to play outside by himself or with friends without the presence of either Anna, Brett, or herself. Except for school, he was living largely an adult life, and she could see that tonight he was feeling a rare freedom.

Tony and Sissy had been with them from the beginning, watching as they left the apartment building and then trailing along, a half-block away, waiting for the right opportunity. Whenever he could, Tony pulled the LeSabre in behind parked cars, hiding, idling, but always keeping them within view, helped by all of the porchlights left on for the children.

"I still don't like this," Sissy said. "Too many people around."

"Relax," Tony said. "We'll wait until they're on their way back to the apartment building."

Sissy opened the paper bag in her lap. "This could be tricky," she said, pulling out the contents and examining them.

"You'll have time," he said. "Just keep cool, and keep the window open."

◆   ◆   ◆

"C'mon, Danny, it's time to get home," Maggie shouted as the boy ran ahead of them down the sidewalk, his plastic pumpkin almost overflowing. They had been out for more than an hour, and she was feeling both the chill of the night and the aftereffects of the night before. She couldn't wait to get back to the apartment and into her robe, sitting in front of the fire.

"Two more, Mom. Honest, that's all."

"That's it, then," she said as he scampered away.

They were some three blocks from the apartment building, having covered homes on both sides of the street. For Maggie, it felt good to have Brett beside her, holding her hand loosely as they walked along. Almost like a real family, she thought, wondering if it could ever be truly that.

He had said little, apparently feeling the same quiet contentment she was experiencing. But she could also sense that he was alert to what was happening around them. He paused frequently to check their surroundings, never allowing Danny to get more than twenty feet from them.

When they were less than a block from the apartment, approaching the parking lot, they saw but took little notice of a car's lights flick on at the far end of the lot. Danny was busily chattering and chewing on pieces of candy from the plastic pumpkin, fighting off Brett's mock attempts to raid his storehouse. "You've got to share, you know," Brett said, grabbing for the candy. Danny squealed and jumped aside.

They were now walking across the parking lot,

one side of which was all but deserted. The car with
the lights was now moving toward them, slowly, still
some distance away, but picking up speed.

Sissy felt the rush of wind in her face from the open
window as the car accelerated. The distance was closing quickly, the headlights now picking up their prey.

"You've got the lighter?" Tony shouted.

Sissy held it up for him to see, but his eyes were
straight ahead, his hands tightly gripping the
wheel of the LeSabre.

"Get set!" he yelled into the wind.

Brett heard the roar of the car's engine before he
actually saw the lights bearing down on them, the
high-beams blinding him. "Maggie!" he screamed,
turning his head away. "Watch out! Grab Danny!"
He could hear the sharp intake of her breath and
saw her lunge for her son.

The car was now no more than fifty feet away,
the driver laying on the horn, giving Brett the
fleeting sense of a freight train rushing down the
tracks, straight at him. He stood, immobilized by
his shock and fear. Maggie had dragged Danny
away, pulling him by one arm, falling, scrambling
on the blacktop, screaming at Brett to move.

Before he could, the car swerved sharply to the
right, racing past him, a black streak, missing him
by no more than five feet. If he had dived that way,
he'd be dead beneath the car's wheels. Paralyzed,
he saw nothing but the flash of an arm out of the
car's open window. Throwing something?

"You bastards!" he shouted at the back of the car, speeding away. Black, that's all he could tell. No make, certainly no license number. It was too dark; it had happened too fast. Turning back, he found Maggie and Danny on the ground, huddled together. But before he could reach them, what sounded like shots began to explode around them. One after the other, a deafening series that seemed to be coming from everywhere, but nowhere. "Duck!" he shouted as he dove to the ground himself, curling up, covering his head. Maggie and Danny did the same.

The shots abruptly ended. Brett raised himself, only then realizing they had been attacked by fire-crackers. The smell of them was in the air, the paper remnants on the pavement, mixed with the pieces of Danny's candy that had scattered every-where. Feeling foolish, Brett wanted to laugh, but choked instead. "It's all right, Maggie. Danny," he said, making his way to them. "They were just fire-crackers. Everything's okay."

She was sitting on the asphalt, Danny in her arms, crying uncontrollably, shaking. She held him tightly, whispering in his ear, trying to calm him. Brett knelt beside them, feeling helpless. "Are you hurt?" he asked. "How about Danny?"

"A few bruises, I think. Scratches, too. But no broken bones."

Danny's sobbing slowly subsided, but his body still shook. Brett ruffled his hair. "C'mon, squirt. Everything's okay. You're safe."

"I should have listened to you," Maggie said, trying to control her own tremors. "We should have stayed at home."

"And I should have kept a sharper eye out," he said. "But, shit, we were almost at the door . . ." His voice trailed off.

"Let's get Danny inside," she said as Brett helped her to her feet. "Get ourselves cleaned up."

Brett took Danny into his arms, and as they walked to the door, he was comforted by only one thought. They could have killed them all, but they didn't.

Later that night, with Danny soothed, bathed, and in bed, and after Brett had returned from the parking lot with as many pieces of Danny's Halloween candy as he could find, Brett and Maggie were in bed themselves. Calm now, fresh from a shower, their bumps and bruises tended, Maggie lay in the crook of his arm, thinking some of the same thoughts that occurred to him earlier.

"If they don't want to hurt or kill us," she wondered aloud, "then why are they trying to frighten us? What for?"

"The sixty-four-thousand dollar question," Brett mused. "It must be tied to the porn ring. Unless it really is some right-wing, born-again zealot out to make life miserable for you.

There are those kind of people around, you know."

Maggie knew he was right, but still, it was hard to believe. "I don't want us to tell anyone about what happened," she said. "Not Barclay, not Jessica, maybe not even Anna."

Brett laughed. "You think you'll keep Danny quiet about this? He'll be all over Anna next week.

With, I'm sure, a somewhat exaggerated version of what actually happened."

"You're probably right," Maggie sighed. "It may be good for her to hear anyway. It'll remind her to keep her guard up."

She turned her head slightly to get more comfortable, allowing her to look up at him. "If we tell Barclay, or even Jessica, they're going to want to chain me up, not let me out of their sights."

"It may not be the worst idea," Brett said.

"Bullshit!" she whispered. "I'm not going to be frightened away, Brett. I have to figure out something to do with Danny, to make sure he stays safe, but I'm not going to crawl into a hole. I won't let them do that to me."

Brett didn't argue. He knew it would do no good.

33

Three nights passed, and Jessica had yet to see the inside or outside of the Edina office building. For the first two nights, her cleaning crew was assigned to a three-story building on Park Avenue, the third night to a car dealership on Lake Street. As she quickly discovered, the work was not easy, in part because the senior members of the crew grabbed the lighter tasks such as vacuuming and dusting, leaving the more odious chores of mopping and bathroom cleaning to the rookie. By the end of each shift, her hands were blistered and her arms and back ached; her clothes were filthy, and her body was covered with sweat. She was exhausted, ready to rush home to a shower and bed.

At least Barclay was letting her sleep in late the next day.

So far, she had worked with the same people: two men, Jake and Larry, and another woman, Evelyn. She still didn't know their last names, but all were older than herself and veterans of the cleaning business. They seldom spoke, but when they did, it was usually in words of single syllables or four letters. They made little effort to get to know Jessica—or Miranda, as she was known to them—or to engage in conversation, which was perfectly all right with her.

On their breaks, however, Jessica was able to pry some information from them: There were three other crews like their own, and together they were responsible for the cleaning of seven buildings. The assignments would vary depending on the whims of their supervisor, who was likely to change their duties from night to night without notice or explanation. That gave Jessica some hope, since it was difficult to picture many more nights at either of the places she had worked so far.

Maybe Maggie had been right in predicting that she might never get to the Edina office. But Jessica didn't want to think about that.

On the fourth night, however, she got lucky. She was preparing to return to the same building with the same crew when the supervisor called her aside. Another woman on another crew had called in sick, and he assigned Jessica to take her place. Within minutes, she found herself in a van with two men she guessed to be in their twenties, one black, whose name was Samuel, the other white, who went by Chip. She recalled the video Brett and Tamara had shot outside of the Edina building nights before, when two men—one white, one black—were shown unloading the Clean Sweep, Inc. van. She crossed her fingers, said a little prayer, and then asked, "Where are we going?" as the van headed south on Lyndale Avenue.

"Near Fiftieth and France," Samuel answered. "Four stories of offices. We each take one floor and work the fourth together. How fast are you?"

"What do you mean?"

"How fast do you work?"

"Fast enough, I guess. Nobody's bitched so far."

"Good. We're paid for eight hours of work, but we try to finish in five. Company doesn't care as long as we do the work. We'd hate to see you hold us up."

"I'll give it my best shot," Jessica said. "But I've never been in the building, you know. You're going to have to show me the routine."

"That won't take long," he said.

She settled back in her seat, considering what she had been told. Four floors of offices, one for each of them and a fourth to share. What about the fifth?

At the time Jessica's van was moving south on Lyndale, Butch Hemrick was driving north in his new Cadillac DeVille, bound again for the uptown area. He wasn't sure he would find what he was after there, but it was a logical place to begin the search.

He had been fortunate the last time to have so

quickly found Amy and her two friends on the bus bench, in the same area, but that had been in daylight and the first place he had happened to look. These kids moved around a lot, he knew, and spotting them now in the darkness and the cold of a near-winter night might be an entirely different story. What's more, he was hoping to find them apart; specifically, he was looking for the kid with the long hair, the one who had flashed his switchblade knife.

Hemrick wasn't spoiling for a fight, but for the answer to a question that had been nagging him since his encounter with Amy. He thought he might have a better chance of getting the answer from one of the boys than he would from Amy herself.

Hemrick crossed from Lyndale to Hennepin on Lake Street, moving slowly, keeping his eyes on the sidewalks, peering into the windows of the lighted stores and fast-food joints along the way. He circled the area three times, parking once to wander through the Calhoun Square mall itself. He saw no sign of Amy or her friends.

Back in the car, he headed for downtown Minneapolis, cruising the length of Hennepin Avenue, and then the area around the Target Center and the bus depot, and finally along Hennepin again, slowing to probe the darkened doorways of the buildings and into theater lobbies and video arcades. Still nothing.

Discouraged, he drove along Washington Avenue, not far from the abandoned grain elevators where he knew many of the street kids escaped from the cold and made their home. He parked near Seven

Corners, another popular entertainment area, and
let the car idle, the heater working, as he waited—
and watched.

As the cleaning van pulled up in front of the
Edina building, Chip, explained the procedures
to Jessica. "I'll take the first floor, Sam here the
second, and you the third. It should take us each
about three hours. We'll take a break and meet on
the fourth floor, then finish up together."

Jessica was out of the van, standing on the sidewalk, looking up, as the two men opened the rear
door of the van for the supplies. "I count five
floors," she said. "Who does the fifth?"

"Nobody," Chip replied. "At least not us. It's
locked up tight."

"Why's that?" she asked innocently.

"Beats the shit out of me," Samuel said, "but it's
one less floor to clean. We just do as we're told."

Jessica grabbed one of the vacuum cleaners out
of the back and glanced across the street. The station's surveillance van was already there, its interior
darkened. She knew Brett would be hearing the
conversation.

As they approached the front entrance, Chip
handed her a set of keys. "The master key will open
all of the third floor offices," he said. "There's
another for both of the bathrooms. Sam will show
you around." Inside the lobby, they found a guard
sitting behind the security desk. He gave them a
small wave and a quick glance, unwilling to take his
eyes off the *Seinfeld* show playing on a small television set on top of the desk. Jessica saw that there

were no other monitors, which probably meant the building had no security cameras in the hallways or offices. At least she could hope that was true.

Chip stayed on the first floor while Jessica and Samuel took the elevator to the third. The corridor off the elevator extended the width of the building, with offices lined up along each side. As they walked along, Jessica noticed there were no office windows facing the hallway, just a succession of closed and locked doors, with the company names in bronze lettering on each of the doors. Twelve in all, she counted. And she had been right: She could see no sign of security cameras anywhere.

"It's the same basic layout on each of the floors," Samuel told her, "although some of the offices are larger, some smaller, depending on the floor. But we've all got the same area to clean."

At the end of the corridor, he opened the door to a small cleaning closet, which he said contained everything she would need, except for the vacuum, which she already had in her hands. "The two bathrooms are over there," he said, pointing to two doors adjacent to the cleaning closet. "And the stairway is back by the elevators, in case they're not working for some reason."

As he started to walk away, he turned. "Oh, yeah. The emergency exit is down this hall. Opens to a fire escape on the back of the building. Not that you'll ever need it." With that, he left her alone, wondering how in the hell she was going to get a look inside the fifth floor.

♦   ♦   ♦

Butch Hemrick had been sitting for an hour, struggling to stay awake in the warm comfort of the Cadillac, his eyes drifting shut to the soft music of the stereo and the steady hum of the heater. Twice he got out to walk in the crisp night air, shaking the drowsiness off, his patience quickly ebbing.

As he prepared to leave, retrace his previous steps, and then to call it a night, he saw three figures moving toward him along the sidewalk. They had emerged from a street-side mission, located in a building with a huge JESUS SAVES sign painted on its brick wall, and were now less than a block away, on his side of the street.

Hemrick couldn't be sure it was Amy and the boys until they passed beneath a streetlamp a hundred feet away. They appeared to be in no hurry, sauntering and chatting among themselves. He waited until they were abreast of the car before he opened the door and quickly slipped out, intercepting them before they had walked more than a few feet. "Hold on," he said, blocking their path.

It took only a split second for them to recognize Hemrick's bulk in the darkness. "Run, Amy!" one of the boys shouted. She darted around and past Hemrick before he could put out an arm out to stop her, as did the smaller of the boys, Popeye. But the other one, Rocky, was trapped, facing Hemrick while also searching frantically for a way to escape himself.

"Keep the knife in your pocket, punk," Butch said. "I only want to talk."

Rocky backed away, eyes moving from side to side. "About what?" he asked, unable to disguise the fear in his voice. Hemrick continued to move toward him, backing him against the fender of the Cadillac, and now stood no more than a foot from him. "Keep your hands where I can see them," he said. Then, "Behind you, against the car."

Rocky hesitated, but did as he was told. He could see Amy and Popeye over Butch's shoulder, standing half a block away, beneath the lighted sign of OSCAR'S BAR.

"What do you want?" he stammered. "I don't got shit for you."

"Yes, you do," Hemrick said. "Tell me where Amy got that coat."

"*What?*" The surprise in his voice was real.

"The coat, the nice coat she's wearing. Where did she get it?"

"How the fuck do I know?" the boy said sullenly.

Hemrick moved so quickly that Rocky felt the pain before he saw the fist move, the blow to the stomach doubling him over. Then his head was jerked back up by his long hair. He tried to cry out, but the slap across the face by the back of Hemrick's hand caught the cry mid-throat, killing it. "Don't screw with me, boy," Hemrick hissed.

Blood was seeping from the edge of Rocky's mouth, and the ringing in his right ear made him dizzy. He fought to keep his feet, but his knees buckled and he slid to the pavement, his head resting against the tire of the car. Hemrick pulled him back up by his ears and in one motion slammed a knee to his groin. His scream pierced the night, and he collapsed again, holding himself, sobbing with the pain.

Hemrick quickly looked around and found Amy and Popeye moving toward him, now less than a quarter of a block away. "Leave him alone, you bastard!" the boy shouted. "We're calling the cops, you fucking scarface."

Butch ignored him and surveyed the street in other directions. No one seemed to be out, let alone responding to Rocky's scream. He knelt by the boy. "Now, who gave her the coat?" he demanded. "Or do you want more?"

Cowering against the car, Rocky mumbled between moans, "The television lady. Maggie Lawrence. She gave her the coat."

"Maggie Lawrence from Channel Seven? You're sure?"

"Yes."

"They talked? Amy talked to this woman?"

"Twice," the boy said.

Hemrick's lips were no more than an inch from Rocky's ear. "What did she tell her?"

Rocky pulled back. "I don't know. I swear. She kept us away."

"Who did?"

"Amy. She didn't want us to hear."

Hemrick rose and lifted the boy away from the car, letting him sprawl on the sidewalk, still holding his groin. "You breathe a word of this to anybody, and you're dead. Understand?"

He got only a groan for an answer.

Jessica worked her way down the hallway, one office after another. Vacumming, dusting, carrying out the trash. Mindless tasks that left her time to ponder the problem facing her. She had decided against doing any exploring until she had a better sense of the building routine. Like when and how often did the guard make his rounds and would one of her coworkers drop by to check on her?

The answer to the last question came first. After less than an hour, she heard the elevator doors open and saw Chip step out. She had just finished cleaning her fourth office and was unlocking the door to the fifth as he strode down the corridor. "Looks like you're moving right along," he said. "Any problems?"

"Besides an aching back, no," she replied lightly.

He took the ring of keys from her. "Let's see how you're doing."

As she followed along, he opened the doors to the offices she had cleaned and went inside each, quickly checking the carpets and wastebaskets, running his fingers along the desktops. He said nothing until he finished his inspection tour. "You're doing okay. But keep moving."

Hardly high praise, but perhaps enough to satisfy him and keep him away for a a while.

As she worked, and when she was sure she was alone, she provided intermittent commentary to Brett via the wireless mike—describing what she was seeing and doing, and occasionally bitching about the amount of work. The exercise was as much a test of the equipment as it was a means of keeping Brett and herself awake and alert.

The guard showed up twenty minutes later. She didn't hear or see him until she was about to leave the fifth office. Suddenly, he was there, filling the doorway, scaring the hell out of her. She gave a little shriek and jumped back. "Goddamn," she said, "where did you come from?"

He smiled and apologized, then introduced himself as Isaiah Roberts. A black man, sturdily built, with a mustache and a goatee, and a silver front tooth that flashed like a beacon when he spoke. "You're new, aren't you?" he asked.

"My first night here," she replied. "How about you?"

"Six months. I've got a day job, too. Drive a yellow cab."

"So what do you do here?" she asked as casually as she could.

He laughed. "Not a hell of a lot, you really want to know. Keep an eye on the doors and tour the building every couple of hours. Checking things out. That's about it."

"Nice job if you can get it," she said, smiling.

"You're telling me," he replied.

Jessica could see that he would like to stand and chat for a while, but she had other priorities. And she wanted to avoid any other questions about herself. "I'd better get back to work," she said. "The guys downstairs want me to keep at it."

"Take care," he said as he moved down the corridor, checking the locks on all of the office doors. She watched until he stepped back onto the elevator, squinting to see if it would take him up or down. It went up, but stopped on four. Did he have access to five? She didn't have the time to wait, and went back to work, moving as quickly as she could. All of the offices seemed pretty much the same, and she paid little attention to the particular companies they housed until she came to one marked DUGGAN CAMPAIGN. Only then did she realize it was located on this floor.

Not as large as some of the offices, the suite contained a receptionist's desk and a private, glassed-in space she assumed to be Butch Hemrick's office. File cabinets lined one wall and a long table was set against another, divided into small partitions, each with its own telephone jack: the telemarketing area, she guessed, where Duggan campaign workers solicited funds, volunteers and votes.

The office appeared unused, at least for a while. The wastebaskets were empty and the carpeting still showed the marks of the last vacuuming. With the door closed, she tried the file cabinets but found them all locked. Hemrick's door was also locked, but one of her keys fit. No surprise since it had to be cleaned, too. She hauled her vacuum cleaner inside and plugged it into a wall socket. Then, with one eye on the outer door, she quickly tested the desk drawers. They, too, were locked. Push come to shove, she suspected they could be picked or forced.

But not now. She had neither the tools nor the time. Nor the know-how.

When Hemrick's Cadillac pulled away, Amy and Popeye ran to Rocky's side. By the time they got there, he was on his knees, struggling to rise. Amy knelt beside him, grasping an arm to support him. "Are you okay?" she whispered. "Can you get up?"

He turned to her, the blood now caked on his

lips. "The bastard kicked me in the balls," he whimpered. "It hurts like a son of a bitch."

Between Amy and Popeye, they were able to get him to his feet and hold him as he gulped deep breaths and held his crotch. "The bastard's fast," he finally said. "I didn't even see the first punch."

Amy took off her coat and put it around his shoulders. "What did he want?" she asked. "Why was he waiting for us?"

Rocky hesitated, then said, "He wanted to know where you got this goddamned coat."

Amy shuddered, suddenly remembering Hemrick's words on the bus bench, his intense interest in her nice new coat. "Did you tell him?"

"I had to, Amy. After he got me in the balls. I didn't know what he was going to do next. The fucker was ready to kill me, for Christ's sake."

She wrapped her arms around him, holding him against her. "It's okay, Rocky. It's okay. What else did he want?"

"What you told her. I said I didn't know, that you kept us away."

Popeye, who had remained silent until then, said, "I'm going to get me a fuckin' gun! I swear, the next time that dude fucks with us, I'll kill him. You hear what I'm saying? No bullshit. I'm going to do it."

Amy began to lead the two of them back to the Jesus Saves mission. "We've got to get you cleaned up," she said. "Find you a place to lay down. Then we've got to make ourselves disappear."

But first, she knew, she had to call Maggie Lawrence.

Jessica waited another twenty minutes, then hurried down the corridor toward the elevators—watching the lights on the wall above them to see if the elevators were in motion. They weren't. The stairway door was immediately to the left of the elevators and opened easily. After pausing briefly in the concrete stairwell to listen, she took the steps two at a time to the fifth floor landing, where she quickly put her ear to the steel door. Hearing nothing, she tried the knob, turning it as quietly as she could manage.

Locked.

She was not surprised. Kneeling down, she studied the lock, then quickly tried to use the master and bathroom keys she'd been given. Again, no luck, but no surprise. The master key did come close; it slid into the slot but refused to turn. She made a mental note to trace the outline of the key on paper when she got back downstairs. Perhaps a locksmith would be willing to make variations of it.

As she worked, she whispered into the wirclcss mike beneath her shirt, hoping Brett could hear what she was trying . . . and failing . . . to do.

Ten minutes had passed. She stood stock-still. What was it? A far-off metallic growl. *The elevator.* It was moving, the grinding of its machinery traveling up the elevator shaft next to the stairwell. "Oh shit!" she muttered, leaping down the stairs, taking them three at a time, grasping for the railing, hoping to keep her feet. She was out of the stairway and out of breath, halfway down the corridor, when the elevator opened and Samuel emerged. Almost too close to call.

"What's happening?" he said as he approached her.

"Nothing much," she said, trying to control her heavy breathing.

But it didn't escape him. "You been running or something?"

"Just finished my sit-ups," she said, thinking quickly. "I try to do fifty of them every night. Keeps me in shape."

He watched her curiously. "The work's not exercise enough?"

She laughed. "It doesn't help take off the pounds in the right places."

"I don't see any extra pounds on you," he said with a slight leer, his eyes traveling the length of her. "You look mighty fine in all the right places."

"Yeah, right," she scoffed, and moved quickly on to the next office.

Like his partner before him, Samuel quickly checked the offices she had cleaned. "You haven't done the toilets yet?" he asked.

She shook her head and glanced at her watch. "Not yet, but I'll be done in the three hours, don't worry."

When he was gone, she quickly got back to work, trying to make up for lost time. She knew there wouldn't be another chance to explore, and didn't know what good it would do anyway. Unless they could get a key to fit the lock, she could think of no way to get inside the fifth floor space. There was the fire escape, but she was not particularly eager to get out on that.

At the moment, it seemed all but hopeless.

◆   ◆   ◆

"Did you hear it all?" she asked Brett when she climbed into the surveillance van after the job was over.

"I think so," he said. "You almost got caught, didn't you?"

"Damn near peed in my pants," she said. "I didn't beat the elevator by more than five seconds."

"Good thing you got your sit-ups in," he laughed.

She grinned. "That was the best I could think of at the moment."

As they paused for a stoplight, Jessica showed him the paper tracing she had made of the key that fit, but did not unlock, the door of the fifth floor. "I don't know," he said, "we can try to make some variations of it, but I wouldn't bet my job on it."

She then described the desk and file cabinets in the Duggan campaign office.

"That may provide us a better chance," he said. "Those office desk locks can be easy to pick if you've got the right tools."

"And if you know what the hell you're doing," she added.

"True enough."

The light changed and Brett drove on, glancing at the fatigued woman next to him.

"What are the chances of you getting back to that building?" he asked.

She shrugged. "Depends on if and when the regular woman gets sick again, I suppose. But the two guys said they liked working with me, that I kept up with them. Maybe they'll put in a good word with the boss."

"I knew you'd make a good janitor," Brett said with a smile.

"Screw you, smartass. I'm sorry now that I won that goddamned argument. I'd like to see you with that mop in your hands, cleaning the toilets. It's not exactly what you go to college for."

34

Maggie got the call from Amy just as she and Brett were preparing to leave for home after the late news. She was standing by her desk, coat on, packing a few things into her briefcase when Brett intercepted the call and quickly handed the receiver to her.

"Amy? Are you okay?"

"I'm okay, but one of my friends isn't," she said, and then briefly related the details of their encounter with Butch on the street. "He beat the shit out of Rocky, made him tell where I got the coat you gave me. He knows that we've talked."

"My God," Maggie whispered.

"We're taking off," Amy said. "I never should have talked to you. It's too damned dangerous now."

"Amy, wait! Give me a minute to think."

Maggie's heart was racing. She sank into her chair and tried to calm herself and gather her thoughts. Brett sat down next to her, watching her quizzically. "Where are you?" she asked, back on the phone. "We're just leaving the station. We'll pick you up and talk this out. You and your friends."

"They're not here," Amy said. "We're staying with some buddies of theirs until we can get out of town."

"Tell me where you are," Maggie pressed. "We have to talk, please."

There was a long pause before Amy finally responded: She was at a pay phone in a pizza place in Dinkytown, a small student shopping area next to the University of Minnesota campus. "We'll be there in fifteen minutes," Maggie said. "Stay put, please."

Grabbing her briefcase and pulling on Brett's arm, Maggie rushed toward the newsroom exit. "Hold on," Brett said, stumbling after her. "What the hell's happening?"

"I'll tell you as we go," she said, still pulling him along. Once outside the station, half-running to the parking ramp, she said, "Butch got to Amy, roughed up one of her friends. They plan to run."

Brett tried to slow the pace to a fast walk. "Does he know about you and Amy?"

"Yes," she said. "He made the boy talk."

"Son of a bitch," he mumbled, at a loss for anything else to say.

As they left the ramp and drove toward Dinkytown in Brett's Explorer, Maggie sat silently for several minutes, thinking. If there was uncertainty before, there was no doubt now that their prey knew his pursuers. Which put not only Amy in greater danger, but herself as well. After the Halloween night scare, that was all she needed.

They had already decided on a plan to protect Danny, at least in the short run. Anna's daughter had agreed to let both Anna and Danny move into the family's home in suburban Apple Valley for an indefinite period. Maggie would pay well for the favor and would see Danny as often as it was possible—and safe.

For his part, Danny had at first resisted the idea, but the scare in the parking lot had given him an almost adult understanding of danger—and he soon agreed to the move. Besides, he was in awe of Anna's teenage grandson, who had already taught him everything he knew about Nintendo and the even more sophisticated video games.

Maggie had arranged for the change in schools, and the move—in secret—had taken place early that morning. She already missed him.

And now there was the question of keeping Amy and her friends safe, yet close enough to be available if needed. "Amy could move in with us," she told Brett, "but there's not room for all three of them. And I don't think she'll part from those two boys."

Brett agreed. "Not after one of them got the shit pounded out of him."

"So what do we do? We can't just let them run. We'd never find them again."

Brett kept his eyes on the road, but said, "My

folks have that cabin near Annandale. They've closed it for the season, but there's no reason we can't reopen it."

"For the kids?"

"Why not?" he said, glancing at her. "It's not that far from here, yet it's pretty isolated."

"Would your folks agree to that?"

"I think so, as long as the place doesn't get trashed."

"We could stock it with food," Maggie said. "And movies and video games. Everything to keep them happy for a while."

"It'll beat riding the rails or living on the streets," he said.

She reached across the seat to give him a quick hug.

After picking up Amy at the pizza place, they drove directly to Maggie's apartment and were now sitting around the kitchen table, sharing a quart of ice cream that she kept in the freezer for Danny. And who knew when he'd be back to eat it?

"How's your friend, Rocky?" Maggie asked.

"Still sore, but okay," she replied. "He got a knee right . . . well, you know, right where it counts."

Maggie smiled. Brett grimaced.

Amy was wearing a Minnesota "M" sweatshirt, identical to the one they had found in the Target bag Nadia had left behind. When Maggie commented on it, Amy said, "We ripped them off together from one of those sports stores downtown. The sales guy saw us, but he couldn't catch us."

Maggie told her they had also found a tape of one of the porn films in Nadia's bag. "I figure Penny must have given it to her before she was killed," Maggie said. "I don't know how else she would have gotten it."

"Was it the one I was in?" Amy asked.

"No. It must be the second one."

Maggie went to her briefcase and pulled out the still photos Brett had made from the videotape, the close-up shots of the other girls and boys in the film. "Do you know who these kids are?" she asked. "Not Penny or Nadia, but the others."

Amy examined the pictures, shaking her head. "No, I've never seen them before."

"They weren't in the film you did?"

She flipped through the pictures again. "Not these, no."

Brett spoke up for the first time. "Where does Butch get these kids?"

"I'm not sure," she said. "Probably off the street. There are little kids like that out there, you know."

"Twelve or thirteen?"

"Hell, yes. Even younger. Their folks are into crack or in jail or whatever. The system can't catch them all, you know that."

Maggie split up the last of the ice cream and then got to the main point. "We don't want you to run," she said, "although we can understand why you want to."

Amy cut in. "You didn't see him! Hell, he could kill one of us the next time. We're not hanging around."

"We don't want you to," Maggie said. "We want you safe, but close by in case we or the cops need to find you."

"*The cops?* Since when did they get involved?"

"They haven't, yet," Maggie replied. "But at some point, they may have to be."

She went on to explain the idea of staying at Brett's family cabin for a time. "This Butch would never know where you are . . . you'd be out of danger. But we would know where to find you if we need you."

When Amy resisted, slowly shaking her head, Maggie again invoked the names of Penny and Nadia. "Penny died trying to expose these bastards," she said, "and Nadia may have killed herself over the guilt of it. And you saw tonight what Butch can do. We need to stop these guys, Amy. But we may not be able to do it without your help."

Amy licked the last of the ice cream from her spoon. "How long would we have to stay at this place?"

"We're not sure," Maggie replied. "Not more than a few weeks, we hope. Time enough for us to bring these bastards down."

"And you'd provide food and everything?"

"Everything you need or want," Maggie promised. "You've just got to leave the place in one piece."

Amy laughed. "We're not jerks, you know. We can take care of things."

"I'm sure you can," Maggie replied.

"Let me talk to the guys about it," Amy said, out of her chair. "I'll let you know in a day or so."

◆   ◆   ◆

Once again, they were all gathered in Barclay's office, slumped in their chairs, each of them showing signs of the stress and fatigue of the past few days. Even Barclay, who was just back from a affiliate news meeting in Dallas, appeared tired and testy from three days of mixing with other news directors—many of them young enough to be his children. "I'm a dinosaur, I know that," he said, "but I'm telling you, these kids speak a different language. All they can talk about are graphics and satellites and set designs and the latest in weather wizardry. I'm not sure any of them would know a real news story if it came up and punched them in the nose."

Maggie, Brett, and Jessica exchanged knowing looks. They had heard this litany of complaints before and waited patiently for him to finish. It usually took about ten minutes, but today it was taking even longer. "You know what they are, don't you? They're news marketers, not news directors. Most of them don't give a shit about the news; they just want to know what it takes to *sell* the news. They're super salesmen, that's all, who just happen to be peddling news instead of used cars."

Maggie knew there was truth in his words, but also an exaggeration of the reality. In many respects, she thought, he *is* a dinosaur, but a lovable one all the same. "C'mon, George," she finally said, "can we get down to business?"

"Sorry," he said, embarrassed to be caught in another tirade. "So fill me in."

Jessica first reported on her night at the Edina office and of possible ways to get access to the fifth floor . . . if she ever got back into the building. "I made a paper tracing of one key," she said. "But a locksmith tells me it's useless. There's one chance in a thousand that he could use the tracing to make a key that would work."

"So what else?" Barclay asked.

Jessica shot a glance at Brett. "Well, Brett here is teaching me how to pick the locks on a desk and file cabinets. Hemrick may keep a fifth-floor key in one of them."

Barclay scowled. "Forget that," he said. "Breaking and entering is a crime, for Christ's sake. If you get caught, we could all be up shit creek."

Jessica and Brett started to argue, but he waved them quiet. "I mean it. No picking locks. You're reporters, not burglars."

Jessica was tempted to tell him about the fire escape at the rear of the building, but held her tongue. If he forbade picking locks, he certainly wouldn't approve of trying to gain entry off the fire escape. Besides, she didn't even know if it was possible.

Brett was on his feet. "I'll say it again, George. It would be a hell of a lot easier, and cleaner, to make Clyde Calder take us in there. He shouldn't have a problem with that if there's nothing to hide."

"What if he refuses?" Barclay demanded, challenging him. "Should we force him at gunpoint?"

"No," Brett said, "just threaten to fire his ass."

"Ha! We'd have a union grievance before you could blink. We have no control over what he does on his own time."

"Even if he's making porn films? That's hardly allowed in the company handbook."

"He could be making Duggan campaign commercials for all we know," Barclay snapped. "We have no goddamned proof of anything."

Maggie jumped in, ending the argument, moving on to a brief description of the beating Butch had given Amy's friend and of Brett's offer to hide the kids away at his family's cabin. "They're going to get back to us," she said, "but in the meantime, Hemrick knows now, if he didn't before, that we're on to him. And that I'm personally involved."

As planned, she neglected to say anything about the Halloween night incident in their parking lot, but did report that they had moved Danny out of the apartment to a safer place. "Why's that?" Barclay asked sharply. "Did something else happen?"

Maggie glanced at Brett. She should have known it wouldn't get by Barclay.

"Well?" he persisted, his eyes moving from Maggie to Brett and back.

Shrugging, Brett decided to confess. "Somebody tried to run us down. In the parking lot, Halloween night. Maggie, Danny, and I. Threw a bunch of firecrackers at us. I thought we were in the middle of a goddamned war. Scared the shit out of us, but nobody really got hurt. A few bumps and bruises is all."

"Mother of God," Barclay murmured. Then, "Maybe we should quit now, call in the cops. It's getting too dicey, too dangerous."

"And be left with nothing?" Maggie said, knowing

she was arguing against her own position of a few nights before. "No way."

"We can still report that Duggan has an ex-con, a child pornographer working for him," Barclay said. "That would be a hell of a story in itself."

"But where would it leave us?" Brett asked. "Duggan would plead ignorance and outrage and fire the guy. He'd probably escape unscathed himself."

"Maybe he should," Barclay said as he got up and walked to the window, staring at the passing traffic outside. "We still don't know that he's directly involved."

"I wouldn't bet your paycheck on it, George," Brett said.

Barclay faced them again. "What do you suggest? That we keep going until one or more of you gets killed?"

"Give us another week," Jessica said. "We still have some leads to follow, some loose ends to tie up. If we're no further ahead by then, we'll get McQueen in here and turn everything over to him."

"Is that all right with you?" he asked, his eyes on Maggie and Brett. They nodded. "Okay, then. You've got one week from today."

Maggie paged through the phone book, finally finding a Dr. Henry Klinkle in the White Pages, with both an office and a home phone number. She punched in the office number and waited for three rings before a woman, sounding harried, answered. "Westside Clinic. Can you hold, please?"

Before Maggie could reply, she was put on hold, serenaded by soothing Muzak-type music. Klinkle was the doctor on the board of Pioneer Properties, the owners of the Edina building, one of those loose ends in the investigation that Jessica had not had time to tie up. Maggie decided to give it a try.

"Thank you for holding." The receptionist was finally back. "How may I help you?"

"Is there a Dr. Klinkle on your staff?" Maggie asked.

"Yes, there is."

"I'm new in town," she lied, "and someone happened to mention his name to me. But they failed to say what type of doctor he is. What specialty."

If the question struck the woman as odd, she didn't indicate it. "Dr. Klinkle is a general practitioner," she said, "a family doctor."

"I see. And how long has he been in practice?"

"Gosh, for many years. I really don't know how many. I'm new here."

"That's okay. I appreciate the information."

"Would you like to make an appointment?" the woman asked, hustling business.

"Not at the moment," Maggie said. "I'll be in touch."

Back to the White Pages and the number of the Minnesota Board of Medical Practice, the agency responsible for hearing complaints against doctors and meting out any discipline. This time she got an answer on the first ring and correctly identified herself to the man on the other end of the line, one Dennis Dunn.

"I want to know if there have been any complaints or discipline against a specific doctor," she said. "Can you provide me with that information?"

"Within limits, we can," Dunn replied. "If a complaint results in disciplinary action by the Board, it can be made public. If, however, the Board fails to discipline, the complaint remains secret."

"Okay," Maggie said. "What kind of discipline are we talking about?"

"The Board has several options. Revocation or suspension of a doctor's license to practice. Censure or reprimand. Fines. Any one or more of the above."

Maggie jotted down notes on a legal pad. "How do I go about checking?"

"That's easy," Dunn said. "Just give me a name."

"Dr. Henry Klinkle. He practices in Minneapolis. At the Westside Clinic."

"Got it," Dunn said. "Do you want to wait while I get the records? Or maybe stop by tomorrow to pick them up?"

Maggie glanced at her watch. "I'll be by tomorrow," she said.

When she looked up, she found Brett standing next to her desk. "So much for Barclay's scenario," he said.

"What do you mean?"

"I just got off the phone with Martin Duggan's ad agency, the one he's used for the last three campaigns."

"And?"

"And they haven't done any television commercials for Duggan in more than a year. Nor has anyone else as far as they know."

"Interesting," Maggie offered.

"What's more," he continued, "the past commercials have all been done through a production house in Chicago. They haven't heard of any spots being done locally."

"Which means our friend Clyde is shooting something other than commercials."

"Exactly. And I think we know what that is."

Across the newsroom, Jessica was also on the phone, speaking with the public relations person for the Minneapolis school system, a man named Hal Hinckley.

"Here's the deal, Hal," she said. "I've got head shots of four kids, grade-school age, I'd say. We'd like to find out who they are and where they live. Their parents' names and all the rest."

"How did you get the pictures," Hinckley asked.

"That's not important. But it's critical to know who they are. It could involve the kids' own safety."

"Sounds serious," he said. "So what do you need?"

"I want someone from the station to visit every elementary school in the city . . . and in Saint Paul, too . . . to see if anyone at the school recognizes the kids in the pictures. I'd like you to clear the way for us by sending out a memo asking for cooperation."

"Jesus, Jessica," he said, "I don't know. That could violate the kids' right to privacy. I'm going to have to talk to one of our legal types."

"Will you get back to me? Quick? I wouldn't be asking if it weren't important."

"How long are you going to be around?" Hinckley asked.

Jessica glanced at her watch. "Not for long. I've got a night job. Just leave a message here or at my apartment."

"Really? You've got a night job?"

"Don't ask," she said.

35

Jessica's luck held. That night, she was back at the Edina building, working with the same two men, Samuel and Chip, who were only too eager to tell her that they had put in a good word for her with the supervisor.

"Thanks, but why did you do that?" she asked.

"Because we like you, kid," Chip replied. "You work faster than the other lady and," he winked, "you're a hell of a lot easier to look at, too."

"He's got that right," Samuel said, grinning.

Jessica laughed off the compliment, unable to believe that anyone would find her the least bit attractive in the wig and the rest of her janitorial attire. At the same time, she knew she would have to be cool, careful not to send the wrong message to the two men. The last thing she needed was to have one or both of them hustling her on the job.

Entering the building, she found the same security guard on duty, again absorbed in whatever was on the television. And again, she was assigned to the third floor. "You know the routine now," Chip said. "Let's see if we can't get done even quicker. Maybe we can catch a beer afterwards."

Jessica didn't need his encouragement. She worked quickly, watching and waiting for either the guard or one of her coworkers to show up. Sure enough, in less than an hour Chip was back, on the pretext of checking her work, but more likely, in Jessica's mind, to get better acquainted. After only a cursory look at what she had done, he spent most of his time asking about her and talking about himself. She was guarded in most of her responses, repeating the lie that she had just moved up from Iowa and knew few people or places in the Twin Cities.

"Then you should let me show you around sometime," he said. "I know a lot of good spots. We could have a good time."

Be polite but firm, she told herself. And lie. "Thanks," she said, "but right now I have to spend every minute I'm not working with my mom. She's got cancer. That's why I moved up here, to take care of her."

"Sorry to hear that," he said. "Is she going to make it?"

"Who knows? She's getting chemotherapy now and is in pretty bad shape. I have to wait on her, hand and foot."

"Maybe we can make it another time, then," he said.

"Maybe so, but right now, I'd better get back to work."

Twenty minutes later, Isaiah the security guard made his rounds of her floor, checking the doors, just as he had done the night before. After a quick wave, she ignored him, bending to her work without so much as another glance up. To her relief, he made no effort to interrupt her and moved on to the elevator.

She allowed another half hour to pass, then put aside the vacuum cleaner and headed for the fire escape. "Here I go," she whispered into the wireless mike. "Wish me luck."

Brett heard her words through the headset cupping his ears. He was alone in the surveillance van, sitting behind the one-way glass window, parked in almost the same spot across from the building. The communication link with Jessica was one-way: He could hear, but could not be heard. He worried about that, but after considerable discussion, they had decided that rigging her up with an earpiece and a receiver would be too cumbersome and potentially too risky. So she was on her own.

"Go get 'em Jess," he said to himself.

She didn't know if opening the emergency exit would trigger an alarm or not, but she knew she had to risk it. After some hesitation, she pushed the wide door handle and braced for the screech of the alarm. There was only silence. But how could she be sure it wouldn't register at the guard's desk downstairs? Give it a few minutes, she thought, propping the door open with her shoe.

She waited, retreating to the main hallway, watching to see if the elevator moved. It didn't. Maybe he was coming by the stairs. Patience, she told herself. If caught, she would simply say that she had innocently stepped outside for a breath of air. They might not believe her, but they couldn't prove otherwise.

After a full five minutes, she eased her body through the emergency door and onto the fire escape, a steel stairway bolted to the brick exterior of the building. She stood stock-still on the steel grid as her eyes adjusted to the darkness. Holding her breath, she strained to see or hear any movement below or above her. There was none.

"I'm on my way," she said, hoping Brett would hear.

The cold wind bit into her skin as she began to climb, the metal railing freezing to the touch. As she passed the fourth floor, she paused again to look and listen, then climbed to the fifth. Her only hope—perhaps far-fetched—was that fire regulations might require that the master office key also open the emergency door from the outside.

She flattened herself against the brick wall to catch her breath. Then, facing the door, she slid the key into the slot and tried to turn it.

It didn't move.

"No luck," she whispered into the mike. "We may be fucked."

She held her watch close to her eyes. Seven minutes had passed since she had first pushed the

emergency door open. Had someone already
found her missing? She looked up. The fire escape
rose above her, apparently all the way to the roof.
What the hell? she thought. Might as well try.

The parapet was two feet high, but she easily
pulled herself over it and made her way slowly,
carefully across the gravel roof, tiptoeing, afraid
footsteps might be heard below, berating herself
for forgetting a flashlight. Hell of a burglar you
are, she thought.

In the middle of the roof, she literally stumbled
over what appeared to be a trapdoor. She knelt
beside it, then duck-walked around it, tracing its
perimeter with her hands, finally finding a handle. She stood and pulled on it. There was give.
She bent over and pulled harder, using all of the
strength her small body could muster.

Someone had forgotten to lock it from the
inside.

The door began to come up, inch by inch.
Jessica leaned back, using her leverage until the
opening was wide enough to put her shoulder
beneath the door and give it a final shove, watching as it fell back on the roof with a crash.

Jesus, she thought, that could bring the troops.

"I found a way in," she whispered to Brett in the
van. "A trapdoor on the roof."

She stared down into the black hole but could
see nothing. Feeling around the edges, she finally
found the rung of a ladder. Gingerly, she put one
foot on it, then the next, descending through the
darkness until her feet found solid ground.

If Barclay could only see her now. She shuddered
at the thought.

Where the hell was she? In a hallway, she figured, moving forward, using the walls as her guide. She came to a doorjamb, then felt the door itself. With a deep breath, she turned the knob and opened the door, finding herself in what seemed to be a large room. The only light was from a red exit sign above another door across the way, the door leading to the stairwell.

Holding the door partially open, she found the light switch, but stopped, debating. Knowing the lights could probably be seen from the street.

Screw it, she thought, flicking the switch.

From the window in the van, Brett could see the fifth floor lights come on. "Way to go, Jessica," he murmured.

Then he heard her voice, giving him a play-by-play of what she saw. "A big room, Brett. Huge. High ceilings. Open, like a gymnasium. But the floor is carpeted. Looks like a playroom, almost. There's a swing set at one end, monkey bars, a sandbox, and a wading pool that's empty."

A minute passed and he heard nothing. Then, "There's a big window and two doors on the left wall, one regular size, one bigger. There must be offices or something on the other side. Let me try the door. It may be locked." He could hear the squeak of a door opening. Another minute passed. "Damn, Brett. It's like a small television studio back here. Two editing suites . . . and let's see, a goddamned control room, almost the size of the one at the station. That's what's behind the big window."

"I knew it!" Brett breathed.

"Hold on," she said. "There's another room at

the end of the hall. Let me get the door." Brett waited. "It's a prop storage room. Beds, couches, desks, lamps . . . all kinds of things. Connected to the other room by the bigger door on the wall."

Engrossed by Jessica's narration, Brett failed until the last moment to see a car pull into a parking place across from the van. And it was not until the car's occupant reached the lighted entry of the building that he could clearly make him out. Clyde Calder, a camera case in one hand, a tripod in the other.

"Fuck me!" he shouted to the empty van. "Get out, Jessica! Now!"

His warning, of course, went unheard.

Jessica moved cautiously through the rooms, jotting down on a small pad the type and brand of equipment she saw. Most of it was top-quality Sony gear, as good or better than the stuff they worked with at Channel 7. Maybe we can trace the ownership, she thought. All of the rooms were open, save one, which she guessed could be an office or a tape storage room. None of her keys fit.

She glanced at her watch. Twenty minutes and counting. Time was getting tight. She knew she had get back to her own floor. Passing back through the small door and into the larger room, she strode quickly to the other end for a closer inspection of the playground equipment she had first seen upon entering the room. And only now, looking up, did she notice the large lights recessed into the ceiling, mostly hidden from view in the shadows. Studio lights that could be dropped down over the playground apparatus.

Suddenly, Jessica thought she understood.

She hurried back across the room, heading for the stairway. She didn't make it. Not before the elevator doors opened. She had not heard it. Caught in the middle of the room, there was no escape.

Clyde Calder stepped out, carrying his tripod and camera case, apparently surprised to find the lights on. Then he saw her. "What the hell?" he said, quickly checking to see if anyone else was there. "Who are you?" he demanded.

"The cleaning lady," she said, surprised Calder had not yet recognized her.

"How did you get in here?" he asked, walking toward her.

It was so strange. Facing a man she had known for years, as well or better than anyone in the newsroom, and not having him know her. It was as if she was transparent.

But she knew it wouldn't last.

Calder was of average height, but years of shouldering heavy cameras left him walking with a slight stoop, making him appear shorter than he really was. His face was deeply lined and dominated by thick, bushy eyebrows and a drooping walrus mustache that reminded Jessica of a New England cod fisherman at the wheel of his trawler.

She slowly moved to her left, away from him, in a direct line to the stairway. "They gave me a key, told me come up and clean."

He stepped into her path, blocking her way. Looking closer. Squinting. "Bullshit," he said, "nobody comes up here to clean." He was now no more than three feet from her. She heard a quick intake of breath. "Jessica?" Confusion in his voice. "Is that you? What the fuck are you doing here?"

"Get out of my way, Clyde, I'm leaving."

"Wait a minute," he said, his momentary confusion over. The light was dawning. "What's going on?"

"I think you know, Clyde. Now move!"

The wind seemed to leave him, the bluster disappeared. "Brett Jacobi's in the van," she said. "He can hear everything." She reached inside her shirt and pulled out the small mike, holding it up. "Aren't you, Brett?" she said, speaking into it as she walked by Calder, keeping her distance.

He made no move to stop her, the fear now clearly written across his face. "Can't we talk about this?" he said. "Give me a chance to explain."

She was at the door to the stairway, hoping it would open from the inside. It did. "Better tell it to Barclay," she said as the door closed behind her. Racing down the stairs as fast as her heavy workboots would carry her, she never paused until she dashed into the lobby. Dropping her keys on the security desk, she said a quick goodnight to the startled guard and was out the glass door before he could reply or react.

Brett was already pulling away from the curb when she hopped into the van.

As the van accelerated, Jessica fought to collect her breath. "I guess I'm out of a janitor's job, huh?" she gasped, but with a grin.

"I guess so," Brett agreed as he checked the rearview mirror and then glanced at her. "Are you okay?"

"Fine now, but I thought I'd die when that elevator opened," she said. "I had no place to go."

"I know, I could hear everything. I felt helpless out here. I saw Clyde go in, but there was nothing I could do."

"Poor Clyde. You should have seen the look on his face . . . when he finally recognized me. Like a ghost."

"I've got no sympathy for Clyde," he said. "He got himself into this mess."

They were now back on the freeway, heading toward the station. Jessica pulled off her wig and scratched her head furiously. "It feels like I've got fleas," she said.

Brett laughed. "Too bad, I was just starting to get used to you in that."

"Yeah, right," she said.

She turned on the van's overhead light and took out her small pad, writing down everything she could remember about the fifth floor. "No question that it's a full production studio," she said. "And I've got no doubt that the playground stuff is the set for one of their kiddie films."

"But we have no proof of that," Brett reminded her. "That's what so maddening."

"Clyde doesn't know that," she replied. "From the look on his face, he thought he was a dead duck."

"I'll call Barclay as soon as we get back to the station," Brett said. "We've—"

Jessica cut in. "Don't tell him how I got in there,"

"I won't, but we've got to get him to confront Calder. It's the only way."

"You're assuming Clyde's going to come back to work," she said. "It wouldn't surprise me if we never saw him again. He looked that scared."

♦   ♦   ♦

Jessica was right. Still in shock, Clyde could only stand and watch the door close behind her. He made no effort to follow her. His mind was whirling, sorting through what he had just seen and heard, digesting it, desperately searching for explanations beyond the obvious.

There were none. Jessica, in disguise, here on the forbidden fifth floor could mean only one thing. His stomach churned and he suddenly felt an overwhelming urge to cry, something he had not done since childhood—except for the day his wife left him a couple of years before. He knew of only one thing to do. He ran to a phone in one of the back editing suites and punched in the number of Butch Hemrick.

"Yes," said the answering voice.

"Butch?"

"Yes."

"This is Clyde. I'm at the studio. There's trouble."

"What kind of trouble."

"I found Jessica Mitchell . . . a reporter from the station . . . up here. Dressed up like a cleaning woman. Wig and everything."

His words were met with silence. "Butch? You there?"

"I'm here," he finally said. "How did she get in there?"

"I have no idea. I came up the elevator and found her here. Took me a couple of minutes to recognize her."

"Is anything missing?"

"I don't know. I'll look."

"Have you talked to the other cleaning people?"

"No. I called you right away."

"Find them. Find out how the fuck she got up there."

"Okay," Clyde said. Then, "This could mean big trouble for me, you know. They must know what we're doing. I could be out of a job."

"That could be the least of your troubles," Butch said. "I'll be there in a few minutes." Then he hung up.

By the time Brett and Jessica got back to the newsroom, they found Barclay gone for the day, but a message waiting for Jessica on her voice mail. It was from Hal Hinckley, the school public relations man, who told her it would not be possible to use the schools to help identify the pictures of the children. "Like I thought," he said, "it's a question of privacy. The lawyers say we would run a legal risk to do what you're asking. Sorry."

Damn, Jessica thought. Now what?

Maybe pass out the pictures to Jonathan Cassidy and other street workers she knew. Perhaps one of them would know one or more of the kids. It was a long shot, she thought, but the best she could come up with at the moment.

As she sat thinking, Maggie sought her out. "Brett told me what happened," she said. "You're doing okay?"

"Yeah, now. But I damn near freaked out."

"I should think so."

"I don't know what I'm going to tell Barclay.

He'll shit tacks when he finds out how I got in."

"Don't tell him anything," Maggie said. "He may not think to ask."

"Don't I wish."

Maggie sat down and made her repeat every detail of what she had seen and done, including a description of the playground equipment. "Can't you just see it," Maggie said. "A bunch of naked kids playing around on that stuff."

"I know. It makes me sick to think about it."

By the time Butch got there, Clyde had checked out the entire floor and had talked to both the security guard and the two other members of the cleaning crew. "They don't know anything," he reported. "They thought her name was Miranda. It was her second night on this job. Claimed she was from Iowa, here to take care of her mother, who supposedly has cancer."

"Shit," Butch said. "Doesn't the cleaning company do fucking background checks?"

Clyde could only shrug. It was not his responsibility.

"How did she get a key to the place?"

"She didn't. She came in from the roof. The trapdoor was still open. Someone must not have locked it."

"Son of a bitch," Butch muttered as he walked into the technical area beyond the wall, Clyde following. "Anything missing back here?"

"Not that I see," Clyde said. "The tape storage door is still locked."

"Maybe she didn't get back here."

"Don't count on that," Clyde said. "No one knows how long she was up here."

Butch slumped into a chair. If Martin Duggan hears about this, he knew, his ass would be grass. For now, he decided, he would say nothing. No sense getting him all worked up again. Besides, what the hell could they prove? That there's a production studio here? So what? There are lots of them around.

Clyde broke into his thoughts. "What do you think I should do?"

"Go back to work. Act like nothing happened. They can't prove anything. If they press you, tell 'em it's none of their goddamned business."

Easy for him to say, Clyde thought. He doesn't know George Barclay.

An hour later, just as Maggie was leaving the Green Room for the studio to do the late news, Jessica caught up with her. "I just thought of something," she said, grabbing Maggie by the arm.

"What's that?" she said, checking her watch. "I've only got a minute."

"The bedroom set. The one the kids were using in the porn film."

"Yeah."

"Remember the bedposts? The intricate carvings? Like a lion's head?"

"Not really," Maggie said. "I guess I was concentrating on the other stuff. But why?"

Jessica's words were rushed, her eyes wide. "I've got to look at the tape again, but I think I saw the same bed in that prop room."

36

Clyde Calder's worst fears were realized when he walked into the station the next morning and was met by an unsmiling security guard, who brusquely told him, "Mr. Barclay would like to see you in the conference room." Calder felt a flash of terror, but then forced himself to relax, recalling Butch Hemrick's words of the night before, "Act like nothing happened. They can't prove anything."

"Okay," he said, "but let me grab a cup of coffee first."

"Sorry," the guard said. "I was asked to escort you directly to the conference room."

"*Escort me?* You're kidding? I know where the hell the conference room is."

The guard shrugged. "I just do what I'm told."

The panic returned. Clyde fought the urge to turn around and run, to escape, never to return. Instead, he followed the guard down the long hallway to the newsroom, ignoring the curious glances of friends along the way. "Can I at least stop by my locker and get rid of my coat?" he asked the guard striding ahead of him. "I'm toasting."

"Sorry," the guard replied over his shoulder.

Clyde shrugged off his coat as they walked, but already the sweat was beading on his forehead and running down the back of his neck. He was getting his breath by the gulp. His feet dragged, as though shackled, each step an effort.

As they crossed the newsroom, he tried to prepare himself. But how could he without knowing exactly what they knew? What they could prove? Stonewall them, he told himself. Tell 'em to go fuck themselves.

The guard opened the door to the conference room and moved aside as Clyde paused, then stepped inside. Barclay was not alone. He was sitting at one end of the long conference table, Terry's table, flanked on one side by Jessica and on the other by Maggie and Brett. All of them were watching him intently, their expressions grim. "Shut the door and grab a chair, Clyde," Barclay said, his voice level.

Calder pushed the door closed, but remained standing. "What's this about?" he demanded with a defiance he did not feel.

"Sit down, Clyde," Barclay repeated.

Calder gave them all another long look, then slid

into a chair at the other end of the table. "This looks like the Inquisition," he said, trying a small smile.

Barclay simply stared back at him.

Calder was wearing the same dark green crewneck sweater Jessica had seen him in the night before, the collar of a white shirt peeking above the sweater top. "C'mon, you guys, what's going on?" he said, shifting uneasily in his chair. "Is this about last night, Jessica?"

She made no reply, but her eyes would not leave his.

Barclay leaned forward, elbows on the table, clasped hands supporting his ample chin. "How long have we known each other, Clyde?"

He seemed to be caught off-guard by the question. "I don't know, George. Five, six years, I guess. Ever since you've been here."

"Have I ever treated you badly? Has anybody here ever treated you badly?"

"No, not at all. The station's been good to me. I've got no complaints."

Barclay hoisted himself up and out of the chair, leaning back against the wall, arms across his chest. "Then why are you doing what you're doing? Fucking the station—me, all of us—over. To say nothing of those poor kids."

Calder rose halfway out of his chair, disguising his fear with anger. "What the hell are you talking about?"

"If you needed money, why didn't you come to me? Maybe I could have helped."

Calder fell back into the chair. "You're making no sense, George."

"Cut the crap!" Barclay growled. "We know

you're working for this Butch Hemrick. We know what goes on in that studio . . . what kind of films you're shooting. We even have a copy of one."

Calder swallowed hard and shook off a droplet of sweat that had found its way to his cheek. "What kids? What films?" His voice was on the edge of panic.

"Let me show you," Barclay said, moving to a corner of the room where a metal stand held a VCR machine and a television set. He hit the PLAY button and stepped back. The first scenes of *Pajama Party* popped up. Calder's eyes were fixed on the screen while the eyes of the others were fixed on him. Barclay allowed several minutes of the tape to run before turning it off. Calder continued to stare at the blank screen. Finally, looking up, he said, "You think I had something to do with that?"

"Yes," Barclay replied simply. "And for the record, you're suspended, effective immediately, until we get to the bottom of this."

"Then I think I'd better get somebody from the union in here," he said. "I'm allowed that under the contract."

"Feel free," Barclay said, "if you're sure you want the union to know about this."

Calder hesitated, but Barclay didn't. "Give me the keys to your locker," he ordered.

"What?"

"Your equipment locker. Give me the keys."

Calder was now out of his chair. "You can't go in there!" he cried out. "That's my personal stuff."

"I'm afraid we can. It's station property. Holds station equipment. We have every right to search it."

Turning abruptly, Calder angrily pulled open the door, only to find himself face-to-face with the security guard, still standing outside. "Don't make me take the key from you," Barclay said. "You're welcome to come along for the inspection."

"I deserve better than this," Calder protested, his eyes searching the room for some sign of compassion. "I've given my life to this place. I've never caused you a speck of trouble, and I've won enough fucking awards for you to cover these walls. Is this what I get back?"

"The key," Barclay said, his hand out.

Clyde picked up his coat and reached into the pocket, pulling out a set of keys.

"Just the one for the locker," Barclay said.

Calder separated one key from the others and handed it to him.

"Let's go," Barclay said.

As ordered earlier, Brett, Maggie, and Jessica remained in their seats, watching as a shaken Calder followed Barclay out of the room—with the security guard trailing behind. "Stay put," Barclay had told them. "I don't want a goddamned parade across the newsroom. This is going to cause a big enough stir as it is."

Maggie got up to close the door and returned to her chair. "What did you make of that?" she asked the other two.

"He looked like a rat with one foot in a trap," Brett said, "trying to claw his way out."

"He's got balls, I'll say that for him," Jessica added. "I'm surprised he even showed up for work."

Barclay had finally agreed to confront Calder

late the night before, after Brett called him at
home to describe Jessica's surprise encounter with
Calder. "We've got to put a scare into him," Brett
had pleaded. "Shake him up. Let him know that
we know. Maybe he'll decide to talk."

Barclay had remained reluctant, even in the
face of the new evidence of Calder's complicity.
His loyalty to his employees was legendary, especially to long-time employees like Calder, who had
helped build the station's impressive news reputation. But he knew Brett was right, and eventually
he succumbed.

"I'll tell you one thing," Jessica said now. "I
don't ever want to get on the wrong side of
Barclay. When he puts his mind to it, he's one
intimidating son of a bitch."

Calder stood back as Barclay slipped the key into
the padlock and opened the door of the storage
locker. Inside, he found an array of station equipment: batteries, battery belts, lights, microphones,
an old tripod, and assorted other photographic
paraphernalia. Nothing unusual there.

Off to one side, however, was a large stack of
videotape cassettes. Fifty or more. Field tapes and
edit tapes, a collection of some of the stories Calder
had shot or edited over the years. As Calder watched,
Barclay picked through them, looking for any that
did not carry station labels or markings. He found
nothing suspicious and stepped back, appearing
puzzled and slightly embarrassed.

"Satisfied?" Calder said from behind him.

Barclay turned. "Give me the keys to your car."

"What?"

"You heard me. Your car keys."

Each of the photographers was assigned a station car—equipped with a phone and two-way radio—to be ready to respond to any emergency at any hour of the day or night.

"For God's sake, George!"

"Save it, Clyde. Give me the keys."

Reluctantly, he again pulled his keys out of his pocket and handed them to Barclay, who led the way to the basement garage. Calder's car was one of several identical Plymouth Voyager vans parked in a line, each of them marked front, back, and sides with the station's logo and call letters.

Barclay opened the rear door of the van. To one side, he found a large silver camera case and tripod. On the other, a canvas bag filled with more video cassettes. "Shooting tapes," Calder said quickly as Barclay began to sort through them. "Just the normal supply."

"Oh, yeah?" Barclay said, holding up two tapes that bore no labels and were of a different brand than the others. "What are these?"

Calder's face seemed to pale in the dim light of the garage. He stepped closer, examining the tapes. "I have no idea," he said. "They're not mine. I don't know how they got there."

Barclay's eyes were unblinking. "It's your bag, isn't it? Your car."

Clyde took a step back. "Sure, but other people use it sometimes. You know that."

Barclay smiled. "Well, since you say they're not yours, you can't have any objection to my viewing them, can you?"

Calder was caught. Trapped. He tried to think of a way out, but found none. "I guess not," he finally said. "As long as you know they're not mine."

"We'll see about that," Barclay replied. Then, signaling the security guard standing off to one side, he said, "In the meantime, I want you out of the building, Clyde. Until we get to the truth. Leave the station keys and all of your gear. We'll let you know when we get things sorted out. You'll hear from either us or the cops."

Calder's defenses seemed to crumble. "You're going to the cops with this?"

"Probably, if we can't pin things down ourselves. I'd stick around town if I were you, Clyde."

Barclay came back to the conference room carrying the two tape cassettes, quickly explaining where he had found them. "They may be nothing, but it's worth a look," he said as he slipped the first tape into the VCR.

"Where's Clyde?" Brett asked.

"Gone," Barclay replied. "For now, anyway."

The first twenty seconds of the tape were blank, the next thirty seconds full of video static. "C'mon," Barclay muttered.

Finally, a picture emerged, immediately recognizable to all of them, scenes from *Pajama Party*. But unlike the finished product they had seen before, the action on this tape was clearly unedited.

"Jesus," Brett said. "It's the original shooting tape."

"No wonder Clyde claimed they weren't his," Barclay said.

"Why would he keep them in his car?" Brett wondered aloud.

"Either he forgot about them or never expected a search," Barclay said.

As the tape played on, they could hear occasional instructions shouted to the children from an off-camera position. Then the tape would go black and restart, with the kids in a different position.

"I can't watch more of this," Maggie said, getting out of her chair.

Barclay stopped the machine. "Somebody's going to have to watch it all," he said. "Both tapes. We need to know exactly what's on them."

Jessica reluctantly volunteered. "I've developed a strong stomach," she said.

Maggie found the Board of Medical Practice in a colonial-style office building on University Avenue, near the dividing line between Minneapolis and St. Paul and just across the street from the studios of one of Channel 7's television competitors. Brett was with her, but chose to wait in the Explorer while she ran in to retrieve the material on Dr. Henry Klinkle.

Dennis Dunn, the man she'd spoken to on the phone, was expecting her and led her to his small private office. "It's not often we get a visit from a celebrity," he said as he offered her a chair. "My wife is a real fan of yours. Won't watch any other newscast."

"Give her my thanks," Maggie said. "We appreciate every viewer, believe me."

Dunn smiled and opened a manila file on his desk. "You asked about a Dr. Henry Klinkle," he said.

"You found something?"

"As a matter of fact, yes." He slid a copy of the file across the desk to her. "Dr. Klinkle had his medical license suspended twice in recent years ... once seven years ago, a second time three years ago. In each case, the license was reinstated after six months."

Maggie spread out the documents, trying to quickly assimilate them.

"As you can see," Dunn continued, "the first suspension was for sexual misconduct, the second—"

"Wait a minute," she interrupted. "What kind of sexual misconduct?"

"Let me look," he said, studying his own copies of the documents. "He was accused of inappropriate sexual contact with one of his patients, a seven-year-old girl. He did not contest the complaint and agreed to the discipline, which also included a mandated treatment program.

"The second, more recent license suspension was less serious. He was accused of improperly maintaining his medical records. From what I see here, he apparently kept a pretty sloppy office when he practiced alone. Couldn't provide records to some of his patients when they transferred to other doctors or clinics."

Maggie was trying to follow along, but got lost in the medical and legal verbiage of the reports, each one about twelve pages long. She knew it would take a couple of hours to sort through it all. "Can I keep these files?" she asked.

"Sure," Dunn said. "But we have to charge you a quarter a page for copying fees."

"I don't think that will be a problem," she laughed as she picked up the report. "The station has deep pockets."

As she was at the door, she thought of one more question. "Who does the actual investigation of the complaints? Your staff?"

"I'm afraid not," Dunn said. "We don't have those kind of resources. Every complaint we get is turned over to the attorney general's office for investigation."

"Really?" Maggie said. "The attorney general? Isn't that interesting."

Later that night, Tony Kolura wandered up and down the aisles of the sprawling Mystic Lake Casino near Shakopee, no more than fifteen miles from their present motel, another dingy place called Sunset Place. He was looking for an empty chair at one of the high-stake blackjack tables, but in fifteen minutes of searching, he had yet to find one. The place was packed, more so than most of the casinos he had frequented in Vegas, Reno, or Tahoe. Of course, there weren't nearly as many casinos around here, but still, he was amazed by the crush of the crowd.

He had waited until Sissy had fallen asleep after the late news before tiptoeing out of the motel room and sprinting to his car. The way he figured it, Sissy would be out cold until she had to get up and piss in the early morning hours, usually about 4:00 A.M. And he planned to be back long before that . . . hopefully with his pockets stuffed with cash.

Tony knew he was taking a chance. Not only would Sissy land hard on him for sneaking away, but if the General ever discovered these gambling forays, he could be in for some serious trouble. Sissy never stopped reminding him of that. But, shit, he'd been sitting on his ass for days, counting his cash and waiting for some action. They'd done nothing, heard nothing, since Halloween night. He was bored and frustrated. And what the hell? He was a total stranger in these parts, and who the fuck could pick him out in this crowd?

This was his fourth visit to one of the local casinos, and each time he had walked away with more than a grand of the Indians' money. Say what you will about Tony Kolura, he would tell anyone who would listen, but never say he doesn't know his way around a blackjack table. Especially compared to some of the yokels who took up table space around here.

He glanced at his watch. Twenty-five minutes had passed, and he was still without a chair. He kept circulating, watching for an opening, sipping on a Diet Coke, the wad of bills hot in his pocket. Finally, he saw an old woman get up to leave and he lunged for her chair, barely edging out a black dude with gold in his ears and around his neck. A few less-than-friendly words were exchanged, but nothing more came of it.

Tony ordered another Diet Coke from a passing waitress, then bought five hundred dollars worth of chips and waited for his first cards. Fuck Sissy. Fuck the General. Like it or not, he was going to have a little fun.

He studied the dealer; he studied the decks as they were being shuffled. But he took little notice of the others at the table, and no notice of the woman across from him. The one who was staring at him.

37

Things began to happen quickly for Maggie.

Amy Boyd called to say she and her two friends would be willing to stay at Brett's family cabin, but for only two weeks, max. "Then we're getting out of town," she said. "Popeye's got a cousin in Texas, and he says we can hang out with him for a while." Maggie tried to argue for a longer commitment, but Amy was firm. "We're out of here before we're up to our ass in snow. Two weeks, max."

Maggie said Brett would pick them up in an hour. "You can stop and shop for anything you want on the way," she said. "Brett will have the money for it."

Before Amy could hang up, Maggie thought of

something more. Something she should have thought of before. "When you made that film," she said, "did you get a look at the people running the cameras or directing you?"

There was a pause at the other end. "Yeah, I guess so, but I don't really remember. It wasn't like I was paying attention. I was scared and there was so much happening. I was like in a daze or something."

"If Brett shows you a picture of someone who might have been operating one of the cameras, do you think you would recognize him?"

Another pause. "I don't know. I'll try."

"Good," Maggie said. "Brett will have the picture when he picks you up."

"Okay. But remember. Two weeks."

Less than an hour later, after Brett had left to shuttle Amy and friends, Maggie was again called to the phone. "Do you want to take a call from a Harry Carlisle?" the switchboard operator asked. *Harry Carlisle?* It had been weeks since she had talked to him. "Sure," she said, "put him through."

"Maggie?" The soft, syrupy voice had not changed.

"Harry. What a surprise."

"Sorry to bother you," he said, "but I have some information that may be helpful."

"What's that?"

"Well, our singles' club had another outing last night. For dinner and a little gambling at the Mystic Lake Casino . . . you know, near Shakopee."

"I know about it, but I've never been there," she said.

"About twenty of us made the trip," he continued,

"and halfway through the evening, one of our members came rushing up to me. Pat McKenzie, the woman who took the pictures. Remember her?"

"Go on, Harry."

"She was quite excited. She said she was at the same blackjack table as the man with the mustache. The one you were trying to locate."

Maggie felt a surge of excitement herself. "Really? Did he recognize her?"

"No, not at all. She led me to the table. I saw for myself. It was him all right."

"So what did you do?" she asked, controlling her voice.

There was a nervous laugh at the other end of the line. "I played detective for you," he said. "I waited until he finished . . . then I followed him to his car in the parking lot."

"No kidding!"

"It was a black Buick LeSabre. License number one-one-zero, L-V-N. I was going to try to follow him, but my car was on the other side of the lot. Besides, I couldn't leave the group."

"Good work, Harry. That's terrific."

"I thought you'd want to know," he said. "Is there anything else I can do?"

"No, except to let us buy you a drink when all of this is over."

"That would be a real pleasure," he said. "I'll look forward to it."

Maggie was back on the phone immediately, calling Timothy McQueen, the detective, and repeating what Carlisle had just told her.

"I'll do a license check right away," he said. "But

if these two are from out of town, I'd be willing to bet it's a rental car."

"Still," she said, "we should be able to learn who rented it and where they're staying."

"Maybe. Unless he used a phony name. I'll get back to you as soon as I can."

It was still early in the afternoon, giving Maggie a chance to more closely examine the medical records of Dr. Henry Klinkle. It came as no real surprise to her that Klinkle's fondling of the seven-year-old girl had happened while he was in private practice in the same Edina office building. The name of the young victim was not revealed, but the report indicated that the sexual touching had occurred on several occasions before the girl finally told her mother, who then reported it to the Medical Practices Board. In the subsequent investigation, several of Klinkle's other young patients were contacted, but no further abuse could be firmly documented.

Before his license was reinstated, the doctor was required to attend weekly sex-offender therapy sessions and to pay a five-thousand-dollar fine. In addition, he was ordered to have no unsupervised medical contact with minor children for a period of three years.

The second offense, four years later, on the surface involved little more than sloppy record-keeping, but as Maggie perused the paperwork, she suspected a deeper problem. The complaint involved a significant number of Klinkle's patients who attempted to change doctors, but whose medical records Klinkle could not locate for the transfers. The Board report did not address the issue of why so many patients suddenly decided to leave Klinkle, but she couldn't help but wonder if it wasn't because the good doctor was up to his old tricks . . . and that word had spread among his patients.

Again, his license was suspended, but again, was reinstated after six months. It was apparently after this latest incident that Klinkle closed his office in the Edina building and managed to hook on with the Westside Clinic.

She sat back, staring at the stack of documents. Now that she knew all of this, she wondered, what could she do with it? While it confirmed that Klinkle was once a pedophile, there certainly was no evidence linking him directly to the porn ring, or to single him out as the doctor who had treated the young girl hurt during the filming. Yet, somehow, Maggie was certain that he was. The key was finding the girl. But how?

She went in search of Jessica, once again finding her behind the computer. As it happened, she was working on the same problem, but from a different direction.

"What are you doing now?" Maggie asked.

"Checking local death records," she said without taking her eyes from the screen.

"For what?"

"For any girl between the ages of ten and fifteen who's died within the past five years."

"I'm not sure I understand," Maggie said.

Jessica turned to face her. "Amy told you that the girl in the film was badly hurt. Hemorrhaging, right? I'm just trying to make sure she didn't die later."

"But why five years?"

Jessica shrugged. "Doesn't take that much more time, and what the hell? Maybe I'll find something else."

"Have you?"

"Not yet, but I'm only back two years."

"Keep an eye out for any death certificates signed by Dr. Henry Klinkle," Maggie said, describing what she had found in Klinkle's disciplinary file and the need to locate the injured girl. "We can't prove anything without her."

"I know," Jessica said. "I've already checked with the schools, and they won't help us with the pictures. Some bullshit about violating the kids' right to privacy. I meant to give Jonathan Cassidy a call. See if he and some of the other street workers will try to find her for us."

"I'll call him right now," Maggie said, heading for the nearest phone.

Cassidy was more than willing to help, promising to stop by later to pick up the pictures and to distribute them to other street workers he knew. "We're a pretty close group," he told her. "We're all trying to get the kids off the street and back home, if possible. At least into a shelter."

"These particular kids are pretty young," Maggie said. "Judging from the pictures, no more than twelve or thirteen, if that."

"That could help," he said. "We don't run into many that young. But you're sure they're from around here?"

"We don't know. But we think they were in town at one point anyway."

Cassidy again pressed her for more details of the investigation. "I really need to know what we're dealing with here. The other street workers are going to want to know."

"And I still can't tell you," she said. "But trust me, it's important or we wouldn't be asking for your help."

"Okay," Cassidy said with a deep sigh. "I'll be by for the pictures as soon as I can."

Across the river in St. Paul, Mike Overby was prowling the halls of the capitol, making his daily rounds, when he ran into Martin Duggan just outside of the attorney general's offices. "Hey, Marty, how's it going?" he asked as cheerfully as possible.

Duggan gave him a wide grin. "Great," he said. "I'd been hoping to run into you. Have you got a minute?"

"You bet," Overby said, although he was immediately wary.

Duggan pulled open the door. "Let's go to my office," he said.

Overby obediently followed him through the reception area and the maze of halls leading to the AG's corner office. Duggan closed the door behind them and said, "Grab a chair, Mike. This won't take but a minute."

Overby had been on a first-name basis with Duggan since his first campaign for office, and while they weren't friends socially, Overby believed he had Duggan's trust and respect. In return, he had made no secret of his admiration for Duggan, although he had taken great pains to maintain his objectivity and balance in his reporting about the man.

"Brian Stringer told me about your visit the other day," Duggan said. "Something about an investigation centering on this office."

Overby shifted slightly in his chair. "Just checking out some rumors," he replied. "Nothing personal. Just part of my job, you know."

"I understand that," Duggan said. "But can you tell me anything more?"

Overby was growing more uncomfortable. "Not really. And even if I knew more, I wouldn't really be free to reveal it."

"Even to an old friend?"

Overby winced. "I'm afraid so."

Duggan got up and removed his suit jacket, throwing it on top of the credenza behind his desk. "You can understand my concern about this," he said. "We run a clean shop. Even a stray rumor can do us great harm."

Overby said nothing.

"Haven't I given you more than your share of exclusives over the years?"

The pressure was building.

"Look, Marty," Overby finally said. "I appreciate what you've done for me, but I honestly don't know what's going on. They won't tell me anything back at the station. Things are about as tight as I've ever seen them. Word is that they just fired one of our veteran photographers, but nobody knows why."

"One of your photographers?" Duggan couldn't hide the shock in his voice.

"Yeah. Clyde Calder. You know him."

"Of course. He's been here dozens of times. You don't know what he did?"

"Not a clue. He hasn't talked to anybody, and the brass aren't saying anything."

Duggan fell back into his chair. While he tried to keep his composure, he could feel the noose tightening. Did Butch know? And if so, why hadn't he told him? Finally, he said, "I appreciate your position in this, Mike, but I do hope—on the basis of our past friendship—that you'll let me know about any smoking guns out there."

Overby was noncommital, but as he left, he couldn't help but wonder why Duggan appeared so upset over the firing of a photographer.

Brett got back to the station shortly before the early news. "Those kids must not have eaten for days," he told Maggie. "I damn near bought out the supermarket. To say nothing of the videos and video games. I even got 'em some new clothes. I hope Barclay's budget is big enough to cover it all."

Maggie laughed. "Maybe they'll like it well enough to stay longer."

"Don't count on it. They kept telling me two weeks was it, not a day longer."

As they talked, Maggie was making her way to the studio, script in hand. She hurriedly filled him in on her conversations with Carlisle and McQueen, and then asked, "What about Clyde's picture?" she asked. "Did Amy recognize him?"

He followed her through the studio doors and up to the set. "She thought so. But she couldn't be positive, even with his big old mustache. She said she'd probably do better if she could see him in person."

"That's something, at least," she replied. "Maybe she'll have a chance before they take off."

Butch Hemrick was at the reception desk in his Edina office when the door flew open and Martin Duggan stood in the doorway, his big body filling it. Butch jumped back, cracking his head against a shelf along the wall. "Jesus Christ, Marty," he yelped, "you scared the shit out of me!" He felt the back of his head for blood but found none.

Duggan slammed the door shut and leaned back against it, breathing deeply, as though he had just run up the stairs. There was no effort to disguise his anger. "Why didn't you tell me about Calder?" he demanded.

Butch, his composure returning, slowly walked around the desk to face Duggan. "What about him?"

"They just fired his ass!" Duggan screamed.

Butch was stunned, momentarily confused. He hadn't talked to Clyde Calder since the night of the break-in, despite two or three attempts to reach him. He had no idea of what had happened at the station. "It's news to me," he said lamely. "I haven't talked to him for a couple of days."

"He hasn't called you?"

Butch shook his head, feeling a shot of pain from the collision with the shelf.

"Why would they fire him? They must know something."

Hemrick's mind raced. Should he tell him about the reporter getting inside and running into Calder? No way. Not now. Play dumb. Duggan would panic, go crazy. Who knows what he would do then? "I have no idea," he finally said. "I'll try to get hold of him again, find out what's going on. It probably has nothing to do with us."

"Sure, and the Pope's a closet Protestant!" Duggan fumed. "I want this place shut down. Now! Lock up that fifth floor. No more films. Hear me?"

Hemrick walked past Duggan and stood by the door to his inner office, a smirk of his face. "Sorry, Marty. No can do. The wheels are already in motion. I've made commitments I can't back out of, not with the people I'm dealing with."

Duggan sank into a chair, exhausted, knowing there was no way he could force Hemrick to do anything. He had to persuade him, to make him feel the same fear he felt. "You want to go back behind bars?" he pleaded. "They'll put you away for the rest of your fucking life! Don't you understand that?"

"Not if I can help it, Marty. You worry too much. I told you, I'll take care of things."

Brett was by Maggie's desk, holding the phone, when she returned from the studio. "McQueen's on the line," he said. "He's got some information."

She dropped her script on the desk and took the receiver. "Yes?"

"Good news and bad news," McQueen said. "I guessed right. The car was rented. From a Budget office in Bloomington, near the airport. Rented to a guy named Tony Kolura. Had a California driver's license." There was a pause. "That's the good news."

"And the bad?" Maggie asked, holding her breath.

"He returned the car this morning."

"Damn!"

"We're now checking every other rental agency in town," McQueen said, "but as you can guess, there are a lot of them. It's going to take a while."

"Maybe they've left town," Maggie ventured.

"Could be," he conceded. "But I've asked our friends at the LAPD to run a check on the guy, just in case Kolura is his real name or some alias he's used before."

"Did the rental agreement say where they're staying?"

"Nope. He apparently told them he was going to be traveling around the state."

"Okay," Maggie said. "Please let us know if you find them."

"Trust me. You'll be the first to know."

38

Young Danny was waiting at the door when Maggie and Brett drove up to the Apple Valley home of Anna's daughter. He raced outside before she could get out of the Explorer, greeting her with a giant hug. "Hey, kiddo," she laughed, pulling herself out of the car, "take it easy. You're going to squeeze the air right out of me."

He held on, arms around her waist, head pressed against her stomach. "Where have you been, Mom?" he demanded, looking up, teary-eyed.

"Busy, Danny. I'm sorry." She bent over and kissed his forehead. "You're okay, aren't you?"

He nodded, but still clung to her tightly.

Although she talked to him on the telephone two or three times a day, this was the first time she had seen him in three days. But from the way he was acting, it could have been three weeks. She felt a new rush of guilt as her own eyes welled. He's too young to be left like this, she thought. *What kind of mother am I?* A pleading glance at Brett brought him to their side.

"Hey, squirt," he said as he picked up the boy and tossed him squealing into the air. "Give your mom a break. She's been working hard."

Anna was now on the doorstep, watching the reunion with a smile. "Don't let the little guy fool you," she said. "He's missed you, but he's doing just fine. He loves his new school and has made a whole flock of new friends."

Maggie knew that was probably true. Apple Valley was one of the newer, outer-ring suburbs, its neighborhoods populated largely by families with younger children like Danny. A quick glance up and down the street was evidence of that.

As they walked into the house, greeted by Anna's daughter and her husband, it also became clear that Danny was feeling right at home. He wasted no time in showing Maggie and Brett his bedroom—decorated with Twins and Vikings banners given to him by Anna's grandson—and in demonstrating his new skills with the video games.

Maggie was feeling less guilty by the minute.

With Anna's prodding, he also displayed some of his artwork from school, along with a note from his teacher to Anna suggesting that his mother might consider moving him immediately into first grade. "Both his reading and math skills are considerably

above others in his kindergarten class," she wrote.
"I'm afraid he might become bored with the present level of teaching."

Maggie told Anna she would think about it—but not before Danny was back in his regular school. "We'll see what the teachers there say," she said.

Because Maggie had to be back at the station for the late news, they said good-bye after just more than an hour's visit. Danny fought back the tears as they left, but Maggie assured him he would be back home just as soon as possible. "Once we catch those bad men who tried to hurt us," she said.

Danny was at the door, watching as they pulled away.

Clyde Calder had disappeared.

After being ordered out of the station, he had returned to his apartment for only long enough to pick up clothes and a few hundred "desperation dollars" he kept hidden away in the pocket of an old sports jacket. His photographer-roommate was working at the time and did not see him come or go, nor had he heard from him since. Except for a few of his clothes, most of Clyde's other worldly possessions remained in the apartment: his furniture, tapes and CDs, his still cameras, even his immense baseball card collection—which filled a large trunk in one corner of his bedroom.

The roommate, Philip LeMere, reported all of this to George Barclay, who listened with interest, but could only shake his head sadly. LeMere, like others, had been unable to learn what sin had prompted Calder's suspension, but he knew that it must have been serious or Barclay never would have done what he did.

"He should be coming back," LeMere told Barclay. "His card collection's worth a lot of money. He's been saving them since he was a kid. It's the only thing his ex didn't get in the divorce. He would never leave it."

Barclay shrugged. "I hope you're right. It won't help him to run."

What LeMere neglected to report was a series of curt messages left for Calder on the apartment answering machine. Messages that LeMere thought could only mean more trouble for Calder, and which he wasn't eager to tell Barclay about. The caller never identified himself and never left a number, but his voice grew more menacing with each message. The first was simply, "Call Me." The last: "Listen, asshole, don't make me come and find you. Call me!"

Like others, LeMere was convinced Calder's gambling was at the root of his problems. He knew hc was deeply in debt and theorized that the station must have found out about it. And that the guy on the phone was some kind of loan shark who was holding a large hunk of Calder's debt.

So, after work, LeMere would make the rounds of the nearby casinos, searching the rows of slot machines, convinced that eventually he would find Calder sitting in front of one, mesmerized, losing whatever money he had left.

Truth was, the slots were the furthest thing from Calder's mind. He was holed up in a small motel north of the Twin Cities, near Cambridge—where he knew no one and no one knew him. Except to eat, he had hardly left the place, spending the hours lying on his bed, staring at the ceiling, or pacing the floor of the small room. By turns, cursing Butch, Barclay, himself, or the spot he found himself in.

Now and then, he would take time out to watch the Channel 7 news, a sad reminder of what he had lost and would never regain.

He had tried to think of any possible way out of this jam, examining every inch of wiggle room, but he had found none. He realized he would never work at the station again and could very well end up in jail—or maybe even dead, if Butch ever felt desperate enough. He had considered running, as fast and as far away as possible, but he knew that if Barclay went to the cops, they would eventually find him and bring him back.

Besides, he had no money beyond the few hundred dollars in his pocket, and that wouldn't last long.

Having exhausted his anger and his options for escape, he finally began to make room for remorse—for his own personal failure, for his betrayal of the station and his lifelong friends there, for his own kids, but most of all, for the children in the films. Until now, he had been able to rationalize his role on the basis that the films would have been made with or without him. He was simply a photographer and editor, a small cog in a porn machine that would never lack for replacement parts.

He was not a pervert. He had gotten no thrill

from standing behind the camera, recording the sexual frolicking of kids young enough to be his grandchildren. He had made himself close his mind, if not his eyes, to it . . . to think only of the professional aspects of the job: the lighting, the framing, the flow of the action. But he knew that was no longer good enough.

He silently bemoaned the day the first casino had opened in Minnesota. In a few short years, the addiction to easily available gambling had turned dozens of decent people into thieves, embezzlers, bank robbers, drug dealers, and—in his case—into a child pornographer.

Only later would he discover that Butch had come to know of his gambling addiction from one of Butch's former prison pals, who worked for the shark who had first bailed Calder out of financial trouble. Butch had taken over his account, and before long, Calder was into him so deeply that there was no refusing any request he made.

That was history. Sad and foolish, but true. While it might help explain his actions, he knew it could not absolve his guilt.

He reached across the bed for the telephone.

Barclay took the call at home, not overly surprised to find Calder at the other end. He had been expecting—no, hoping—for it.

"Brett gave me your home number," Calder said. "You have time to talk?"

"Of course," Barclay said. "Where are you?"

"In some shithole motel near Cambridge," he said. "I couldn't stay at the apartment."

"I know. LeMere told me you'd taken off. He's worried about you, been out looking for you."

"I'll call him next," Calder said.

Several seconds passed without further conversation. Barclay guessed he was working up his courage, and he was not about to rush him. Finally, he heard Calder's voice again, clearly choked up. "George, I can only tell you I'm sorry. There is an explanation for what I did, but no excuse. I know that now. I feel the worst about the kids, but I'm also terribly ashamed of what I've done to you and the station."

He hardly paused for a breath. "You were right on the other day. You've always been decent to me. You're a class guy, and you're right . . . I fucked you over. You don't deserve all of this. I should have known better, but I didn't."

There was another long pause before Barclay asked, with no sympathy in his voice, "So what are you going to do about it?"

"Anything you want. You tell me. I don't want to run. I'll face what I have to face."

"Come in tomorrow, first thing in the morning. To the conference room. The same people will be there, plus one. A cop who's been working with us."

Barclay could hear the sharp intake of Calder's breath. "It's going to come to that at some point, Clyde. Better sooner than later. Get it behind you."

"Okay," Calder said. "But no security guard this time, all right? Let me walk in like a man."

"You've got it," Barclay said. Then, almost as an afterthought, "Did you have anything to do with the harassment of Maggie Lawrence? The truth, now."

"What?"

"The stuff that's been happening to Maggie. The threats and all the rest."

"God, no. I swear it. I would never be a part of that. You've got to believe me!"

Barclay did. "How about this Butch? Could he be behind it?"

"Not that I know of," Calder said. "But he's a mean bastard. I wouldn't put it past him."

"Okay," Barclay replied. "Be here at nine in the morning, sharp. No security guard."

Barclay spent the next twenty minutes back on the phone, arranging for Brett, Jessica, and Maggie to be at the morning meeting. Maggie argued against McQueen's presence, but Barclay would have none of it. "I know I gave you a week," he said, "but we can't wait any longer. Not with Calder ready to tell all. It's time we give McQueen everything."

"What about our story?" Maggie persisted. "Are we going to give that up?"

"I hope we don't have to," he replied. "But, yeah, if it's a choice between that and getting these slimeballs behind bars, then I'm willing to give it up."

Maggie couldn't believe her ears. George Barclay was renowned for his disdain of news people and cops working too closely together ("What happens when we have to report on them?"), but in this case, he clearly had had a change of heart. She didn't really blame him, knowing what was at stake, but still, the thought of possibly losing their story after all of their time and effort was too painful to consider.

"There must be some way we can protect ourselves," she said.

"I'll try," Barclay said. "Maybe McQueen will cooperate. But, either way, we can't wait any longer."

As much as she missed her son, it was comforting to Maggie—and somehow more honest—to no longer have to sneak around the apartment at night, with either she or Brett moving between bedrooms for quick and quiet lovemaking. Now, and for the duration of Danny's absence, they could go to bed together and get up together, enjoying their newly-found intimacy without fear of discovery or embarrassment. But, of course, she knew it could not last . . . that Danny's return would also likely mean the end of Brett's stay.

Was she ready for that? For Brett to be gone, out of her daily life at home? She didn't want to think about it, but now, as she lay comfortably in his arms, she knew she must. With the progress of the investigation and with Calder's apparent willingness to talk, the end of the story could not be that far off. And with it, hopefully, an end to the danger facing Danny and herself. Brett would no longer be needed to watch over them.

Turning her head toward him, she whispered, "What happens when all of this is over?"

His eyes were half-closed with sleep, but snapped open, meeting hers. "What do you mean?"

She propped herself up on her elbow, looking

down on him. "I think you know what I mean."

"I suppose I'll have to go back home," he said. "It wouldn't be quite proper for me to stay on, would it?"

"I guess not," she said, falling back onto the pillow. "But it will seem strange not having you here. I'll miss you."

"Really?" he said with a grin. "That's nice to know."

To this point, neither had discussed the future or their feelings toward the other in any definitive or intimate way. Love was a word still unspoken; so far, they had allowed their bodies to do all of the talking.

For his part, Brett could not forget her earlier rejection of him, almost two years before. Much had changed since then, of course, but he could not bring himself to think of a more lasting relationship for fear of yet another disappointment. Try as he might, he could not rid himself of his doubts—that this new bond of theirs was only the result of bizarre circumstances, of being thrown together in close quarters and in the face of danger.

Were it not for the threats, would she be lying next to him now?

In many ways, she remained an enigma. He certainly knew more about her early life now than he had only a few weeks before, but there were still gaping holes. Despite his urging, she never spoke further of Danny's father or in much more detail about her life on the street. She would simply say, "That's the past. I don't want to think about it."

But *he* had to think about it, to know about it.

How could he plan a future with a woman when he still knew so little of her past?

For Maggie, the idea of another long-term commitment was no less frightening now than it had been when she'd first come to Minnesota. Try as *she* might, she could not rid herself of the last scars—or was it memories?—of Mick Salinas. Perhaps it was the lingering mystery of his disappearance, but she could not shake all thoughts of him. He would pop into her mind at the most unexpected times, as she read the news, as she stood at the stove, even as she lay like this, next to Brett.

Could she ever commit to another man while the shadow of Mick Salinas still hovered nearby?

"I think we should wait until this is all over," Brett said now. "If it ever is. Then step back and try to figure things out. I'm not sure we can do that right now. We need for this to be done, behind us."

Maggie knew he was right. That she felt the same. But she said nothing. Instead, she pulled back the covers and once again let her body do the talking.

39

At Barclay's request, Timothy McQueen got to his office almost an hour before the others were due to arrive. Barclay wanted time alone with him, to explain what they had learned so far about the child porn ring and to plead for McQueen's cooperation in keeping the story a Channel 7 exclusive.

"We've put our heart and soul into this thing," he said, "to say nothing of countless hours and a hell of a lot of initiative. We don't want to lose it. We don't want to see it on the front page of the *Star-Tribune* or the *Pioneer Press* . . . or leading the news of one of our competitors before we have a chance to report it."

McQueen claimed to understand, but said he

could make no promises. "If what you've told me about this porn ring is true, it's going to have to involve more of the department than just me. To say nothing of other departments. I'll try to keep a lid on it, but that's the best I can do."

Barclay suspected that would be his answer. He had spent most of the night worrying about it, tossing and turning, sleeping little, knowing that bringing McQueen in at this point would put the story at great risk. After Maggie had hung up the night before, both Jessica and Brett had called him to argue against it, pleading to give them the week he had promised. But in the end, he felt he had no choice: that in this case, his responsibilities as a journalist were outweighed by his duties as a common citizen.

"So let me get this straight," McQueen said, checking the notes he had made on a long legal pad. "You have a tape copy of a child porn film which you say was made here in the Twin Cities, in Edina to be precise." Barclay nodded as McQueen went on. "You say an ex-con by the name of John Hendrick, a.k.a. Butch Hemrick, a convicted pornographer, is one of those responsible, and that he's now a top campaign aide to the attorney general."

"Nice, huh," Barclay said as McQueen made a mock wipe of his brow. "Nothing like a little political scandal mixed in. Duggan's a big man at the capitol."

"Tell me something I don't know," McQueen said. "It could get dicey. But you're not sure if Duggan himself is involved."

"Directly involved," Barclay said, correcting

him. "He must know something about it since this Hemrick works for him, and since his goddamned campaign office is in the same building."

"Okay," McQueen said, making a new note on his pad. "Moving on. One of your employees, a Clyde Calder, is also involved . . . as a photographer. And he'll be here in a while to 'fess up."

"He said he would be."

"And you also know of a girl, a minor, who took part in one of the films, not the one in your possession, who has identified this Butch Hemrick, and who may be willing to testify to that fact. Correct?"

"We know where she is," Barclay said. "We don't know if she'll testify. If she is willing, we want to get her on tape first."

"She also believes Penny Collins was killed, perhaps by this Butch, because of her involvement in the films, and because she may have been ready to report it to the police."

"And," Barclay added, "because she may have stolen the tape that is now in our possession. But neither we nor this girl have proof that she died for those reasons."

McQueen got up and walked around the office, stretching his legs. "What else?" he asked.

"There was another girl, another young runaway, who supposedly took part in both of these films. Her name was Nadia Vaughn, from Madison, Wisconsin. But she committed suicide at her home several weeks ago."

"No shit," McQueen whispered. "Bodies all over the place."

Barclay leaned back. "We also know that a studio

and control room exist on the fifth floor of the building. One of our people has seen it, and Calder will confirm it. Also, that a bed similar to one used in the film was seen in the prop room on the fifth floor."

McQueen stopped his pacing and went back to his chair. "You mentioned a doctor . . . somebody named Klinkle."

"Henry Klinkle. He used to have an office in the same building. Once, seven years ago, he had his license suspended for fondling a seven-year-old girl. We think he could be the doctor who treated the little girl hurt during the second film, but again, we have no proof. He's also on the board of the company that owns the building."

"And the little girl, the one who was hurt?"

"We're trying to find her, or someone else who saw her get hurt. We think we have her picture, but, so far, she's still missing."

The detective shook his head in admiration. "You guys have done a hell of a job. We ought to hire the whole lot of you."

"It wasn't me," Barclay said. "It was Maggie, Jess, and Brett. They did it all."

"Speaking of Maggie," McQueen said. "Have you been able to tie the two people stalking her to any of this? That was your theory, wasn't it?"

"It still is," Barclay said. "But, no. We haven't made a direct connection. We just don't know what else it could be."

Calder was there a few minutes before nine, wearing a sport coat, dress shirt, and tie for the first time in

Barclay's memory. Looking more like a frightened job applicant than a possible felon, he shook hands with Barclay and McQueen, then slunk to a corner of the conference room and sat silently, waiting. Maggie, Brett, and Jessica showed up moments later, along with Barclay's assistant, Teresa Jensen, whom Barclay had asked to record the meeting.

"I've already told Mr. McQueen most of what we know," Barclay said once they were all seated. "I've also asked him to do whatever he can to protect our story, and he's promised that he will. But he says he can't guarantee anything."

"That's what we're afraid of," Maggie said. "We want guarantees."

McQueen shrugged. "What can I say? I'll do my best. But from what George has said, this case could involve several police jurisdictions, maybe even the BCA and the feds. It's going to be hard keeping all of those genies in the bottle."

When Maggie tried to press her protest, Barclay waved her quiet. "Forget that for now," he said. "We want to hear what Clyde has to tell us."

As he began, Calder refused to look at Barclay or any of his former coworkers. Peering straight ahead, and in a voice that was barely audible, he told them how his gambling addiction had led him to Butch Hemrick more than two years before. "Between the slots and my divorce, I was broke and up to my ass in debt. Big-time. I was fresh out of credit at the casinos, but didn't have enough sense to stop playing those fucking machines. Couldn't stop dreamin' of hitting one of those big old jackpots. And Hemrick kept feeding me the dollars until I was into him so deep I was drowning."

"Did Hemrick know then that you were a photographer?" Barclay asked.

Calder moved his eyes for the first time, turning to Barclay. "Sure. He'd seen me at Duggan's news conferences. He knew exactly who I was and what I could do. It turns out his old photographer had left him and gone back to California."

When his debts reached more than ten thousand dollars, Calder continued, Hemrick put the arm on him. "That was a year or so ago. He told me he wanted either the money, right then and there, or my services. Shoot and edit a couple of films for him, he told me, and he'd forget the debt. I didn't find out until later what kind of films they were, but by then it was too late. I was into him even deeper."

Brett leaned across the table, anger in his voice. "When you found out what kind of films they were, why didn't you tell him to fuck off?"

Calder laughed. "You don't know Butch. You don't know what kind of friends he has. Give him the chance and he'd play pool with your balls."

Barclay stood up. "Hold on a minute, Clyde. Maybe we should show Mr. McQueen the kind of film we're talking about." With that, he slipped the *Pajama Party* tape into the VCR and prepared to let it roll. "We won't watch the whole thing now," he said, "but enough for McQueen to get the idea. Teresa, perhaps you should step out of the room for a few minutes."

All of them except McQueen and Calder turned their backs on the TV, unwilling to watch even a portion of the film again. Barclay let it run for about fifteen minutes, then turned the VCR off and called Teresa back into the room. And to McQueen, he said, "We'll provide a copy of the full tape to you. You can then watch the rest of it, if you can stomach it."

McQueen turned to Calder. "Did you participate in the production of that film?"

"Yes. I shot and edited it. Others arranged the music and prepared some of the graphics."

"What others?"

"I only know their first names. Most of them fly in from California for the final mix."

McQueen pressed on. "Have you participated in other films like this one?"

Calder was stoic. "One other one. It was shot after the one you just saw."

"Do you have a copy of that?"

"No. They're locked up. At the studio."

"Can you get a copy?"

"No, Hemrick has the only key."

"Barclay tells me a young girl may have been hurt in the second film. Is that true?"

For the first time, Calder displayed some real emotion. His head hung and his voice cracked. "Yes. She began to bleed. Really bleed. It was pretty bad. She got hysterical. So did the other kids. I tried to help, but Butch told me to stay back."

"So what happened then?"

"Butch called a doctor, some friend of his. But the bleeding had pretty much stopped by the time he got there."

"Do you know the doctor's name?"

"No, I never heard it. But he's a big guy, fat. Bald with a double or triple chin. His whole body shook when he walked, I remember that."

"So you could identify him, if you saw him again?"

"Sure."

"Do you know the girl's name?"

"No. I never knew any of their names."

McQueen paused in the rapid-fire interrogation, catching his breath. Barclay was impressed. "Goddamn, McQueen, you sound just like a prosecuting attorney."

The detective ignored the comment and went back after Calder. "What about Martin Duggan? What connection, if any, does he have to all of this?"

Calder shrugged. "I don't know. I've never seen him around the fifth floor. But Butch works for him. He must know something."

"But to your personal knowledge, he's never taken part in any of this?"

"That's right."

"Hemrick has never mentioned his name in connection with the films?"

"No."

McQueen took off his sports jacket and loosened his tie, pacing around the table. "How about anyone else? Other crew members?"

Calder followed McQueen's lead, shedding his sport coat and loosening his tie. "Like I said, most of them came from out of town, California, I think. Two other backup photographers, an audio guy, and a few others in the control room. That's why Hemrick wanted me, I guess. A local guy to tie it all together."

The interview went on for twenty more minutes, McQueen leading, but others at the table asking occasional questions. Finally, they felt they had elicited all of the information they could get from Calder.

"So what happens now?" Clyde asked, slumped in his chair, visibly tired and shaken.

"That depends," McQueen replied. "I could put you under arrest right now, I suppose, but that could be a little tricky since the actual crime appears to have occurred in Edina. That's not my jurisdiction."

"Is there any chance of making some kind of a deal?"

"That's not up to me," McQueen said. Then, after a pause, "Did you have something in mind?"

Calder straightened up. "Well, there's going to be another shoot."

All heads turned his way. "When?" Barclay demanded.

"Soon. Unless Butch has canceled it. That's why I've been at the studio so much lately, trying to get things ready."

"Using the playground set?" Jessica asked.

"Yeah."

"When, exactly?" Barclay asked again.

Calder tightened his tie and slipped his sport coat back on. He seemed to have regained some of his confidence. "I guess I thought that information could be the basis of a deal." He had obviously thought of this well in advance.

"Exactly what are you proposing?" McQueen asked.

"Butch has been trying to get hold of me. Left a slug of messages at the apartment. I suppose I could try to hook up with him again, maybe work some kind of an inside deal with you guys on the day of the shoot."

"You mean let us inside?"

"That's what I was thinking of. But maybe Butch doesn't want anything to do with me anymore. He sounded pretty hacked off on the messages."

McQueen looked around the table. "This is out of my league," he said. "I'm going to have to put some kind of a task force together. Including somebody from the U.S. Attorney's office." Then, looking at Calder, he asked, "How much time do we have?"

"Only a few days, if it's still on schedule."

McQueen again. "Can we trust you to stick around?"

"If I was going to run," Calder said, "I would have done it by now."

"Okay. Get back to Hemrick. Try to set it up. I'll get a meeting together as quickly as I can."

"Can I be part of that meeting?" Barclay asked. "To try and protect our story?"

"I don't see why not," McQueen said. "I'll let you know the time and place."

Before leaving, McQueen collected a copy of the porn tape from Brett along with copies of the two unedited shooting tapes they had found in Calder's trunk. He also asked Teresa Jensen for a copy of her recording of the meeting. She promised to get it to him by that afternoon.

As Maggie walked him to the front lobby, his pocket cellular phone, no larger than the palm of his hand, buzzed. He stopped and put the tiny instrument to his ear, as Maggie waited. "McQueen here." He tucked the phone between his shoulder and ear and quickly made some notes on his legal pad. "Okay, thanks."

Slipping the phone back into his pocket, he said, "That was the office. They found the new car-rental agency."

Maggie looked at him expectantly.

"An Avis office downtown. Just a few blocks from here. The same guy, Kolura, got a Chevy Lumina yesterday morning." He repeated the license number and told her the license and a description of the car were already being distributed to squad cars in Minneapolis, St. Paul, and the suburbs. "Everybody's been told to follow but not stop the car. We want to know where they're staying. Unless he's got the car tucked away somewhere, we should run across it soon."

"Have you heard anything on Kolura himself?" she asked.

"Not yet. The guys in L.A. said they'd get back as quick as they could."

It's taken long enough, Maggie thought, but everything seemed to be coming together now.

"Where the fuck have you been?" Hemrick's words screamed out at Calder across the telephone line.

"Take it easy, Butch. I just got back in town."

There was truth in Calder's words. He had no more than walked into his apartment before making the call. "I don't know if you've heard, but I got my ass fired. I needed some time alone."

"I heard. But don't you ever check your god-damned answering machine?"

"Not until now. I told you, I wanted to be alone."

"So what the hell happened at the station?" Hemrick demanded.

Calder recited a story as close to the truth as he could manage: That he had been confronted by Barclay, who accused him of making kid-porn films and suspended him on the spot. "Shit, the only evidence he had was Jessica finding me in the studio. I denied everything, just like you told me to, but Barclay was set on getting rid of me. I'm not going to take it lying down. I'm going to get the union involved and get the suspension lifted. Maybe get Barclay fired in the process. He had no right."

He said nothing about the tapes or the other evidence the station had collected. And certainly nothing about Timothy McQueen.

"That's it?" Butch asked skeptically. "That's all they had?"

Hemrick knew for himself, of course, that Maggie had talked to Amy and that Jessica had gotten a look at the fifth floor studio. But he was unaware of anything beyond that.

"That's all I know about," Calder lied. "I'm telling you, it stinks."

He hoped Hemrick was buying the story, but Butch's next question made him wonder. "You're being straight with me? You know what happens to people who try to fuck me over, right?"

"Would I screw with you, Butch? I'm broke, I've got no job, and I'm into you up to my ass."

There was a long pause, then, "I don't think they've got shit," Hemrick finally said, as though trying to convince himself. "We have to go ahead with the next shoot. I've got no choice."

"You're sure that's smart?" Calder asked innocently. "Why don't you wait awhile?"

"I can't. I've got a deadline to meet. Everything's set, everybody's flying in."

"Do you want me to work it?" Calder asked.

"Fuck, yes. Who else have I got?"

40

Tony loved the smell of a new car. Better than any goddamned perfume, that's for sure. Bottle it and he'd buy it. Okay, so the Lumina wasn't brand-new, but still, it was new enough to carry that indefinable scent that inevitably brought him back to the day his old man brought home the '73 Olds Cutlass, the first new car young Antonio had ever been in. He'd sit in that car for hours, breathing in the fragrance until somebody chased him out. What the hell? It was one of the few pleasant memories he had of growing up—but even that didn't last long. Within a few months, somebody came around in the middle of the night and repossessed the damn thing, putting them back into a rundown old Chevy Impala.

He would never forgive his Pa for losing that '73 Olds.

Tony was on his way back to the motel after a quick stop at a Chinese take-out a few miles away. Flush from another winning night at the casino, he was feeling as content as he had in days. The weather had warmed up a bit, Sissy was laying off of him, and he'd found a new and hip radio station on the Lumina's FM dial. The world wasn't so bad, after all.

Darkness was still an hour away, and traffic was light. He didn't notice the black-and-white squad car until he was within a mile of the motel, and even then, he paid little attention. He wasn't speeding and—to his knowledge—had missed no stop signs or committed any other driving error. To be safe, however, at the next intersection he took a right instead of the left that would have led to the motel. Then another quick right. The squad hung with him, although well back. He felt the first prickling of uneasiness.

He kept going, debating as he drove. Staying well away from the motel, moving slowly and aimlessly, his eyes never leaving the rearview mirror for long. The cop was still there, following along, but making no effort to stop him and pull him over.

What to do?

Call Sissy, that's what. He spotted a bar and restaurant coming up on his right and pulled into the parking lot, looking over his shoulder to see if the cop would follow. He didn't, continuing down the road without an apparent glance in his direction. *Was it his imagination?* He sat in the Lumina for a few minutes more to see if the squad would return. When it didn't, he got out and walked into the bar, finding a pay phone just inside the entrance.

Sissy answered on the first ring, listening as he quickly related what had happened. "You must have done something to make him suspicious," she said.

"No fucking way. I've been driving like an old lady, you know that."

"Why else would he be following you?" she demanded. "They can't know anything about us, and you just picked up the car, for Christ's sake."

"I know, but I'm telling you, he was on my tail for miles."

"Stay where you are for an hour or so," she advised. "Then keep your eyes open when you head back. It's probably nothing."

By the time Tony returned to his car, two things had happened: the sweet odor of the chicken chow mein take-out, now more than an hour old, had replaced the Lumina's new car smell, and an unmarked squad car had found its way to the far end of the parking lot. Two others were sitting, lights out, in either direction on the road Tony would have to take.

To his credit, Tony was extremely cautious. He alertly surveyed the parking lot and again sat in the car for several minutes, allowing his eyes to adapt to the darkness and watching for anything unusual. But to the Burnsville cops, this was old hat. With the darkness, three cars, and an intimate knowledge of the local geography, they knew there was virtually no chance of them being spotted . . . or of Tony losing them.

They were right. Despite his vigilance, Tony could see no sign of a tail as he took a long, round-about route back to the Forest Green motel. In fact, he was feeling quite satisfied with himself, and knew that Sissy would be impressed, as well.

But he still wondered why that cop had been following him in the first place?

McQueen got the word from the Burnsville PD a few minutes later, along with a request for additional instructions. "We can keep an unmarked car there for the rest of the night," he was told, "but we're going to need help after that."

"Good," McQueen said. "Will you also have 'em keep track of who comes and goes? The license plates?" Wouldn't it be nice, he thought, if somebody like Butch Hemrick dropped by to tie all of this together. "I'll be back in touch in the morning."

With that, he immediately put in a call to Maggie at the station. "We found them," he said. "At a place called the Forest Green Motel in Burnsville."

"That's great," Maggie replied.

"What do you want to do?" he asked. "We've got them covered for the night, but I don't know about tomorrow and beyond. Should we go get them?"

Maggie was afraid of this question. What good would it do now? What could they prove? Nothing, yet. "I don't know," she finally said, repeating her concerns to McQueen.

"You're right," he replied. "With what we have,

there'd be no chance in hell of ever getting a judge to sign a search warrant. And we probably couldn't hold them for that long. But at least you'd have a chance to confront them."

"Can you give me some time?" Maggie asked. "I need to talk to the others."

"How about an hour? I'll be here 'til then."

There was division in the ranks. Barclay and Brett favored bringing Sissy and her boyfriend in immediately in hopes of getting something out of them or, at the very least, scaring them out of town. Maggie and Jessica thought otherwise. "It would be useless," Maggie now argued. "It might chase them away, but we still wouldn't know what it's all about. Who's behind them."

"They have to be tied to the porn ring," Brett said. "What else could it be?"

"Then why haven't we been able to connect them?" Jessica said, speaking up for the first time. "Calder says he knows nothing about these two, and we've never spotted them together with Butch or hanging around that Edina building. As far as we know, the first time Butch learned of Maggie's involvement was when he beat up that kid. And the threats against her started long before that."

They were interrupted by a page for Maggie. It was McQueen again. Maggie put his call on Barclay's speaker phone. "I thought you should know this right away," he said. "I just talked to the LAPD. Kolura is apparently the guy's real name. He's got a long record, mostly small stuff, but including one cocaine bust, and . . . get this . . .

three years in a federal pen for distributing child pornography. He got out in '91."

Brett let out a low whistle. "If that doesn't prove a connection," he said, "I don't know what does."

"They're faxing me his record," McQueen continued. "I'll get a copy over to you as fast as I can."

While he was still on the speaker phone, Maggie repeated the essence of the internal debate. "I don't know," McQueen said. "With what we know now, I'd string it out for a while. If they are connected to the porn films, it would be nice to pull them in with the same net we're going to use on the others."

"But how do we keep track of them?" Maggie asked.

"Let me try to figure that out," McQueen replied. "And, George, the first meeting of the task force is tomorrow morning at nine, at the government center."

"I'll be there," Barclay said, without hesitation.

McQueen knew putting the task force together would not be easy. He wanted to keep the group as tight as possible, yet large enough to include representatives from all the affected jurisdictions. He also knew that the feds—once they learned the facts—would want to take charge, since the production and distribution of child pornography were primarily federal offenses. But they'd have to get in line.

McQueen stood by the door of the government center meeting room as the participants began to drift in: his own department's chief of detectives, a deputy

Hennepin County sheriff and one of the assistant
county attorneys, the chiefs of the Edina and
Burnsville police departments, a lead investigator
from the state Bureau of Criminal Apprehension,
and a field agent of the FBI. None of them had been
told anything in advance, except that the meeting
was of the utmost importance with far-reaching
implications.

Barclay was the last to arrive. McQueen met
him at the door and quickly introduced him to
those he didn't already know. Then he locked the
door and opened the session. "I may be the lowest-
ranking guy here," McQueen said, "but since I've
been working this case from the beginning, I suppose I should get things going."

When the buzz around the table subsided, he
said, "I should first emphasize the absolute need
for confidentiality. What you are about to hear in
this room must be dealt with carefully or we risk
the loss of a major bust."

He went on to briefly explain how he had come
to be involved, reporting on the threats against
Maggie—but without mentioning her film. "That's
why George Barclay is here," he continued. "He
believed then, and still does, that the harassment
of Maggie Lawrence could be connected with
Channel Seven's ongoing investigation of a child
pornography ring operating in the Twin Cities.
Ms. Lawrence, it turns out, made some mistakes as
a street kid living in Los Angeles years ago. Barclay
believes the threats to publicly expose her past
have been aimed at forcing the station to give up
its investigation."

Referring to the notes he had made the day

before in Barclay's office, McQueen recited everything they so far knew about the porn ring, anticipating the collective gasp at the mention of Martin Duggan's name. "I should make it clear that we don't know if he is personally or directly involved, but we do know that his aide, this guy Butch Hemrick, is at the heart of it. At least if we can believe the girl, Amy, and Calder, the photographer."

Before accepting any questions, McQueen slid the tape of *Pajama Party* into a VCR and rolled it. "You'll be shocked by what you're about to see," he said, "but you'll also understand the need for quick and effective action by all of us."

The group sat in absolute silence from the beginning of the tape to the end, with only occasional glances away or at one another. When the final scene was over, the Edina police chief, a man named Bernie Fallon, looked at McQueen and said, "I can't believe it. You're telling me this piece of shit was made in my town?"

"I'm afraid so," the detective replied. "Another one, just like it, came later . . . and still another is planned for the next few days. And who knows how many more were made in the past?"

Others at the table reacted with the same outrage and disbelief. "How could it have been going on for so long without a leak?" McQueen's boss, chief of detectives Allen Burr, wanted to know. "Our sex squad should have gotten wind of it."

McQueen could only shrug. "Barclay's people are the ones who did it," he said. "Using the computer and some damn fine grunt work. Starting with the murder of Penny Collins and going from there. Which brings us to Mr. Barclay himself."

Barclay stood at the end of the table and made
his pitch to preserve the story. "When all of this
comes down," he said, "we want to be the only ones
reporting it, at least on that first night. We think we
deserve it. As McQueen says, you wouldn't all be
sitting here if it weren't for the work of our people.
You want your arrests and we want our story . . .
but we won't have the exclusive if any word of this
leaks to the other media."

One by one, each participant pledged to maintain secrecy, although acknowledging that others
in their departments would have to be made aware
of the investigation. "We'll do our best for you,
George," the BCA agent, Virgil Krupp, said. "But
with an operation of this size, it could be risky."

Barclay took only slight comfort from that, but
knew he could do or say little more.

It was at this point that the FBI agent, George
Endorf, spoke up. "Like the rest of you, this is the
first I've heard of this. If it's all true, the Bureau
would have to take primary jurisdiction. These are
clearly federal offenses we're talking about. While
some of your local laws would no doubt apply, the
major responsibility for prosecution would rest
with the U.S. Attorney's office."

In the face of several groans from around the
table, he quickly added, "But we're perfectly
happy to work with all of you. After all, you've got
more resources than we do. And it's your commu-
nities that are being affected. For the record, however, I must tell you that we're going to be deeply
involved, not simply interested bystanders."

Having heard that, and in the wake of a barrage
of other questions, the group tried to formulate

two alternative plans—one assuming Clyde Calder could give them access to the next filming, the other assuming he couldn't or wouldn't. Once McQueen or Barclay heard from Calder, they said they'd put him in touch with the U.S. Attorney's office to discuss a possible plea bargain. "I'll try to get the appropriate search warrants," Endorf, the FBI agent, said. "But what do you want to do about Martin Duggan?"

After considerable debate, they decided to do nothing until they had made the bust ... until Butch Hemrick was in custody. "Maybe he or somebody else will talk," McQueen said. "But don't count on it. And without it, we may have no direct link to Duggan."

In the meantime, it was decided to put Hemrick under loose surveillance and to seek permission to tap his telephone. The Burnsville chief said he would continue to monitor the movements of Sissy and Kolura and keep tabs on any visitors they might have, day or night.

For his part, Barclay promised that Maggie Lawrence would try to persuade Amy Boyd to testify, if she was given immunity, and that they would continue to search for the other children who may have been involved in the film, especially the young girl who was hurt.

"What about the doctor, this Klinkle guy?" the deputy sheriff asked.

"If Calder agrees to cooperate," McQueen said, "he should be able to tell us if he's the right guy."

After another hour of discussion, they agreed on specific plans and duties and named Timothy McQueen to work with the FBI in coordinating their continuing efforts. They weren't sure how much time they had, but they knew it would be short.

The cabin was tucked away in a forest of scrub oak and spruce, fronting the south shore of Apple Lake, five miles outside of Annandale, which was some forty miles west of the Twin Cites. Maggie and Brett had taken a dirt road off the main highway, twisting and turning through the heavily wooded countryside, every now and then catching a fleeting glimpse of yet another lake through the curtain of trees.

It wouldn't be long, Maggie knew, until the lakes would turn to ice two or three feet thick, dotted with small, ramshackle fishing houses or lone fishermen standing patiently, some would say forlornly, over holes in the ice, slapping their sides and stamping their feet for warmth while waiting for an elusive fish to bite. Already, a thin layer of the ice had formed along the shorelines, edging farther out with every sub-freezing day and night.

The cabin was impossible to spot from the road, lying at the end of a long, meandering driveway. It was larger than Maggie had expected, looking like a Swiss chalet sitting on the edge of the lake. Its exterior was of varnished half-logs, with dark brown shingles and shutters. A stone chimney clung to one side of the cabin, a thin trail of smoke rising from it.

Amy was sitting outside as they drove up, hunched over on a picnic bench, sipping a cup of coffee. Clad in a new pair of coveralls Brett had bought for her, she appeared far healthier than the last time Maggie had seen her. Even from a distance, Maggie could see that her cheeks had regained some of their color and her eyes some of their luster. Her hair was combed and, surprise, the rings had vanished from her nose.

"What's up?" Amy asked as they approached her.

"We need to talk again," Maggie replied. "How are things going?"

"Fine. Rocky and Popeye are out in the canoe, fishing."

"Best they not fall in," Brett said. "They'll die of hypothermia."

For the first time, Maggie saw Amy laugh. "You mean they'll freeze their asses. Don't worry. They're wearing life jackets. Neither of them knows how to swim."

"Do you have everything you need?" he asked.

"No problem. It's been great. We eat and sleep and watch videos. And fish."

Amy led them to the cabin and into an imposing combination living and dining room, dominated by a high, vaulted ceiling and by the large stone fireplace on one wall. There were also three bedrooms, a bath and sauna, and a loft overlooking the living room. Maggie quickly noticed that the floors were swept and the dishes done; the place appeared spotless.

"Nice to see you taking care of things," Maggie said.

"I told you we would," Amy replied as she threw two more logs on the smoldering fire, then sank to the floor next to it, watching as the flames grew. "So what do we need to talk about?" she asked.

Maggie described the recent events and explained that the police were now fully involved in the investigation. "They want you to testify about what you saw and did during that first film, Amy. And they want you to identify Butch as one of the people responsible."

When Amy started to protest, Maggie quickly added, "Nothing will happen to you, Amy. They'll give you immunity from any kind of prosecution. You'll face no kind of punishment, and you won't have to worry about Butch anymore. He'll be behind bars."

"But what about my folks?"

Maggie had expected the question, but had no ready answer. "I'm not sure, Amy. We'd have to face that when the time comes. Perhaps they wouldn't have to know. You're a juvenile, so you won't be identified by name in the media. But even if they do find out, I promise I'll be there with you."

Amy shook her head defiantly. "That's not good enough. They'll never understand, never forgive me."

"C'mon, Amy," Maggie said with some irritation. "What you're doing to them now is far worse. They don't know from one day to the next if you're dead or alive. It's a living hell for them."

Amy returned her anger. "Don't give me a god-damned lecture," she spat out. "I've been getting those all my life."

Maggie was not cowed. "It's time to turn your life around, Amy. Now's the chance. And you can do it. Face this and make amends with your folks, if you can. Do it for Penny and Nadia, if nothing else. They'd want you to, I know."

Amy began to cry, softly but steadily.

Maggie knelt beside her on the floor, feeling the heat of the fire. "You can't keep on running, Amy. Living on the streets. Not forever. I found that out years ago. You're a bright girl. There's still time to turn things around."

Amy looked away. "What about Rocky and Popeye? What happens to them?"

Brett, who had been standing apart, said, "We'll try to help them, too. If they want help. But you can't tie your life to theirs forever. Maybe they'll follow your lead."

Amy got up and wiped the last of the tears away. "What do I have to do?" she asked, resigned.

"Nothing," Maggie said. "Just stay here for now. We'll come and get you when the time is right. I'll be with you. But, please, don't take off on us."

"I won't," she promised. "But I can't say the same for the guys. They want to go to Texas. They may not stick around."

"That's up to them," Maggie replied. "But don't let them talk you into going with them."

"You've got my word," she said.

As Maggie and Brett were on the road, returning from the cabin, George Barclay was on the phone with Clyde Calder. "I talked to Butch," Calder told him. "He seems to have bought my story. Says he wants me back for the new shoot."

"Do you believe him?" Barclay asked.

"I don't know. I don't trust him, but he does

seem desperate to get this film done. Apparently he's on some kind of a deadline that he can't delay."

"When is it?"

"In three days. In the afternoon."

"Okay," Barclay said, "here's what you should do." He gave him the name of the assistant U.S. attorney he was supposed to see, a woman named Jennifer Sievers. "Give her a call. She'll discuss some kind of deal with you, assuming you live up to your end of the bargain."

"I will, trust me."

"But watch your ass end," Barclay told him. "Make sure Butch isn't tailing you when you meet with the lady."

"Don't worry. I won't take any chances. I'm already scared shitless."

41

That evening, after the early news, Barclay brought them all together in the conference room, reporting first on his morning meeting with McQueen's task force and then on his conversation with Clyde Calder. "We've got three days to get this story together," he said. "The cops will do their thing, but we've got to do ours."

They spent the next few minutes assessing what they already had on tape. It didn't take long, because there wasn't much there. The porn film itself, which would have to be carefully edited for use on the air, and the outside shots of the Edina building, with Butch and Calder going in. That was about it, so far.

"Tough to make a story for television out of that," Barclay said. "Let's talk about what we need."

"Don't forget, we also have footage of the Penny Collins murder scene," Jessica said. "That will fit in somewhere, since Penny was involved in both of the films."

"But be careful not to tie her death directly to her part in the films," Barclay warned. "We have no evidence of that."

"What about Amy Boyd?" Jessica asked.

Maggie shrugged. "She's agreed to testify, but I didn't dare ask if she would tell her story on tape. The timing wasn't right. She was too shook up as it was."

"If she does agree," Brett said, "we'll have to cover her face and disguise her voice. She's scared stiff her folks will find out."

"Get back to her," Barclay ordered. "And take a photographer this time."

While they had file tape of both Hemrick and Duggan in their political roles, it was decided that they should also get additional hidden camera footage of both of them, in case it was needed for the story. "And how about Dr. Klinkle?" Maggie asked. "We may need some shots of him, too."

"We'll get Calder inside the clinic," Barclay said. "To make sure he's the right guy. Then we can pick him up coming or going."

He also asked Jessica to begin working on a first draft of the story. "It won't be easy, with everything still up in the air. But I'd like to get started, knowing what we know, and making some assumptions about what we'll have on tape three days from now. I don't want to put this thing together at the last minute. Maggie and Brett will give you a hand, I'm sure."

Jessica swallowed hard, but didn't argue. "I'll give it a try," she said, "but I'm going to need all of the help I can get."

Maggie was exhausted. All of them were. For the past week or more, they had been working fourteen-to-sixteen-hour days, an especially difficult task for Maggie, who was still expected to be bright and chipper for each of her newscasts. Several times, she had considered asking Barclay for an evening off, for a chance to rest and recuperate, but she couldn't forget the promise made to him weeks before: that she would not let the investigation affect her anchor duties.

The November rating period was in full swing, their performance tracked each night by the overnight ratings and closely examined the next day by Nicholas Hawke and others sitting high up in management heaven.

So far, they had nothing to complain about. The ratings dominance they had established in October was holding up in November, despite an abysmal showing by the network in its prime-time programming, which led into the local news. Translated, that meant literally tens of thousands of viewers were making a deliberate effort to switch from the other networks to see the local Channel 7 news.

In an effort to ease the pressure on her, Alex Collier had begun to read more than his share of the news, giving Maggie time to breathe and to conserve her energy, allowing her to appear more animated than she actually felt. She told Collier that she owed him one, but he would have none of it. "Believe me, I know what you're going through," he said. "I only wish I could do more."

If nothing else, the continued ratings success apparently was keeping Hawke at bay. The general manager had stayed away from the newsroom, and out of Barclay's hair, since his last tirade of weeks before. Barclay knew it couldn't last forever, but he hoped it would extend at least through what promised to be nerve-wracking days ahead. There was so much to do and so little time.

But Maggie, like the others, was almost too tired to think about it.

Jonathan Cassidy was waiting in the lobby when Maggie arrived at the station the next morning, looking far better than she felt after another short night. From all appearances, he was a changed man, almost: well-scrubbed, clean-shaven with fresh clothes that were pressed and color coordinated, and a belt instead of the rope holding up his pants.

"Your wife or mother must have gotten after you," Maggie said, smiling.

Cassidy blushed, glancing down at himself. "She did. My mother. Told me I couldn't walk around looking like I did. Especially when I was coming to see someone like you."

"That's sweet," Maggie said, leading him to a pair of chairs on the far side of the lobby. "Do you have something for us?"

He waited for her to sit before he took the other chair himself. "I do, actually," he said. "We found two of the four kids in the pictures."

"Are you kidding me?"

"No. But it wasn't me. Another one of the street workers, a woman who works out of a Catholic shelter, knew both of them. One of the girls and one of the boys."

"Does she know where they are now?" Maggie asked.

He held out two of the pictures. "She thinks so. The little girl, Merilee Townsend, is in a foster home in the suburbs. Columbia Heights, I think. I've got the address. It's about her fifth foster home, the woman says. The boy, Jason Schuster, is back with his parents, unless he's run away again. I've got his address, too."

"That's great work, Jonathan. I hope you'll pass on our thanks to the lady."

"I will," he said. "And we're still looking for the other two."

"Good," Maggie said, explaining that the FBI and police were now involved in the investigation and that she would turn over the children's names and addresses to them. He wanted to know more, but she declined. "You should know in a few days. And then you'll understand the importance of what you've done for us. And for the kids still out there on the streets."

As Maggie got up, Cassidy gave her a sheet of paper with the children's names and addresses, but appeared hesitant to get up and leave himself. After waiting, she asked, "Is there something else, Jonathan?"

"Not really," he said, finally rising. Then, shyly, "You're not married, are you?"

Maggie was taken aback, but touched. "No," she

said with a gentle smile, "but I am in a relation-ship."

"Really? Then I heard wrong, I guess."

"It hasn't been that long, Jonathan. And not everybody knows."

"That's too bad," he said, looking away. "I thought we might have dinner or something."

She gave his arm a quick squeeze. "That's still possible. Once this is all over. It would be a nice way for all of us to say thanks."

From the look on his face, Maggie knew that wasn't exactly what he had hoped to hear.

Later that morning, Brett was once again inside the surveillance van, along with Tamara Swain, the same photographer who had staked out the Edina office building with him. Now they were outside of the Westside Clinic, waiting for Clyde Calder to emerge. He had arranged a last-minute appoint-ment with Dr. Henry Klinkle, claiming to have an extremely sore throat.

They had been sitting there for more than an hour, Tamara once again huddled behind the camera at the shooting window. "What the hell can be taking so long?" Brett wondered aloud.

"When's the last time you've been to a doctor?" Tamara asked. "They just love to keep you waiting. Makes them feel important or something."

Another twenty minutes passed before Calder finally walked out of the clinic and climbed into the van. "He's the guy," he said. "The same one that Butch called to treat the little girl."

"You're sure?" Brett asked.

"Positive. Although I think he's added one more chin."

"He didn't recognize you?"

"No way. But he did wonder why he couldn't find anything wrong with my throat. The strep test didn't show anything, but he took some blood for another test. He says he should know the results in a day or two."

"He may not be around to get the results," Brett said, glancing at his watch. It was almost noon. "I hope he goes out for lunch."

They were not disappointed. Forty-five minutes later, Klinkle emerged, wrapping the belt of an overcoat around his large body. He stood for a moment, checking the weather, breathing the fresh air, before moving on toward the parking lot.

"I've got him," Tamara whispered, as the camera followed Klinkle along the sidewalk and through the parking lot to his car. "You should have thirty or forty seconds of useable stuff," she said.

"That'll be enough," Brett said with satisfaction. "More than enough."

The Burnsville cops keeping an eye on the Forest Green motel had no idea why they were there. They had been told nothing except to monitor any movement by the occupants of Room 113, a man and a woman, who were driving a '97 dark blue Lumina sedan parked immediately in front of their unit. They knew it must be important, however, since it was costing the department a mountain of overtime: two officers, one in an upper-floor room with a clear view of ll3's entrance and another sitting in an unmarked squad car in a Hardee's parking lot adjacent to the motel. Two cops, twenty-four hours a day.

And for what? The pair almost never left the room, and when they did, they would drive no more than a few blocks to a drugstore, a video store, or to some take-out joint. There had been only one exception: Late the night before, the man had driven to the Mystic Lake Casino, staying for a couple of hours before returning to the motel, stopping nowhere in between.

The officers would change the stake-out car every eight-hour shift, always parking in a somewhat different location to avoid detection. So far, they were sure they had not been spotted.

The other part of their job was more difficult: to note the license number of every car that came and went from the motel, day or night, and to feed those numbers back to their base every two hours. The plates the cop in the squad couldn't pick up with his binoculars were left to his partner inside the motel. Fortunately, the motel was somewhat off the beaten track, and at this time of year, there was not much traffic in and out.

So for the most part, they simply sat and waited. And watched. Why they didn't know.

If the cops outside were bored, they had nothing on the two people inside. But by now, Sissy and Tony had become accustomed to the monotony, having formulated a routine that would help keep them both sane and off each other's back. Up by ten, no earlier unless there was some special assignment, check the front desk for an envelope or message, spend an hour working out with Jane Fonda, another hour reading the morning newspapers cover to cover, lunch, then the afternoon soaps and talk shows, the news, dinner, and a movie for the evening. In bed by 10:30, after the news.

On some days, especially after one of his nocturnal visits to the casino, Tony would manage to squeeze in an afternoon nap and shower. Sissy would spend the time with a stack of magazines now almost two-feet high.

They seldom talked and rarely had sex, never if Sissy had anything to say about it. They had quit worrying about when the next message might come or who their employers were. As long as the cash kept flowing, they were satisfied—content now to dream of what they could do with their stash once they were finally back in California.

Although she never spoke of it, Sissy planned to use her share to open a "dating" service in L.A., one with a little class and a top-shelf list of girls and clients. After all, she knew the business from top to bottom, although admittedly she had spent more time at the bottom than she had at the top. But she could learn. She had the contacts and knew the girls. All she needed was a small honey pot, which was now growing larger by the week.

As for Tony, well, between his earnings and his casino booty, he figured he had enough to leverage a first-class, big-budget film of his own. One he'd produce and direct himself. Not just another fuck film, but one with a real story to it. X-rated, maybe, but better than most of the porno crap in the video stores now. He knew there was a huge market out there; he just had to tap into it.

Like Sissy, he never talked about his plans. He was afraid she'd want a piece of the action, and there was no way he'd go for that. If he never saw her again after this gig, it would be all right with him.

Tony being Tony, it no doubt would have surprised him to know that Sissy felt exactly the same way.

Both cops spotted the big car at the same time: Sonny Sprague in the squad car and Bruce Lessor in the room upstairs, although Sonny would later admit he was damn near asleep when the Lincoln swept past him and into the motel parking lot. But the flash of the headlights had brought his eyes wide open.

Neither man would have paid particular attention had it not been for the hour: 2:42 A.M., the middle of the dog watch, and the first car to enter the lot since midnight. "You see him?" Sprague said into his radio. "Got him," Lessor replied "ninety-seven Lincoln Continental. Dark blue or black, I can't tell which from here."

The Lincoln doused its lights as it came to a stop outside of the motel office. The driver was out of the car and through the office door before Sprague could put the binoculars to his eyes and focus. Even then, in the dark and with the car parked at an angle, he could not make out the license plate.

"You're going to have to get the plate number," he told Lessor. "I can't see it from here."

"Okay," the other officer said. "But it's going to take me a minute to get down there."

A minute was too long. The driver was back outside and into the Lincoln before the last words were out of Lessor's mouth. "Shit," Sprague muttered, knowing his partner would never make it in time. "He's already moving out," he said into the mike. "I'm going to have to follow him to pick up the plate."

Putting his Crown Victoria into gear, he took off, surprised that the Lincoln was already so far ahead of him. "Fucker's pushing the pedal," he said to himself as he continued the pursuit. The Lincoln was doing seventy-five in a fifty-five-mile-an-hour zone, apparently oblivious to the pair of headlights behind, keeping pace. Sprague knew he should stop the bastard, but he didn't know if he was supposed to. Their orders were simply to get the license numbers.

Screw it, he thought, the son of a bitch could kill somebody, and then where would I be? He flicked on his flashing lights and siren and gunned it, pulling up close behind the Lincoln, watching as the car moved quickly to the curb, slowed, and then stopped.

Before leaving the squad, he punched the car's license number into his computer, which quickly told him the car was not stolen and was registered to a Richard Wycross. And that there were no warrants outstanding.

Still, he was cautious as he approached the car, standing slightly back from the driver's open window, his holster unsnapped. The beam of his flashlight caught the man's face: white, middle-aged, graying hair, and mustache. His hands were on the steering wheel. Sprague leaned forward, hoping to catch a whiff of alcohol. He couldn't.

"May I see your driver's license, please," he said. The license confirmed the computer report: Richard Wycross, born in 1938, with a Minneapolis address. "Know how fast you were going, sir?" The man shook his head. "Seventy-five in a fifty-five zone. I'm afraid I'm going to have to cite you."

The man shrugged his shoulders but then asked, "How long have you been following me?"

Funny question, Sprague thought. "Long enough," he said as he returned to the squad car to write out the ticket.

Once Wycross had driven off with his ticket, Sprague returned to his car . . . and then to the motel, yawning all the way. He'd seen the last of Richard Wycross. To him, it was no more than another ticket, no more than another license number to add to the list.

He just wished he could be home in bed.

42

Two days to go . . . and counting. McQueen was in continuing contact with Barclay. Things were happening quickly.

The feds had obtained search warrants for the Edina building, for both the fifth floor and for Duggan's campaign office, and for the Westside Clinic and home of Dr. Henry Klinkle.

Clyde Calder had arranged a tentative plea bargain with the U.S. Attorney's office, specifying one year in a minimum security prison and ten years' probation in return for his full cooperation with the bust and for his eventual testimony against the other defendants.

Butch Hemrick was under constant but discreet surveillance by a combination of FBI and BCA

agents, and a federal judge had approved taps on
the telephones at both Hemrick's home and the
Edina offices. In addition, records of his telephone
calls for the past two years had been obtained and
were now being analyzed.

Hennepin county deputies, in plain clothes,
were monitoring all in-coming flights from
California at the Twin Cities International airport,
cross-checking the manifests against any names
that might also appear in the logs of Hemrick's
telephone calls.

With the addresses Cassidy had given to Maggie,
FBI agents had been able to locate one of the two
children, Merilee Townsend. She was in protective
custody as the search continued for the boy, Jason
Schuster, who apparently had taken off again, and
for the two other unnamed children who had participated in the *Pajama Party* film.

Maggie had promised to bring Amy Boyd back
to town for questioning by the FBI, but only after
she had agreed to be interviewed on camera.
Maggie was again en route to the Annandale cabin
with a photographer—in hopes of persuading
Amy.

The Burnsville police were faxing McQueen and
Barclay the names of the owners of every vehicle that
had stopped at the Forest Green Motel since their
surveillance began. McQueen was checking them
for any criminal records, while Barclay was to look
for any familiar names. So far, neither had come up
with anything.

Much to Barclay's relief, there had been no
sign of a leak. McQueen told him none of the
agencies had received any calls or other inquiries

from the newspapers or other television stations. Barclay could only hope it would last.

At the Annandale cabin, Amy was proving to be as difficult as Maggie had feared she would be. At first, she outright refused to be interviewed on camera, threatening to renege on her promise to testify and instead take off for Texas immediately. Maggie was undeterred, patiently explaining that Amy's identify would be protected: Her face would never be seen and her voice would be altered and made unrecognizable to anyone, even to her parents.

Still, she resisted.

"Look," Maggie said, trying a new tack, "a lot of kids and parents will be watching our story. What better way is there to warn them about the dangers of getting caught up in something like this than to hear it from someone like yourself? Someone who has been there and who's survived it.

"Maybe hearing it from you will keep some other Penny or Nadia . . . or another Amy . . . from getting involved. From ending up dead. Think about it, Amy. It could happen, it could help."

They were sitting on the cabin's picnic bench. But this time, the two boys were there, listening in. "She's making sense, Amy," Rocky said, surprising Maggie. "And what the hell can it hurt? She says Butch isn't going to be around for a long time."

"You're sure no one will be able to tell who I am?" Amy asked.

"Positive," Maggie said.

Amy was clearly undecided. On one hand, she

didn't want to disappoint Maggie, the one adult she had come to trust in her time on the street, who had given her money and even the coat off her back. On the other hand, the thought of her folks ever finding out, no matter how unlikely, scared the hell out of her. She looked again at Rocky and Popeye. "You're sure I should be doing this?" Both boys nodded. "Okay," she said, "Let's do it."

Maggie breathed a deep sigh of relief and nodded to the photographer, who immediately headed for the cabin to begin setting up the camera equipment.

Tony found the envelope at the motel's front desk. Larger than the ones they normally received. It came as no surprise that the clerk had just come on duty and could provide no clue as to who had left it or when. Tony decided to take a flyer. "Why don't you call the guy who was here and ask him?"

"He's probably home sleeping," the clerk said. "He'd kill me if I call him now."

Tony took out a twenty-dollar bill. "There'll be one of these waiting for him, too. When he comes on tonight."

The clerk fingered the bill, then tucked it into his pocket. "Okay, I'll call you after I talk to him."

Tony thanked him and took the envelope back to the room, reporting to Sissy on what he had done. "That was stupid," she said. "What if the General finds out?"

He should have known what she'd say. "How can he? He doesn't know the fucking clerk. And, shit, we'll be in another motel by the time he makes the next payment."

Sissy could only shake her head. Loser.

The envelope contained the usual amount of cash, along with a key and a note, the longest one yet.

> We are tired of waiting for results. The enclosed key will open locker number 6 at the downtown Minneapolis bus depot. In the locker, you will find ten video cassettes, copies of the one you left for Maggie Lawrence. Beginning tomorrow morning, you will anonymously distribute one tape to each of the television stations in the Twin Cities, to the two daily newspapers, and to the alternative newspapers, *City Pages* and *City Business*. The addresses are listed below.
>
> Enclosed in each tape will be a copy of the following message: 'Please cue into this tape fifteen minutes and you will find a woman, although younger, who bears a startling resemblance to a Twin Cities television anchorwoman, performing unspeakable acts. We trust you will be interested in exposing this wanton woman for what she was . . . and is.
>
> Signed,
> God's Witnesses.

They both read the note again. "Son of a bitch," Sissy whispered. "They're not going to fuck around, are they?"

"What do you mean?" Tony said. "They've *been* fucking around. Now they're finally getting down to business."

"You think that's what they've wanted all along? To chase her out of town?"

"Must be," Tony agreed.

"Then why didn't they do this in the beginning?"

Tony shrugged. "Got me. Maybe they thought the threats would be enough."

"And who in the hell are God's Witnesses?"

Tony was tiring of her questions. "How should I know? If they're some right-wing, born-again weirdos, they sure as hell have money to spare."

Sissy sank back onto the bed. She could picture people all over town sitting down to look at the tape. The surprise. The laughter. The leering. Word would travel as fast as the goddamned Concorde. Give it a day and Maggie would be a laughingstock, regardless of whether one picture or one word was ever printed or broadcast. She would have no choice but to leave, in embarrassment and disgrace. But where would she go? The tapes would never be far behind.

Stupid broad, she thought. Why hadn't she taken the threats seriously? Save herself and that kid of hers from all of this. Despite herself, Sissy felt a pang of pity for the woman. What had she done to deserve this? Made a success out of her life, that's what. Unlike some of us, she thought ruefully. But what the hell could she do without getting herself in a jam? The wheels were already in motion.

This time, it was Tony who had the question. "Why don't they just mail the damn tapes? Why make us deliver them?"

Sissy had wondered the same thing. "They must want to stay away from the mails," she said. "Worried about getting the postal inspectors on their ass. That's all I can figure."

At that moment, the phone rang. It was the clerk at the front desk. "Randy, the night guy, says the man was in and out in a flash. Dropped the envelope on the desk and beat it. He didn't get any kind of a look at him at all. Sorry."

Tony was disappointed, but not too badly. Maybe it was better that he didn't know. As long as the money kept coming.

The interview with Amy was going well. Despite her earlier reservations, she appeared poised and unafraid in front of the camera, answering Maggie's questions honestly and concisely. Her story was not unlike Maggie's own of years before: hungry and homeless, with no money, no clothes except those on her back, and no place to turn until she met a man named Butch—who offered her five hundred dollars to appear in a film with several other youngsters.

"Did you know what kind of film it would be?" Maggie asked.

"Yes. He didn't try to hide it."

"And you still did it?"

Amy stared straight into the camera, defiantly. "I needed the money. I hadn't eaten in days. I was living in a cardboard box under a bridge. I couldn't go home, and I didn't want to steal. I didn't know what else to do."

"How did this Butch find you?" Maggie asked.

"Through my friend, Nadia. He was giving her money for drugs."

"To appear in his films?"

"Right."

"Were you taking drugs?"

"No way. But Nadia was hooked. She needed the money for drugs. I needed it for food."

"Where is Nadia now?"

Amy voiced cracked. "She's dead. She committed suicide a few weeks ago."

The photographer signaled Maggie from behind the camera. He had to stop to change tapes. "You're doing fine, Amy," Maggie said during the break. "Are you okay?"

She took a deep breath and whispered, "I think so."

The camera was set up inside the cabin, with Amy sitting directly in front of one of the wide front windows, the bright sunlight making a halo around her head and leaving her face in a shadow. Electronic effects would wipe out any remaining features.

With the camera rolling again, Maggie asked, "Did you also know Penny Collins, the girl who was found murdered in the park a couple of months ago?"

"Yes. She was my friend, too. And Nadia's."

"Did she also appear in these films?"

"Yes, two of them that I know about. So did Nadia."

Maggie knew she had to be careful now, remembering Barclay's cautions, but she felt the question had to be asked. "Do you know who killed Penny Collins?"

There was a long pause. "Not that I can ever

prove. But I know she was planning to go to the police. To tell them about the film."

"Why would she want to do that?" Maggie asked.

"Because she saw a little girl get hurt during the filming. A real young girl, a kid, during one of the sex scenes. She felt horrible about it. So did Nadia."

Amy went on to detail the girl's injury and then, at some length, to describe the film she herself had appeared in. "All of the girls were supposed to be Barbie dolls, you know, each one of us dressed up in a different outfit. Then we met a bunch of boys who were supposed to be Ken dolls. It became a Ken and Barbie party. Everybody ended up naked, doing horrible things. It was pretty sick."

After several more questions, when it became clear that Amy was beginning to tire, Maggie decided to wind up the interview. "Why have you decided to come forward now?" she asked. "To testify in court?"

"I'm not really sure," she said. "I'm scared, I guess, that the same thing that happened to Penny could happen to me. And I'm sorry now for what I did. Ashamed that I was part of it. I thought this might be a way I could make up for it, to say I'm sorry."

At the Forest Green Motel, Tony and Sissy were hunched over a map of the Twin Cities, figuring out the route they would follow the next day. Using a highlighter pen and the addresses provided to them in the note, they connected the dots between

the various television stations and newspapers, trying to decide on the most efficient way to get to all
of them.

"This could take hours," Tony grumbled, staring down at the map. "Damn near every one of
them is in a different part of town."

Sissy scoffed. "What's the difference? You got a
hot date someplace?"

"Fuck you," he said.

They had already decided to take turns dropping off the tapes, making themselves as inconspicuous as possible in the process. "Get in and out
in a hurry," Tony said. "Those receptionists will
never remember who left it. They get deliveries all
the time."

Sissy, who unlike Tony had pretty much stayed
out of sight until now, could only hope he was
right. She didn't want anything to screw up her
plans for back home.

George Barclay was at his desk, trying to concentrate on the list in front of him, a list McQueen
had sent over with the names of all the registered
owners of vehicles that had come and gone from
the Forest Green Motel in the past twenty-four
hours. Barclay had intended to get to the list earlier, but a thousand other things had gotten in the
way. Not only preparing for coverage of the raid,
but a host of other newsroom matters that
demanded his immediate attention. He felt like a
clumsy juggler, dropping more balls than he
caught. Finally, he had to close his office door and
tell his secretary to hold all of his calls.

McQueen had jotted a note on top of the list. "Can't find anybody here with a criminal record, at least not in this state. They all seem to be solid citizens." Seeing that, Barclay was tempted to put the list aside, but he decided he should wade through it anyway. There were about thirty names in all, along with ages and addresses and the times of arrival and departure from the motel.

He ran his finger down the list, seeing no names that meant anything to him. Until he came to the final entry: Richard Wycross, 3320 Alameda Avenue, Minneapolis.

Why was that name familiar?

He read on. Wycross had arrived at the motel at 2:42 A.M. and departed at 2:44 A.M. *Two minutes?* A notation said an officer was forced to pursue him to get the license number and in the process gave him a speeding ticket.

Richard Wycross?

Barclay searched his memory. Where had he heard the name? It couldn't have been that long ago. A letter or a call from a viewer? Could be, but he didn't think so. A politician or P.R. flack? Maybe, but that didn't seem right either. He was driving himself nuts. Finally, he got up and opened the office door, summoning his assistant, Teresa Jensen. She would know. "Tell me," he said. "Who in the hell is Richard Wycross?"

She gave him her famous you're-losing-your-mind look. "You just met him a few months ago," she said.

"I did?" His mind was blank.

"Of course. At the broadcasters' reception in

August. He's the new general manager of Channel Thirteen."

Son of a bitch! Barclay thought his legs might crumple beneath him. *That was it!* Richard Wycross. A New York dude who'd been sent in by the parent conglomerate to fix things at Channel 13, now a poor third in news ratings among the local network affiliates. A guy as old or older than Barclay himself. Gray-haired with a mustache and flushed face, who Barclay remembered was drinking more than his share of the reception champagne. Because of the large crowd, he had been able to do no more than say hello to the man, but from his looks and bearing, Barclay had immediately written him off as another corporate fixer who didn't know or care a damn thing about the local market or local news. With all of the recent mergers in broadcasting, the business was overflowing with carpetbaggers like him—buttoned-up assholes whose only job was to boost a station's bottom line.

"Are you okay?" Teresa asked, watching him closely.

"Yeah, I think so," he said, suddenly aware she was still there.

"Why were you asking about him?" she wanted to know.

"It's nothing. I just came across his name and couldn't place him."

"I think you need some time off, boss."

"You're right about that," he said.

Retreating to his office, he again closed the door behind him. His mind was twirling like a top. What in the hell was Richard Wycross doing at that motel in the middle of the night? He couldn't be shacking up, not in two minutes. Nobody is that quick. Could it be that he had some connection with this Sissy and Kolura? Hard to believe, but what else? And who had more to gain from scaring Maggie Lawrence so badly that she'd get the hell out of town? Why hadn't he thought of it before?

He rushed out of the office and across the newsroom to Computer Central, breathing hard by the time he got there, finding Jessica at her usual place. "I need a favor," he puffed. "Put that old computer into high gear and give me everything you can on Richard Wycross, the new GM at Channel Thirteen, and everything there is to know about the station's parent company. I think it's Prestige Broadcasting."

Jessica was making notes. "What's going on, George?"

"I'm not sure, but I think we may have just found the missing piece to our puzzle."

"Tell me more," she said.

"Not now," he replied. "Just get me the information."

Two hours later, Jessica was in Barclay's office, a sheaf of papers in her hands. "Here's the dope," she said, passing the papers to him. "Wycross's background seems fairly typical for the big hitters. Ivy League education, Princeton to be exact. Began his career in sales at one of the New York network stations, then went on to a string of other stations, never staying long at any one place,

eventually working his way up to general manager
at one of the affiliates in Cheyenne. That was ten
years ago."

Barclay's eyes were on the papers she had given
him, trying to keep up.

"He kept on moving," she continued, "to ever
larger markets. Even worked at one of the networks for a while, in their affiliate relations department. Hooked up with Prestige Broadcasting a
couple of years ago, apparently as a trouble-
shooter, a turnaround specialist they'd dispatch to
any of their stations that were in trouble."

Barclay felt some small satisfaction. His original
assessment of the guy had been right on. He knew
the type. He'd even worked for one or two of
them in his earlier life.

"I know somebody at one of his stations,"
Jessica said. "A reporter in Denver. We went to
Northwestern together. She tells me the guy's a
prick of the first order. Came in, cut their staff to
the bone, and had them covering every sleazy
story in town. They had a big party when he finally
left."

"What about Prestige Broadcasting?" Barclay
asked.

"I'm still working on that," she said. "But I did
run over to one of the brokerage houses to get a
copy of their annual report. This should get you
started."

Barclay took the glossy-covered report from
her and began to thumb through it. Prestige was
not a broadcasting giant by today's standards, but
big enough and still growing: eight television stations and sixteen radio stations, spread across the

country. He looked at the pictures of the corporation's officers, but recognized none of the names or faces except Wycross's, who was listed as a vice president of affiliate performance.

In other words, the company gunslinger.

"Okay," he said, flipping the report on the desk. "Good work. Give me half an hour and we'll get together with Maggie and Brett."

Then he reached for the telephone.

43

McQueen answered the call on the first ring. "I think we've got something," Barclay told him, quickly reciting the news of Richard Wycross and Prestige Broadcasting. "I can't figure out why else he'd be there at that time of night. He must have dropped off a message of some kind. Or maybe money."

The detective listened without interruption, but then said, "I suppose there could be other explanations."

"Like what? He only stayed for two fucking minutes."

"You've got a point. But what do you want us to do?"

"I don't know," Barclay said. "That's why I called you."

"Give me a minute to think," he said.

The line went silent for what seemed to Barclay like an hour. Finally, McQueen was back on. "I'll tell you what. We'll get the Burnsville PD to find out who was on duty at the motel. Maybe he or she will be able to tell them something."

"But tell them to be careful," Barclay cautioned. "Those two are still living there. We don't want to spook them."

"Don't worry. They can handle it."

Twenty minutes later, Jessica, Brett, and Maggie were once again packed into Barclay's office, listening with growing anger and disbelief as he repeated what they had learned about Wycross.

Maggie was outraged. "You mean all of this has been because of the stupid ratings? He's put us through this to get me off the air and out of town, to get rid of a competitor? Forget about me. Think of what he's done to Danny. I can't believe it!"

"I couldn't either," Barclay said. "Until I stopped to think about what's at stake. If getting rid of you could mean a few more rating points for them, especially if they came out of our hide, it would be worth millions and millions of dollars over the long run."

Brett started to say something, but Maggie cut him off. "Wait a minute. You say his name is Wycross? I talked to him, for Christ's sake. Not more than a couple of months ago. He was pitching me for a job at another one of their stations, in Chicago, I think. I told him thanks but no thanks, that I was happy here and hoped to stay for a long time. He was ever-so-polite, even thanked me for taking the time to talk to him and wished me well. That dirty bastard."

"That's when he must have decided on another approach," Barclay said bitterly.

Brett finally got the chance to speak. "If you're right about this, then I was wrong. There must be no connection to the porn ring. But if not, where did Wycross get Maggie's film? Where did he find Sissy and Kolura? It doesn't make any sense."

"Maybe we'll have the chance to ask them someday," Barclay said. "But that's not what is worrying me now."

"What do you mean?" Jessica asked.

Barclay leaned well back in his chair. "If Wycross stopped at the motel to leave a message or money, it makes me wonder what's going to happen next?"

"You mean a new attack on Maggie?" Brett asked.

"Exactly. If he's looking at the ratings, he must be getting desperate."

"Goddamn," Maggie murmured.

"I'll talk to McQueen again," Barclay said. "Make sure those Burnsville cops keep a tight watch on them."

When Maggie returned to her desk, she found the light blinking on her voice mail. She hit the button and listened. It was another electronically altered voice, different than the others but no more distinct. And this time, it carried a warning, not a threat. "Ms. Lawrence. Be careful. Protect yourself. Have someone at the bus depot tomorrow morning. Stop them." Maggie played it again, then again. A male voice, she thought, but thoroughly disguised.

What was he talking about? What bus depot? Protect herself from what? Stop who? She called Brett to her desk and asked him listen. He could make no more sense of it than she could. Nor could Jessica. "Better take it to Barclay," Brett said. "So he can let McQueen know."

"What can he do?" she asked. "He's got enough on his plate already."

Brett shrugged. "Somebody's trying to tell you something. It could be what Barclay was worrying about. I think he'd want McQueen to know."

Maggie made a recording of the voice and carried it to Barclay's office. He was gone, but she left a note. *"Brett thinks you should hear this,"* it said, *"and let McQueen know. We don't know what it means. Maggie."*

Clyde Calder was standing high atop a twelve-foot ladder, adjusting the lights over the playground set in the fifth floor studio. He'd been working at it for the past two hours, with Butch standing below him, supervising, occasionally shouting a curt order to change this or that. Calder was used to it; Hemrick was a perfectionist when it came to lighting.

So far, Hemrick was treating him—and preparations for the shoot—as though nothing had happened. He had questioned Clyde no further about his encounter at the station or about what he'd been doing since his firing. Amazingly, he appeared absolutely at ease, apparently confident that everything was in order and on schedule.

Calder was not about to give him cause to worry.

Hemrick told him the first of the crew was due to arrive from California that night. The audio man, the video switcher, and two other camera operators. The others, he said, would be here by the next afternoon, giving them a full twenty-four hours to make final preparations. "This has got to be a first-class production," he said. "No glitches, no delays."

Now, as Calder climbed down the ladder, he asked, "When will the kids get here?"

"Two hours before the shoot. Enough time to get them made up and briefed on what they're supposed to do."

Again, Calder learned, there would be no script, no narration. The children would be given general instructions and then set free to romp around the playground, performing sexual acrobatics at the direction of Butch on the floor. The camera work would be cinema verité style, with the music and graphics to be added later, as part of the final edit.

"Where did you find the kids this time?" Calder asked as casually as he could.

"Around," Butch replied vaguely. "It's a good group. We've used some of them before. They'll know what to do."

As Clyde took down the ladder and headed for the prop room, he heard the telephone ring in one of the back edit rooms. Twice, then three times. "Are you going to get the phone?" he asked.

"No, let it ring," Butch said. "It's probably some damned charity."

More than likely it was Martin Duggan. He had already left three messages on the campaign office phone and two more at Hemrick's house.

The bastard was running scared, and Hemrick didn't want to waste his time talking to him. Duggan didn't know the kind of clients he was dealing with or the kind of money involved. If he did, he wouldn't be begging to shut down the shoot.

Butch knew that in another forty-eight hours or so it would be all over. He'd be home free. Maybe then he'd think about closing the place down for a while. Let things cool off—and get Duggan off his back.

Late that afternoon, McQueen got hold of Barclay before Barclay could reach him. "One of the Burnsville detectives talked to the night clerk at the motel, a kid named Randy Striker. He confirms that your guy left an envelope for the couple in 113. Mr. and Mrs. John Tremaine, as they're now calling themselves. Said it was a large envelope, but that's about it."

"He didn't get a look at the guy?" Barclay asked.

"Not really. He ran in and out. But he did report one interesting thing."

"What's that?"

"It seems the day clerk called him at home this morning. Woke him up. Said our Mr. Tremaine wanted to know the same thing . . . if he got a good look at the guy."

"What?"

"You heard right. It seems Kolura doesn't know who's been leaving the messages either."

Barclay was befuddled. "I don't get it."

"Neither do I, but that's what the kid said."

After mulling that over for a moment, Barclay told him about Maggie's message, repeating it verbatim.

"The bus depot?" McQueen said. "What's that about?"

"I don't know," Barclay replied. "But it's too weird to ignore."

"Man, I've got my hands full with the task force. I don't know what I can do."

"Give me one of your guys," Barclay pleaded. "Somebody who can be in contact with the Burnsville cops. If Sissy and Kolura start heading toward downtown in the morning, we want to know about it. We want to be at the bus depot."

There was a long pause at McQueen's end of the line. "What time tomorrow?"

"It's anybody's guess. Eight o'clock, I suppose. Unless you hear from Burnsville sooner."

"Fuck it," he said. "I'll be there. I'll meet you at the station."

McQueen was right on time. So were the others. They all gathered in the conference room to wait, the detective's cellular phone on the table in front of him. "The Burnsville cops will call me here if there's any sign of movement," he said. "All we can do is wait."

As they sat, McQueen updated them on the task force operations. "Calder's keeping in touch with us. He says Hemrick is getting things ready and seems to suspect nothing. Part of the crew was supposed to come in last night from California, the rest of them today. Our people at the airport are keeping watch."

"What about the telephone taps?" Barclay asked.

"Not much happening now," McQueen said, "although his telephone records show a whole flock of calls to California in the past couple of months. The FBI's working on those as we speak. Martin Duggan has also left several messages for him, but so far, Hemrick hasn't returned them, at least not from one of the phones we're tapping."

"Wait a minute," Barclay said. "What if Duggan has picked up some rumor and is trying to get word to Hemrick? As the AG, he could sure as hell hear a rumor about something as big as this."

"You've got a point," McQueen said. "I'll see what the FBI guys think."

"What about the plans for tomorrow?" Brett asked.

"The FBI's in charge. We'll have plenty of people there: inside, outside, on the roof, on the fire escape. We found the architect of the building and have a complete set of blueprints . . . so we know every nook and cranny in the place.

"The plan is to wait for the taping to begin, then make our move. Calder will be wired and will give us the go-ahead. If he can't let us in for some reason, we'll bust in. We've got all of the warrants in place."

"What about us?" Maggie said. "What do we get?"

McQueen deferred to Barclay. "We'll be taping everything on the outside from the surveillance van," he said, "and then, we'll follow them in, once we're sure it's safe and secure. If nothing leaks, we should have the whole thing to ourselves."

Barclay knew there was the possibility of getting sued by the owners of the building for entering and taping without permission, but in this case, he decided the potential reward far outweighed the potential risk. Once the public learns what was going on in there, he doubted there would be much support for a suit from the owners. Especially if—as they suspected—Martin Duggan was one of them.

The two Burnsville cops had been alerted that something might be happening that morning, that the couple in 113 could be on the move. So both officers were in their unmarked cars, waiting patiently in the Hardees' parking lot. In the past hour, both men had consumed two sweet rolls and two cups of coffee, and one of them, George Levy, was already feeling the need to piss. While it would take him only two minutes to get in and out of the restaurant's john, he was afraid to risk it. They'd been told not to screw this one up.

To his relief and to the delight of his bladder, the couple emerged within the next three minutes and climbed into the Lumina parked in front. Levy quickly punched in McQueen's cell phone number. "They're leaving now," he said. "I'll keep you informed."

The Lumina pulled out of the motel parking lot and into traffic, heading north, toward Minneapolis. Both squads waited, then fell in behind, allowing several other cars to move between them, but always keeping their quarry in view. The Lumina was moving slowly, well within the speed limit, with Tony and Sissy demonstrating no awareness of being followed.

When the car entered the access ramp to Interstate 35W, Levy made another call to McQueen. "They're on the freeway, still heading your way." Even though they would soon be out of their jurisdiction, the Burnsville officers had been ordered to keep following the car until it made a stop.

As soon as he received the second message, McQueen led the group out of the station, bound for the bus depot, McQueen in his car, the others in Brett's Explorer. "If they do show up, you stay outside until we know what's going on," McQueen had told them. "I'll have help there, so just stay cool until I give you the word."

The depot is located in the heart of downtown Minneapolis, not far from the Target Center arena. Parking places were at a minimum, but with time Brett managed to find a meter nearby. They knew it would take Tony and Sissy twenty minutes or more to get there . . . if, indeed, they were coming at all.

"So who do you think the mystery voice belongs to?" Barclay asked Maggie.

"I have no idea," she said. "I wish I knew."

The question had troubled her all night. If the warning was accurate, it had to come from someone close to Wycross or to Tony and Sissy. How else would he know about their plans? But if he was some type of an accomplice, why would he be warning her? Why now and not before? It just didn't figure. Maybe, she thought, the whole thing was some kind of bizarre trap.

Brett had been quick to argue against that idea. "What kind of trap could it be?" he'd said. "With all of us and the cops around?"

Maggie had had no answer, although the thought of Danny, alone and relatively unprotected, did cross her mind. But she quickly dismissed it; no one could know where he was. They had taken too many precautions.

Barclay was the first to spot the Lumina in the side rearview mirror. "They may be coming up behind us," he said. "Turn the other way."

The car was past them before they could get a look inside. But from the rear, they could see there were two people, a man and a woman. Like Brett before them, they apparently were searching for a parking place. The car circled the block twice before they finally gave up finding a place on the street and pulled into the Target Center parking ramp.

Out of sight for now.

44

McQueen was slouched in one corner of the bus depot, hands in his pockets, eyes constantly moving. Two other detectives he had borrowed from the sex crimes unit were mixing with the small crowd, watching for any signal he might provide. The Burnsville cops were already gone, having left after reporting to McQueen that the Lumina was in the ramp and parked.

The Minneapolis bus depot was like most others in the country: Dingy, dirty, and depressing, consisting of one large open space with long rows of steel-mesh chairs in the middle and, off to one side, another group of chairs with tiny TVs attached to the arms. The ticket counter occupied one wall, a group of vending machines and a small deli another, with the doors leading to the bus garage taking up a third. Stuck away in one corner was a group of lockers.

To McQueen, most of the people there seemed either very young or very old, apparently too poor or too feeble—or both—to drive or to take a plane wherever they were going. Or maybe they just liked to ride the bus. He checked his watch. Ten minutes had passed since they'd parked. Were they really coming? There were only two entrances, both easily within his view. Having seen the picture of Sissy, and knowing a general description of Kolura, he had no doubt he would spot them quickly. Then, he had decided, he would simply watch and see what they did.

Five more minutes went by before they came through the door on the right, Sissy first, Tony following. They stopped briefly to look around and get their bearings, then headed directly toward the lockers. McQueen sauntered after them, keeping his distance, discreetly signaling the other two detectives.

If the couple was worried about being followed or watched, they showed no sign of it. There was no hesitation, no wary glances beyond that first sweep of the depot. They walked slowly along the lockers, examining the numbers, finally stopping in front of number six. As Sissy stepped back, Tony pushed a key into the slot and turned it, pulling the door open. McQueen was no more than ten feet away as Tony reached into the locker and pulled out a black leather satchel. With a quick glance at Sissy, he zipped open the bag and held up what looked like a small package.

It was then that McQueen decided to move. With a quick nod to the other detectives, he stepped up behind the pair. "Excuse me," he said, holding his badge at eye level as they turned to face him, "I'm Detective Timothy McQueen with the Minneapolis police department. Are you Sissy McGowan and Tony Kolura?"

Surprise. Shock. Terror. All three emotions passed across their faces within the first three seconds. A split second later, Kolura tried to bolt—but was easily blocked by McQueen's partners, who were standing on either side of him.

"These are Detectives Richards and Tanori," McQueen said. "Also with the Minneapolis police department."

Although still shaken, Sissy by now had regained some of her composure. "What do you want with us?" she demanded. "We weren't doing anything wrong."

"Are you Sissy McGowan?" McQueen repeated.

"What if I am?"

"And are you Tony Kolura?"

"I don't have to tell you shit!" he hissed, braver now.

"I'm afraid you do," McQueen said. "You're both under arrest on suspicion of stalking and harassing Maggie Lawrence."

A small crowd of the curious began to gather. Not wanting to prolong things or create a scene, McQueen quickly handcuffed the pair. "You'll have to come along with us now," he said as he began to lead them away, reading them their rights as they walked. One of the other detectives picked up the black satchel.

Sissy held back. "This is an outrage!" she screamed, looking back at the crowd for sympathy. "We've done nothing. Is this the way you treat tourists here?"

McQueen smiled, pulling her along as gently as possible. "Shush now, Sissy," he said. "You'll have plenty of time to talk later."

"Fuck you, pig!" she shouted. "How dare you do this?"

For his part, Kolura had quieted and was trying to be more diplomatic. "I'm telling you, there must be some mistake," he calmly told one of the other detectives. "We were simply here to pick up some parcels."

"Right," he said tiredly. "We'll be sure to keep them for you."

From the Explorer, Maggie and the others had watched as Sissy and Tony went through the doors and into the depot. They knew they were supposed to await some kind of signal from McQueen, but Maggie quickly grew impatient. "I'm going over there now," she said after several minutes.

"I'm not sure that's wise, Margaret," Barclay said.

She opened the car door and stepped out. "Maybe not, but that's what I'm going to do."

Brett tried to follow, but Barclay held him back. "Let her go," he said. "She's entitled to this."

She waited for the stoplight to change and then strode across the street, planting herself outside the same door Sissy and Tony had entered. She could only hope McQueen would bring them out the same way.

Several more minutes passed. She stepped aside

as others came in and out of the door, ignoring the startled looks of recognition on some of their faces. Finally, she caught a glimpse of McQueen's green sports coat through the glass. Then he was there, gripping Sissy's arm, her wrists in front of her, cuffed together.

Maggie stepped in front of them and grabbed Sissy roughly by the other arm. "I'm here, Sissy. Look at me!"

She would forever remember the moment. The utter astonishment, then fear, on the woman's face. Then what? Almost a smile. Twelve years disappeared in a whisper. They were back in the warehouse, the stench of oil surrounding them, Sissy smiling and saying, 'We try to watch out for one another.'

But the years—and life—had not been kind to Sissy. She was heavier now, her skin pasty and worn, her eyes even harder, if that was possible, with dark, half-moon circles settling in below them.

How could it have come to this? The girl who had once saved her life now accused of trying to ruin it. Sissy tried to turn away, but Maggie held her eyes, refusing to release them. "Why have you done this?" she whispered. "Please, tell me."

Tony, standing behind Sissy in the grasp of the other detective, leaned over her. "You don't have to talk to her," he said. "Tell her to get fucked."

"C'mon, Maggie," McQueen said, moving between them. "We've got to go."

"No!" Maggie said, refusing to move. She had waited too long. "I want to know. What did I ever do to you, Sissy? Tell me!"

Sissy finally turned to her, eyes flashing, her

words venomous. "I've got nothing to say to you. You hear me? I don't even know you. Now get the fuck out of our way."

By then, Brett was beside Maggie, gently pulling her aside. "That's enough, Maggie. Let it go."

She shook off his hand, but made no attempt to follow as McQueen led the pair away to two parked squad cars. She couldn't trust herself to walk. Her legs were weak, almost numb, and she could not control the tremors that shook her body or the tears of anger and pain that flowed so freely down her cheeks.

McQueen placed Sissy and Tony in separate squad cars, with plans to keep them apart for as long as possible. They could be held for thirty-six hours or so without official charges, which would keep them out of trouble for the time being while allowing him to prepare for the next afternoon's porn ring raid.

Sissy, sitting behind the wire mesh in the squad car, had said nothing since her angry outburst at Maggie. And as McQueen studied her in the rearview mirror, she appeared confused and lost in thought, staring blankly out the side window, occasionally muttering to herself.

He was right. She was thoroughly confused, unable to comprehend how this could have happened. The questions overwhelmed her: How had the cops found them? And when? And how could they possibly have known about this morning's bus depot pickup? It made no sense to her, especially now when she knew she wasn't thinking straight.

She needed time to clear her head, to talk with Tony to get their stories in sync. But would she be allowed to see him? She doubted it. She would have to get a lawyer and hope that the General, whoever and wherever he was, would somehow come to their rescue.

Would Tony talk? Try to make a deal for himself at her expense? She wouldn't put it past him, the bastard. Should she consider doing the same? She would first need to know more. Like how much do the cops actually know? And did they have any real proof? If they did, why had they waited until now to pick them up?

Sissy could see her dream of the dating service disappearing. The lawyer would cost money, no doubt about that, and who knew if she'd end up spending time in a goddamned Minnesota jail. Or a federal prison. She knew they would examine the tapes in the bag, and that Maggie would confirm that both she and Sissy were minors when the film was made. Could she and Tony be accused of possessing child pornography with the intent to distribute it?

Stalking was one thing, but the thought of the other scared the hell out of her.

Tony could see the back of Sissy's head in the squad car directly ahead of them. Like her, he was still in a state of shock. But unlike her, he had a pretty good idea of how the cops had tracked them down. It had to be the tail that he thought he had lost a few nights before. They must have stayed with him somehow. But he had no notion of what had prompted them to follow him in the first place, or how they knew they would be coming to the bus depot this morning. There had to be a leak somewhere.

Many of the thoughts passing through Sissy's mind were also passing through his: the need for a lawyer, the possibility of a deal, the hope that the General would find a way to get them out of this mess. After all, the whole thing had been his idea, not theirs. But what leverage did they have? They didn't even know who the hell he was.

Of one thing Tony was certain: He was not going back to federal prison. One three-year stint had been enough. He would do anything to save himself from another.

Once the two of them had been booked into the county jail, McQueen took personal charge of the satchel seized at the depot. He opened one of the packages and found the cassette and note, knowing immediately upon reading it what the tapes contained. He hurriedly checked the satchel into the evidence room with strict instructions that no one was to examine it without his personal permission. Then he called Barclay and told him what he had found, reading him the note.

"God's Witnesses!" Barclay fumed. "That's blasphemy bullshit."

"Of course it is," McQueen said, "but from the looks of it, they were going to take them around to every media outlet in town."

"My God," Barclay said. "She would have been destroyed."

"Wouldn't have helped her image, that's for sure," McQueen said. "But they're all here now, under lock and key."

"What have you done with Tony and Sissy?"

"They're locked up, too. We'll let 'em cool off for a while and then see what they have to say. But with the bust coming up, I'm not going to have much time."

"You've got to make the time," Barclay said. "If there are more of those tapes around, we've got to find them and destroy them. And those two may be the only ones who know."

"How about Wycross?" McQueen said. "If he's behind this, he should know, too."

"But you don't have enough to arrest him, do you?"

"Probably not, but you may know enough to scare the shit out of him."

"Do I have your permission?" Barclay asked.

"Be my guest," McQueen replied.

The more Barclay thought about the idea, the more he liked it. Not that it would necessarily succeed, but what could he lose? He had to stop the flow of those tapes somehow, and what better way than to go to the source? And time could be at a premium. When Wycross learned that Sissy and Tony had been picked up, and the tapes confiscated, he might very well try another method of distribution. Like mailing the goddamned things.

Barclay put in a call to Wycross at Channel 13, only to be told by his secretary that he would be out of the office all morning. "I have a somewhat

urgent message for him," he said. "Would you tell
me where I could reach him?" When the secretary
hesitated, he added, "I'm sure he would want to
know about this as soon as possible."

The woman finally relented. "He's at the Athletic
Club downtown. At a Chamber of Commerce meeting. It should be over by eleven o'clock."

Barclay glanced at his watch. He had twenty
minutes, and the Club was no more than a ten-
minute walk away. "I'll try to catch him there," he
said. "Thanks very much."

He briefly considered telling someone else
about his mission, but decided against it. Nicholas
Hawke might hear about it from Wycross, but he
would deal with that later.

Covering the distance in even less than ten minutes, Barclay stood across the street from the
Athletic Club, in front of a hotel parking ramp,
halfway hidden behind a pillar. He figured Wycross
may well have parked in the ramp, and since he
didn't want to confront him in the Club itself, waiting for him here seemed to be the best option.

He didn't have long to wait. Within ten minutes, Wycross walked out of the Club and stood on
the sidewalk, chatting with another man Barclay
didn't know. Then he came across the street,
alone, walking directly toward the ramp, taking no
notice as Barclay emerged from behind the pillar.
Barclay guessed the man would never recognize
him. They had met only that once, in the midst of
the large crowd at the reception.

He was right.

They boarded the elevator together and got off
on the same floor. Checking to make sure no one

else was around, Barclay waited until his prey had walked about fifty feet before overtaking him. "Hey, there," he said, "you're Richard Wycross, aren't you."

Wycross stopped and turned, puzzled. "Yes, I am. Why?"

"I'm George Barclay, the news director at Channel Seven."

Wycross's face immediately clouded over.

"We met at the broadcasters' reception a few months ago. Remember?"

"I'm sorry, I don't. What can I do for you?"

"I have some information you'd be interested in."

"Then make an appointment," he said smugly, turning away. "I don't hold conversations with competitors in parking ramps."

Barclay stood still, but said, "The cops picked up Tony and Sissy this morning at the bus depot. Confiscated a satchel full of tapes."

Wycross stopped and turned back, scowling. "What are you talking about? What tapes?"

"The ones you or somebody in your employ left there. The ones you told Sissy and Tony about in the note you left for them. You know, the other morning at the Forest Green Motel."

"You're full of shit," he said defiantly, although clearly shaken.

Barclay walked closer to him. "The motel was staked-out, Richard. Or should I call you Dick? Or maybe Ricky? Which do you prefer?"

"Fuck you and your mother, too, Barclay."

Barclay grabbed the lapels of his camel-hair coat and pulled him to within an inch of his nose. "Listen, sleazeball. The cops saw you arrive and leave. They even gave you a fucking ticket. The desk clerk knows that you left an envelope for Sissy and Tony, and the cops already know what the note said. My guess is, when pressed, Tony and Sissy will say that the same person who left the note has been instructing them on a whole lot of other dirty tricks, all aimed at Maggie Lawrence and her young son. Including one that could have killed them."

Wycross struggled to free himself from Barclay's grip, but with Barclay's bulk, he was no match. Barclay finally took a deep breath and threw him across the fender of a car. Then he stood and watched as Wycross slowly picked himself up.

"What do you want from me?" he asked, cowering against the car.

Barclay had been waiting for this moment. "Listen carefully. I want the original tape and any other copies you have on my desk this afternoon. Delivered by you, personally. Then I want you to resign as general manager of Channel Thirteen and as vice president of Prestige Broadcasting, effective today. Blame your health or whatever you'd like. And I want to know where you got the tape and how you found this Sissy and Tony. Unless you do all of those things, the cops will be at your door before the day is out. I swear to God they will."

If Wycross thought he was bluffing, he didn't show it. In fact, Barclay himself was impressed with how convincing he'd been. Maybe, he thought, he shouldn't be giving the asshole a chance to get off the hook after all. But, no, it was the only way he knew to get the tapes and avoid any publicity.

"Do you know what you're asking?" Wycross whined. "To give up my job? I've got a wife and kids in college."

"You won't have trouble finding another job," Barclay said. "There's a big demand for pricks like you. Besides, you have no choice."

Wycross was nervously brushing off his coat. Defeat was in his eyes, but he was not yet ready to concede. After all, he still had the tapes. "Can't we make some kind of a deal here?" Desperation was in his voice. "You get the tapes and we forget the whole thing?"

"No way," Barclay said. "I told you what the deal was. You're wasting my time."

"How do I know the cops still won't come after me?"

"I guess you'll have to take my word," Barclay said.

Wycross stood silently for several minutes, frantically trying to find some room between the rock and the hard place. In the end, he couldn't. The prospect of an arrest and the public humiliation of a trial, to say nothing of the possibility of jail time, was more than he could risk. His career would be destroyed, his family devastated, whatever the eventual outcome. "Okay," he said finally, "I'll do what you say, but I can't tell you where I got the tape or how I found those two people."

"Why not?"

"Because I could end up worse than arrested. You understand what I'm saying?"

"I don't believe you," Barclay said.

562

RON HANDBERG

"Then call the fucking cops. Because I won't
. . . I can't tell you."

Barclay studied him. Was he bluffing now? He
didn't think so. He was too frightened. "That
means more tapes may still be out there," he said.

"I can't help that," Wycross replied. "But I think
I have them all."

Barclay considered it a few moments more. "Okay,"
he finally said. "But I want the tapes and a copy of
the news release announcing your resignations in
my hands before three o'clock this afternoon."

"You'll have them," Wycross said as he began to
walk toward his car.

Barclay called out after him. "One more thing.
Tell whoever you got those tapes from that I'll be
waiting to get them next. You hear me?"

Wycross nodded and got into his car.

Maggie and the others could not believe what
Barclay was telling them. "You actually roughed
him up?" Maggie said.

"Not that much, really. Just enough to get his
attention."

"George! I can't believe this," Jessica said. "It's
so unlike you."

He shrugged. "What can I say? I was pissed off."

It was now early afternoon and they were sitting
in Barclay's office, awaiting Wycross's delivery of
the tapes and the news release.

"He wouldn't tell me who gave him the tapes,"
Barclay said. "But I assume it's some old broadcasting buddy of his or somebody from the parent
company. We'll probably never know."

"So we'll never know if we have all the tapes," Brett said. "One could pop up anytime."

"I'm afraid so. But I don't know what else to do."

"What is Prestige Broadcasting anyway?" Maggie asked as she picked up the company's annual report from Barclay's desk and began to thumb through it.

"Another one of the new media conglomerates," he said. "With the FCC's new ownership rules, they're popping up all over. Mega-owners, money guys who collect radio and TV stations by the dozens. Part of the technological revolution. It won't be long before we're all working for one of them."

Maggie flipped through the pages, studying the graphs and charts and pictures. "Do you mind if I keep this for a while?" she asked.

"Find something interesting?"

"Maybe. I'd just like to have more time with it."

Only Brett noticed the flush rising in her cheeks.

45

The day had arrived. And so had the first sign of a leak.

McQueen said a reporter from the *Star-Tribune* had gotten wind that something big was about to break, although he didn't know what and wouldn't say where he'd gotten the tip. But he was beating the bushes with a vengeance, calling in favors from anyone and everyone he knew in the pursuit of the story.

"I'm not sure how long we can keep the lid on," McQueen told Barclay. "The guy is everywhere. I'm getting calls from every which way."

Better a newspaper reporter than a television reporter, Barclay thought, since the paper could print nothing until the next morning. That would at least preserve their exclusive through the early evening news. But if the newspaper was hot on the trail, he guessed one of their TV competitors would probably not be far behind.

He was counting the hours.

To McQueen, he said, "I don't know what to tell you. I'm having enough trouble keeping it quiet here and getting our own people ready. Do your best, I guess."

With the help of Maggie and Brett, Jessica had completed the first draft of the background piece that would follow their live and taped coverage of the porn raid itself. Her story incorporated carefully edited footage from the *Pajama Party* porn film and the personal stories of Penny, Nadia, and Amy, including excerpts of Amy's interview, plus hidden-camera shots of both Butch Hemrick and Dr. Henry Klinkle.

It would also include a prominent mention of ex-con Hemrick's long and close association with Attorney General Martin Duggan, although the AG himself would not yet be accused of anything. However, because they feared he would leak something, they had decided not to seek Duggan's reaction until after the actual raid.

Barclay had checked Jessica's script twice himself, and had asked the station's attorney to review it, as well. This was one story he wanted to get right. With their suggestions in hand, she was now rewriting the piece . . . preparing it for the final edit.

Barclay had assigned Brett to produce the live coverage after the raid, with Maggie and Jessica sharing the reporting duties from the scene.

Three photographers would also be there, one of them working out of the surveillance van, the other two following the FBI and the cops into the studio.

"Have we forgotten anything?" Barclay asked Brett.

"Not that I know of," Brett said. "I think we're all set."

So was Butch Hemrick, although he was slightly troubled by the telephone call he had finally accepted from a highly-agitated Martin Duggan, who had barely been able to control his voice. "A *Star-Trib* reporter just left my office. He's trying to pin down a lead that something big is about to bust today. He doesn't know what and came over here to shake my tree. But I told him I knew nothing."

"He's chasing phantoms," Butch had told him, knowing what a nervous Nelly Duggan was. Still, he couldn't escape a moment of uneasiness.

"It's too much of a risk," Duggan had pleaded. "Call it off."

"Sorry, Marty. Everything's in place."

And it was. The entire crew was there, putting the finishing touches on preparations. In a few hours, the children would be there, and soon after, the filming would begin. Hemrick was convinced this would be his best yet. Certainly the most elaborate and expensive. With the marketplace demanding more quality, Hemrick was determined to meet the demand.

He walked over to Clyde Calder, who was setting

up a camera on one side of the playground. "Any problems?" Hemrick asked. "You've checked all the systems?"

"Three times," Calder replied. "Video, audio, everything. It's looking good."

Hemrick smiled and turned away. He couldn't wait to get started.

An hour later, as Martin Duggan paced his office, his secretary rapped on the door. "Sorry to bother you, Mr. Duggan, but—"

"I told you I didn't want to be disturbed," he snapped.

"But—"

"What is it?"

"Two gentlemen are here to see you. From the FBI."

Special Agent George Endorf walked past the secretary and into the office, introducing himself and his partner, Michael Johnson.

"This is a surprise," Duggan said. "Did we have an appointment?"

Endorf waited for the secretary to close the door behind her. "No, sir. We didn't. We're here to take you into custody as a material witness in a federal felony case. We'd like you to come along with us."

"What?" Duggan's expression was one of utter disbelief. "What the hell are you talking about?"

"With a federal court order, we've been monitoring the phones of John Hemrick. We were able to overhear and record your call to Mr. Hemrick earlier this morning."

Duggan sank into his chair. He thought his heart would jump out of his chest. "What call? I haven't spoken to Mr. Hemrick this morning. There must be some mistake."

"I don't think so, sir. And we can't allow you to make any additional calls. That's why you'll be in custody for at least the next several hours. You will be free to call an attorney later in the day."

Duggan didn't move. It was all over. He knew that now. He'd been right. They're going to raid the place. He was already thinking of what he could tell his family.

"If you'll get your coat," Endorf said. "We'd like to move along now."

"What about my appointments? My job here? I can't just pick up and leave."

"I'm afraid you'll have to. We don't want to create a scene."

Duggan rose slowly from the chair, wondering at that moment if he'd ever sit in it again.

The surveillance van, with Brett and Tamara Swain once again inside, arrived at the Edina building shortly before noon. Calder had told them the filming was due to begin at three, with the kids arriving a couple of hours before that. Brett wanted to get tape of them going in, if that was possible, although their faces would have to blanked out before the story could go on the air.

While Brett couldn't see them, he knew the area was already overrun with FBI agents and cops from several other agencies—hidden away in nearby buildings or in trucks or vans not unlike their own. He had no communication with them, but he was in contact with the station's other two photographers and Maggie and Jessica, who were parked down the street in the Wendy's lot.

Barclay was back at the station, overseeing the final assembly of Jessica's story and maintaining communication with McQueen, who was in the area somewhere. Barclay had already relayed the news that Duggan was in federal custody and would remain incommunicado until the raid was over. Mike Overby had been assigned to try and find him later for comment, although Barclay doubted he would be available.

In the newsroom, tension was high and escalating by the hour. Even now, only a few of the staff knew what was about to come down, although everyone suspected something big was in the works. The rumors had been circulating for weeks. That Barclay himself was closeted in one of the editing rooms was in itself a clue, along with the fact that Jessica, Maggie, Brett, and several photographers were among the missing, and that the six o'clock producer had been told to leave a seven-minute hole in the newscast.

In addition, one of the station's live mini-cam trucks had been ordered out of the garage and told to stand by in an area of south Minneapolis, ready to respond to a summons at a moment's notice. All communication was limited to cell phones, out of fear that radio messages could be more easily intercepted.

The sky was about to fall in.

♦   ♦   ♦

The *Star-Tribune* reporter, Charlie Tucker, was getting desperate. He'd busted his ass and so far had almost nothing to show for it. But he knew something was about to happen. Every news-gathering instinct, gained from twenty years of reporting, told him so. Sources who were normally available and loose-lipped were now either closed-mouthed or nowhere to be found. He wasn't sure where to turn next.

To this point, he knew only that child pornography was somehow involved in it all, as was Channel 7. He was tempted to call the station and try to weasel the information out of some of his friends there, but he decided that would be too boldly unprofessional. Besides, if it was a major story, they wouldn't tell him anyway.

Instead, he returned to the office of the attorney general. If anybody would know what's going on, he should, although he had pleaded ignorance earlier in the day.

He found the AG's office quieter than usual, and Martin Duggan's secretary looking preoccupied and worried. She told him Mr. Duggan was gone for the day.

"Can you tell me where?" Tucker asked.

"I don't know," she said. "He left here a few hours ago, with two men. He didn't say where he was going or when he'd be back."

"What men?" he asked.

"I'm afraid I can't tell you that," she replied, looking even more uneasy.

"What the hell's going on around here?" he asked irritably. "No one will tell me a damned thing."

She shrugged and turned away.

"What about Hemrick? Is he around?"

"No," she said, turning back. "But he may be at the campaign office."

"I'll try him there," Tucker said, heading for a telephone in the press room.

The children began to arrive shortly after one o'clock. Three girls and three boys, coming separately or in pairs. Tamara Swain followed each one with her camera as they entered the building, trying to avoid faces or shoot slightly out of focus. There was still no sign of any law enforcement types, although they knew they were there in force.

Inside, Clyde Calder watched as the children got off the elevator, accompanied by one of the beefed-up group of security guards now patrolling the building and monitoring traffic in and out. He remembered having seen two of the kids before, but all of them were fresh-faced and laughing. And so young. They could as easily have been arriving for the first day of school.

Hemrick was there to greet them, tussling their hair, tweaking their cheeks, joking with them. But as he was leading them to the dressing room, one of the security guards got off the elevator and said, "Mr. Hemrick, you have a call down in the campaign office from someone at the *Star-Tribune.* He's trying to locate Mr. Duggan."

Hemrick stopped. "He should be in his office," he said.

"The guy says he's not. He claims it's important."

Hemrick seemed puzzled. "Have him leave his number. I'll call him back."

"Yes, sir," the guard said.

Tucker had no sooner hung up the phone than it rang again. He picked it up quickly. "Hemrick? That was fast."

"No, Mr. Tucker. This is Special Agent George Endorf of the FBI."

"Really? Then you must want somebody else."

"No, I want you. I need a favor. I would ask you not to answer this phone again. And not to speak to Mr. Hemrick, should he try to contact you elsewhere."

"What are you talking about? How do you know I called him?"

There was a long pause. "We are operating a court-approved wiretap of Mr. Hemrick's telephones. It is crucial that he have no contact with you or other members of the media for the next several hours."

Tucker was beginning to see the light. "What's going on here? Is this what I've been trying to track down all day?"

Endorf, who had been told of Tucker's many phone calls, said, "It could be."

"And Hemrick's in the middle of it?"

"It could be," Endorf said again.

"And you want me to ignore it? Think again, friend."

"If you insist on speaking to Hemrick, you could jeopardize an important federal and local investigation. With significant consequences."

"I don't give a fuck. I want the story."

There was another long pause. "Wait ten minutes. Then call George Barclay, the news director at Channel Seven. He'll be expecting your call, and will provide you with access to the story. But, please, do not answer the phone or speak to Hemrick."

"You've got a deal," Tucker said.

Hemrick tried to return Tucker's call three times in the next half hour, but got no answer at the number he'd left. He then tried the city room at the *Star-Tribune*, but they had no idea where he was. "He's on the run somewhere," was all they would say. Hemrick left a message. Next he called Duggan's office, hoping to get his secretary, if not Duggan himself. But the secretary had gone home early, another woman in the office told him. She wasn't feeling well. And the woman had no idea where Mr. Duggan was. Hemrick's calls to Duggan's home and his health club provided no results either.

Something didn't feel right, he told himself. But time was growing short. The kids were ready and the crew was getting itchy. He couldn't delay much longer.

"You're going to have company," Barclay told Brett over the cell phone. "A guy named Tucker from the *Star-Tribune*."

"What?"

"He'll be coming to your van. I had to fill him in. He was going to screw things up for the FBI. I had no choice. Besides, he'll give us full credit in the paper."

"You're the boss," Brett said, holding up his watch in the darkened van. Twenty minutes to three.

"Good luck," Barclay said.

The studio lights were on. The cameramen and the control room crew were ready. The children, now fully dressed, were on the playground set, standing around the equipment, talking as they waited. If things went as planned, they would soon be shedding their clothes and partaking in a different sort of game.

Calder, with a tiny wireless microphone attached to the inside of his shirt, was providing a countdown of sorts to McQueen and Endorf in the FBI control center outside. He had been instructed to report when all of the children were naked and the filming had begun. He was then to give them exactly three minutes before he opened the fifth floor door. They would take care of the rest.

Now, however, as he watched Hemrick across the way, Clyde began to worry. Butch seemed visibly upset, pacing back and forth, glancing at his watch. Sweat had begun to form on his forehead, which Calder didn't think was the result of heat from the lights. He had never seen him this way before, and wondered if he was losing his nerve.

Had something gone wrong?

"Can we get going, Butch?" one of the other cameramen asked. "I've got a flight back to California tonight."

"Yeah, yeah," Butch said. "Give me a minute."

Calder turned his back and whispered into the

mike. "Something's not right up here. Butch could be chickening out."

"We're set in here, Butch," came a voice from the control room. "Anytime."

Hemrick gave one more look around, then said, "Okay. Stand by. We'll get this show on the road."

"Never mind," Calder whispered again.

Hemrick got the kids into the positions he wanted them and then backed off to the edge of the set. "Okay," he called out again. "Let's have action!"

As Brett stared out of the van window, he could see three men enter the front door of the building. Even from here, seeing them from the rear, he knew they were FBI guys. They had that look. They must be taking care of the security guards, he thought.

Less than a minute later, the wide back doors of a moving van across the street opened and at least a dozen men in blue coats with FBI emblazoned on their backs jumped out, some running to the front door, others around to the back, to the fire escape and the roof. Others soon emerged from buildings across the street.

"Are you getting all of this?" he whispered to Tamara.

"You bet your ass," she said from behind the camera.

Tucker, the newspaper guy who was now with them, leaned over their shoulders. "What's going on?"

"They're moving in," Brett said.

"Let's go, then."

"We can't. Not until they give us the all-clear."

At both ends of the street, squads of Edina police suddenly appeared to erect barricades, blocking traffic from either direction. Other officers were now stationed outside the front door of the building, letting no one in or out.

It wasn't that long ago, Brett thought, that he and Maggie were standing in the darkness outside that same door. How time flies.

Calder was in a jam. He couldn't both follow the action with his camera and still keep an eye on his watch. He thought about two minutes had gone by since he had whispered "Go!" into his mike, but he had no inkling if he'd been heard outside with all of Hemrick's screaming inside. With Butch shouting instructions to the kids, Calder circled the set, using a special harness to keep his camera steady, moving ever closer to the side of the room by the door, still unsure of how much time remained.

Finally, he got a glimpse at his watch. Ten seconds to go. The longest ten seconds of his life. He backpedaled slowly across the floor, moving further away from the set, hearing Hemrick shout after him, "Where the hell are you going, Clyde?"

In one motion, he slipped the camera and harness off and raced to the door, flinging it open. He was greeted by a wall of blue jackets, pushing past him, rushing into the big room, assault weapons at the ready. "Police! FBI! Stay in place!"

At the same moment, he heard the splintering of the trapdoor on the roof above. There was pandemonium. Naked children were running in every direction, screaming, trying to cover themselves. Members of the crew, cowering, holding their hands high. Blue jackets still streaming through the doors. More coming in from the fire escape and down the ladder from the roof.

In the middle of it all, Butch Hemrick. He had not moved, and now stood, cuffed and shackled. Under guard. Bewildered. Frightened. He fastened his eyes on Calder. "You dirty fuck!" he shouted.

Calder gave him a long look at his middle finger and then darted down the stairs, meeting Maggie, Jessica, the two photographers, and the newspaper guy on their way up. "Join the party," he said, knowing the party was over for him.

It was a story made for television. It had everything. Action. Excitement. Drama. Importance. Moreover, it was theirs and theirs alone. And it would not have happened without them.

Realizing that, the police and FBI did everything possible to accommodate them: parading Hemrick and the other suspects in front of their cameras, pausing to give them a good look, allowing them to tape the extensive search of the facilities, making Endorf and McQueen available for lengthy interviews.

All before the first of their television competitors had arrived on the scene.

George Barclay could not have been prouder.

Maggie and Jessica anchored the live reports from outside the building for the early and late news, utilizing both the exclusive footage of the raid itself along with Jessica's lengthy background report. While Jessica had tasted such glory before, for Maggie, it was the most satisfying moment of her career.

Attorney General Martin Duggan was in seclusion, unavailable for comment. Before the night was out, rumors were swirling that he would resign, possibly by the next day. And federal officials were hinting that a grand jury would be asked to consider an indictment against him, the seriousness of which would likely depend upon Hemrick's willingness to cooperate.

Simultaneous with the raid, Dr. Henry Klinkle was arrested at the Westside Clinic, and he, too, was now behind bars, awaiting a preliminary hearing. The children were also in custody and were being held in juvenile detention pending possible charges.

But perhaps most important, at least to Maggie, were the more than one thousand cassettes of pornographic filth found in the fifth-floor storage room, which were seized and eventually would be destroyed.

If only someone had done that with her film.

46

When Maggie struggled out of bed the next morning, she found Brett already at the kitchen table, the front page of the *Star-Tribune* spread out in front of him. "Good morning," she said, leaning over to give him a hug and kiss at the same time. "Did we make big news?"

"Take a look," he said.

CHILD PORN RING BUSTED
CHANNEL 7 INVESTIGATION CREDITED

Charlie Tucker's story covered all of the now familiar ground, providing a dramatic re-creation of the raid and its aftermath, using color photographs lifted from Channel 7's videotape. He listed all of the suspects, but centered his attention on Butch Hemrick and Clyde Calder, reporting on Calder's plea agreement and the central role he played in providing information and access to the feds. He also included excerpts of interviews with both Maggie and Jessica about their roles in the investigation.

> Maggie Lawrence, the Channel 7 anchor, said reporter Jessica Mitchell had first heard rumors of the porn ring months ago, and that she only became involved after the murder of Penny Collins, a young runaway who had appeared in an earlier film. "It was Jessica's story from the beginning," Ms. Lawrence said. "I was just happy to help out."
> For her part, Ms. Mitchell said "without Maggie's contacts with the families of the runaway children, we never would have broken the case or the story."

There was also a long sidebar on the relationship between Hemrick and Attorney General Martin Duggan, including the fact that Duggan had personally persuaded the parole board years before to release the man then known as John Hendrick, a convicted child pornographer, and later employed him as his campaign treasurer. State and federal officials, the story said, were now poring over the financial and campaign records seized in the raid. And Duggan had scheduled a news conference for that afternoon, reportedly to announce his resignation.

It took the better part of an hour for Brett and Maggie to get through it all.

"Hell of a story," Brett said. "Congratulations."

"You didn't get your share of the credit," Maggie said sadly. "We couldn't have done it without you, you know."

"Aw, shucks, ma'am, it was nothing. Besides, I live behind the scenes, you know."

Maggie knew this could possibly be the last day Brett would be sharing her bed and breakfast. With Sissy and Tony in custody and Wycross out of the way and out of town, there was no reason not to bring Danny home from his exile in Apple Valley. And no reason for Brett to stay on any longer.

She wasn't sure she was ready for that.

"I need a shower," she said. "How about you?"

"Funny you should ask. I was thinking the same thing. But I need somebody to scrub my back."

"You found the right gal," she said, taking his hand.

McQueen was in Barclay's office when Brett and Maggie arrived at the station late that morning. He was full of information: Hemrick and the rest of the California crew were due to be arraigned before a federal magistrate soon, with bail expected to be set high enough to keep them all behind bars. But so far, none of them was talking, and all had retained lawyers.

"The county attorney is also considering state charges," he said. "So when the feds get done, we may get a crack at them, too."

Juvenile court officials, he said, were still trying to figure out what to do with the children. Most of them were already living in foster homes or on the streets.

"But that's not really why I'm here," he added. "We need to talk about Tony and Sissy."

"I'd almost forgotten about them," Barclay said.

Maggie hadn't.

"I can't hold them much longer without charging them," McQueen said. "We did get a search warrant for their motel room and found a big stash of cash along with copies of some of the earlier notes they'd received. But frankly, we don't have that much evidence against them. Not without Wycross, and now he's out of the picture."

"And if you were to charge them," Barclay said. "The whole business about Maggie's film would come out, wouldn't it?"

"Probably. If they have an attorney who's worth a shit. He or she would make hay with it."

Maggie spoke up. "I really don't care if they go to jail. But I would like to try to make a deal with them."

"Like what?" McQueen asked.

"I want the chance to meet with Sissy alone. I also want them to turn over the money they made out of this to some charity, maybe to one of the shelters for runaways. And I'd like to see them put on a plane to California, with the promise never to bug me again."

McQueen shook his head. "I can try. But I'm not sure any promise they make would ever be honored."

"I know that, but they must be scared. They

don't really know how much you have on them. After all, they were planning to distribute pornographic material."

"All right," McQueen said. "I'll pay them each a visit and let you know."

Nicholas Hawke was waiting outside Barclay's office as McQueen left. Impeccably dressed as always and sporting a big smile, he had Jessica with him, one arm around her shoulder, holding her close, not seeing the grimace on her face. "I just wanted to tell you all what a marvelous job you've done," he said, pulling Jessica along into the office. "It was a hell of a show yesterday, and I can't tell you how proud I am of you."

They all mumbled their thanks while searching for a way to escape. Especially Jessica. Barclay wanted to smack him in the teeth.

"Best of all," he continued. "We did a fifty-eight share last night! The biggest audience we've had for one of our news program in years. The whole town is talking."

"That's nice to hear," Barclay said. "But we didn't really do it for the ratings."

"Oh, you news people," he laughed. "I knew you'd say that."

Jessica gracefully pulled away from his grasp and started to leave the office, but Hawke wasn't finished. "Did you hear that Dickey Wycross quit over at Channel Thirteen?"

Dickey?

"No kidding?" Barclay said. "Too bad."

"His company must have pulled the plug on

him because of their horseshit ratings. Shows you how brutal this business can be."

You don't know how brutal, Barclay thought. Then he smiled.

Later, when Maggie was alone, she made two telephone calls. The first was to Nadia's parents in Madison, to tell them about the raid and the arrests. "It wouldn't have happened without you," she told Mrs. Vaughn. "And without Nadia. The papers I found in her room made it possible. I hope that's of some comfort to you."

Next she called Amy, who was still living at the Annandale cabin. She was to be interviewed and put in protective custody by the FBI later in the day.

"Did you see the story last night?" Maggie asked.

"Did we ever," she said. "It was great. Especially seeing Butch walking out in handcuffs. All of us were cheering here."

"Your friends are still there?"

"Yeah, but they're leaving tomorrow. For Texas. But they say they'll be back."

"Good," Maggie said. "By the way, did you recognize yourself?"

"No, none of us did."

Maggie paused for a moment, then said, "When this is all over, Amy, I hope you'll be back in touch with me. If you want me to, I'd like to help you. Maybe we can get you back in school and back with your folks."

"Maybe," she said. "Let me think about it."

"That's all I can ask," Maggie said.

◆   ◆   ◆

Sissy was already sitting in the small room in the county jail complex when Maggie walked in. She sat hunched over in her chair, barely glancing up at Maggie as she came through the door. The hours in jail had not helped her appearance. If anything, she looked even older and more haggard than she had at the bus depot.

Maggie said nothing as she slipped into a chair across from her. The silence hung in the air, almost palpable. Sissy would not look up again. Her eyes were focused on her clasped hands atop the table.

Finally, with her eyes still lowered, Maggie heard her say, "I'm only talking to you because it's part of the deal. *You got that?* I'd do anything to get out of this fucking place and back to California."

Indeed, both she and Tony had agreed to all of Maggie's demands, with two exceptions: Tony had insisted on keeping the money he'd won at the casinos, and both had demanded enough money to get back to California. The rest had already been donated to charities of Maggie's choice. Sissy's dream of a dating service would have to wait.

"I don't want a long conversation, Sissy. I only want to know one thing and you can get out of here. But I want the truth."

Looking up, finally, Sissy seemed surprised. "What's that?"

Maggie took a deep breath. "Did you tell Mick Salinas, the guy I was living with in L.A., about our film?"

Sissy started to giggle, then to laugh, softly at first, but then loudly, her head thrown back. Maggie could only sit and wait until she finally stopped.

"Tell him about it? Shit, I showed it to him. At least your part of it. I tried to blackmail him, for Christ's sake. But he told me to fuck off. Said they could show it on the six o'clock news for all he cared. Your boyfriend got real angry, Maggie. Damned near threw me out of his office. And then he left you, didn't he? Ha! You and that baby of yours."

She began to giggle again as Maggie got up and left the room.

47

Once in the air, the Northwest flight to Chicago took less than an hour, but more than that for the cab ride from O'Hare to downtown in the midst of the morning rush hour. For Danny, sitting between Maggie and Brett in the back of the cab, it had been his first flight, and he couldn't stop talking about it. They let him chatter on, laughing at his exuberance and occasionally trying to answer one of his many questions about the plane and how it managed to stay up in the air. By the time they got downtown, he had already decided on a future career as a pilot.

Barclay had agreed to let her and Brett make the trip as long as she was back in the Twin Cities in time to read the late news. "We're still in the rating period, you know." She'd said that wouldn't be a problem, although she had given him no reason for the day away. "We just want to get out of town for a while," she had told him. "Let Danny see a little bit of Chicago."

It was close to 9:30 A.M. when the cab dropped them off in front of the Sears Tower. Danny craned his neck in an effort to see the top, amazed when they told him it was the tallest building in the world. "Can we go all the way up?" he begged. "Please?"

Maggie said they would later if they had time, but they had to make a stop first.

The elevator, packed with people on their way to work, took them to the twenty-first floor, where they and several others got off. Maggie paused to get her bearings and then walked to the right, Brett and Danny trailing behind her. She stopped in front of a pair of massive glass doors, the name PRESTIGE BROADCASTING inscribed in fancy gold lettering across the face of them.

"You're sure you want to do this?" Brett asked.

"I'm sure," she replied. "I didn't come all of this way to stop now."

"What do you want us to do?"

She thought for a moment, then said, "Stay out here, okay? But within view. I don't want to put Danny in the middle of a scene."

With that, she pushed open one of the doors and walked into a large reception room, where an older woman with badly-dyed red hair and half-glasses draped around her neck was sitting behind a highly-polished mahogany desk. "May I help you?" she asked.

"I'd like to see Michael Salerno," Maggie said.

"Do you have an appointment?"

"No."

"I'm sorry, but Mr. Salerno's in a meeting and can't be disturbed at the moment."

"Yes, he can," she said. "Tell him Maggie Lawrence is here."

The woman looked at her curiously, but seemed intimidated by Maggie's hard stare back. "May I tell him what this is about?"

"He'll know," Maggie said. "Just get him."

The receptionist picked up the phone and punched in a three-digit number, turning her head away as she whispered into the receiver. She had no sooner hung up then a youngish man in a double-breasted blue suit appeared at the far end of the reception area, his eyes fastened on Maggie.

How long had she waited for this day? How many sleepless nights and long-suffering days? Month after month, year after year. Praying he was still alive and that someday they would meet again.

She walked across the room to him. "Hello, Mick."

It was as if time stood still. Everything seemed to freeze in place. Then, just as quickly, it was in motion again. His eyes had left hers only once, to quickly glance at Brett and Danny waiting outside the glass doors.

"Hello, Maggie. This is a surprise."

His voice had the same deep resonance. A radio voice, his teachers used to tell him. Or a preacher's. Full and throaty. "Why don't you come back to my office?"

She turned toward Brett and Danny. "First, take

a look at your son, Mick. It's the last time you'll ever see him."

He smiled slightly, and pointed down a hallway. "It's this way."

He had not changed that much in six years. He remained a startlingly handsome man. If anything, better looking now than before. More mature, of course, but something else, too. His eyes seemed of a darker blue, his waist even trimmer. And he carried himself with greater confidence. He would turn women's eyes in any crowd, but then again, he always had.

They were now sitting in his corner office, spacious and impressively decorated in oak and leather, looking out at the facades of other downtown skyscrapers. He was leaning back in his chair, hands clasped behind his neck.

"So how did you finally find me?" he asked.

"From your picture in the Prestige Broadcasting annual report. Corporate vice president of news. Not bad, Mick."

"I've worked for it," he said.

"I bet you have."

He brought his hands from behind his head to the top of the desk, clasping them together, fingers interlocked. For the first time, he appeared slightly uncomfortable. "Look, I'm not going to try to explain why I took off, Maggie. It's history and I won't relive it."

"I now know why you took off," she said. "But I have to admit you had me jumping through hoops for a long time, trying to find you. To know whether you were dead or alive. To know what I'd done to make you run from Danny and me. You even changed your name. Were you that afraid I'd find you?"

"I'm sorry about the boy," he said. "He deserves a dad."

"I hope he'll have one soon," she said.

"The guy out there now?"

"Maybe."

Mick got up and stared out the big window, his back to her. "So why did you come now? You need money or something?"

"No, Mick. Hard to believe, but I may even have more money than you do."

He turned around. "Then what is it?"

Any uncertainty Maggie had felt before disappeared now. The tremors were gone. She had no fear. "Don't be cute. Please. I talked to Sissy. We know what Richard Wycross did. I bet he reported to you, didn't he?"

"No, as a matter of fact. To a guy one step up."

"But you knew what he was doing, didn't you? You knew about the film, you knew about Sissy. She says you damn near threw her out of your office back in L.A."

He turned back to the window.

"You're the one who found her, aren't you? The one who got her and that Tony to come to Minneapolis. You gave Wycross and the two of them everything they needed to scare the hell out of us."

"I don't have to listen to this," he said, still facing away.

"Yes, you do," Maggie said, undeterred. "But I have to give you credit, Mick. You only wanted to scare me, not destroy me. Was it because of Danny?

It certainly couldn't have been because of any feelings for me.

"You're the one who left that final message,
aren't you? The mystery voice. Warning me about
the bus depot. You must have thought Wycross
had gone too far. You just wanted me out of town,
for the sake of a few rating points, but you knew
those tapes would destroy whatever future Danny
and I had. Were you afraid I'd come after you for
the support you've never paid?"

He came around the desk and sat on the edge
of it, not two feet from her. "You have no proof of
any of this," he said.

"I don't need proof, Mick. We're not in a court-
room here. But I wanted you to know that I know.
And that someday Danny will, too, when he's old
enough to understand what his father did to him
and to me. I hope he won't hate you, but I suspect
he will."

He leaned into her face, his lips pressed
together so tightly the words had trouble getting
out. "I loved you. You know that. We'd still be
together if you hadn't been in that fucking film.
How could you have ever done that?"

She pushed him away. "Why didn't you ask me
then? I would have told you. We could have talked
about it. Maybe I could have made you understand."

"Never. I wasn't going to marry a whore!"

Her hand moved so fast and with such force
that she surprised even herself. The blow to his
face knocked him back, almost off the desk.
Before he could recover, she was standing over
him. "Don't you ever call me that, you bastard!

And don't you ever try to hurt Danny or me again . . . or I swear I'll be back. And not just to talk."

With that, she got up and walked to the office door. Turning back, she was pleased to see that his cheek was already reddening and puffing out. "You know something?" she said. "You are a real piece of shit."

Then she was back into the reception area and out of the glass doors, back with Brett and Danny.

"Are you okay?" Brett asked, looking into her eyes.

"I'm fine."

"You're sure?"

"I'm sure," she said.

Then, grabbing each of their arms, she said, "Let's go home, guys."